Books by
Martha Wells

WHEEL OF THE INFINITE
THE DEATH OF THE NECROMANCER
CITY OF BONES
THE ELEMENT OF FIRE

Forthcoming in hardcover

THE SHIPS OF AIR

MARTHA WELLS

THE WIZARD HUNTERS

BOOK ONE OF THE FALL OF ILE-RIEN

An Imprint of HarperCollinsPublishers

EOS
An Imprint of HarperCollins*Publishers*
195 Broadway
New York, NY 10007

Copyright © 2003 by Martha Wells
Excerpt from *The Ships of Air* copyright © 2004 by Martha Wells
ISBN: 0-380-80798-X
www.eosbooks.com

First Eos paperback printing: June 2004
First Eos hardcover printing: May 2003

HarperCollins® and Eos® are trademarks of HarperCollins Publishers Inc.

Printed in the U.S.A.

HB 05.12.2023

To Liz Sharpe and Carolyn Golledge

THE
WIZARD HUNTERS

 Chapter 1

Vienne, Ile-Rien

It was nine o'clock at night and Tremaine was trying to find a way to kill herself that would bring in a verdict of natural causes in court when someone banged on the door.

"Dammit." A couple of books on poisons slid from her lap as she struggled out of the overstuffed armchair. She managed to hold on to the second volume of *Medical Jurisprudence,* closing it over her finger to mark her place. The search for the elusive untraceable poison was not going well; there were too many ways sorcerer-physicians could uncover such things and she didn't want it to look as if she had been murdered. Intracranial hemorrhage seemed a good possibility, if a little difficult to arrange on one's own. *But I'm a Valiarde, I should be able to figure this out,* she thought sourly. Dragging the blanket around her, she picked her way through the piles of books to the door. The library at Coldcourt was ideal for this, being large, eclectic, and packed with every book, treatise and monograph on murder and mayhem available to the civilized world.

The entry hall was dark except for a single electric bulb burning in the converted gas fixture above the sweep of the stairs. The light fell on yellowed plaster walls and rich old wood and a blue-and-gold-patterned carpet on polished stone tile. Coldcourt was aptly named and Tremaine's bare feet were half frozen by the time she made it to the front door. She had let the housekeeper have the night off and now she regretted it, but she had had no idea it would take this long to arrange things. At this rate she wouldn't be dead until next week.

The unwanted person was still banging. "Who is it?" she shouted, wondering if he could hear her. Coldcourt had been built as a country house and its walls were thick natural stone to withstand the Vienne winter. It was part of an aging neighborhood of small estates just outside the old city wall and sprawled in asymmetrical crenellated and embellished glory across its poorly kept grounds. The door was several inches thick, old oak plated with not entirely decorative embossed lead, proof against bullets and other less solid assaults. The windows above the door were heavy leaded glass threaded with silver, the blackout curtains fixed tightly. All buildings had the blackout curtains, stipulated by the Civilian Defense Board, but the other protections were peculiarly Coldcourt's. Though all its wards against sorcerous attack were no help in the current situation.

A muffled voice replied, "It's Gerard!"

"Oh, God." Tremaine leaned her forehead tiredly against the chill wood surface. As executor of her father's estate, Guilliame Gerard had been her guardian until she was twenty-one, but she had seen him only infrequently these past few years. Her first thought was that her supervisor in the Siege Aid group must have written to him.

Tremaine had joined the Aid Society because they worked in the bombed-out areas of the city searching for survivors or bringing supplies to the fire brigades and the War Department's rescue teams. It was hard, desperate work, and many of them, even experienced men like constables or fire brigade members or former soldiers, were killed by unexploded bombs or collapsing buildings. A small woman who had never been very good at games in school shouldn't have been able to last a week. Tremaine's life should have ended with no more fanfare than a line in the casualty columns of the newspapers. Anything else would surely lead to a Magistrates' investigation which might uncover even more unpleasant facts about her family's immediate past than had already been exposed; that was the last thing she needed. But Tremaine had been in the Aid Society for six months.

She probably still couldn't hit a lawn tennis ball properly, but she could climb, scramble over, under, and through rubble like a squirrel, dodge flying debris, and when a ghoul had leapt out at her from a half-collapsed cellar the instinct to beat it to pieces with a lead pipe had triumphed over the will to die.

But after six months of near-death-but-never-quite experiences, her supervisor had told her she was due a month's leave before she could enlist for another term. Tremaine had protested with a patriotic fervor that her old friends in the theater would have admired, those who were still alive anyway. But she had given in when she had seen the look in the woman's eye. The supervisor was the Duchess of Duncanny, used to managing estates on a grand scale, and she had been trained as a hospital nurse early in the war. She was too perceptive by far and Tremaine had looked into those old eyes and thought, *She knows. She knows why I'm here.* It was time to leave the Aid Society and find some other way.

She must have contacted Gerard. "Shit. Shit, shit, shit." Wincing, Tremaine turned the heavy key and drew the bolts.

Gerard slipped in, by habit pushing the heavy door shut quickly so a betraying light wouldn't escape. The outskirts of Vienne were considered an unlikely target area and Tremaine hadn't heard any bomb warnings on the wireless earlier.

He was a tall man, in his early forties, with dark hair just lightly touched with gray. His tie was askew and his tweed jacket stained with dark patches. His spectacles caught the light as he stared down at her in consternation. "Tremaine, I'm sorry to burst in on you like this, but something terrible has happened."

They broke the wards, she thought, staring at him blankly. *The palace is destroyed.* A bubble of hysterical laughter grew in her chest. It was over. There would be no messy inquests or embarrassing articles in the papers to avoid. The Gardier had won and she could bash her own head in with a rock and no one would think twice about it. "The palace was bombed."

"No." Gerard gave her an odd look. "Oh no, not that terrible." He took a sharp breath, gathering his thoughts. "I've just come from the project. The last test sphere was destroyed."

"Oh." Tremaine wet her lips, trying to catch up. He meant the Viller Institute's Defense project outside the city. She gathered the blanket around her and fumbled the large book into a more comfortable grip, trailing Gerard further into the hall. "Do you need me to write a bank draft?" she asked vaguely. There were people in the city who did that and handled the other business affairs of the Institute, but perhaps those offices had been hit or evacuated. "I thought the government requisitioned anything you needed now."

Gerard stopped to face her impatiently. "Tremaine, listen to me—" He blinked as he took in her appearance. "Is that your nightdress?"

"It's a smock. An artist's smock." Most of Tremaine's clothes were worn-out; the couturier she had patronized had closed down and left the city and she hadn't had time or inclination to stand in the lines at the stores for months. "I— Never mind. Now . . . what's happened?"

"The sphere we were using for the experiment was destroyed," Gerard explained. "The Riardin prototype of the Viller sphere, the last one we had."

That time she understood him. "Was destroyed?" Suddenly angry, Tremaine dumped *Medical Jurisprudence* on the marble console table. "What the hell do you mean 'was destroyed'? By who?"

"By Riardin." His face grim, Gerard adjusted his spectacles. "It killed him and self-destructed."

Tremaine let out her breath and pinched the bridge of her nose. "Moron," she muttered. But it didn't surprise her. It was hardly the first time this project had killed someone.

"He was overzealous," Gerard admitted, "but he was the best we had. I'm now the highest-ranking sorcerer on the project." He took a deep breath, as if he was still trying to take stock of that himself.

Tremaine looked up at him, frowning. Lodun University had been sealed off by its own wards and lay under heavy sorcerous siege by the Gardier. It had been impenetrable for the past two years and no one had been able to get close enough to discover whether the sorcerers and townspeople trapped inside were still alive or not. Since then sorcerers who could be spared from the border and coastal defenses were in short supply. Gerard was more than competent, but he wasn't up to the flamboyant Riardin's level. One of the benefits of suicide was not having to watch while what was left of her friends went before her. "Gerard . . ."

"The other spheres were specifically keyed to Riardin. He built them, he worked with them. There's no time to build another for me." His expression was grave. "I need the Damal prototype."

"Oh." Arisilde Damal had been the greatest sorcerer in the history of Ile-Rien. Tremaine had called him Uncle Ari. She stared at Gerard for a moment, nonplussed, then realized he was asking for her permission. "Well, yes. Of course."

Gerard started for the stairs, halting in confusion when Tremaine veered back toward the library, still dragging her blanket. He demanded, "You don't keep it in the vaults upstairs?"

"It gets lonely. It's cold and dark up there. That's probably what made the two early spheres die, you know." There had been three original spheres constructed by Edouard Viller, Tremaine's foster grandfather, kept in the secret storerooms in Coldcourt's attics. Two had quietly died in their years of inactivity and the last had been destroyed by Arisilde Damal himself in the course of a powerful spell. When Tremaine's father, Nicholas Valiarde, had endowed the Viller Institute to continue Edouard Viller's work, Arisilde had worked with the natural philosophers employed by it to re-create Viller's original design.

Tremaine led the way into the library. The books had overflowed the floor-to-ceiling shelves long ago and invaded the parlor next door and several rooms on the second floor, but the main part of the collection was still housed here. Though it badly needed dusting it was still the coziest room in the house, with colorful antique Parscian carpets and overstuffed armchairs. It was also the only room without blank spots on its walls where paintings had been taken down, silent reminders of the imminent danger of invasion. Following the instructions her father had left behind, Tremaine had had his art collection removed to a sealed hidden vault below the Valiarde Importing offices in Vienne, along with some of the furniture, the older books, her mother's jewelry and other valuables. Since then Tremaine had had the feeling the house was an empty shell, nothing left behind, including herself. She went to the glass-fronted cabinet against the far wall and opened a drawer to search for the key.

"Sorry to burst in on you like this. I know you're on leave from the Aid Society." Gerard glanced at the meager fire in the grate and the pile of books surrounding her armchair. "Are you writing something again?"

"Uh huh." Tremaine gave up on the key buried amid the welter of pencil stubs, scraps of paper, and several decades' accumulation of unidentifiable odds and ends, and popped the lock on the cabinet doors with a hard jerk. The sphere rested on an upper shelf, crowded in with old yellowed notebooks and folios. It was a small, croquet ball–size device formed of copper-colored metal strips, filled with tiny wheels and gears. She lifted it off the shelf, her fingers going a little numb with the mild shock of the power shivering through the metal. She breathed on it and the sphere warmed to her touch.

She gathered it against her chest as she shut the cabinet door. "No magical locks? No secret devices?" Gerard said a little sadly as he stepped up behind her. "The Valiardes have come down in the world."

"No, really?" Gerard had been a trusted crony of her father, so he was entitled to the observation, but Tremaine still felt more than a twinge. "Just stab me in the gut while you're at it, why don't you?" she muttered.

"Sorry." He actually sounded sorry as he accepted the

sphere from her. He added wistfully, "I was rather fond of the secret magical locks."

"So was I." Tremaine looked into the sphere, watching the blue and gold lights chase each other along the metal pathways. Alchemy and natural philosophy were powerfully mated in the design; she hadn't a clue how it did what it did. This particular sphere had never been part of the Institute's studies. Uncle Ari had given it to her when she was a little girl, the day her pet cat had died of old age. He had said it would be cruel to prolong the cat's life but that this could be her friend too. *It won't catch mice but it can purr,* he had told her. Uncle Ari hadn't always been playing with a full deck of cards, but he had been very sweet. He had been the first sorcerer to begin the Viller Institute's great project and one of the first to die of it. She said, "Give it a minute to warm up."

Gerard watched her gravely. "I handled this one when Arisilde first charged it, but that was years ago. Is it easy to work with?"

She shrugged. "I never had any trouble with it. But then I never used it for spells. Not real ones." You didn't have to be a sorcerer to make the sphere work, but you did need to have some latent magical talent. Tremaine's great-grandmother had been a powerful witch, and all her mother's family had had talent to one extent or another, though her mother had been an actress rather than a sorceress. As a child, Tremaine had had enough magic to make the sphere find lost toys and produce small illusions and colored light shows, but even that ability had faded with lack of practice. She supposed she would never see the device again. "Any progress?" she asked, not expecting an optimistic answer. "Besides Riardin blowing himself up. Not that that was progress but—"

Gerard knew her too well to take offense. "I think we're close. The experiment Riardin was conducting— He was approaching the spell from an entirely new angle." He shook his head, pulling his spectacles off to rub his eyes. "We're very close to deciphering Arisilde's architecture."

"So you'll know exactly what killed Uncle Ari and my

father." Tremaine turned the sphere, watching the sparks travel deeper into its depths. It was active tonight, more so than she had ever seen it before. Perhaps because she hadn't had it out since last year. *Last year? Maybe it's been longer than that.*

"They wanted to save us from this, Tremaine," Gerard said quietly. He gestured at the blackout curtains tightly covering the library's narrow windows. "From this war."

"I know." Nicholas Valiarde and Arisilde Damal had been the first to discover the early traces of the Gardier, that faceless enemy that appeared out of nowhere, that attacked without reason with power that destroyed conventional weapons and magic alike. That had been years before the devastating attack on the city of Lodun, before the small country of Adera had been overrun and forced to serve as a Gardier staging area for attacks on Ile-Rien.

Tremaine didn't blame Nicholas and Arisilde for what had happened afterward. It had been an accident, a series of miscalculations on the part of two men who had been treading a fine line between life and death all their lives. With a sigh, Tremaine held the sphere out to Gerard. "Uncle Ari never wanted to make weapons."

He took the sphere from her, handling it carefully. "It may sound overdramatic, but this could be the salvation of—" He stared into the sphere with consternation. "It's gone dead."

"No." Frowning, she took it back. She shook it a little, making Gerard wince, but then he was used to the more delicate and temperamental instruments constructed by Riardin and the others who were trying to duplicate Arisilde's work. "It's fine." She held it out, showing him the lights moving deep within the device.

Gerard took the sphere again and Tremaine leaned over it, frowning as the life faded out of it. She shook her head in annoyance, taking it back from him. "It worked for you before, didn't it?"

She shook the sphere again and he hurriedly stopped her. He said, "Perhaps . . . I haven't worked with it in more than ten years." He blinked, struck by the enormity of the possible disaster. "If that's the case . . . We have no working spheres to continue the experiment."

"You mean it's forgotten you?" Brows drawn together, Tremaine held it out to him again. "Try to use it while I'm holding it. Something simple."

Gerard rested his fingers lightly on the sphere, frowning in concentration. For a moment Tremaine thought nothing would happen. Then a swirl of illusory light drifted across the fine old carpet near the hearth, sparkling like fayre dust, making both the fire in the grate and the electric bulb in the lamp dim and shiver.

Gerard let out his breath and released the sphere. The light vanished. "It still knows me but it apparently wants contact with you also." He met her eyes, his face serious. "Tremaine, I hate to ask you this, but . . . it's vital for the continuation of the experiment. We're so close to success—"

Tremaine looked around at the library, gesturing vaguely. She couldn't afford to get involved in anything right now. "I'm sort of in the middle of something—"

"—I know it's dangerous, but if you could—"

Dangerous. Tremaine stared at him. *That's perfect.* She nodded. "Give me a few minutes to get dressed."

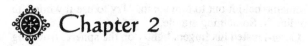

Chapter 2

Isle of Storms, off the Southern Coast of the Syrnai

We'll see you at the moonrise," Ilias said, and thought, *I hope*.

In the water below, Halian was balanced carefully on the bench of the dinghy, bobbing in the ripples that washed against the rocky wall of the sea cave. He was a big man, weathered by sun and sea, his long graying hair tied back in a simple knot; Ilias had never thought of him as old, but right now worry made Halian show his years. "Are you two sure you know what you're doing?" he asked, handing up the coil of rope.

Ilias chuckled, reaching down out of the crevice for it. "I'm never sure we know what we're doing." The jagged hole of the cave entrance lay only twenty paces or so beyond the bow of Halian's little boat, allowing in wan morning light and the dense fog that lay like a wool blanket over the blue-gray water. The rock arched high enough to allow entrance to their ship the *Swift*, but the bottom was dangerous with submerged wrecks.

Longer ago than Ilias or anybody else alive could remember, the back of the cave had been a harbor, part of an old empty city that wove through the caves, much of it underwater. But now the stone docks and breakwaters were obstructed with the wooden skeletons of wrecked ships, all jammed together in one rotting mass. The stink of decay hung in the cool dank air, concentrated in the fog that some wizard from ages ago had caused to form around the island. The sudden gales and bad currents that frequently trapped ships and drew them in to their deaths gave it the name the Isle of Storms.

Halian didn't appreciate the attempt to lighten the mood. "You know how I feel," he said seriously, sitting down again in the boat as it rocked gently in the low waves.

"It'll be all right," Ilias told him, exasperated. When Halian had brought this up to Giliead last night, it had caused one of those long polite arguments between them where both parties are actually on the same side and there is no hope of resolution. Ilias had no idea how it had worked itself out; he had gotten fed up and gone to sit out on the wall of the goat pen with the herdsmen.

From the crevice above Ilias's head, Giliead's voice demanded, "What did he say?"

Ilias stretched back to hand the rope up to him through the narrow passage. "He said we're suicidal idiots."

"Tell him thanks for his support," Giliead said, but the words didn't have any sting to them. "And love to Mother."

Ilias leaned out again to relay this, but Halian rolled his eyes, saying, "I heard him, I heard him." He took up the oars as Ilias freed the mooring line. His expression turning rueful, he added, "Just take care."

Ilias smiled. Halian had faith in them; he was just tired of funeral pyres. "We will."

Without looking back, Halian took two quick strokes toward the cave entrance, the little boat already starting to vanish into the fog. Ilias braced his feet on the slick rock and pushed himself up through the opening into the cramped passage above, finding handholds in the mossy chinks in the stones. Giliead was waiting there, sitting on his heels and digging through the supplies in their pack. The crevice stretched up into the rocky mass over their heads, disappearing into shadow when the dim gray light from the opening below gave out. "Ready?" Giliead asked, shaking his braids back and awkwardly maneuvering the pack's strap over his head and shoulder. He was nearly a head taller than Ilias and the confined space was almost too small for him.

"No," Ilias told him brightly. The crevice was not only too small for Giliead, it was too small for the distance weapons they would have preferred to bring; bows and hunting spears would never fit through here. They both had their swords strapped to their backs, but drawing them in the confined space was impossible.

Giliead's warm smile flickered, then straight-faced he nodded firmly. "Me neither."

"Then let's go."

The climb went faster than Ilias remembered, maybe because this time he knew it would end. Searching for a way out of the caverns last year, they had discovered this passage by accident, not knowing if it led to a way out or a dead end somewhere deep in the mountain's heart. It was pitch-dark and the stone was slick with foul water that dripped continuously from above. After a time the sound of the waves washing against the cave walls below faded and the only noise was their breathing, the scrape of their boots against stone, and an occasional muttered curse due to a bumped head or abraded skin. It was hot too and nearly airless, and Ilias felt sweat plastering his shirt to his chest and back. Bad as it was, it was still easier going up than it had been last year going down.

Giliead called a halt at what they judged was halfway up and Ilias wedged himself onto a shelf of rock invisible in the dark, bracing his feet against the opposite side of the crevice. Shoving the sticky hair off his forehead, he realized his queue was coming undone and he took a moment to tighten it and pull the rest of his hair back. After some struggling, he managed to unsling the waterskin and take a drink. He handed it up to where Giliead was shifting around, still trying to fold his larger body into a comfortable position, and slapped it against the other man's leg to let him know it was there. When Giliead handed it back down, Ilias asked, "What did you and Halian finally decide last night?"

"That I'm bullheaded and he's worse." There was rueful amusement in his voice. Since Halian had married Giliead's mother five years ago, becoming his stepfather and the male head of the household, things between him and Giliead had occasionally been tense. There wouldn't have been a problem if Giliead had still had his own household with his sister Irisa, but living under what was now Halian's roof had caused some friction.

"Bullheaded? I would have picked the other end." Ilias was only a ward of the family, Giliead's brother by courtesy rather than blood, and therefore able to remain stubbornly neutral. He had come to Gil's house of Andrien as a child; his own house had been a poor one with far too many children to support, especially boys. He and Gil didn't look much like blood brothers either, since Ilias's ancestors had come from further inland, where people were smaller with lighter hair and skin, and Gil's people came from the bigger, darker strain that had been planted here on the coast since before the first boat was built.

Giliead snorted. Ilias could hear him shifting around uncomfortably again. Finally Giliead added, "He understands that I just want to be sure."

Ilias finished the unspoken thought hanging over both their heads. "That Ixion's not back." It was the first time either one of them had said it aloud, though Ilias knew they had both been thinking it since earlier this season when the rumors had started. Stories of smoke from the island again, of the bodies of curselings like those Ixion had bred washing up on isolated beaches. It wasn't just talk, either; in the past few months fishing boats had gone missing far more often than they should, with no survivors and no signs of wreckage in any of the places where small boats usually came to grief. Then a trading fleet of six ships from Argot had failed to arrive and two small coastal villages of gleaners had been found deserted, the huts burned and the boats broken into kindling. Nicanor, lawgiver of Cineth, and his wife, Visolela, had asked Giliead to return to the island to see if another wizard had taken Ixion's place here.

"He can't be back," Giliead pointed out reasonably. "I cut his head off. Nobody comes back from that."

Ilias remembered that part, in a hazy way. Lying across

Giliead's lap in the sinking gig, the water in the bottom red with blood, he had a clear picture of Ixion's head under the rowing bench. They had never talked about that, either. "Dyani told me you threw it to the pigs."

"The pigs we eat?" Giliead sounded dubious.

Ilias didn't take the bait and after a moment his friend said quietly, "Three days after we got back I took it to the cave and the god told me to bury it at the place where the coast road met the road to Estri. That's when you started to get better."

"Oh." Ilias scratched the curse mark on his cheek. He remembered Giliead being gone then and everyone refusing to tell him why. Even after all this time, the memory of Ixion's malice and power gave him a cold feeling in the pit of his stomach. That the man could be dead and in at least two pieces and still be trying to hate him to death.

As soon as Ilias's fever had abated enough for him to get up, he had walked to Cineth to turn himself in and get the curse mark, the silver finger-width brand given to anyone who had been cursed by a wizard. Giliead had caught up with him halfway there and tried to stop him, but Ilias had refused to listen. He hadn't meant to make himself a walking symbol of their failure but maybe it had turned out that way; it still seemed like something he had had to do, though Ilias couldn't say why even to himself.

He shook his head, trying to drive off the uncomfortable reflections. At least the curse mark had stopped Visolela from trying to convince the family to sell him off into marriage somewhere inland. "Crossroads, huh," he said thoughtfully, keeping his tone light. "I guess the god figured the bastard's shade would get confused and wander around in circles."

"Shades can't cross running water anyway."

Ilias heard Giliead's boots grate on the stone as he shifted, ready to start the climb again. Giliead hadn't meant for Ilias to come with him this time. He had, in fact, invented a story about a dull trip along the coast to Ancyra, which would have been more convincing if Giliead wasn't such a lousy liar. Cornered and forced to admit the truth,

Giliead had still maintained adamantly that Ilias shouldn't come with him. Ilias had spent the last few days countering arguments, calling bluffs, topping dire threats with even more dire threats, ignoring pleas, and foiling a last-ditch attempt at physical restraint by battering the bolt off the stillroom door. Everybody else had refused to take sides, fearing retribution once Giliead wasn't around to protect them. Halian and Karima, Giliead's mother, hadn't interfered either, both knowing that the only thing more dangerous than going to the Isle of Storms was going to the Isle of Storms alone.

That Giliead would go, with help or without it, had been certain; it wasn't just that he had taken the duty of Chosen Vessel personally ever since he had first discovered what being one meant. Ranior, who had been his father before Giliead had been named a Vessel, had died from a wizard's curse. It had been the first real curse that Giliead had ever faced and probably the first time he had started to blame himself for things he had no control over.

Ilias took another drink from the waterskin, slung the strap back over his head and shoulder and pushed himself up to follow. "That's rivers and streams that shades can't cross, not seas."

"Seas don't run?" Giliead countered.

He had a point. Ilias thought for a moment, feeling for the next handhold. "They're salty." But as he leaned against the warm rock, he felt a vibration. He hesitated, pressing the side of his face against the stone. Somewhere, deep inside the mountain, something was thrumming. Like a giant heart beating fast in panic.

"What would salt have to do with—"

His throat suddenly dry, Ilias whispered tensely, "Gil, listen."

Giliead stopped. Ilias could sense him listening silently to the telltale vibrations in the stone. After a moment he answered softly, "I feel it." He let his breath out in resignation. "I hate being right."

"I hate you being right too," Ilias told him briskly, bracing his feet and feeling for the next handhold. At least they didn't have to wonder about it anymore; knowing for certain was a relief. Though it sure cut all the joy out of the debate over the seaworthiness of shades. "And Halian thought he wouldn't have anything to worry about the rest of the year except the drainage problem in the hay fields."

"Well, that's a pretty serious drainage problem," Giliead said, deadpan, as he resumed the climb. After a moment, he added, "It's not him. It's another wizard that came to take his place."

"I know." Ixion alive had been bad enough. Ixion, dead, headless and really, really annoyed was unimaginably worse.

After another long stretch of darkness and groping for hand- and footholds and occasional slips on the slimy rock, Ilias realized he could make out Giliead's outline above him. *Nearly there*, he thought. *Too bad this was the easy part.*

The gradual increase in light let their eyes adjust from the impenetrable darkness to the dim grayness of the upper cave, just visible through the cracks above. Giliead found an opening large enough for them to wriggle through and paused, listening intently, then cautiously edged upward to peer out. There was room for only one of them at a time and Ilias waited below, braced awkwardly, nerves tight with tension. Giliead's heritage as the god's Chosen Vessel made him proof against curses, but not Ixion's curselings. If something had heard them climbing up through the cave wall, if it was waiting up there like a civet at a mousehole, all he would be able to do was pull Giliead's body back down after it bit his head off.

Giliead motioned that it was clear and climbed up through the crack. Breathing a little easier, Ilias followed, pulling himself out onto a ledge in the large cavern. The dim light came from above, through shafts and cracks that led up to the surface of the mountain. Conical columns of rock hung from the cave roof like icicles, hundreds of them, the light-colored ones glittering with myriad crystal reflections.

It courted terrible luck to say "so far so good" so Ilias just knelt, dumping the coil of rope off his shoulder and un-clasping the climbing hook from his belt. Giliead paced along the edge, looking for the best spot to go down. The cave was about four or five ship lengths across, the far side hard to see in the dim light. They knew it was just like this one, sloping down into the abyss, pocked by cracks and crevices, ledges and sheer faces of rock. They had no idea how deep the cavern was and personally, Ilias didn't care to find out. The dank cold air drifted up out of it like a breeze from the netherworld, raising gooseflesh on his sweat-slickened skin. They would use the rope to go down the cliff to the inner passages' entrance, about forty paces down this side.

Ilias took a deep breath as he tied off the climbing hook. Except for the rush of wind through the shafts higher up, it was silent. Last time they had been able to hear the pound-ing of Ixion's engines all through this part of the caves. "At least it's quiet," he said, keeping his voice low. He glanced up when Giliead didn't answer. His friend was sitting on his heels near the edge, head cocked to listen, his brows drawn together in consternation. "What?" Ilias asked softly.

Giliead glanced back urgently. "You hear that?"

"The wind?" Except it was growing steadily louder. And it didn't howl and moan like it should through the narrow rocky openings. It was more like . . . a roar.

Giliead came to his feet suddenly, staring toward the north side of the cavern, where it wound deeper into the mountain and the darkness was absolute. Something was moving there, something very, very big. Ilias's breath caught. "Not the wind."

It was already too late to get back down into the crevice. Giliead flung himself against the wall as Ilias rolled back to crouch against it. They both froze. The roar that sounded like rushing wind grew louder until it hammered off the stone walls and inside Ilias's head. Heart pounding, he pressed hard against the rock.

It came out of the darkness with a steady, inexorable motion, an unbelievably huge oblong shape, black as night.

It was narrow at the front, but the middle swelled to take up almost half the cavern. It had to be walking on the cave floor, however far below that was, but its gait was smooth and impossibly even. Ilias couldn't see anything that looked like an eye or worse yet, a mouth, but it wasn't fea-tureless; he could see pockmarks and the long ridges of ribs running horizontally through its body.

Giliead's thigh brushed against Ilias's shoulder and he looked up, startled, to see his friend easing away from the wall. Ilias reached up to grab his belt. "Gil," he whispered through gritted teeth.

"I want a closer look." Giliead mouthed the words, though surely the thing couldn't hear their voices over its own hollow roar.

"Are you crazy?" Ilias mouthed back, and tightened his grip.

Giliead pressed his lips together in exasperation but didn't force the issue.

It was already moving past, the bulk of its middle part narrowing again at the rear. It had a jagged ridge along its back and a cluster of long sharp-edged fins where the tail should be. As its mass slowly vanished into the darkness at the other end of the cavern, Ilias let go of Giliead and they both eased to the edge to watch the slowly disappearing bulk. His voice hushed, Ilias said, "That's . . . that's . . ."

Giliead drew a sharp breath. "Bad."

"Bad," Ilias agreed. He leaned out, trying to see the creature's legs. It was too dark in the bottom of the cavern to make them out. "You think it was here last time? Maybe in those tunnels we couldn't get to from this side?" Like all wizards, Ixion had used his curses to make things. Live things. Distorted awful things that were always hungry. With Ixion dead, there was no way off the island for most of his curselings and the waterpeople tended to kill the ones that could swim.

Giliead frowned. "Maybe. I thought cutting off the water to the vats would take care of anything he had down there." He swore under his breath. "I wonder what else I missed."

"It wasn't your fault," Ilias said, though he knew Giliead wouldn't believe him. "Besides, most of them should have eaten each other by now. Maybe it came from somewhere else." The idea that it wasn't dangerous wasn't worth suggesting.

Giliead watched the last glimpse of the thing disappear in the cavern's shadow, his mouth twisted ruefully. "We're going to have to do something about this."

"All right." Ilias nodded. "How?" he asked, just to hear what Giliead would say.

"We'll think of something." Giliead turned back, picking up the fallen climbing hook and setting it in a solid chink of rock. Ilias leaned on it to keep it anchored and Giliead tested it cautiously with his weight, then swung over the side and started down. "We killed that leviathan, didn't we? It was . . . almost as big."

Watching him climb down the sloping wall into the dark abyss, Ilias whispered after him, "That was mostly an accident and you know it." It was crazy, but this new thing made Ilias think of a flying whale. It had moved like a whale too, sliding smoothly through the air. Except it was far bigger than any whale he had seen around the outer islands or washed up dead on the beach. The leviathan that had gotten confused in the spray and unintentionally murdered itself on the spar of the *Dare*, and not done the ship a lot of good either, hadn't been half so big.

Ilias waited until Giliead reached the shaft about forty paces below, then went over the edge after him. It was a quick, scrambling climb, requiring you to place your feet carefully to keep from sending loose fragments of rock skittering down the wall. He reached the wide square-cut mouth of the shaft where Giliead was anchoring the bottom end of the rope and dropped to the floor. "What does something that big eat? People?"

"It could eat everybody in Cineth and it wouldn't be enough to fill a belly that size," Giliead argued, leaning out of the opening to yank at the hook until it came loose.

Ilias collected the rope. There hadn't been any word of large numbers of sheep or cattle going missing, so the thing hadn't left the island. Yet. "It's got to be eating something." Even if the thing didn't eat people now, after living in this place something would probably teach it.

Ilias slung the rope over his shoulder and they started down the shaft. It had been hollowed out of the cavern wall, perhaps as an air passage to the chambers of the old city, and sloped steeply down. There was just room for them to walk abreast and the ceiling was only a little above the top of Giliead's head.

The light was gray and dim by the time they reached the first cross passage and they both paused, listening. "Something's different," Ilias said softly.

Giliead stood poised in the join, brows knit thoughtfully, one hand on the wall of the shaft. "The air's coming from the wrong direction."

The breeze came from up the cross passage instead of down, not from the lower caves where Ixion had done his work. Ilias had gotten almost used to the taint of corruption in the air, but now he could smell hot metal and an overlay of something bitter and acrid. "Smell that?"

Giliead nodded, unslinging his pack to dig out one of the pitch-coated torches they had prepared earlier. "This part of the passage was closed off before. I thought it might go to the other caves, the ones closer to the surface, but it was blocked." He took a step down the cross passage into that damp cool breeze. "It's not blocked now."

"That's odd." Ilias stared into the darkness, thinking it over. Giliead was talking about the time when he had been alone down here. Ilias's memory was hazy on everything that had happened after Ixion had caught him and Giliead had never spoken of the details. Whatever was down here, Ilias could do without the return visit to Ixion's workroom.

They got the torch lit with flint and tinder and started down the passage, wary of sudden pitfalls or traps in this unknown territory. Soon the shaft lost its square shape and began to look more like a natural tunnel, the walls growing rougher and narrowing until they had to turn sideways to slip through. It slanted down, first gradually, then dramatically, and they had to scramble down nearly vertical slopes.

When the passage widened out again it was abrupt and they suddenly found themselves in a larger chamber. Ilias fell back a pace, drawing his sword to cover Giliead's back as his friend lifted the torch to check the knobs of rock overhead. Things often hid in the ceilings of the big chambers in the lower caves, waiting to drop on whatever passed below.

As they made their way cautiously forward, Ilias's foot knocked against something that rolled away. He spared a quick glance down and reported tersely, "Bones." His eyes widened as the flicker of light revealed more of the chamber floor. It was covered with bones. "Uh, lots of bones."

Giliead turned around, trying to look in every direction at once. There were two other tunnels intersecting here and it was a good spot for a trap. "What kind?"

Ilias glanced around, studying the remains with a practiced eye. The odor of decay that hung in the air all through the caves made it impossible to judge how recent the death was. He nudged a skull out of a pile with the toe of his boot. It looked human, except for the elongated jaw and the fangs. The bones didn't appear that old, but the scavengers in the lower caves would strip any carcass they found within hours and many of the long bones were broken or chewed. "Howler," he said. "Nothing looks fresh, though." He frowned at a skull, then leaned down to pick it up. It had a neat hole drilled through it, just above the right eye. "What does that look like to you?" he asked Giliead, holding it out.

Giliead spared it a glance, brows quirking. "Like something bored into its head and ate out the insides?"

"That's what I thought." Mouth twisted in disgust, he tossed the skull back into the pile. "Which way?"

"The air is coming from this one." Giliead picked the tunnel on the far left. "What's that smell?" he muttered.

"I still can't place it. Bitter, isn't it?" Ilias paused to sheathe his sword and while Giliead kept watch, he used his knife to scratch a trail mark on the floor. The trail marks were a language all their own, the individual lines telling which direction the maker had come from, which direction he went, what his name was and what he was looking for. Ilias wrote the mark to say they were looking for trouble, which he thought summed up the situation nicely.

Not that Halian or anybody else will be coming through here to appreciate it, I hope, he thought, getting to his feet and following Giliead into the next tunnel. Giliead had made Halian swear on his grandmother's ashes not to come after them if they didn't come back. Ilias hoped that Halian would hold to it, even if it meant their bodies were lost and their souls trapped here forever.

The acrid odor in the air became thicker as the tunnel floor slanted even further down. "So say you're Ixion—" Ilias began.

"I'd rather not, thanks, I have enough problems of my own." Giliead lifted the torch to chase away the shadows overhead.

"—and you're sitting around one day in your dark dank cave, watching the howlers and the grend hump and kill each other, and you think, 'Hello, I'll make something that jumps on people's heads and bores through their skulls and eats out the insides.' Why does that happen?"

"Because he's a wizard and that's what wizards do," Giliead said patiently. "What else—" He stopped abruptly.

Ilias froze, a hand going to his sword. He heard it too, a muted click of claws against stone. He drew the weapon, shifting to stand back to back with Giliead, his eyes on the rock above their heads. There would be tunnels up there, the openings hidden in folds and shadows. "Back or forward?" he whispered. The passage was too narrow to fight in.

"Back—" Giliead began. Then from the direction of the bone chamber, two lean man-sized shapes appeared at the edge of the torchlight, the flame reflected in mad hungry eyes. "Forward!" they finished in unison.

Ilias let Giliead worry about what was ahead and kept his eyes on the passage behind them as he backed away. The firelight threw leaping red-tinged shadows on the howlers' slick mottled green hides, which he knew were disconcertingly like human skin to the touch. The creatures had the elongated heads and long spidery hands of harmless rock lizards, but their jaws were heavy with vicious fangs and their claws were like razors.

These howlers warily kept their distance, as if they had been hunted before. *That's all we need, for these things to get smart,* Ilias thought in exasperation. He shouted, darting forward. The one in the lead took the bait, springing at him, hands reaching. Ilias ducked under the sweep of its claws, thrusting his sword upward and skewering it in the belly.

It recoiled with a screech, lurching into the wall and clawing at the rock. He dodged back as it struck the ground; the others fell on it as prey, maddened by the scent of blood.

Warily watching the dark shapes tear at the frantic creature, Ilias heard Giliead curse and risked a look over his shoulder. The tunnel came to an abrupt end not far ahead. "Damn," he breathed, turning back. The wounded howler writhed at the bottom of the snarling heap.

"Down here," Giliead said sharply, sweeping the torch along the ground in a haze of sparks. At the base of the boulders blocking the passage were openings in the rock. He leaned down, thrusting the torch into the largest, then jumped.

Ilias scrambled down after him, sliding, then leaping down to level ground. Giliead had found a large, low-ceilinged tunnel, wide enough for them to make a stand. Giliead cast the torch behind them and drew his sword as the first of the howlers leapt down to the chamber floor.

Driven wild by the fresh blood, the howlers lost all ability to coordinate their attack and came at them in a confused rush. Ilias took the first one with a straight thrust into the chest. As he pulled his sword free it went down, still clawing for him. He blocked a blow as another ran at him, half severing its arm, then spinning close to slice its head off. Ducking under the next creature's wild swing, he took its leg off at the knee and risked a look around as it fell.

Giliead freed his sword from a creature's chest with a hard shove from his boot. He shifted to close the distance between them as Ilias eyed the howlers warily.

Seven of the creatures sprawled limp and bleeding on the ground as the others withdrew to the far side of the chamber, hissing and growling. Ilias frowned, watching as they stooped and weaved, their heads bobbing in what looked like a strange dance. "What the . . ." Giliead muttered. Ilias shrugged, baffled, as one by one the howlers crept back up the rocks into the upper tunnel.

Ilias pivoted, trying to see the rest of the chamber as Giliead grabbed up the torch again. "Are they trying to get above us?" he demanded. Howlers never gave up prey.

"They didn't even take the dead ones, that's—" Giliead cocked his head, lifting the torch higher. "You hear that?"

After a moment, Ilias nodded. It was faint, but he could hear a humming, like disturbed bees.

"We've found it," Giliead said softly, absolute conviction in his voice. He stepped forward and thrust the torch against the wall, grinding it out.

As his eyes adjusted, Ilias could make out the shape of a tunnel in the far wall, gently limned with a pearly white light. He heard Giliead move toward it. *Right,* Ilias thought, taking a deep breath. *This is what we came for.* He would have rather fought howlers. He followed Giliead's quiet footsteps.

The tunnel wound around, slanting downward, and the humming grew steadily louder. Ilias thought he could hear a faint metallic banging as well. The strange white light grew brighter until the last turn revealed it spilling from a jagged gap in the low ceiling. Ilias stared at it in dismay. That light, without the flicker and color of real flame, was something only wizards made.

Giliead stepped around it, moving forward. Ilias followed more cautiously. The ability the god had given Giliead to sense the presence of curses had kept them alive on more than one occasion and Ilias was trusting to it now.

Ilias stopped at the edge of the pool of light, craning his neck to look up. Far overhead he could see reflections on white crystalline stone clinging to an arching cavern roof like so many frozen water droplets. This had to be some other part of the central cavern. A shadow passed over the opening and Ilias ducked back hastily. From somewhere above two voices spoke a rapid spate of words in an unfamiliar tongue with a strange harsh sound to it. Cineth had trade from everywhere but Ilias didn't think he had ever heard speech like that before. He edged away from the spot of light as Giliead motioned urgently for him to hurry.

Ahead there was another narrow opening in the side of the tunnel and Giliead climbed the rock to look through. He froze, the set of his shoulders telling Ilias he had seen something shocking. Ilias twitched, impatient to know the worst. Finally Giliead moved aside and Ilias swung up to push in beside him. What he saw made his eyes widen. A hysterical scream seemed the only appropriate response, but he settled for swearing softly under his breath. It was much, much worse than he had ever imagined.

The opening looked out on a large cavern, the floor only about twenty paces below this level. It was filled with people, dozens of them. They swarmed around a huge structure of bare metal ribs supported on a high scaffold. From the shape outlined by the metal bars it might be a giant ship, maybe a barge, except that the lines were subtly wrong and it was just stupid to build a ship out of metal. The worst part was that they were using curses to construct it; several men, if they were men, had some kind of small torch that emitted a fire so brilliant it was like a captured star. They were playing the torches over the metal, as if melting it into place.

Ilias shot a worried look at Giliead. His friend's grim expression was just visible in the reflected light. *Yes, we're in trouble,* he thought. So many wizards.

But not like Ixion. He had looked and dressed just like a normal man and had even managed to fool everyone into thinking he was one for a time. The people below were anything but normal. Their clothes were drably colored, all dull browns, and they wore half masks of some kind of dark-colored glass over their eyes. Their hair, if they had any, was gathered up under baggy brown caps. Ilias was sweating in the warm damp air but the men below were covered up as if they expected to have to plow through a snowy mountain pass. Their sleeves came down to reach their gloved hands, the collars went up nearly to their chins, leaving only the pale skin around the mouth, nose, and throat exposed.

And their wizard lights were different from the ones Ixion had used. His had been small silent misty wisps of illumination that floated on the cave breezes; these were giant things a good two paces across, set in metal holders driven into the rock or on high metal stands. Looking at them was like trying to stare into the sun and they made a low hum, the source of the strange noise.

Then as Ilias watched, a group of howlers came out of another tunnel dragging a bundle of metal poles, watched over by a pair of wizards. The white light gleamed off their slick mottled skin and mad eyes. These wizards had tamed the howlers, then, just as Ixion had.

Then one suddenly dropped its burden, crouching and snarling. A wizard stood nearby, unrolling a coil of black rope; he shouted a warning and pointed at the creature. The noise and sudden movement attracted it; with snakelike quickness it darted at him.

Just as it leapt on him another wizard pulled something dark out of the sheath at his belt, pointing it at the howler. Ilias flinched back at a sudden sharp report. *That's a new one,* he thought, glancing at Giliead, who was wincing at the echo that reverberated through the cavern. His ears still ringing, Ilias looked back in time to see the howler reel and fall, its legs kicking spasmodically. The other howlers didn't go after it, but huddled in a group, hissing in alarm. Ilias wet his lips. *At least now we know what taught the howlers to be wary of people.*

Some wizards were herding the others back to work, as if it was a normal occurrence. One gestured for two of the others to haul the howler's victim away. He was limp, though the creature had barely touched him and there was no blood trail on the stone; they dragged him by his arms with his head hanging back to bounce on the ground, as if they knew he was dead or didn't care. *Or that curse, weapon, whatever it was killed him too.*

He looked up at Giliead. Ilias had seen wizards kill before, but curses always took time to work. If they didn't, he and Gil would be dead several times over. He nudged the bigger man's arm with an elbow and mouthed, "What was that thing?"

Giliead shook his head, equally baffled. He leaned down to say in a nearly voiceless whisper, "Some of them aren't wizards. Some are slaves, see?"

After a moment of study Ilias nodded. The ones who were doing the herding all wore leather belts with the odd-shaped sheaths attached, often with other pouches and metal implements. The ones being herded didn't have such accoutrements. They were also the ones doing all the actual labor, using the cursed tools, carrying pipes and poles and heavy cables. The others pointed and gave orders and watched, or scribbled things on small square boards they seemed to use as miniature portable writing desks. They also moved more confidently, shoulders stiff, jaws squared. Not so many wizards as it had looked at first, then. *Still too many,* Ilias thought.

A touch on his shoulder made Ilias jump and he realized he had been staring in horrified fascination for some time. His legs were stiff from crouching so long. He scrambled down the rock after Giliead and they retreated back up the tunnel, to just before the chamber where the howlers had fought them and fled. They sat back against the rock under an overhang, squeezing in shoulder to shoulder, more for comfort than any need for concealment. "Well?" Ilias said, keeping his voice low.

Giliead took a deep breath, then said softly, "I didn't know there were that many wizards. Anywhere." Ilias felt him shrug helplessly. "I didn't know they could work together like that."

Ilias swallowed in a dry throat. This wasn't one lone wizard, come to take Ixion's place and make use of his leavings, to prey on the shipping and the towns and villages along the coast as he had. A wizard like that could be killed if you were clever and careful. They had done it enough times before. This was an army of wizards. The scars on his back ached with the thought of it. "It's war."

Giliead nodded and rubbed his forehead. He was badly disturbed and trying to hide it. "We've got to get word back to Nicanor and Visolela. Not that we have much to tell them." They could send messengers to the other city-states and all the holdings throughout the Syrnai. Giliead shook his head in frustration. "We've got to find out when the attack will start."

"We've got three days to scout around." The *Swift* would be picking them up at the next moonrise on the opposite end of the island. "And we've got the advantage now since they don't know we're here." He sensed Giliead looking down at him and added, "We hope."

Chapter 3

Vienne, Ile-Rien

After Tremaine had dressed and they had experienced the usual difficulty with the starter handle of Gerard's old sedan, they set out for the Institute. It was faster to skirt the edge of the city and as Gerard drove, Tremaine leaned back in the cracked leather seat and watched the dark streets go by. This quarter still looked relatively normal, if murky and oddly quiet. There had been no blackout sirens tonight, but only a few streetlamps were lit and they saw no one except for the civil defense and the army patrols.

As they drove a short distance up the end of Saints Procession Boulevard there were more cars, more people and even a few cafés open. The old casino, converted to a military canteen, was a spot of light and gaiety in a block of fashionable shops that had been closed for months as the owners and customers fled the city. Other than that, this end of the boulevard looked strangely undisturbed by the war, the old stone façades undamaged, as if they had been removed from the scene and preserved in a glass case. The few passersby walked under the potted trees in groups or couples and there was music and laughter from the canteen and the scents of coffee and chocolate in the cold damp air. But in the distance, over the roofs of the lower structures and the mists that hung above the streetlamps, she could see the ruin of the Grand Opera. Her eyes would never grow accustomed to the gaps in what should be a perfect dome; it was like seeing an old friend with an arm missing. Of course she had seen that too.

The Institute's project lay outside Vienne, a long drive through dark twisty country lanes, past old estates, farms, vineyards and a couple of small villages. Patchy clouds occasionally obscured the moon and stars and a rainy wind tore at the treetops. The air had the heavy wild scent of the country, laced with smoke. It would be a wonderful thing if the Institute was successful, but Tremaine wasn't an optimist by nature or nurture.

Her first hint that her family life would not be a normal one had come when she was seven. Her mother Madeline had died and her father had disappeared for a year. She had lived with Uncle Arisilde then and he had assured her that her father was still alive no matter what the newspapers might say. She had realized later that Nicholas had gone after her mother's murderers and that her peripatetic existence with Arisilde, wandering the byways of Vienne, tramping through fields and forests, with occasional visits to Lodun where they stayed in the strangest places and met the oddest people, had kept her alive. That quirky and self-effacing Uncle Arisilde was a powerful sorcerer and that he was hiding her from her father's enemies, some of whom were powerful sorcerers themselves. One day Arisilde had taken her back to Coldcourt and they found her father there, and that was that.

She had never found out what had happened to those enemies. Nicholas Valiarde had never set foot on a stage but he had been a born actor, taking on different roles and personas the way other men changed their coats. He had done work for the Queen at times, but Tremaine had grown to understand that his public persona of gentleman adventurer was just that, a persona. He wasn't one of those noble rogues with a heart of gold who were portrayed in novels and plays, though he could maintain that act when it suited him. The reality was that he had been and to a large extent still was a lord of the criminal underworld—dangerous, implacable and ruthless.

After a time of staring hypnotized at the night landscape, it occurred to Tremaine that Gerard must be exhausted from making this drive once already tonight and she offered to take the wheel.

"I didn't know you could drive," he said, gratefully pulling over to the side of the narrow country road. "Did you learn in the Aid Society?"

"I drove supply trucks for a while," Tremaine told him, blundering into the spiky hedgerow while climbing out of the passenger-side door. Staging an accident with her truck would have been a possibility, but everyone had been so disparaging of her ability to learn to drive it in the first place that she hadn't been willing to give them the satisfaction. She disentangled her cap from the thorns and stumbled around the front of the car.

Gerard climbed into the passenger seat. "This past six months for you must have been—"

"It's the same for everyone." Tremaine pulled the door shut with a grimace. She sounded like a bad melodrama. *Don't mind me, even though my leg's blown off, I'll stagger back to the front line.* She fumbled with gears and got the car pointed back to the road.

"With the skills your father taught you, I thought you might go into the Prefecture or the Intelligence Service. Though I was glad you didn't." Settling back in the seat, Gerard added ruefully, "They aren't making any headway from what I've heard and the attrition rate is even higher than the Aid Society."

Tremaine had never considered that as a serious possibility. It wouldn't have worked, anyway. She hadn't wanted her death to ruin some vital operation or get anyone else hurt or killed. That was the last thing she needed. "I was never as good at that sort of thing as you all."

Gerard snorted. "You weren't there to see my spectacular failures. I was lucky Nicholas was there to save my— Well, that's all over with now." He must have sensed she wanted to change the subject. "What are you writing?" he asked.

"Ah . . ." Natural honesty did not run in the family so Tremaine wasn't sure how she came to be saddled with it, at least when it came to speaking with Gerard. She guided the car past a couple of slow-moving farm carts. It was safer to bring supplies into the city after dark. Branches caught on the windscreen and the bonnet as Tremaine edged the car close to the ditch, and one of the drovers lifted his hat in thanks, barely visible in the light from his kerosene lamp. It gave her time to think. "I was playing around with . . . doing another play." She winced again, glad it was too dark for Gerard to see her face.

"Another adventure?"

His voice still sounded unconcerned but Tremaine knew in her gut he had read the titles of the books piled around her chair in the library. Gerard hadn't been one of Nicholas Valiarde's chosen few for nothing. "Maybe," she said offhandedly. Tremaine's plays and serials had all been romantic adventure fare, with lost cities, undiscovered fayre islands, and other fantastic elements. Not exactly something one read *Medical Jurisprudence* for. "Something different, you know."

Fortunately Gerard was tired and he soon began to drift off. Tremaine had been out here several times when the Institute first acquired the land and had to backtrack only once. The car was stopped twice by Civil Defense patrols, cautioning her to use the headlamps sparingly, and once by the regular army as she neared the old estate that housed the project grounds. Bringing the car to a halt, Tremaine fished for Gerard's authorization papers in the litter in his dispatch bag, glad for the electric torch the soldier shined into the car. She handed him her identity card and Gerard's papers. He checked them over briefly with the torch, then directed the light for a moment on Gerard, who snored. "Looks in order, madam. Hold up a moment while I get the corporal."

"All right," Tremaine replied dispiritedly, thinking *Miss, it's miss. I'm twenty-six, I only look forty.* Her mousy brown hair didn't look any better for the bad bob she had gotten not long ago. If she had just continued to cut it herself with the kitchen shears, it would have at least looked neat. She was pale from the winter too but so was everyone else. She probably didn't look like a Gardier spy, at least. There were warnings in the papers constantly that there were Gardier spies in the cities, there to get information on defense plans and troop movements on the Aderassi border, and to kill sorcerers.

The soldier carried their papers over to the truck parked off under the trees and she heard the voice of the corporal as he checked their documents again. "They've hit the coast too, Chaire again. It's likely they'll take another run at Vienne before midnight."

"No, not again." The soldier sounded as resigned and weary as Tremaine felt.

"Yes, just came in on the wireless."

The bombings on the seaport of Chaire had started only a few months ago. The two things that had most puzzled the Institute's researchers since the war began was where the Gardier had come from and how they were concealing their bases. Airships now also came from the captured territory of Adera, but at first they had always come from over the Western Ocean. They still made their attacks on the Western Coast that way, but as far as their allies in Capidara could tell, the dirigibles were not passing over their territory at any point. Speculation in the newspapers had covered everything from a secret undiscovered island, an underwater city and a hitherto-unnoticed continent that submerged at will. If the Gardier came from further away, from some hidden city, then that still left the fact that they appeared to be supplying and launching many of their airships from the middle of the open sea. After three years of fighting, Ile-Rien still knew little about them, not even what they called themselves; the name *Gardier* had been given to them by the newspapers and was a Rienish corruption of an Aderassi slang word for "enemy."

Ile-Rien had been invaded before. During the Bisran Wars, troops had crossed the borders and pushed inward as far as Lodun, overrunning towns and villages, burning witches and priests. She had read the history, seen the ancient great houses pockmarked by cannonballs. But nothing prepared you for this.

Many of the standards of the Ile-Rien sorcerer's arsenal, like the charm that ignited gunpowder, were useless against the Gardier. Only illusions or defensive wards seemed to succeed against the airships and attempts to work magic often drew their attention. And one of the Gardier's most devastating spells caused engines, gun mechanisms and electrical equipment to spontaneously explode. Now traveling the shipping lanes to and from allied nations was suicidal and the few surviving factories were hard-pressed to provide new munitions.

The soldier returned and handed over the papers. "Thank you, madam. Careful now. It's a good night for a bombing."

It might have been the soldier's warning or Tremaine's inherited paranoia, but as the road left the woods and hedgerows behind for an open down, she switched the headlamps off. The sloping field ahead, bleached of any color by the moonlight, led down to another shadowy curtain of trees, the dark sky chased with clouds stretching above it. Tremaine's foot slammed onto the brake before her brain processed what her eyes had just recorded; outlined against a stray cloud was a long cylindrical shape, the jagged ridge down its back tapering into knifelike tail fins. Gerard jolted awake. "What is it?"

"Airship, dammit." Tremaine craned her neck to look out the windscreen. It was low, perhaps only a hundred feet above them. She wished she hadn't stopped so abruptly; surely a sudden motion was more likely to attract attention than a slow one. She was very glad Gerard's car had a silver-gray body and a dingy gray bonnet; it should blend in with the grassy field.

Please no firebombs, Tremaine thought, watching the airship draw closer. After so much time in the Aid Society she should be used to air raids, to the noise and the smoke and the smell of death, but maybe that was something no one got used to. The damn thing was passing directly over them, as if drawn to the surely near-invisible shape of the car by her fear. It was too dark for a shadow to fall over them but Tremaine gritted her teeth, feeling it anyway. She started as something clanked on the floorboard. "What the hell?" she whispered. The clanking turned into rhythmic clicks.

"It's the sphere." Gerard sounded quietly aghast. He fumbled for it in the dark.

The Gardier could detect spells and the sphere, old and fading, was held together with nothing but magic. "Kick it," she urged him.

"I'd rather not."

Tremaine's stomach twisted with tension. She had seen too many people get blown up to want to die that way. And certainly not with Gerard in the car, and not with the sphere needed by the Institute. *Come on,* she told it silently, *stop clicking at the airship. You're going to get us all killed. And no, I'm not being ironic.*

There was one last reluctant click and the sphere shuddered into silence. Gerard breathed, "That was close."

Tremaine twisted around on the seat, looking out the back to see the airship passing over the crown of the hill behind them. It must have moved out of the sphere's range. She took a deep breath in relief, then realized the airship was going in the wrong direction. She frowned, glancing at Gerard. "It's not going to Vienne?"

"Bel Garde." His voice was grim as he turned to look back. "It's just over that rise, on the other side of the woods."

It was a suburb of Vienne, one of the most beautiful. Remembering the last time she had been out there, Tremaine pictured old houses with wild green summer gardens centered around the ruins of an ancient and picturesque stone keep. "There's nothing there," she protested.

She couldn't read his expression in the dark, but she saw him shake his head. "An arms depot."

"Stupid place for an arms depot." The first blast echoed over the hills, jarring her teeth. The flash lit up the sky for an instant. "Ex–arms depot," Tremaine muttered, turning around and putting the car back into gear. "How did they know it was there?"

She heard his tired sigh. "Their intelligence sources are excellent."

Wonderful, she thought sourly. She could have lived without knowing the newspapers were right about the spies.

Tremaine didn't see the turn for the Institute's drive until the last instant and skewed the car into it, almost landing them in the ditch.

"Sorry." She winced, noticing Gerard was still gripping the dash.

"That's quite all right." He took a deep breath. "Once you get past the bridge, just turn into the woods to the left. We keep the vehicles under the trees to keep from drawing any airships down on the place."

Peering into the dark, Tremaine managed to find an open spot and deposit the car in it without incident. She collected the sphere from the floorboards and trailed after Gerard, following the beam of his electric torch over the uneven ground. She stumbled over the remains of an old brick path and a stone flower bed border, more confirmation that they were on the grounds of the old estate that housed the Institute. They passed out of another copse of trees and emerged to see the outline of a ruined great house against the moonlit velvet background of the sky. It was a forest of towers and sharply pitched roof lines and half-collapsed walls etched against the night.

The past few hours had been surreal enough already; now Tremaine found her attention roaming, trying to turn this into a scene for a play or a magazine serial. Foolish. The theaters had been closed for months and only a few of the magazines were still in operation. Not that people didn't still want stories. In the Aid Society, as they had huddled around the kerosene stove in the shelters during their rest breaks, there was always some new volunteer who discovered her identity and begged her to tell him the ending of her last serial in *Boulevard.* The final three numbers of it had never been printed when publication was suspended for the war.

They were now walking on a dirt path through winter-dry grass, drawing closer to another large dark shape outlined against the sky, this one with the curving roof of what had been a large stables. Abruptly the sphere in Tremaine's hands trembled and heat flashed through the metal, intense enough for her to feel it through her gloves. She swore, juggling the thing awkwardly.

"What is it?" Gerard demanded, pausing.

"Did we just pass through some wards?" Tremaine managed to get the sphere tucked under her arm, where the thickness of her tweed jacket protected her from the sorcerously hot metal.

"Yes." He stepped closer, directing the light down on the sphere. "It reacted again?" he asked, his voice tight with excitement.

"I think it ate one of them."

A loud crash from the direction of the dark building made Tremaine nearly drop the sphere. A door spilled light and shouting people. Gerard whirled, yelling, "It's all right! We've got the Damal sphere and it reacted to the wards."

The men gathering, some of them in military uniforms and armed with rifles, now rapidly backed away. Tremaine looked around at the respectful breathing room she, Gerard and the sphere now had, bewildered. *What the hell is the matter with them?* she wondered. The sphere's metal cooled rapidly in the night air and she shifted it into a more comfortable hold. She followed Gerard through the quietly murmuring crowd toward the door.

She stepped into a long building, high-ceilinged and bare, lit by strings of electric bulbs hanging from the rafters overhead. She could hear the distant roar of a generator and realized the wards must have blocked sound from escaping as well as guarding against magical attack. The floor was hay-strewn packed dirt and the air was full of dust. There were doorways leading into other workrooms and tables along the walls where men and women worked busily in groups.

For some reason Tremaine hadn't thought there would be this many people here. She was glad she had put on what passed for her best outfit: a dark tweed jacket and skirt. Unfortunately, the stout walking boots didn't exactly go with it. *But then the "dowdy old maid" look never goes out of style,* she thought in resignation.

A tall slim young man with short straw blond hair hurried up to them, demanding, "Did you get it?"

Unperturbed, Gerard touched her elbow to bring her forward. "Tremaine Valiarde, this is my colleague, Breidan Niles."

"An Arisilde Damal sphere," Niles said, ignoring Tremaine in favor of the device she was holding. He touched the metal reverently. "The other prototypes were before my time."

"Yes, thank you for reminding me of that." Gerard sighed and took the sphere from Tremaine. "The sphere will let me manipulate it, but it's still keyed to Tremaine."

Niles stared at her, as if seeing her for the first time. With his well-tailored suit, narrow features and slicked-back hair, he looked exactly like the kind of man who should be decorating a café society party or a court reception, but if he was here, he was either a sorcerer or a philosopher or both. Light brows drawn together in consternation, he turned back to Gerard. "Have you considered the possible consequences?"

Gerard lifted an ironic brow. "I assure you, I've thought of nothing else for the past few hours."

"Is she aware—"

"She's just spent six months in the Aid Society," Gerard informed him dryly, "I assure you she is perfectly aware."

Yes, I'm a bloody heroine, Tremaine thought, stepping past them. It made her wonder how many of history's favorite heroes were just incompetent suicides.

About midway down the length of the building was a wooden platform and she strolled toward it, Gerard and Niles still arguing behind her. She stepped up on it and leaned on the railing. Below was an open area of packed dirt, dug several feet down below the level of the floor. The cold air rising up from it touched her cheeks. Resting on the bare earth was a round narrow band of dull-colored metal, enclosing an open space perhaps ten feet wide. There was nothing inside the band but more dirt, disturbed by footprints and the marks of what looked like a garden rake. Tremaine caught the slaughterhouse scent of blood and suspected they hadn't cleaned up quite well enough after Riardin's accident. This would be where it happened, then. This was Arisilde Damal's last Great Spell.

There were alchemical symbols that she couldn't read roughly scratched or etched onto the metal band. Around the outside, pieces of paper, scribbled over with notes and sections of sorcerous adjurations, were tacked down with various makeshift paperweights—small stones, pencils, cups and saucers, walnuts, a woman's shoe. Representing three years of work by teams of sorcerers and philosophers and sorcerer-philosophers of the Viller Institute, desperately trying to re-create Uncle Ari's work.

Nicholas Valiarde had caught the first hints of the Gardier's presence in Adera, nearly four years before they had appeared so devastatingly in the sky over Lodun. Nicholas had never committed anything to paper, never wrote letters or took notes that involved his work, even when it was legal, so the details of how he had discovered them were largely unknown. His only close confidant in his self-appointed mission had been Arisilde Damal. Damal had been a force to be reckoned with when he was a young man half dead and drugged to the gills on opium; then he had been older, sober and mostly sane. If you were going to pit yourself against an organization of mysterious and deadly sorcerers, he was the man to have at your back. It had been then that Arisilde began to work on this spell ring.

Tremaine rubbed her eyes. Since conventional spells had little effect on the Gardier, whatever Arisilde had been building here, it had to be something special. It had certainly killed him and Nicholas during its first test seven years ago, vaporizing them utterly, without leaving any unpleasant remains for the bystanders to deal with. This evidently had not been the case with Riardin.

Nicholas and Arisilde had died still thinking they were dealing with a criminal organization of sorcerers and not the first scouts of an invading army. Now three years after the first strike that isolated Lodun under its wards, Adera had fallen and Bisra and Parscia had come under heavy attack.

"When can we get this over with?" Tremaine asked, turning back to Gerard and Niles. Seeing their expressions, she corrected herself hastily: "I mean, when can we, ah, start the test." She gestured vaguely back at the ring.

Niles glanced at Gerard and said guardedly, "We can be ready in an hour."

It was more like three hours. Gerard and Niles weren't quite as in charge of all aspects of the experiment as they would have liked to be. There was a long argument with Colonel Averi, the army liaison, who had the extremely valid point that all sorcerers were desperately needed for the defense of the population and the support of the troops on the Aderassi front, and if this spell was going to use them up like matches, then maybe it wasn't such a good idea. But the beleaguered Crown had given a carte blanche to the Institute three years ago at the start of the war, and revoking that would mean a long drive into the city, talking a way past the security provided by the Prefecture at the Defense Department, a visit to the palace, talking a way past the Queen's Guard, and a discussion with the Queen. Everyone seemed to know Gerard and Niles were going to win, but the colonel felt compelled to make the argument anyway.

Tremaine drank black terribly bitter coffee to stay awake and sat near the side room that housed the wireless, where a group had gathered to listen to the reports of the Gardier's bombing of Chaire, Bel Garde and the eastern side of Vienne. There were more rumors of the royal family's evacuation to Parscia, more reports of the number of people leaving the capital.

Tremaine wandered away from the group around the wireless, tired of listening to it. Niles was the only one who seemed excited about the sphere. The Institute smelled of failure and dying hopes.

Nearby at one of the worktables a young woman was examining what looked like a small chunk of crystal. Her bobbed hair was dark red and she was dressed even more drably than Tremaine in a dull-colored skirt and jacket and clunky shoes. Tremaine wandered close, looking at the crystal. The girl glanced up, startled, and dropped it.

"I'm sorry!" Tremaine dived to recover the object just as the girl pushed her chair back and bent forward. They bonked heads.

Tremaine sat back with an embarrassed smile. "I think I'll just get out of your way."

Rubbing her forehead and smiling back, the girl picked up the crystal and dropped it on the desk. "It's all right. If we did break it, it would at least tell me something."

Tremaine picked up the blue-veined crystal, holding it to the light. "What is it?"

"It's a piece of one of the crystals they found in the wreckage of that Gardier airship that went down a few months ago." The girl pushed loose strands of hair back with a weary sigh. "Everyone thought it would be the big breakthrough to finding out how they resist our magic, but nobody can tell how the crystals are used or what they do. I guess when it shattered in the crash any spells it had just vanished without a trace. They've gotten so desperate, they've even let me take a look at it." Her rueful expression turned self-conscious and she added, "I'm training to be a sorceress. I'm Florian."

"Tremaine Valiarde." It was just a shard of crystal. It could even have been a chunk of glass, as far as she could tell. *You'd think the Gardier would have something complicated, like the spheres.* "I didn't even know any airships had ever been captured. But I haven't been paying much attention to the news lately."

"There wasn't much left of it. There was a big storm over the mountains in Adera and its protective spells must have failed; it was torn apart. An Intelligence patrol found it and they grabbed everything that looked important." Florian picked up the notebook that lay nearby and scratched out a couple of words. "The mechanical bits

were pretty ordinary. The crystal shards are the only unusual thing." Depressed, she added, "We don't even know
if they're dangerous."

"Dangerous?" Tremaine repeated thoughtfully. She
brought the crystal to her eye and peered through it at the
lightbulb overhead.

"It hasn't done anything to me," Florian admitted,
sounding disappointed.

"Tremaine?"

She turned, startled at the familiar voice, and found herself staring up at Ander Destan. "Ander, what are you
doing here?" she demanded, getting to her feet hastily.

"I work here." He grinned at her. He was a tall handsome man, only a few years older than Tremaine, with dark
hair and laughing eyes. "You sound shocked."

Tremaine had sounded aghast. Ander had been a fixture
in the café society of artists, actors and writers that
Tremaine had inhabited before the war, though his family
had been a little too beau monde to approve of his pastime.
In Ander's social set, associating with the people of cafés,
salons and theaters was slumming; for Tremaine it had
been a part of her career, and for her father part of his protective coloration. Though she and Ander had been almost
close at one point, that seemed a lifetime ago now. It was
nice to know he was still alive and well, but he knew a little too much about her past for comfort.

Years ago before her father had disappeared, Tremaine
had been kidnapped and held in a private institution for the
mad. She had been there for nearly a week, until she had
stabbed an attendant in the neck with a hypodermic needle
and escaped by jumping out a window. She had recovered
from her ordeal at Coldcourt, only to discover that the
story that she had been voluntarily committed was making
the rounds of society. The Prefecture could do nothing,
since the institution had the forged documents to prove
their version of the story and she had nothing but her word.
Her father had been out of the country at the time; when he
had returned he had heard her adventures without a great
deal of visible sympathy. But this time Tremaine was old

enough to recognize the newspaper reports for what they were, to know that it was no coincidence when the institution burned down and several key members of the staff were found floating in the river, minus vital body parts. A surviving employee was found to be guilty of arson and murder and subsequently hanged for it. Arisilde had made a "tsk tsk" noise and said that Nicholas had always liked things neat and tidy.

She had never told any of her friends the truth and Ander had, of course, always treated the matter with a civilized delicacy. Tremaine would have preferred it if he had flat out asked her if she was insane. She managed to say, "I thought you were in the army." Ander was dressed as a civilian, in a tan pullover sweater and a leather jacket.

"Well, I am. I'm in the Intelligence Corps, attached to the Institute to keep an eye on the sorcerers. Like Tiamarc here." Smiling, he turned to the man who had stepped up beside him. "Tiamarc, this is Tremaine Valiarde, the playwright."

"Oh, really?" Tiamarc smiled. He was sandy-haired and handsome under his spectacles, though he didn't have Ander's air of Ducal Court Street polish. "Anything recent?"

"Nothing you would have heard of," Ander told him with a grin before Tremaine could gather her wits enough to answer. "The old-fashioned blood and thunder stuff for those old ex–music hall theaters."

"Yep, that's me," Tremaine managed, feeling as though Ander had just identified her as a leper. She cursed herself for being oversensitive. Ander had sat in many of those old ex–music hall theaters watching her blood and thunder stuff, so he didn't mean anything by it.

Tiamarc's polite expression didn't alter but Tremaine could tell he had lost interest. Florian, on the other hand, tugged on Tremaine's sleeve and whispered excitedly, "Really? Which ones?"

Before Tremaine could answer, Niles strode up from the other end of the building, bellowing, "Tremaine, we're ready!"

"Nice meeting you," Tremaine told Florian, absently setting the crystal back on the desk. "Got to go do this thing."

"Thing?" Ander asked, lifting his brows.

"The experiment."

Holding the sphere, Tremaine stood with Gerard in the metal circle. Niles moved around the circumference, making a few last checks of the notes tacked down around the outside, and everyone else was crowded up to the railing. Tremaine saw Florian had managed to fight her way to a spot in the front and was watching with her brow creased in concern. Ander stood nearby with a deeply worried expression. Tremaine felt horribly awkward and self-conscious under all those combined gazes, especially Ander's. She couldn't tell if he was worried that she would die or that she would do something stupid, or a combination of both. She just wished they could get on with it.

Finally Niles nodded to Gerard and climbed back up to the wooden platform. "Ready?" Gerard asked Tremaine, watching her gravely. Sweat was beading on his brow and he looked more nervous than she felt.

You could stop it, a traitor voice whispered in her head. *Just say no.* Maybe it was the Voice of Reason, but that had never had much power over her. Tremaine shrugged. "Let's go."

Gerard took a deep breath, then touched the sphere.

Her stomach lurched and a rush of cool air struck her, passing through her without impact, as if her body were made of gauze. There was nothing under her feet and her hair streamed up and she just had time to realize that this bizarre sensation was vertigo from falling when she hit something.

The first lungful of salt water clarified the situation completely. Tremaine surfaced, thrashing and gasping for air. It was day, bright blue sky laced with white clouds arched above and this was the ocean. Choppy blue water lay in every direction. In the distance was a rocky cliff-lined coast. Closer there was an island that seemed to be nothing but several peaks of graduated heights, all wreathed in dense mist. "Gerard!" Tremaine yelled, and went under again. She fought her way back up and remembered to tread water. Shrugging out of her jacket helped. She took a deep breath, went under, and wrestled off one boot; that helped too. She surfaced, her throat burning from inhaled salt water. "Gerard!" she shouted again.

"Here!"

She saw him swimming toward her and thrashed awkwardly to him. "What the hell happened?"

"I . . . I don't know." He had lost his spectacles and his dark hair was plastered to his head. "Do you have the sphere?"

The sphere . . . Oh, God. Tremaine looked around as if it would be floating nearby. "I must have let go of it!"

"All right. It's all right." He sounded as if he was reassuring himself as well as her. "Give me your hand, we can call it."

Tremaine nodded and reached for him, lacing their fingers together as Gerard whispered the words of the brief charm. They bobbed in the water, Tremaine turning her face away as the low waves crashed into her. "Did it work?"

"I'm not—" The sphere surfaced a few feet away with a splash. "Thank God!" Gerard let go of Tremaine and grabbed for it before it could go under again.

Watching him, Tremaine asked, "There's an island that way, should we swim?" It seemed the thing to do, though she had never swum that far in her life.

Gerard twisted to look. "Island? It could be a promontory."

"Whatever. Shouldn't we start—"

He shook his head. "No, now that we have the sphere, we need to give the spell a chance to reverse. I timed it precisely—"

"Precisely? Gerard, what happened? This was supposed to be a weapon, not a transportation—thing!" Tremaine demanded, keeping her head above water with difficulty. "Hold on." She went under again to get rid of the other boot.

As she surfaced, Gerard asked anxiously, "Are you all right?"

"Boots," she explained succinctly. "What happened to the spell?"

"Ah, yes. Well, something . . . something unexpected has happened."

"You think?"

"Yes, sarcasm always helps a situation like—" His face went deathly still. "Tremaine, look."

Her head whipped around, following his gaze. "The Gardier."

The airship hadn't been there a moment ago. It hung low, heading away from them, its black mass silhouetted sharply against the blue sky. The ridge and fins made jagged outlines and the long square cabin hung low underneath the swollen belly of the hull. "Where did it come from?" Tremaine realized she had whispered. It wasn't likely to spot two heads bobbing in the waves, as high as it was and pointed away from them, but she had instinctively tried to sink as low as she could in the water and still keep breathing. The thing moved slowly but something made her think of a wasp, heavy with venom and searching for prey.

"It just appeared. I saw it." Gerard stared after it. "There was a flash of light and it popped into existence. . . . Just like we did."

"Like we did?"

Gerard was muttering, "Gardier attacking the coast always come out of the west and return that way. If that's west— Wait!" He floundered, splashing her, frantically digging something out of a pants pocket. He produced a compass, shook it to get the water out, and examined it avidly. "That is west!"

"The spell sent us to Chaire? Except that isn't Chaire." Tremaine frowned at the island, the distant rocky coastline. The country around the port city of Chaire was flat. Then Tremaine's startled brain put two and two together. "The spell sent us to where the Gardier come from."

"Wait, look!" Gerard pointed.

Tremaine squinted against the sun. There was a dark blot moving out of the mist around the island's peak. "It's another airship—"

Tremaine hit the ground with a jarring thump, drenched by gallons of seawater. The downpour ended abruptly and she looked around, dazed. They were back in the Institute's building, in the center of the spell circle. Gerard was sprawled a few feet away, dripping wet, still holding the sphere. They stared at each other, stunned.

There was a whoop of joy from somewhere above and Breidan Niles vaulted the railing, slipped in the mud caused by the deluge of seawater and landed beside them with a splat. "What happened?" he demanded. "Where—"

Gerard dropped the sphere, grabbing the other man's shoulders to shake him. "It's a translocation spell!"

"I gathered that, but where—"

From the railing, Tiamarc burst out, "That's impossible!" Both Gerard and Tremaine stared up at him blankly. Tiamarc added, "But isn't it?"

"Where did you go?" Niles demanded.

Tremaine saw the salt water had soaked the notes tamped down around the outside of the circle and that the ink was running. She gasped and grabbed Gerard's shoulder. "Oh, no! The spell— The water—"

Shaking his head, Gerard told her, "Those are only the working notes. We have several typescript copies of everything."

"Oh." Tremaine sat back, shoving her dripping hair out of her eyes. "Never mind."

"Where did you go?" Niles demanded again.

Tremaine's dazed brain was still trying to catch up. She shook Gerard's sleeve again. "Arisilde did a translocation spell before. He told me about it—"

Gerard nodded, his face intent. "I remember his description of that. I thought he used an old fayre ring—"

"And a sphere. The spell destroyed the sphere but—"

"They could still be alive." Gerard met her eyes. "Nicholas and Arisilde."

Tremaine opened her mouth but no words came.

"WHERE DID YOU GO?" Niles shouted, shaking Gerard.

"I don't know." Gerard let go of him, sitting back and shaking his head in amazement. "Niles, it was broad daylight."

Niles rubbed his brow, trying to comprehend it. "My God."

"We saw two Gardier airships, one coming from an island, one going toward it," Gerard told him. "It could have been returning from Chaire. One of their bases, Niles." He shook his head, smiling in wonder. "It wasn't a weapon. Arisilde Damal was creating a translocation spell to take us to a Gardier base."

Arisilde never wanted to make weapons, Tremaine thought, remembering her own words.

 Chapter 4

Isle of Storms

I still think it's alive," Ilias said thoughtfully. He was stretched out on a shelf of rock, head propped on his arms, watching the scene below. This was another branch of the great cavern that wound through the mountain and their vantage point was a small tunnel opening about fifty paces up the wall. Below was a ledge, part natural and part augmented by wooden platforms, lit by wizard lights. One of the flying whales was anchored to the edge, enormous and silent, floating like a tethered thunderhead in the damp air. About thirty paces or so below the makeshift dock and mostly lost in shadow, a dark river cut through the cavern floor. "I think it's breathing."

Lying next to him, Giliead lifted his brows skeptically. "I think that's your imagination." From this angle they could see the flying whale didn't have any legs, that the edged tail fins seemed to be how it moved itself through the air. The purpose of it was easier to discern now too: There were places in its body that the wizards rode in. They got aboard it with a gangplank that stretched from the cliff to an opening in the squarish belly that hung along the lower part of it.

For some time several wizards had been going in and out and now the slaves were carrying aboard wooden boxes and metal containers from stacks on the platforms. Giliead shook his head, studying the creature with a frown. "They put this thing together somehow."

"They fed it," Ilias argued, scratching his head vigorously. They had rolled in mud to kill any scent that might attract the attention of the captive howlers and it itched like mad, especially in hair. "From those vats." The large metal vats, each as big around as a decent-sized hut, stood against the cavern wall not far below their ledge.

After two days of carefully creeping through the tunnels and passages to spy on the wizards' mostly incomprehensible activities, they still didn't know much about them. They had found the place where the wizards had cut through into the tunnels of the lower city, perhaps to reach the old harbor cave, but they hadn't been able to get a look at the smaller passages on the west side of the main cavern. It was the place where the wizards seemed to have their living quarters and it had to yield more clues than these large work areas. It was also where the slave quarters must be, so there had been no hope yet of releasing any of them.

As far as they could tell, there were at least fifty wizards and more than sixty slaves here, scattered all through this section of the caverns. It was hard to estimate their numbers when it was so difficult to tell the wizards apart, but right now there were five working on the platforms below, two supervising the slaves and the other three going in and out of the flying whale. There was at least one other whale, the one they had seen swimming in the air through the big cavern, and they had found two other large caves with platforms like this.

All those wizards working together, Ilias thought again, still overwhelmed. He and Giliead had been killing them for fifteen years now and they had never come across wizards cooperating before, not real ones. They always hated each other even more than they hated normal people. He would have been sick with the thought of it if there hadn't been so many other things to be horrified about.

He told Giliead, "And Ixion put things together too. Never that big, but still." It was the vats that made Ilias doubt. They were too much like the ones that Ixion had used to make his curselings, though they hadn't been able to see what was in these yet.

"I know, but this is . . . different." Giliead let out his breath in frustration. "We're not going to have much to tell Halian and Nicanor."

"There's an army of wizards ready to overrun the coast with giant flying whale monsters. I think that's all the telling they can handle."

Giliead lifted a brow at him. "You know what I mean. We should know where they come from, why they're here." He shook his head a little, frowning. "Or at least where they're going to attack first."

Ilias scratched the stubble on his chin, dislodging a few flakes of dried mud. They had overheard plenty of conversations, not that any of it had been intelligible. If the wizards were calling Cineth or Pirae or any of the other coastal cities by their names, they hadn't heard it. "If we could just get closer—" He started at a sudden crash from below, wincing as he saw what it was. "Oh, not again." A few years ago he and Giliead had killed a wizard near Ancyra who had cursed people to dance themselves to death, a fairly horrible way to go; at least these wizards took their victims quickly, though that didn't make it any easier to watch.

The crash had been one of the slaves dropping a crate. Now he backed away from the furious wizard advancing on him.

Then the slave stumbled back into the metal stand supporting a curse light. It swayed over and both wizard overseers shouted in alarm. The slave made a wild grab for it but the heavy light tipped. As the white part smashed against the stone, the curse escaped in an abrupt burst of sparks. A little fire leapt to life on a bundle of tarps piled near the crates.

The platform suddenly boiled with confusion. The slaves retreated in terror while the two wizards pressed forward, ripping off their jackets to beat at the small fire. The other three wizards ran out of the flying whale, shouting at each other, frantic, panicked. The howlers screamed, probably because everyone else was.

Completely baffled, Ilias stared at Giliead. "They're afraid of fire?"

"I'll say." Giliead watched in amazement. "I almost took a burning arrow in the chest once and it didn't scare me that much."

Ilias shook his head. It was such a small fire. "How do they cook?"

"Very carefully?"

The little fire died under the wizards' frantic efforts. Abruptly all the lights on the platform went out, the buzzing hum they emitted dying away. In the dimness figures still milled in confusion but at least the yelling stopped. Tiny lights sprang to life, held in the hands of the wizards.

Without the buzzing, their speaking voices were audible. As others herded the slaves and howlers away, three of them held a brief agitated conversation, playing the lights over the heavy metal cylinders stacked waiting on the far side of the platform. Then they followed the others, leaving the cave in darkness.

Except for the glow of light from the open door in the flying whale's belly.

Giliead sat up, nudging Ilias excitedly. "This is our chance."

Ilias let his breath out in resignation as he pushed himself up off the rock. "I was afraid you'd say that."

While Giliead cached their pack and waterskin in the bottom of the vertical shaft, Ilias crept out to scout the cavern floor. The shadows were deep and there was cover along the rocky bank of the narrow river, mostly old rockfalls and some boulders that might have been recently dislodged by the wizards' construction efforts. The whale hung over the cavern, impossibly huge for something so quiet; its presence made the back of Ilias's neck prickle. They would have to cross under its shadow to get to the platform, like coneys trying to sneak past a hawk; that would be a terrible time to find out it really was alive.

Giliead joined him and they made their way along the bank of the river, staying low. The channel was deep and narrow and the quick-flowing water stank of grend filth. It must come from near Ixion's chambers and probably led back into the old city.

Ilias tried to stay as close to the ground as possible as they crept under the whale's bulk; seeing Giliead unconsciously duck as he looked up at the thing's belly made him feel less irrational. It was too dark to see anything up there anyway.

The wooden supports of the dock platform were easy to climb, offering plenty of handholds. Ilias reached the top first, peeking cautiously over the edge. The chill sorcerous light from the flying whale's door illuminated the platform, revealing the stacks of boxes, the metal cylinders, the spidery outlines of the stands supporting the quiescent lights. It gave the shadows a sharp outline, as if they were all knife-edged. The smell of burning still hung in the air, though there was an odd unfamiliar taint to it. The wood creaked as Giliead climbed out onto the platform and Ilias scrambled up after him, staying in a crouch, listening intently. They exchanged a wary look but nothing moved in the shadows.

Giliead went toward the crates nearby and Ilias crept forward cautiously to the shadowy vats and canisters on the far side. The vats stood back against the rock wall, looming in the dark. He touched one cautiously; the metal surface was chill. Reluctantly he pressed his ear to the side, but he couldn't hear anything stirring within. Ixion's vats had bubbled and churned constantly, so maybe these weren't the same after all. He felt around it, looking for a way to see what was inside. All he could find was a small wheel near the bottom, above a pipe. The wheel refused to turn, and though he examined it as best he could, he couldn't tell how it was locked.

They searched the rest of the space, Ilias taking one side and Giliead the other, picking cautiously through the stacked boxes, pipes and other strange objects. Then a hiss from the other side of the platform called Ilias over.

Giliead was crouching by the broken lamp. He held up something so Ilias could see it in the light that came from the flying whale. It was the charred end of a black rope with odd-colored bits poking out. In a low whisper, Giliead explained, "These are connected to all the lights. I think when this one broke it started the fire."

"Huh." Ilias took it and sniffed it cautiously. It did smell of burning. He handed it back. "What's in the crates?"

Giliead shook his head. "Couldn't get any open without breaking them. I don't want them to know we were here. Not yet."

That left only one thing to search. They both looked at the open door into the flying whale's belly. Ilias swallowed in a dry throat. "Well . . ."

Giliead took a sharp breath. "I know."

Ilias tried not to step on the black ropes as they crossed the platform, but it was hard to miss them in the dark. One of them squished unpleasantly underfoot and he winced, but it didn't burst into flame or break.

They reached the edge of the gangplank together. All they could see through the doorway was a dull-colored metal wall. Ilias hesitated, wiping sweaty palms on his pants, and found himself hoping fervently again that the creature wasn't alive. Walking voluntarily into its belly seemed less suicidal that way. He looked at Giliead, whose expression said he wasn't feeling so sure of himself either, which made Ilias feel even worse. He nudged him with an elbow and said in an almost voiceless whisper, "Are we sure this is a good idea?"

Giliead shrugged and shook his head, which Ilias interpreted as "No, but we're doing it anyway." He took a tentative step onto the plank and Ilias checked the set of his sword and followed.

Giliead stopped in the doorway, head cocked to listen. For such a large creature—or thing—the flying whale was oddly silent. He leaned back and whispered, "No guard curses." Ilias nodded and eased through the door after him. These wizards didn't seem to use such things to protect their territory; the only ones Giliead had found while they had been here were old, left by Ixion or his predecessors.

Inside was a long, low-ceilinged chamber, half filled with the containers they had watched the slaves load, lit by a few small white bubbles of curse light attached to the ribbed metal ceiling. The floor was covered with a thin soft stuff like cork that dampened any sound their boots might have made.

Well, it's a cargo hold, Ilias thought, but after watching the slaves load it he supposed they could have known that without actually coming in. He moved down a row of crates as Giliead took the other side. The crates were stacked above his head, secured with ropes and nets to hooks in the floor. Ilias tried not to brush against anything even though Giliead had said there were no guard curses to injure intruders or alert the wizards to their presence. The strangeness of the place, the odd scents, the cold light, made his shoulders tight with tension and his nerves twitchy. There wasn't anything to see but the crates and he circled back around.

Giliead had found a metal door in the wall to the far right. He listened at it a moment, then gave it a cautious push. It creaked loudly, making Ilias's stomach do a nervous flip-flop, but it revealed only a dimly lit corridor, with more doors off each side.

Giliead took a deep breath and consulted Ilias with a look. Ilias shrugged. They had come this far, they might as well go all the way.

The corridor was narrow and low enough that Giliead had to duck under the light bubbles. The wizards, who mostly seemed to be between the two of them in height, would have barely enough clearance themselves.

One of the doors stood partly open, revealing a darkened chamber, and Ilias leaned into it for a look. The dim light from the corridor fell on a narrow room lined with big shelves fixed to the wall with metal brackets. From the gray blankets and cushions he realized they were beds. Cold and lonely beds, thinly padded, narrow, and meant only for one person each. "This is how they sleep?" he whispered, glancing back at Giliead. "No wonder they're all so irritable."

Giliead looked too, made a thoughtful noise, and continued cautiously up the corridor. Ilias followed, pausing to look in the other open doors. It was all the same. The lack of personal possessions or clothes might be explained by the thing still being uninhabited, but there were hardly any colors at all except gray and brown. No painting on the walls, no color in the rough weavings they slept on or the padding on the floor.

It was another way these wizards were unlike Ixion. He had liked comfort and had covered his chambers with fine linens and silks, beautifully woven carpets and painted tiles. It made Ilias wonder what these wizards used their power for, what all this labor was in aid of.

At the end of the corridor was another dim chamber lined with metal vats, with pipes leading up into the ceiling. A heavy odor hung in the air, detectable even over the foul stink of the mud on their clothes and skin. Ilias couldn't identify it, except that it was heavy and dark and clogged his nose and throat.

"Let's try up here."

"What?" Ilias glanced around to see Giliead had found a ladder, set back between two of the vats. He stepped closer, seeing it led up the wall through a hole in the ceiling and into an empty space that glowed with a diffuse orange light. It looked exactly as he imagined a giant beast's belly would appear from the inside. "Try what up there?" he asked dubiously.

"Come on." Giliead started up the ladder and Ilias followed reluctantly.

Giliead climbed up onto the floor above, the metal creaking faintly. Ilias poked his head through the opening warily, but the sight was disappointing. It was only a long straight narrow passage built of flat metal bars, with walls of some kind of slick brown fabric. It seemed to run the whole long length of the creature.

Sitting on his heels, Giliead studied the corridor thoughtfully. "Still think it's alive?"

Ilias climbed up to sit on the narrow metal catwalk. He touched the wall tentatively but jerked his hand back with a grimace. "It feels like skin. Dead skin."

Giliead leaned close to the wall, running a hand over it thoughtfully, with the air of someone who did this every day. "Huh."

"Well?" Ilias demanded.

"It could be skin," he conceded, getting to his feet. "Come on, let's see what's up here."

After a short time of searching it became apparent that these narrow metal catwalks and skin walls made up most of the bulk of the creature. Ladders at intervals led up to more catwalks and more brown walls, fading into murky dimness in the stretches where the curse lamps weren't lit.

Giliead's hopes were raised when he climbed cautiously up to one of the dark stretches, only to find yet another identical catwalk and another ladder. Coming back down to the lighted area, he said with a grimace of frustration, "This isn't telling us anything, is it?"

Ilias agreed, leaning around Giliead to see up through the opening. "At least down below there were things to look at."

"We'll go down again. If there's something to tell us where they came from, it'll be there."

A faint sound from back down the catwalk made them both turn.

A man's head and shoulders suddenly popped up from the opening below the last ladder, facing away from them, no more than twenty paces away. He was dressed in the brown clothing of the wizards, though his cap had been pushed back and the eye coverings were hanging down around his neck. He had dark hair, clipped close to his head, and his skin was moon-pale, as if he had spent all his life underground. Ilias ducked instinctively and Giliead fell back a step toward the ladder behind them. But the wizard had already pulled himself up and turned to step onto the catwalk. He froze, staring right at them.

Ilias couldn't read the man's expression in the dim light,

but he could imagine it. For a long heartbeat nobody moved, then Giliead said matter-of-factly, "Shit."

The wizard gasped and fumbled at the sheath at his belt. Ilias saw the hilt of one the curse weapons and knew they were dead. He pulled his knife, drawing back for a desperate throw, when Giliead snatched it out of his hand. He looked up in shock to see Giliead grab the curse-light bubble above his head, yanking it down so the black rope was visible. He put the knife against it in obvious threat. *That can't work,* Ilias thought, whipping back around to face the wizard.

The man had frozen, one hand still on the weapon, his expression horrified.

Ilias threw a wary look up at Giliead. "It worked," he whispered.

Giliead took a sharp breath, acknowledging the danger. "Get down the ladder," he said softly.

Ilias slid past him, careful not to jostle his arm. "Do it. If you turn your back on him—"

"I know."

Ilias reached the ladder, catching hold of a rung and setting one foot on it. "Ready," he said. The wizard shifted nervously, his hand still on the weapon's hilt.

Giliead sliced the cord. The curse popped loudly and the light winked out. White sparks showered down as Giliead yelled and dropped the knife. Ilias heard the wizard shout in horror and feet pounded on the walk but he was already swinging down the ladder, dropping to land lightly on the padded floor. He saw a large room, with tables and benches and walls lined with metal cabinets. Two doors, one directly in front of him and one behind. Just as Giliead landed behind him, the door on the far side of the chamber swung open and there stood three wizards.

They weren't wearing the eye coverings or caps, so it was easy to see their expressions of complete astonishment. Ilias registered that they weren't identical after all; one was taller than the others, another more squarely built, and the third had beard stubble showing starkly against the whiteness of his skin.

Giliead swore under his breath and grabbed for another light bubble. Ilias dived for the other door, their only clear exit. He could still hear the wizard on the catwalk above the thin metal ceiling, yelling like a madman. He was afraid to see what the other three were doing. He hit the door with his shoulder, feeling the wood crack. The room went dark as it burst open, sending him staggering into another narrow corridor. He looked back desperately, but Giliead was already shoving through the door behind him.

They ran, banging open the doors, looking for anything like a way out and finding only tiny unlit chambers filled with shadowy incomprehensible objects. Then Ilias shoved a door open to see a small room with a wide square window looking out into the darkness of the cavern. "Gil, here!"

Footsteps thudded down the metal floor behind them as they tumbled through the door. Giliead tripped over Ilias in the confined space and they both hit the floor in a heap. Ilias struggled to his knees, yanking the door closed and fumbling at the unfamiliar bolt, just managing to slide it home.

He fell back as the wizards pounded on it from the other side. It looked stronger than the other doors but they didn't have much time. Giliead was already struggling to stand, heading toward the window. Ilias lurched to his feet, looking around for something else to block the door.

The walls were lined with cabinets but when Ilias tried to pull them down across the door he discovered nothing was movable. He turned to Giliead, who had stopped at the window set at an angle in the far wall. He was swearing in frustration.

"What is it?" Ilias stepped up beside him, reaching for the metal bar that was just outside. He flinched when his hand banged into an invisible barrier. He fell back a step, thinking it was some protective curse, then realized the openings were covered with clear glass. "Oh, no."

"We need something heavy." Giliead turned around, trying to pull down one of the shelves. It refused to give, too firmly attached to the wall.

Ilias turned, looking around again, and saw a rough gray rock with crystal shards growing out of it, mounted in a metal stand atop one of the cabinets. It looked heavy. He reached for it but Giliead turned suddenly and knocked his arm away.

Ilias stepped back, knowing that look. "It's cursed?"

Giliead stared at it, eyes narrowed. "Yes, there's something . . . I'm not sure what."

That was all Ilias needed to hear. "Great, we picked a room with a cursed rock." Ilias moved back to the window, drawing his sword. He struck the glass with the hilt. Tiny cracks appeared, but it didn't shatter. Two more blows had the same effect.

While Ilias battered at the unbreakable glass, Giliead turned away to drag open one of the narrow doors in a cabinet, revealing metal drawers. He gave one a hard yank and it came loose, spilling papers covered with brightly colored markings onto the floor.

Giliead awkwardly lifted the drawer above the angled window, and Ilias hurriedly sheathed his sword to steady it. "Together," Giliead said as they lifted the clumsy battering ram. "Now!" They smashed the metal down, shattering the glass barrier.

The floor jerked under them suddenly, throwing them both backward. Ilias's fall was cushioned by landing on Giliead but the metal drawer clipped him in the temple. Dazed and seeing black patches hovering in his vision, he struggled to push himself up. "Did we do that?" he gasped, his uppermost thought that the beast was alive after all and reacting to the injury.

Giliead lifted him off as he sat up. "No, no, we couldn't have." The battering at the door had stopped with the abrupt movement of the whale, but now it resumed with renewed fervor. As Ilias climbed to his feet and wrestled the drawer up again, Giliead stared down at the papers on the floor, then grabbed one off the pile. "Ilias, these are maps! This is what we've been looking for."

"Take some and come on!" Ilias hefted the drawer and Giliead steadied it from above. One blow took out the rest of the glass panel. Ilias ducked as Giliead slung the drawer back against the door. He grabbed the metal rails, lifting himself up onto the ledge, then realized Giliead wasn't behind him anymore. "Gil!" He looked back over his shoulder. "Come on, now!"

"Right behind you. Hold it." Ilias wriggled involuntarily as Giliead shoved a couple of folded maps under his belt into the back of his pants. "Go!"

Ilias swung out of the opening, hung for a moment from the metal bar, looking for a good flat landing spot. The lights were shining brightly from the platforms now and shouts from that direction told him their exit would be witnessed. He aimed for the riverbank, then dropped.

He landed hard, letting his upper body go limp and rolling to absorb the shock, feeling the sharp edges of the loose scree jab into his ribs and back. Winded, he sprawled to a stop just as Giliead hit the ground heavily behind him.

Dazed, Ilias lifted his head to see the cavern illuminated with a strange red-orange light. Incredibly, the glow emanated from the center of the flying whale. Barely conscious of the wild cries of alarm from the platform, he watched flame suddenly blossom under the creature's skin, its metal bones visible now through the illuminated hide. Giliead dragged him to his feet, staring up at the thing, muttering, "Oh no."

They're afraid of fire, Ilias thought in horror. Now they knew why. "We did that," he gasped.

Giliead gave him a push. "Run."

They ran down along the rock-strewn riverbank. Ilias looked back just as a fireball erupted from the creature's spine and it tipped sideways, sliding ponderously down onto its dock. Fire burst outward from it, enveloping the platforms, climbing the cavern walls. He turned back, pounding toward the shelter of the rocks as burning metal rained down like fiery hail.

Giliead reached the boulders at the edge of the river and Ilias was right behind him when something struck him in the back. It knocked him to the ground and he slid in the rough gravel, scraping his arms. Raw pain radiated from his shoulder and he rolled, clawing at it, desperately trying to wrench out the fragment of hot metal. Giliead leaned over him then, slapping his hand away. He wrenched the fragment out himself and hauled Ilias to his feet. Then Giliead froze, staring back at the base of the platform.

Feeling blood trickling down his back, Ilias followed his gaze. A man staggered on the cavern floor below the burning platform. In the blaze of orange light Ilias saw his clothes and surely the flesh beneath were charred from the fire; he must have jumped from the dock or fallen from the whale almost in time to avoid the blast. Wizard or not, Ilias had a stomach-churning moment of guilt and pity; then the man raised his hand and a light glinted starlike in his palm.

Something came out of that star and faster than thought streamed toward them, a shadowed distortion in the air, expanding to push smoke and flaming metal aside. Giliead shouted, shoving Ilias back even as the curse struck him.

Ilias launched himself over the rocks but the wave hit, slamming him down into the stone. He knew he was rolling down the steep muddy slope, then nothing.

 Chapter 5

Port Rel, Western Coast of Ile-Rien

T he giant gray wall of the ship's hull seemed to stretch out and up forever, the upper decks and the three gray-painted stacks lost far above the spotlights' glare. The light was a little muted, the outlines of the ship a little blurred, and Tremaine found herself squinting. The distortion was more than could be accounted for by the heavy mist in the cold night air.

There was a ward of concealment laid over the huge bulk of the ship, a very slight one to escape the Gardier's ability to detect the presence of sorcery. From above, it distorted the ship's form to an empty square of water at an open dock, concealing the presence of the spotlights and dampening the sounds of welding and labor.

"Beautiful, isn't she?" Captain Feraim said, studying the gray bulk looming above them fondly. "Had a few voyages before the war, never sailed since. They brought her in to add ballast because she was so bottom-heavy from her engines."

Tremaine nodded. "I remember reading about her, before the war." The *Queen Ravenna* had launched only a few months before the first Gardier bombings. She had been built to be the star of the Vernaire Solar Line, to carry passengers in speed and comfort between the ports of Ile-Rien, Parscia, and across the ocean to Capidara. Now that the Gardier patrolled the sea-lanes by air, no one traveled to Capidara. If Tremaine had thought about it, she would have supposed the *Queen Ravenna* to have been trapped in another country's port or destroyed along with so much of the navy, the other commercial shipping and the three smaller Vernaire passenger liners. It was hard to believe she had rested quietly in hiding here in the port city of Rel for three years.

It was hard to believe that only a few years ago there had been time and money to build such things, and that people had taken pleasure trips on them without fear.

"Yes," Gerard said, folding his arms as he studied the great ship. "I heard she was to be refitted as a troop carrier, but there was never anywhere to send troops. Until now."

"She's still the fanciest lady on the sea. They didn't have the labor to finish the refit." Captain Feraim turned and started back down the dock with a sigh. "About time she had a chance to show her stuff. In the open ocean she's faster than an airship, faster than anything we've seen the Gardier use. Before all this happened, she was designated a last-chance evacuation transport." He glanced back at them with a slightly twisted smile. "Meaning they were going to send her out but didn't expect her to make it past the blockade."

Tremaine and Gerard followed Feraim, Tremaine pulling up the collar of her pea coat against the damp cold. Activity around the giant gray hull was hushed but hurried as repairs were made and supplies carried aboard for the upcoming voyage. Tremaine shook her head, bemused. It was hard to believe it was really happening.

It had been a whirlwind week. Secret meetings, Gerard and Niles and others rushing back and forth between the palace and the Institute, shifting the location of the experiment to the Port of Rel.

One of the first discoveries was that the sphere did not have to be inside the circle to initiate the translocation. As long as the sphere was within a certain distance, it could begin the spell. They could also trigger the reverse adjuration separately, as long as they were within a few hundred yards of the spot the circle occupied, whether it was here or there. Wherever there was.

Tremaine, Gerard, Tiamarc and a few others had been through three times in a small tug dubbed the Pilot Boat, allowing various sorcerers to experiment with drawing buoys through and sending them back, testing how long the doorway would stay open. They hadn't seen the Gardier's airships again, but then there hadn't been a bombing along the coast for three days.

Tomorrow they would take the Pilot Boat through one last time, the final preparation for the expedition that would carry the first of the teams of soldiers and sorcerers who would scout the Gardier island in preparation for the attack. For the past few months the frequent bombings along the coast had kept ships from reaching the open ocean and prevented Capidara from sending in supplies and munitions. This was only one small base, but if they could destroy it, there would be a hole in the Gardier blockade. And this would be the first time Ile-Rien had managed to capture anything belonging to the Gardier except for that one mangled airship; there was no telling what they could find there.

Feraim gave them a casual salute and headed off down the dock toward the old warehouses that served as the naval headquarters. "You should get some sleep," Gerard told Tremaine as they started away in the opposite direction. "It's going to be a long day tomorrow."

"I will. You aren't going back to the boathouse tonight, are you?" Further down the boardwalk, where a sandy beach hugged the curve of the cove, there was an old resort hotel, closed since the war. The Viller Institute had taken it over as a headquarters, since the assembly rooms had more than enough space for their work. In the daylight it was a picture of decayed gaiety, with fading white paint, broken red tile on the roof, and several stories of large balconies and open verandas. At night it was just large, gloomy and dark. Tremaine didn't mind the gloominess; she was used to Coldcourt after all, though the ghosts there were all part of the family.

"No, I'm just going to stop by and talk with Niles before I turn in." Gerard sighed as they started up the first flight of stairs that climbed the terraced ground up to the hotel's veranda. There was just enough moonlight to see the steps; gaslit lampposts with ornamental ironwork that looked as delicate as spun sugar should have lit the way, but they were kept turned off to avoid Gardier attention. The white beach below lay still and empty except for the steady creep of the surf and the occasional abandoned bathing machine. Off to the right was an amusement pier, closed and abandoned like most of the town, the dark windows of the restaurants and theaters throwing back no reflections. There were no lighted windows visible anywhere, though there were workmen, sailors, naval officers and most of the staff of the Viller Institute in these buildings. Even the sound of the sea was muted. The place was overlaid with sorceries, small ones, charms of concealment and darkness and silence. Wards to warn, and confuse and disguise. No great spells, nothing active to attract the Gardier's notice.

Tremaine gripped the railing to keep from stumbling on the uneven boards, though a couple of men had been through to hammer the loose planks down. "I suppose they're nearly done with the design of the new spheres."

Gerard nodded. "Thank God." Once Arisilde's sphere had demonstrated the proper way to activate the spell, they had been able to pinpoint the defects in the others that the Institute had constructed. One of Niles's tasks was to build his own sphere to take the place of Arisilde's. "Once that's done you can go home."

"Right, home." Tremaine let her breath out slowly, wondering how much she could safely say. So far the sphere had stubbornly refused to let Gerard use it alone, so Tremaine's place in the project had been assured. So far. "I rather like it here."

"Here?" Gerard glanced at her in mock-horror as they climbed the last steps to the dilapidated veranda. It was distinguished by long clay basins and tubs empty of plants, with a forbiddingly boarded-over solar and a general air of forlorn desolation.

"Well, not here." The hotel's gas lines had been turned

off, so none of the radiators worked and the rooms were cold and damp and smelled odd. The kitchen's modern refrigerated iceboxes installed before the war had also failed drastically and they were depending on infrequent ice deliveries from the military outpost in Rel. She added cautiously, "But I'd like to stay with the project."

"I'm sure we can find something for you to do," Gerard said, sounding a little surprised as he opened one of the double doors. Blackout curtains hung just inside, so it was like stepping into a pit. "I thought you'd want to get back to your play."

"Oh, that." She gave Gerard a sharp look but couldn't tell if he was probing for information or not. She followed him as he fought his way through the curtains and into the marble-floored foyer. The two bulbs left in the lobby's elaborate chandelier shed light on fine but dusty wood, faded blue plush couches and armchairs and unpolished brasswork. Reddish marble columns soared upward into shadows that hid the figured arches of the ceiling. Tremaine scratched her head. "I . . . decided to put that off. I can always go back to it."

Despite the gloominess of the lobby, the inside of the hotel exhibited more signs of life. Tremaine could hear voices and the distant buzz of a wireless from the direction of the lounges and ballrooms where the Institute had established their main work areas. Drifting above one of the reservation desks was a tiny wisp of blue sorcerous spell light, dimming even as she noticed the glow, forgotten by the sorcerer who had summoned it. Below it someone had drawn alchemical and mathematical symbols in the dust on the granite counter.

Gerard paused to study her gravely. "I was optimistic at first too, but you know . . . the chances of discovering what happened to Nicholas and Arisilde—"

"I know. That's not it." Tremaine shook her head, looking away. She knew the few Institute members who realized who her father was had the idea that she was breathlessly expecting to encounter him and Arisilde at every trip through the doorway, but Tremaine wasn't that naive. She knew the chance that either was alive was still small.

She was saved from further explanation when Tiamarc stepped out of one of the cross corridors, deep in conversation with Breidan Niles. While Tiamarc wore a disreputable-looking sweater and flannels, Niles's impeccably cut suit made him look as if he had just stepped out of an exclusive tailor's shop on Saints Procession Boulevard. Tremaine had no idea how he managed it; she knew he had spent the whole day crouched on the floor of the dusty ballroom poring over spell diagrams and reams of notes. Niles spotted them and waved imperatively. "Gerard, listen to this."

Tiamarc turned to Gerard, smiling. His fair hair was tousled and there were shadows under his eyes from weariness. Despite that, his voice was full of energy and excitement as he said, "Great news! The test I performed last trip was conclusive, all the others agree. The destination site is not a fayre realm."

"How is that great news? Now we don't have a clue where it is," Tremaine said. The astronomy work Tiamarc had completed on the Pilot Boat's first trip had eliminated the possibility that the destination was somewhere in the opposite hemisphere. The stars were completely unfamiliar. Gerard and the others believed that the airships' recent passage to and from Chaire had caused the spell to tune in to the spot, like a wireless operator tuning in to a distant signal. They had also discovered that physically moving the spell circle would move the target point in the other world. Moving from the estate outside Vienne to Rel had shifted the target point substantially closer to the island when they arrived in the other place.

Frowning, Gerard took off his spectacles and cleaned them absentmindedly. "That eliminates a number of the potential spells we could do. The fayre realms are far more susceptible to wide-scale sorceries than the mortal plane."

Niles nodded. "I know, but it does seem to prove the multiple-dimension theories of Vortal and Igbenz."

"You can't use my sphere anymore," Tremaine said, just to see what would happen.

Everyone stopped to stare at her for a moment, then went back to their conversation. "I don't think it's a proof of those theories, just because we know it's not a fayre realm," Tiamarc objected, shaking his head. "It could be another etheric realm within our world-structure, just not one associated with fayre."

Niles frowned. "Oh, really, I don't think so. Vortal and Igbenz's theory fits so many of the spell's projected parameters—"

Tiamarc noticed the orphaned wisp of spell light and extinguished it with a sharp gesture. "I've got to go up to my room and get that copy of Negretti's *Etheric Principles*. I'll be back in a moment."

"We'll meet you in the ballroom," Niles called after him as Tiamarc started up the wide sweep of the stairs. He turned back to Gerard. "If it is another world, and not another etheric level within our world, it's even more of a mystery where Arisilde Damal acquired the spell's basic structure."

Gerard nodded. "Yes, and I wish we knew how the Gardier airships manage the portals—in the one that was brought down there was no evidence of the ring or of any device like the spheres, just the broken pieces of crystal from above the steering console."

"Yes." Niles frowned. "But I would say the spell has to be of Gardier origin. The operative characters don't resemble anything we've ever seen before, at least not without access to the Lodun Libraries."

"My father probably stole it from the Gardier," Tremaine said absently, studying a broken fingernail.

"What?" Niles stared at her.

"Ah." Tremaine suddenly realized she had spoken aloud. She hadn't thought they were listening to her. As usual, people never listened to you when you wanted them to, only when you didn't. "Well . . ." she began, hoping something would come to her. Nothing did. "Well . . ." she tried again.

Niles turned to Gerard, who adjusted his glasses self-consciously, and said, "Well . . ."

Tremaine held her breath, afraid he would get stuck there too, then he continued, ". . . Tremaine's father was the first person to discover the Gardier's activities."

"Really?" Niles frowned, glancing back at her as if expecting to see some sort of evidence of this on her countenance that he had previously overlooked. "I thought Nicholas Valiarde was an art importer who funded Arisilde Damal's work in the Viller Institute."

"He was," Tremaine agreed readily. "He did." The public version of events was that Nicholas had been just a gentleman adventurer who had made the mistake of helping Arisilde test his last Great Spell. Nicholas had always meant to keep the Valiarde name clean, but after years of living a variety of double lives, too many people knew too many pieces of the truth. And after her mother's death he had become careless.

Gerard's brows quirked and he cleared his throat. "He occasionally did work for the government." He took Niles's arm and turned him back toward the hallway.

"Work for the government involving art?" Niles asked, with another baffled glance back at Tremaine.

"Uh . . ." Tremaine nodded.

"I'll see you in the morning," Gerard said over his shoulder as he hauled Niles along.

"Good night," Tremaine called, and he gave her a backhanded wave as he disappeared down the hall. She started up the grand staircase with a shake of her head. Once they finished constructing the new spheres, her part would be over unless she could think up some other job to do here. Unfortunately the Institute needed sorcerers or scholars of etheric theory, or people trained in mechanics, philosophy or astronomy. Tremaine had an average education in writing and letters. *I can't even make decent coffee.* Being a member of the family that had bankrolled the Institute's nonmilitary endeavors and who owned the patent on the Viller-Damal Sphere, she could probably hang about anyway, but that would surely get awkward.

It had put a real crimp in her plan to kill herself, that was certain. There had been a profound relief and a wonderful freedom in giving up, in resolving not to strive anymore for goals she couldn't define even to herself. Now she seemed to be weighed down with hopes again. Not the least of which was that Nicholas and Arisilde might really be alive, lost in that other world somewhere.

Tremaine paused on the stairs, thinking about it. She wasn't sure she believed there was a chance at all, if she wasn't just seizing on it as a convenient excuse in case someone tried to send her home before she wanted to go. *Maybe I can learn to make coffee,* she thought ruefully, continuing up the stairs.

Muttering "I hate my life" under her breath, she reached the third floor and tramped down the dusty carpet toward her room.

Only one of the glass lily light fixtures still had a bulb and it was at the end of the dim hallway. She stopped in front of the door, digging in her pocket for the latchkey. As she touched the door, she felt it give slightly. Tremaine frowned, running her hand lightly down the smooth wood to the lock. It had taken her at least five minutes of struggle last night to get the damn thing open; she knew it fit tightly. Then her fingers found the scoring on the metal that the shadows in the hallway concealed. The lock had been clumsily forced.

Half chilled, half intrigued, Tremaine stepped slowly back. *Oh, I don't need this right now.* Getting murdered had never been near the top of her list as a viable suicide option. How embarrassing, if this was another old enemy from her family's checkered past, come to enact vengeance on Nicholas Valiarde's daughter. And incidentally disrupting the Institute's vital work and causing Tremaine the humiliation of difficult explanations to people who already thought her a little odd. It had happened to her before. She wasn't anxious for it to happen again.

There were people who were supposed to take care of this sort of thing for her. Tremaine knew Gerard wasn't her only guardian. He had been given the legal responsibility but she knew there were others who had been assigned to watch over her and she suspected Gerard knew who they were, though he had never said. Doubtless they had lost track of her between the confusion in the city and her abrupt removal from Coldcourt. She had a telephone exchange she could call to summon their assistance, but it was a little late for that. She swore under her breath. There were ways for her to take care of this herself and dispose of the body without anyone being the wiser, and she wished she had listened better to her early lessons so she knew what they were. *Dammit.*

She debated screaming and decided against it. It would be better to trap the intruder inside the room. She edged away, moving silently back to the nearest door. That should be Tiamarc's room. Still keeping a wary eye on her own door, she reached out to knock.

It swung open at her touch. *Oh no,* was Tremaine's first thought as she looked down the short hall into the darkened room. She saw a figure sprawled on the floor. Then *this just happened.* She fell back a step.

Her door swung open suddenly and a man stepped out. He was tall, compactly built, dressed in dark clothes and a long coat, his hair cropped short and oddly wearing a pair of driving goggles. He started toward her without hesitation, reaching out a gloved hand to grab her.

Yelling for help, Tremaine bolted back up the corridor, feeling the dusty carpet catch maddeningly at her clunky boots. Like a chase in a nightmare, she could hear him only a few steps behind her.

She threw a look back just as a door opened and Florian stepped out, wearing a flower print bathrobe. The man careened into her, sending them both sprawling on the floor. One of her father's rules had always been "never fail to take advantage of a fallen enemy," and almost before this shot through her thoughts, Tremaine skidded to a halt. The man brutally shoved Florian away, the girl yelping and curling up into a protective ball. Tremaine looked around wildly, then grabbed one of the spindly-legged side tables, upsetting the vase atop it and sending up a flurry of dust and dried flower petals. She smashed it down on the man's head just as he climbed to his feet.

Instead of going down, he shook his head, dislodging the splintered fragments, and reached for her again. Tremaine stumbled back, appalled. The wood was light but the table had had a thin marble top, which she had felt connect with a satisfying thud. The man should have a cracked skull at least. Florian uncurled and kicked at his legs, her expression white and desperate in the dim light. He swatted at her, giving Tremaine a chance to grab up the fallen vase. As he turned back toward her she swung it by the neck, the heavy stoneware body catching him squarely in the chin.

His head jerked back and his return swing caught her in the cheek, slamming her sideways into the wall. She slid down the wainscoting, hearing Florian's yelp of dismay.

The sound of the shot was like thunder in the close corridor.

Tremaine sat up, her head aching from the blow and the noise, feeling the pounding of running feet in the floorboards. *Finally,* she thought. She looked up blearily as Florian crawled toward her, giving the man who lay flat on his back a wide berth. "Are you all right?" the other girl gasped.

Tremaine nodded, pressing a hand to the knot of pain in her cheek. "Yes, sort of," she admitted. She blinked and saw Gerard and Niles leaning over the intruder, with Ander trying to look over their shoulders. He was holding a pistol. Colonel Averi and two of the soldiers assigned to guard the Institute personnel pelted up the corridor to join them. Tremaine asked Florian, "Did he hurt you?"

"No, if you don't count the terror." Florian lifted Tremaine's hair aside and winced. "Oh, that's a big bruise."

"It'll add distinction to my appearance," Tremaine managed.

Florian helped her stand and Ander turned to them, asking worriedly, "Are you all right?"

"Oh, fine." Tremaine pushed her hair back, trying to see

past him to the man on the floor. There was an ugly red hole in his chest where the bullet had struck. "Who is he?"

Ander shook his head, looking back at the corpse. "No idea. I was coming up when I heard the commotion. I called for Gerard and Niles, but I was the only one who was armed." He turned to Tremaine and smiled with relief. "I'm glad you two aren't hurt."

Still trembling a little, Florian was self-consciously pulling her robe closed over her flannelette nightgown and tying the belt. "It happened so fast."

Niles had stepped into Tiamarc's room with one of the soldiers. Now he returned, grim-faced. "Tiamarc's dead. His throat was cut."

Florian made a faint noise and Tremaine felt her stomach roil. She hadn't known Tiamarc well, but she was glad she hadn't seen his body more closely. She said, "He—that man—was in my room. He must have found Tiamarc first." She followed that thought to its logical conclusion and felt worse. "I suppose he was just . . . moving down the hall, one room at a time."

"That's . . ." Florian hugged herself, uncomfortable. "Let's not suppose that."

"You walked in on him?" Averi demanded, staring at her. He was an older man than most of the other military personnel assigned to the Institute, with a perpetually grim expression, thinning dark hair and cold blue eyes. The Institute usually tended to get raw recruits or men who had been wounded and sent behind the lines to recover; Averi seemed to be an exception and Tremaine wasn't sure why.

Tremaine shook her head. "I saw someone had forced the lock on my door and I was going to go for help. He must have heard me."

Colonel Averi went to examine her door, crouching to look at the lock. He frowned, glancing at her. "How did you know it was forced?"

"I felt the scratches on the lock," she told him. When he continued to stare in disbelief she added honestly, "I'm a very suspicious person," not knowing how else to explain it.

"She is," Ander agreed. At Tremaine's expression he winced, and added, "Sorry."

Gerard stood up from his examination of the intruder, his mouth set in a thin line. "This man is a Gardier."

Colonel Averi turned a shade of red that indicated either shock or extreme rage and turned away, taking one of the soldiers by the arm and giving orders in a harsh undertone, sending the man running off down the corridor.

Tremaine stepped forward, inserting an elbow into Ander's side to edge him out of the way so she could see. The man sprawled on the ground looked ordinary enough, pale from the winter and maybe a little ill. His cropped hair was short, but not so short as to be out of fashion in a city where most of the men were in the army. "How can you tell?" she asked, warily fascinated.

"He's resistant to spells," Niles answered her, his eyes still intent on the dead man. "He has no counter talismans or antietheric agents on him but he got past the wards against intruders."

"I hit him with that tabletop and the vase, and it barely slowed him down," Tremaine said as Florian nodded confirmation. "Is he a sorcerer?"

"Gardier don't send their sorcerers into battle," Gerard told her. "At least from what we can tell. He's probably had protective spells cast on him."

"The ones we faced on the Aderassi border sure did." Ander reached to pick up the goggles the man had worn, which had fallen next to the body. "These are aether-glasses of some sort, aren't they?"

Tremaine frowned. The bulky crystal lenses were a modern substitute for gascoign powder, a substance that sorcerers placed in their eyes in order to see the etheric traces left by wards or active spells.

Florian looked up at the others, her brow furrowed. "But if he was here, he has to know about the project?"

"I'm certain he did." Gerard pulled off his spectacles and rubbed his brow. "Poor Tiamarc wasn't a powerful sorcerer; he would hardly have been a target for Gardier assassination with Niles and me here. There was no reason to kill him except to delay the project. The question is whether this man had a chance to notify his superiors." He shook his head, looking worriedly at Niles. "Dammit, it could already be too late. We should make the last survey trip immediately."

Ander frowned. "Can't we skip it and send the advance scouting team in now?"

"We have to make this last trip or the advance scouting team will be the advance suicide team," Gerard countered briskly. "We haven't been taking these survey trips simply to gather information. They're essential to stabilizing and widening the etheric world-gate, not to mention opening it in different locations once the Gardier discover its existence. The spell parameter that prevents transfer into solid objects only protects us so far."

"Oh, I like that," Tremaine said before she could stop herself.

"What?" Ander stared at her incredulously.

" 'Etheric world-gate,' it just sounded . . . never mind."

Colonel Averi gave her an annoyed look. "We're not in one of your plays, Miss Valiarde. Focus, or you're just a liability. This is a deadly serious business."

Tremaine's brows drew together. "I know it's serious," she said mildly. "I've got the bruise to prove it."

"You're not taking it seriously," the man persisted.

Tremaine met his gaze, her eyes cold, her self-consciousness dissolving abruptly. She smiled. "Sure I am."

"The Gardier killed her father, Colonel," Ander said suddenly, startling her by how offended he sounded. He gazed sternly at the older man. "Of course she takes it seriously."

Averi stared at him, then turned to Tremaine stiffly. "I apologize."

Tremaine shook her head, wishing Ander hadn't brought it up. His defense had knocked the fight right out of her. "It's all right."

Niles was digging in his pockets, pulling out a pen and a notebook stuffed with loose paper. "Ander, Colonel, Tremaine, be quiet." He turned to Gerard, saying urgently,

"You'll need a secondary sorcerer, someone who's familiar with the spell."

"I'd rather have you here in case something goes wrong."

"I can do it, I can go," Florian spoke up suddenly. As everyone turned to her, she looked a little overcome by her own temerity but forged on. "I've been reading all the documentation and studying the structure. I'm sure I could trigger the reverse adjuration if I had to."

"You'll have to do," Niles said, though Gerard looked like he wanted to protest. "Just stay long enough to make sure the larger gate parameters are stable."

"Right." Gerard nodded. He took a sharp breath. "Let's go."

A half hour later Tremaine and Florian sat huddled on crates in the cavernous boathouse, watching the Institute personnel ready the Pilot Boat for its last voyage. It was a small steam tug with a crew of two, Captain Feraim and his mate, Stanis. It didn't take up much room at the dock, which had been meant for the large pleasure boats that took holiday travelers on excursions up and down the coast.

On the big flat platform above the boat's slip, another version of the spell circle had been laid out on carefully painted removable wooden panels. She could hear a few people moving around up there, though they were too far back from the railing for her to see them. She heard Averi's voice, and then Niles's.

Tremaine sighed, folding her arms. She had dressed in tweed knickers and an overjacket over a lighter middy blouse, the outfit she usually wore on board the boat and her only one that was vaguely suitable for it. Florian wore a long jacket and sweater over a pair of bloomers. It was cold now but it would be significantly warmer once they crossed into the other world, though the sea breezes could sometimes be brisk. It was the last time she would see it, she realized. The fine china blue sky, the darker color of the sea, the mysterious peaks of the island and the cliffs in the distance. She touched her aching jaw thoughtfully.

"It was nice of Ander to stick up for you to Averi," Florian commented.

Tremaine nodded, still distracted. "Sure."

"Except it didn't seem like you needed anybody to stick up for you."

"What?" That got Tremaine's attention. Her mouth twisted ruefully. "Maybe not."

"So were you two together? You and Ander," Florian asked, looking at her.

Tremaine sighed, shoving her hands deep in her pockets and leaning back against the wall. "No. People thought we were. Sometimes I thought we were." Ander had always behaved as if she was an utterly normal, completely conventional girl. At times, when her father was coming home disguised as a dustman every other night or was off plotting the downfall of some small foreign principality, this had been welcome; it had helped her pretend she was normal. Later, when she had craved an actual acknowledgment of who she really was, it had just been smothering. "I never felt like . . . he really knew me."

Florian was nodding. "I can see that. He doesn't listen to you when you talk." Her brow furrowed as she tried to explain what she meant. "Or really, he listens, but he never seems to hear what you say. No, that's not what I mean. It's . . . he says what he thinks people expect him to say. Maybe that comes from being in the Intelligence Service. He can't tell what you expect him to say, so it never quite comes out right."

Tremaine stared at her, not sure whether the revelation was unwelcome because it wasn't true or because it was.

Florian misread her silence and looked embarrassed. "Sorry. I should just not—"

Maybe it was unwelcome because it was a little too similar to Tremaine's own situation for comfort. "No, it's all right—"

Colonel Averi and Niles came down the stairs from the upper level, with Captain Dommen, Averi's second-in-command, trailing them.

With a harried expression, Niles sorted through an armload of folios, saying, "We've risked everything to make the portal large enough to bring their troopship through. It would be kind of them to supply enough troops to make it worthwhile."

Averi's permanently angry expression was firmly in place. "We were lucky to get the troops we have. Not everyone at Vienne Command believes this is anything but a waste of rapidly failing resources." Tremaine couldn't tell if he was angry because he agreed it was a waste or because he didn't. She also hadn't heard Niles swear before, so the imprecation the sorcerer muttered in editorial comment as he dug through his armload of papers was a little shocking.

Captain Dommen shook his head with a frustrated frown. He was younger than Averi, tall, dark-haired, very much the dashing officer type. Like Ander and Niles, his family was beau monde, and he looked it in his carefully tailored uniform. "I'll make some calls. I know a few people who have influence in the Ministry. If they're still in town—"

Averi paused, and again Tremaine couldn't tell if he appreciated the suggestion or not. Then he nodded sharply. "Yes, try that."

"We're ready," Ander called from the deck. "Come aboard."

Tremaine got to her feet, distractedly looking around, though she didn't usually bring anything with her.

Stanis, an awkward young man with the dark hair and olive skin of Adera, tossed a coil of rope aside to step to the gangplank and help them aboard. Tremaine smiled and Florian thanked him. From the amount of attention paid, Tremaine thought that Stanis would have badly liked to ask Florian to coffee or dinner or anything else, but none of them had any free time.

They stepped through the hatch into the main cabin where Ander was doing a quick check of the supply lockers. The cabin was small and crowded, holding a chart cabinet, the wireless, a galley table bolted to the floor and the shelves of reference texts that Gerard, Tia-marc and the others had used to make their observa-tions. Stanis hurried down the steps into the engine compartment.

As Florian went to take a seat on the padded bench against the far wall, Tremaine turned to see Ander reload-ing his pistol. Her hands clenched in her coat pockets and she felt a nerve in her face jump.

He saw her expression and looked puzzled. "Afraid of firearms?"

"Yes." She hated to give further weight to the image Ander now had of her as some kind of twitchy feather-head, but she had been avoiding guns lately. Explaining that she was afraid if she touched one she might give way to an overwhelming impulse to blow her own brains out would hardly go over well either. She knew Feraim had one too, but he kept his out of sight in his coat pocket.

Ander shrugged slightly, tactfully dropping the sub-ject for all the wrong reasons. "It's all right," he said kindly. "I just want to have something on hand if we run into trouble."

Gerard, stepping into the cabin behind them, frowned and said, "If by 'run into trouble' you mean the Gardier, we'll be dead before you could use that thing."

The Gardier's most devastating spell was the one that could detect and destroy mechanical equipment at a dis-tance. If the little tug came within range of a Gardier airship, it would be sunk before they could activate the return spell. *Not to mention the whole plan of scouting and attacking the base would be circling the drain at that point,* Tremaine thought sourly. *If they see us there, they'll know we've dis-covered their secret.*

"The Gardier might not be the only thing we have to worry about." Ander smiled engagingly. "I like to be pre-pared."

"How nice for you," Gerard said shortly. Tremaine man-aged to control her expression, but she noted Florian had to turn and peer earnestly out the porthole at the empty dock. He continued, "Come on, Tremaine, we need to get under way."

Tremaine obediently followed him through the short passage into the steering cabin. It was as unimpressive as the rest of the little boat, though the wheel and the brass were polished and it looked to be in good repair. The glassed port showed them the dark wooden walls of the boathouse and the last of the navy crew leaving through the door out onto the dock. As Gerard shut the hatch, he muttered, "If anyone is going to be fumbling around with a pistol, I'd prefer it to be you rather than that overconfident young man."

Tremaine smiled. "He is a captain in the Intelligence Service, you know."

"I'm afraid that making his acquaintance years ago when he was only an upper-class layabout may have colored my opinion." Taking the sphere out of its protective leather case and setting it carefully on the bench, he glanced at her sharply. "Why on earth did you tell him you were afraid of firearms? I know Nicholas taught you to shoot."

She looked away, thinking about Ander. If his past affected even Gerard's view of him, she wondered how much it weighed with men like Averi. And did Ander realize that? And did she give a damn? She shook the thought off, realizing she hadn't answered Gerard. "I just didn't want to carry one. Like you said, if the Gardier see us, it's not going to do any good."

Captain Feraim stepped into the cabin from the hatch that opened out onto the deck. "We're ready." He eyed the sphere a trifle suspiciously. Feraim had been with the project long enough to hear how the experiments with the previous spheres had ended and being near this one always worried him.

Tremaine picked up the sphere, feeling it warm at her touch. *This one won't hurt anybody,* she thought. Well, not anybody she knew. She wondered what it would do to a Gardier.

Gerard consulted his pocket watch. "All right. Tremaine?"

As Feraim used the speaking tube to warn Stanis in the engine room, Tremaine held the sphere out to Gerard. She watched his face as he concentrated, touching some mental connection to the spell circle carefully duplicated on the wooden panels in the boathouse. She knew when he took a sharp breath that the transition would be in the next instant.

She would never get used to the fact that they could travel so far while standing still.

Tremaine let go of the sphere and grabbed the table as a sickening lurch of vertigo hit her stomach. An instant later the boat met the water with a tremendous splash. *They got the altitude wrong again,* she thought in annoyance, squeezing her eyes shut and taking deep breaths to keep her last meal down.

Gerard caught the sphere, then cursed suddenly. Tremaine looked up. Her own curse died unspoken as she saw the wall of gray water outside the port.

The wave towering over them broke over the bow and Tremaine ducked back instinctively as the sea crashed into the port. She straightened up warily, watching the foam retreat across the deck. The boat was cresting a wave now and they were looking into an angry purple-gray sky, the clouds low and heavy.

"Storm," Feraim commented succinctly as he fought the drag on the wheel. "All the luck."

Tremaine swayed into the rail as the boat dipped into the next trough and rose on another wave. The peaks of the island, even more thickly wreathed in mist than usual, lay some way off their bow. Tremaine had no idea how far, not being enough of a sailor to gauge distances over water. The edge of the storm lay just past the island and she could see where the clouds dissolved into blue and the sun glittered off the water. "Gerard, look—" she pointed.

"I see it," Gerard muttered. "We're on the very edge of the storm. That's oddly coincidental."

Feraim cursed at a squawk from the speaking tube. He grabbed it, listened a moment, then threw it down.

"Stanis needs help in the engine room. We're taking on water."

Tremaine looked at Gerard, seeing the worry on his face. *It was that drop,* she realized. They must have come through the doorway at exactly the wrong moment, just above the trough of a wave, and the fall had been much harder because of it.

"I'll go below," Gerard said, tucking the sphere under his arm and swaying as he started toward the door to the aft cabin. "I can do a binding spell on the hull, that should help."

Tremaine started after him, lurched as the deck moved underfoot, and caught herself awkwardly on the railing. "Do you want me to come along?"

"No, stay up here."

He staggered as he opened the cabin door and Tremaine caught a glimpse of Florian's worried face. Gerard closed the door behind him and she turned back to the frightening view out the port.

The boat troughed and crested again, their vision blocked by another spray of water and foam. Suddenly something else appeared on the water. Tremaine stared. *What the hell. . . .* She gasped, pointing.

There was another boat out there, cresting the next wave. It had sails, purple ones, and she could see figures frantically trying to furl them. It had no smokestack and even in the gray light she could see red, green, and gold painted designs on the wooden hull.

"Stanis, what's going on down there?" Feraim was shouting into the speaking tube. "This storm's not natural," he growled.

The other boat vanished in the trough, leaving Tremaine pointing at empty sky and water. She tried again. "I saw a—"

Then something else filled the port, dropping out of the storm-wracked sky like death. It was a Gardier airship, black against the gray clouds, less than a hundred yards away.

Tremaine gripped the railing, thinking sourly, *just as things were getting interesting.* It hung there, a fragile fabrication of duralumin, linen and membranes, protected by a sorcery that left it untouched by the wind that made the heavy wood and metal of the compact Pilot Boat creak with strain. Feraim was shouting, hauling hard on the wheel, and that was the last thing Tremaine remembered.

✻ Chapter 6

Tremaine dreamed she stood in the bow of the *Queen Ravenna,* the whole bulk of the great ship behind her. It was night, and under the clear chill moonlight a strange landscape of sharp hills rose across the water to either side, as if the *Ravenna* had sailed up a fjord. Tremaine glanced down and saw that the sea, dark and still as a sheet of glass, was far closer to the railing than it should be. She turned around and saw to her horror that the ship was sinking. Slowly, silently, with only a slight backward tilt to the deck, the ship was disappearing beneath the inert blackness, the water already up to the railings on the A deck. All the electric lights were out in the main deck and above, and she knew that the moment to give the warning had passed her by, that she had stood here with her back turned while the water got into the engines and the generators. There were no people on the deck or in the water, but the lifeboats were still in place. She could see everything in the moonlight that shone, cold and clear, out of a cloudless and starless night sky. *I did this,* she thought. *I brought us to this.* She turned back to the bow to see a man stood there now.

She knew it was her father though she couldn't see his face. He told her not to jump, that the suction might pull her down with the ship, but to stay on as long as possible, to wait until the bow went under, then simply step off. That sounded like something he would know, so she waited until the cold still water rose above her waist and the deck dropped smoothly away from under her feet. Nicholas held her hand as they swam to shore, and it wasn't nearly so far away as it looked.

Cold salt water splashed her in the face and Tremaine woke to a screech of stressed metal and splintering wood. She groped at the crazily tilted deck, realizing she was crammed into the back corner of the Pilot Boat's steering cabin. Her head pounded and she couldn't tell how much of her skewed perspective was the angle of the deck and how much was a concussion. *Gardier, storm, dead,* she remembered. Except of course with her luck, her death was going to drag out horribly and painfully. "This is what I get for putting things off," she muttered disgustedly as she struggled to push herself upright.

Glass from the shattered windows covered the deck and the ceiling was sagging. Waves washed through the empty port just above her and she knew the boat must be wedged atop something. The door to the aft cabin was crunched, splintered on the edges as the sides of the hatch had pressed in on it. She looked around vaguely, freezing when she saw Captain Feraim. He was tangled in the broken wheel, covered with glass and blood. "Captain!" She dug her fingers into the uneven boards and hauled herself toward him.

She reached him, grabbing on to the broken end of the wheel's post to stay upright. As she tried to feel for his heartbeat she realized blood was running down the deck, mixed with seawater to stream in rivulets between the boards. He was cut to ribbons from the port's shattered glass.

I was standing right beside him. She stared down at her hand, wet with his blood. She didn't have a scratch on her.

"Tremaine!" It was Florian, somewhere outside the cabin.

"In here." Remembering that Feraim had always carried a pistol on these trips, Tremaine steeled herself and put her hand into the pocket of his greatcoat. She drew out only a handful of warm fragments of twisted metal that stank faintly of gunpowder. Of course, the Gardier had used their favorite spell.

Cursing, she pushed away from the wall, managed to

grab the brass-lined doorframe. Her stomach gave a warning lurch as she stretched to step over Feraim's body. She was just beginning to realize the enormity of the disaster. *We can't let the Gardier get the sphere. Not Arisilde's last sphere.* If it hadn't already been destroyed; the spell might have shattered its mechanical parts too.

Tremaine pulled herself through the door and onto the open deck. The wind had died and white clouds of fog hung in shrouds above the choppy gray water. She saw Florian climbing up the sharply angled deck by holding tightly to the railing. The other girl had a bloody nose and the beginnings of a black eye. Tremaine grabbed her arm and they steadied each other. "Are you all right?" Florian asked, blinking unsteadily at her.

"I'm fine." Tremaine realized Florian was staring at her bloody hand and she wiped it on her middy. "Captain Feraim's dead." The Pilot Boat was jammed against a reef; she could see the black rock under the bow, green-gray waves washing steadily against it. The rock disappeared into the mist only a few yards past the bow, but she could see gray shapes of boulders in the dimness. "We're on that island," she said blankly, then shook her head, trying to get her brain moving. The boat wasn't covered by Gardier and the airship was nowhere in sight, though with this mist that meant nothing. "Where's Gerard?"

"I think he was still down in the hold. I was in the other cabin and I got knocked out." Florian stumbled and caught herself on the bent railing as the boat shifted under them. She sounded dazed. "I couldn't find Ander or Stanis—"

"We've got to get off this boat." Still gripping the other woman's arm, Tremaine slid cautiously down toward the hatch that opened into the stern cabin, bracing her feet against the wall. Florian stretched across to grab the railing, helping Tremaine stay upright as she reached the hatch.

Tremaine shoved at the unresponsive door, then let go of Florian to throw her whole weight against it. It still didn't budge. Florian added her weight and after three tries, the door popped open, revealing the tumbled cabin with books and charts slung every which way. Tremaine aimed herself at the hatch that led down to the hold, let go, and staggered across the angled floor, fetching up against the far wall.

Florian stumbled in after her, catching herself against the table still bolted to the floor. "Tremaine, careful."

"Get a bag and grab things." She waved helplessly at the lockers across the cabin that held the emergency lamps, rations and other equipment. The wireless, of course, was shattered to bits from the spell.

Tremaine turned to the closed hatch, hoping it wasn't jammed like the other one. She heard Florian rummaging in a cabinet, then the other girl said, "Here's a rope." The loose coil hit Tremaine in the back of the head for emphasis.

"Oh, good." She caught it against her waist as it unraveled and looped a length around her shoulder. Wood cracked and the boat shifted ominously, underlining the urgency. Tremaine grabbed the door handle and shoved with all her strength, almost flinging herself down into the dark hold when it swung abruptly open. The stepladder had been twisted and wrenched off its support and she could see water lapping at the bottom. "Gerard!" she called desperately.

"Tremaine?" She heard thumps and bangs from the compartment, then Gerard appeared below. She tossed the rope down to him, glancing back to make sure Florian was tying the end off on the bolted table leg. The case with the sphere hung over Gerard's shoulder in a makeshift sling fashioned out of a sheet.

Tremaine steadied the rope as Gerard climbed, bracing herself against the cabin wall. Florian slid to the opposite side of the hatch to grab the sorcerer's arm and help him pull himself up. "Stanis is down there, dead," Gerard reported, his voice grim as he got shakily to his feet and steadied his spectacles. His clothes were soaked and he had a bleeding cut on his temple. "He was down below, near the engine when the Gardier's machinery destruction spell engaged."

Tremaine grimaced. *Stanis.* "The sphere wasn't affected?"

"Apparently not. I was leaning over it when the spell hit, and it even seems to have protected my watch." He tapped the object in question, still hanging intact from his vest pocket. He shook his head with a bitter expression. "If we had only known it could do that—"

"We could have kept it next to the engine." More vital information they couldn't tell the Institute. And she had the suspicion they were too far from the target point to trigger the reverse adjuration to take them back home. When they had tested the distances on earlier trips the target point had had a radius of less than a mile, and the island had been much further away than that. Tremaine pulled up the rope and collected it into an awkward bundle. "Gerard, we've got to"—the boat shifted again with a great crack of abused wood and metal, punctuating her words—"go."

"Yes, of course." He made sure the sling with the sphere was still secure, then hauled himself across the cabin toward the hatch on the port side. "Captain Feraim and Ander?"

"Feraim's dead," Florian told him, climbing back to the other side of the cabin. She tore open one of the cabinets and grimaced when she saw the rifles stored there were now nothing but pieces, trickling out of the open rack. She moved on to the next. "We haven't found Ander yet but—" Her foot knocked against something, scooting it across the floor to land in the middle of the cabin. Tremaine stared at it. It was the grip of a pistol.

"Ander's," she said with a wince. "He wasn't down below?"

"No. He must have been washed overboard. Poor boy," Gerard said grimly, turning back to the hatch. "Come on."

Florian gave Tremaine a stricken look, then shook herself and turned back to the cabinet. Tremaine climbed across the cabin to help as the other girl dumped the wireless operator's manuals out of their canvas satchel. *I can't think about it right now.* She helped Florian stuff in cans and packages of provisions, matches and the medical kit.

The door grated against rock as Gerard finally forced the port hatch open. Through it Tremaine could see gray daylight and fog drifting over the dark rock wedged under the boat. The railing all along that side was crushed.

The deck shifted abruptly and Tremaine staggered. Florian caught her arm, keeping her from falling into the cabinets. Florian muttered, "That wasn't good."

"Now," Gerard said, motioning urgently to them, "we're slipping off."

"Go, we're right behind you!" Tremaine pushed off the wall toward him, shouldering the satchel of provisions. Florian grabbed one of the oil lamps and struggled after her.

Gerard climbed out of the hatch, making his way cautiously through the shattered wood to the knob of rock that was holding the hull in place. Tremaine took his supporting hand gratefully and scrambled after him.

Just as Florian jumped down out of the hatch behind her the boat shifted again. She yelped and Tremaine and Gerard both grabbed for her, Gerard catching her arm and Tremaine her jacket flap, pulling her to safety. The hull ground slowly down the black rock. With a great crack and a screech of abused metal, the boat slid away from the reef, rolling away into the waves. "That was close," Florian breathed, stumbling a little as she gained her balance on the wet rock.

Tremaine nodded in relief. Continuing its long slow roll, the boat capsized, gray foam washing over the scarred hull. They retreated hastily, Tremaine looking back to see the wreck fading into the fog.

"Well, that's that," Gerard said wearily. He took the oil lamp from Florian and they carefully picked their way along the ridge. "I just hope this protrusion is actually attached to the island." He paused, looking around at the fog, trying to get his bearings.

"I guess we're not close enough to swim to the target point and go back through the portal?" Tremaine asked hopefully, squinting to see off into the mist.

"No, the island is several miles outside the circle's radius." Gerard pressed his lips together, studying the dim white sky.

"Did anybody see where the airship went?" Florian asked.

"They must have lost us in the mist," Tremaine told her, trying to ignore the sick sensation in the pit of her stomach. "Besides, if they knew about the Pilot Boat, they must know at some point there's a force coming through after us to attack them." She remembered her dream, the *Ravenna* sinking slowly beneath a still sheet of black water. They had to keep the sphere away from the Gardier. Looking at the innocuous bundle slung over Gerard's shoulder, she said, "It might be better to smash the sphere now."

Gerard shook his head slightly, still distracted. "We have to get word back to Rel." He turned to her, smiling a little ruefully, and adjusted his spectacles. "And I personally would be afraid of what the Gardier might do if they managed to find even one of the pieces."

Oh, there's a lovely idea, Tremaine thought, grimacing. As they continued, the rocky ridge widened out, more boulders appearing on either side in the wash of dull gray waves.

Gerard halted abruptly. Tremaine leaned around him to see the ridge dead-ended into a rough waist-high wall, constructed of dark stone.

"What is it?" Florian asked, puzzled. "Is that a breakwater?"

"Whatever the purpose, it's man-made." Gerard sounded deeply worried. Beyond it was a rougher, obviously natural wall of lava rock, disappearing into the fog about thirty feet above their heads.

"I saw another boat caught in the storm," Tremaine said, remembering it suddenly. Spots of purple and gold against the storm gray water. "It was a sailing ship. I don't think it was Gardier."

Gerard stared at her. "You're sure?"

Tremaine nodded. "Well I didn't have a chance to snap a photograph, but yes, I'm sure."

Florian pushed the hair out of her eyes, biting her lip thoughtfully. "So . . . There's people here? Besides the Gardier?"

Tremaine and Gerard both turned to look at her. "We hope? Or not?" Florian added uneasily.

"It's . . . hard to tell at this stage," Gerard admitted as he started forward again. Tremaine took a deep breath, adjusted the strap of the satchel on her shoulder and followed.

As they drew closer she saw the blocks forming the wall were huge, each close to twenty feet long, though they were only a foot or so wide. *Like stone logs,* Tremaine thought, puzzled, running her hand over the rough surface. She couldn't see any mortar holding them together, but the wall seemed stable just the same. On the other side was a path, just wide enough for three people to walk abreast. Gerard climbed over onto it and she followed him, then turned to help Florian scramble over.

"This could be some sort of pavement, but it's hard to tell," Gerard said, brows drawn together as he studied the smooth stone surface under their feet. "I wonder . . . If that wasn't a Gardier craft you saw, if they were also under attack or simply in the wrong place at the wrong time."

Tremaine leaned against the wall to retie her bootlaces. "I hope it didn't sink." *I hope not everybody is as doomed as we are.* She shouldered her bag again. "Which way?"

"We need to get as far away from the wreck as possible." Gerard glanced up and down the path. They could see about twenty feet in any direction, if that. The waves appeared out of an ocean of cloud to wash against the ridges and scattered boulders. It was quiet except for the distant scrape that must be the hull of the capsized Pilot Boat rubbing against the reef. "Unless we want to try scaling that cliff . . ."

"I vote not," Florian put in, gazing up at the sheer rock wall.

"Quite." Gerard adjusted his spectacles. "Widdershins way is usually appropriate in these situations."

"These situations?" Florian asked with a puzzled glance at him.

"Situations in which we don't know which way to go," Tremaine explained, knowing Gerard's sense of humor.

They followed the path to the left. After a short time it

curved inward, leaving the sea, turning into a twisting passage through high rock walls, heavily shadowed by short deformed trees and curtains of dark foul-smelling vines. The walls were dotted with niches, square-cut and obviously meant for some purpose, but while some were high enough to hold lamps, others were at waist height, or only a few handspans above the ground.

The passage turned and dead-ended suddenly into a large square plaza. At the far side was a crude blocky structure made from more of the black stone logs, the only feature a large forbidding doorway in the center. The gray daylight illuminated a few paces of the dark tunnel within. The rock walls on the other sides were the same as the passage they had just come through, except on the left the rock dropped away to reveal a narrow canal. "It seems to be deserted," Gerard commented warily. The edges of the stones were weathered and softened by time and there was no sign of any living inhabitants.

Her eyes on the view ahead, Tremaine stumbled a little on the uneven paving blocks. It was hard to see the full extent of the building; the concealing swaths of fog disguised where it left off and the dark cliffs began. Gerard stopped near the doorway and Florian moved over to the canal, Tremaine trailing after her.

It was just wide enough for a large rowboat. The far bank seemed to be made of more of the stone logs like the building, though heavy dark green bushes and palms grew atop it. The fog kept them from seeing anything beyond that. The canal itself was choked with reeds and other vegetation and the water smelled stagnant and foul. A bright green snake with black diamonds along its back slipped through the stems of the weeds as she watched. "First sign of life," Florian commented, not sounding enthused at the sight. She shivered and rubbed her arms briskly.

"Gerard, the Gardier didn't build this place, did they?" Tremaine demanded. The corners of the stones were rounded, moss and sand collected in niches and cracks; it looked ruinously old. "It's not what I expected." She wasn't sure what she had expected, but it wasn't this. She realized she hadn't imagined their enemies living in very different circumstances from themselves.

"You're right, this looks more like the remains of a long-dead civilization," Gerard answered. He made a gesture and a wisp of spell light leapt to life above his head. "We'll have to chance that it's uninhabited by the Gardier or anyone else. We need to get under cover."

Florian looked as uncertain as Tremaine felt, but they didn't have much choice. Gerard stepped inside the doorway, the spell light drifting ahead of him.

The passage beyond was high-ceilinged and dry, the natural rock walls smoothed to roughly square precision by long-ago hands. "Hmm," Gerard commented, and moved further into the tunnel. "I don't suppose the emergency supplies included electric torches, batteries and a carbide lamp."

Florian glanced into the satchel doubtfully. "Umm, no. Should we light the oil lamp?"

"Let's save it for now." After a short distance the passage turned to the left and Gerard paused, patting his pockets. "Compass, compass."

"Wait, I've got one." Tremaine dug in her coat and pulled out the small brass compass.

Gerard consulted it, Tremaine taking the lamp so he could record the direction in his battered notebook. He smiled slightly as he tucked the notebook back into his coat. "Your father used to carry small explosives in his dress suit."

"Those were the good old days?" Florian offered dubiously.

"A long long time ago." Tremaine handed Gerard back the lamp. She would rather not explain the facts of Valiarde life to Florian.

Gerard sighed. "Quite."

They moved down the new passage, the light from the entrance fading quickly behind them. A cool steady breeze came from somewhere ahead. Tremaine tugged on the strap of the satchel again, wishing the spray hadn't drenched her stockings. There were several more turns that

Gerard carefully recorded, then the passage widened. Tremaine had barely noticed the ceiling was higher, that the wispy white spell light no longer reached the walls to either side. Then they turned a corner and the passage opened suddenly into a great dark echoing space. The light reached another waist-high wall not far in front of them.

Gerard gestured for the light to drift up as they moved forward slowly. It gave them tantalizing glimpses of the chamber beyond, of stone bridges, galleries, rows of pillars. Columns, built of bundled masses of the stone logs, supported a bridge that crossed overhead and led away into darkness. From the wall a wide stairway curved down and ended in a floor of polished black stone. No, not stone, Tremaine realized, seeing a drift of seaweed floating atop it. Murky water, still as glass. The whole place was half-submerged.

Tremaine stared, thinking, *This is Kimeria.* There had been a scene in her last play, cut due to the theater's inability to stage it, where the characters, while exploring a hidden fayre island, encountered a sunken city. This was very close to how she had pictured it.

"Wow," Florian said softly.

"My sentiments exactly." Gerard shook his head slightly, his frown thoughtful. "The air is still fairly fresh. There must be an opening to the outside somewhere close."

Tremaine nodded. "It smells like salt water. Really stale salt water." While it looked a great deal like her imaginary city, this place didn't bear much kinship with the little ship Tremaine had seen. She had only caught a glimpse of it, but she clearly remembered the colorful sails and the painted designs on the prow. Whoever had built this wasn't an admirer of color or ornament, or at least not the kind of ornament that she could appreciate.

"Hold on." Gerard gestured at the spell light again, dimming it to a negligible gray spark.

The moments stretched as Tremaine waited for her eyes to adjust. Florian shifted restlessly beside her and Tremaine bit her lip as the darkness seemed to press in. Then she saw the dim radiance from the far side of the chamber, a gray reflection of the wan daylight outside. She pointed. "There! See it?"

"Ah, yes." Gerard waved the light back to life, the white glow washing over the dark stone again. "If we can jump to that broken column there at the bottom of the steps, we can reach the top of that wall." Briskly he added, "Come along."

They climbed cautiously down wide steps streaked with damp muck and managed the first jump to the broken column that poked up above the dark water.

Taking a wavering step to the next block, her mind still on the coincidental resemblance to her play's setting, Tremaine said, "I wonder what kind of people lived here." Above the waterline small pale lizards flashed away from their light.

"Humans, you mean?" Florian asked, taking Gerard's outstretched hand to help her to the next block. "This place looks like it was built by giants."

"There is evidence of a race of giants that inhabited part of Ile-Rien and the Low Countries hundreds, perhaps thousands of years ago," Gerard admitted. "They've found similar remains on the Tiakar Plateau in Parscia. Not underwater, of course."

"That's comforting." Tremaine nodded, not comforted at all. She was having a hard time not imagining large clawed hands reaching up out of that water and grabbing them. The still surface seemed made for something horrible to burst up out of it. The fact that this had actually occurred in her play didn't help.

Florian gave her a skeptical glance. "If they were still here, there'd be brackets for lamps, or pipes, or electric wires, or something. They couldn't live in the dark."

"Albino giants that can see in the dark, like bats," Tremaine countered.

"With fangs?"

Gerard paused to indicate a doorway between two of the huge pillars, leading into a small room empty except for seawater. "That doorway and the tunnel passage would not accommodate giants."

"Oh."

Gerard had to douse the spell light again to let them get their bearings, but the daylight was even brighter this time. There was another bridge, this one with a roof, blocking their view, but once they passed under it they could see the gray light was coming through an archway at the top of a low ramp. The breeze carried the dead fish smell Tremaine associated with every seaport she had ever visited.

They reached the ramp without anyone falling in, but the slick muck covering the stone made it a far more difficult proposition than anything else so far and Tremaine was glad for her rubber-soled half boots. Florian drew a little ahead as she and Gerard scuffed and scraped their way to the top, so that when they reached her the girl was standing transfixed by the sight ahead.

Tremaine took a startled breath. It was an enclosed cove, a lagoon sheltered by a high rocky vault arching overhead. A jagged opening at the far end allowed in daylight and fog drifting in from the open sea. The shore of the cove had once been a harbor; she could still see the stone platforms and breakwaters built out into it, the square pillars sunk into the water as pilings where the ships had once tied up. Now those platforms and the narrow slips between were jammed with wrecked hulls, wooden skeletons of craft of all different sizes. The wrecks formed a forest of broken masts, decaying sailcloth hanging like shrouds, rotted ropes like spiders' webs. Some were capsized and submerged, some were smashed in heaps up on the stone bank, as if dropped there by a terrible gale. At least no one could doubt now that she had seen a ship, Tremaine decided ruefully, looking over the destruction.

"Good God," Gerard murmured.

The smell of rot tinged the breeze that came from the sea entrance. This was old carnage, Tremaine realized with a little relief. Still, the destruction was disturbing on a whole other level, like the crater the Gardier's attacks had caused in Riverside. "Must have been some storm," she commented uneasily.

"More than one storm, surely." Florian squinted at the cave's entrance.

"Not a storm," Gerard said. He studied the devastation, brows knit. "A trap. Powerful spells drew these ships here. If I could find the etheric signatures . . ." He fished in his coat pocket and drew out a pair of aether-glasses. Pulling off his spectacles, he held the glasses up to his eyes, turning to view all of the large cave.

"The Gardier?" Tremaine wondered. "But it's not recent." Everything looked old and settled and rotted. But surely not as old as the barren submerged stonework in the chambers behind them. Mist drifted off the dark water like smoke.

"There are inimical forces other than the Gardier, but yes, this looks like something they would have been a party to." Gerard's voice was grim. Still holding the glasses up to his eyes, he started down the curving ramp into the cavern.

Tremaine followed, stepping over splintered boards and rusted piles of metal, wishing for a pistol. Or maybe a shotgun. The water lapped against the wood and stone, giving the impression of constant shadowy movement among the wrecks. They all looked like fairly simple craft. No sign of paddlewheels or engines, and most seemed to have only one or two masts, though it was hard to tell. Simple fishing boats, maybe. Many had faded designs painted on the hulls in gold, green, blue. *Red sails,* she thought, looking at the faded tatters festooning the spars of a broken mast. *I wonder if that means something different from purple.*

Preoccupied, Gerard said, "Yes, the latest activity was some time ago. Perhaps more than a year. There's a few etheric signatures remaining that are just starting to fade."

Tremaine felt pinpricks of unease climb up her back. "Oh, good. So whoever did this could still be around." As if the Gardier weren't trouble enough.

Gerard nodded abstractly, tucking the glasses away and putting his own spectacles back on. "There are layers over layers of activity. Whoever did this preyed on the shipping for some time."

"But why? What's the point of it?" Florian asked suddenly. She had crouched down near a broken hull jammed up onto the stone dock. Its lower half was still submerged and Florian was looking through a gaping hole in the side.

Surprised at her incomprehension, Tremaine waved an arm at the destruction. "To steal the cargoes, like the coast scavengers who wave lanterns on stormy nights and make the ships think it's a safe landing when—"

"Yes, I know, but look." The girl pointed and Tremaine went to her side to peer over her shoulder. As her eyes adjusted to the dimness inside the wreck, she saw what Florian meant.

The exposed section of the hold was full of broken crates, barrels, smashed pottery. Rotted bolts of fabric lay tumbled in piles near rusted metal heaps that still glinted with buried jewels. Florian leaned forward and picked up a small grime-encrusted object. She rubbed it with her thumb and it gleamed a dull red. "This is a ruby, I think." She glanced up at Tremaine, her eyes worried.

Tremaine stood slowly, looking around. "So whoever did this wasn't interested in loot." She rethought several of her assumptions and she didn't like the new conclusions. "I don't see any bodies, or bones." Even if most of the corpses had been washed out to sea, there should still be some remains, tangled in the ropes or smashed under the fallen masts, trapped inside the splintered overturned hulls. Florian tossed the gem back into the hold and rubbed her hand vigorously on her jacket flap as she got to her feet.

Maybe somebody buried them, Tremaine thought as they moved on. Hopefully after they were dead. They proceeded along the dock, stepping over the broken masts and shattered decking. Tremaine kept an eye out for bodies but though the smell of rot and decay seemed to worsen, she saw nothing that resembled human remains. After a short time the wan daylight and their spell light revealed another opening in the cave wall. It was smaller than the one that had led them here, not a square-cut doorway but a rough opening that looked as if it had been knocked through the solid rock.

It was dark and dank and somehow even more unpleasant than the passage through the remains of the underground city. The spell light seemed to penetrate the blackness only reluctantly and Tremaine could see pools of green stagnant water collecting on the rough rock further up the passage. "Well?" She glanced back at Gerard. "Do we try it?"

Florian wrinkled her nose. "It smells worse than the other one."

Tremaine had to agree. "And it looks like it goes down."

"Not very encouraging, is it?" Gerard too eyed it without enthusiasm. "It doesn't seem to be part of the constructed area. Let's keep moving. We'll try this one only if we have to."

They continued on. It was darker toward this end of the cove, as a heavy fold in the rock ceiling overhead blocked the gray daylight from the entrance. The wall of the cave curved backward and there were more boulders and rockfalls to obscure the view. Tremaine squinted and made out another square doorway in the shadow, about ten feet up the wall. What looked like a rockfall below it was actually another ramp, covered by debris.

"This one looks more promising," Gerard said, pausing at the top. The passage looked dry and it seemed to curve upward. It was smaller than the others but there was still room for them to walk abreast.

As they started along it, Florian asked, "You think the Institute will send someone after us?" She sounded carefully casual. "Once Niles gets his sphere to work?"

Tremaine looked at Gerard, walking between them. The flicker of the spell light made it hard to read his expression, but she could tell his frown was grim. "I'm sure they'll try," he said.

"And that would be a bad idea?" Tremaine asked bluntly. She didn't think Florian wanted it sugarcoated either.

"The Gardier were waiting for us," Gerard admitted reluctantly. "Our multiple trips to test the spell and the sphere before pressing an attack may have been a mistake."

Tremaine heard Florian take a sharp breath of dismay. She felt a sinking sensation herself. "We had to make the tests, Gerard. They couldn't send a troop in blind. You and Niles didn't do this."

"She's right, Gerard," Florian seconded firmly. "There was no other way."

He smiled a little ruefully. "Thank you, both." He sighed. "I think—" He paused. "Do you feel that breeze?"

"Yes." Florian lifted her hand, feeling the flow of air. "It's damp." She wrinkled her nose. "And it smells awful."

Tremaine sniffed and winced. The stink had an unfortunate resemblance to rotten eggs.

After a few more steps the light revealed a square opening in the corridor wall and another passage winding off through the rock. "Should we try that?" Florian wondered.

"No, let's keep to this one for a while," Gerard decided. "The breeze is still coming from this direction."

They had only gone some ten paces or so further when he pointed ahead, saying, "There. More doorways."

Just visible at the edge of the light the passage opened up to a wider chamber, with three more dark square openings in the wall. The damp breeze was coming from the one directly ahead. Tremaine began, "So should we—"

A low animal howl echoed through the passage.

Tremaine froze, Gerard and Florian jerking to a halt beside her. The sound came from somewhere in the darkness up one of the new tunnels, well past the reach of their light. *Ack,* Tremaine thought, her throat too paralyzed to make the sound aloud. Gerard reached out, taking her sleeve and then Florian's, indicating they should both draw back. As they started to move back step by step, he slipped the sling off his shoulder, starting to unbutton the sphere's case.

God yes, hurry, Tremaine thought, seeing what he meant to do. She could hear stealthy movement now, soft scrapes and rattles against stone. As he freed the sphere from its cover, she reached out to put her free hand on it. The metal was warm and tingling with power.

They made it almost to the first doorway they had passed. Suddenly dark figures burst out of the tunnels ahead, howling in high keening voices. Light exploded from the sphere, starkly outlining the tunnel. Captured in it as if in a frame of film were half a dozen human-shaped creatures. Their skins were a slick green-gray, their heads long and narrow, their open jaws bristling with fangs.

Before Tremaine could yell in alarm a concussion of sound and physical force followed the light. She felt the sphere spin out of her grip as the creatures confronting them were blasted backward and she was shoved the other way, slamming into Florian. She tumbled down the tunnel, landing hard on her shoulder, the breath knocked out of her.

Florian had landed beside her but there was no sign of Gerard. Tremaine sat up, gasping for breath. The spell light still hung abandoned further up the tunnel, flickering as if tossed by a hard wind. In the dimming light she could see that despite the backlash the spell had worked; several of the creatures sprawled in bloody heaps on the ground. Others out of the direct line of fire lay stunned, some further down the tunnel dizzily climbing to their feet. She still didn't see Gerard. "Where is he?" she demanded.

Florian, struggling to stand, pointed down the other tunnel entrance. Tremaine looked and in the dim light saw Gerard about twenty feet up the tunnel where the blast had thrown him, just pushing himself to his feet. In the sandy dirt near him the sphere spun like a top, throwing off blue sparks. Tremaine stumbled up just as Florian gasped in alarm.

Further up their passage past the fallen creatures, human figures moved toward them. There was just enough light from the spell wisp to see they wore dark brown uniforms. After an instant of blank shock, Tremaine's mind formed the word: *Gardier.*

She fell back a step, looked toward Gerard. He started toward her then stopped, reading her expression. She looked back at the Gardier. They hadn't seen Gerard. Beside her Florian, leaping to the same conclusion, breathed, "Distract them."

Tremaine raised her voice to a shout: "Oh no, it's the Gardier, run!"

Tremaine didn't know she could move that fast. She was gripping Florian's sleeve, hearing the other girl's harsh gasps for breath, pelting down the tunnel. They spilled out into the cove, tumbling down the rock-strewn ramp, somehow managing to stay on their feet. Tremaine pulled Florian to a stop at the end, knowing they couldn't run blindly. Florian hovered at her side, looking around wildly for someplace to go. Hiding in one of the wrecked ships was putting themselves in a trap, going into the water was pointless, they couldn't reach the opposite end of the cove and the tunnel that led to the surface fast enough. . . . Tremaine tugged Florian into motion as the creatures howled behind them and they raced for the tunnel they had passed earlier.

They reached it and ran through the dark, puddles of slimy water splashing underfoot, the uneven rocky floor threatening their balance. Gray light fell sporadically from cracks and fissures above, but the shadows were heavy. Tremaine caught her boot on something and pitched head-long, landing heavily on the rough rock. Florian kept hold of her jacket, dragging at her until she got her feet under her, and they ran.

They burst out into a wider cave, much of it lost in the dark. A shallow stream crossed the muddy floor and the ceiling was festooned with moss. Straight ahead a rockfall led up to another tunnel opening nearly twenty feet up the wall. *We can't make that,* Tremaine thought desperately. They were going to have to try.

They splashed across the stream, the mud catching at their feet and taking away any margin they might have had for scrambling up the rocks. Tremaine's boot caught on something and she staggered, falling to her knees, pebbles sliding away under her scraped hands. Florian rammed into Tremaine, grabbing her arm to pull her up.

Something gray burst out of the shadows and struck the

nearest creature, slamming it into the ground and rolling with it into the stream. The creature squealed and the water turned dark with blood. The others spun, crouching and snarling. The gray thing leapt up, resolving into a human shape, not quite as large as their pursuers.

My God, that's a person, Tremaine thought in shock, knowing it from the way it moved. It was a man with a wild mane of tangled hair, covered with patches of the gray-green mud and slime from the cave walls. It—he tossed his hair out of his eyes, backing rapidly away from the thing still shrieking and writhing in the stream. He circled around the others and they hesitated, growling, shifting back and forth, torn between the ambulatory prey and the fresh blood flowing into the muddy water. Tremaine gasped, sense returning, and pushed at Florian. "Go, go," she whispered.

Florian made an incoherent noise of agreement and turned, scrabbling for a handhold among the rocks. Tremaine gave her a push from behind, her own muddy boots slipping on the stone. Most of the creatures made their choice, leaping on their dying comrade, but one turned back toward them with a snarl, attracted by the movement. The man shouted and waved his arms and the creature rounded on him. It swung a clawed hand at him and missed as he ducked away.

Help, Tremaine thought vaguely, climbing after Florian, rocks sliding away under her scraped hands. She couldn't believe they weren't dead yet. She scrambled up the last few feet as Florian pulled her arm. They tumbled through into the new tunnel together and Tremaine looked back to see the creature close with the man, saw him dodge under its wild grab to slash at its abdomen. It staggered back and went down, dark blood spilling. Two of the others abandoned the carnage in the stream to leap on this new diversion.

Bright light flared behind them and Tremaine whipped around, blinking. She found herself staring at a group of men, several holding heavy handlamps.

More Gardier. They wore brown uniforms with heavy

boots, close-fitting caps covering their heads, belts with pouches and containers and bits of what looked like mountaineering equipment hanging off. They looked just like the few bad grainy photos she had seen in the papers.

Tremaine turned, waving wildly and yelling to the man in the cave below, "Run! Get out of here!"

He hesitated for a heartbeat, staring up at her, then bolted across the stream. The creatures feeding on their fallen comrades hissed as he dodged around them.

A Gardier shoved past Tremaine, knocking her into the cave wall. Others charged by, hurtling down the slope. She looked back. Florian was flattened against the opposite wall of the cave and there were three Gardier still looming over them expectantly. One of them barked an order in a language she didn't understand. She and Florian both must have looked blank rather than rebellious, because he repeated in awkward, badly accented Rienish, "Hand . . . up."

"What?" Tremaine managed. She had time to notice two of the men had pistols pointed at her.

"Hands up," Florian clarified in a whisper. She straightened slowly, lifting her hands above her head.

Oh, right. Tremaine stumbled to her feet, putting up her hands. *That's it for us.*

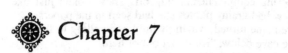

Chapter 7

Making sharp gestures with their pistols, the Gardier directed Tremaine and Florian to move a short distance up the curving tunnel to a wider cave. Stumbling in the dimness with her hands up, Tremaine saw a jagged tear in the wall that opened into the large chamber they had just come through. The things that had chased them were still there, gathered on the far side of the stream. They were eerily quiet except for an occasional low hiss, ducking their heads and peering up at the Gardier. Caught in the electric lamplight, their eyes looked greedy, hungry and hostile.

The Gardier in charge stepped to the edge of the opening, unclipping one of the devices from his belt and fumbling with it. He had several to choose from, all little metal boxes with triggers on them, like fancy cigar lighters. Reluctantly, growling, the creatures left their meal and moved away down the other tunnel. Joining the hunt. *God, they work for the Gardier,* Tremaine thought, exchanging an appalled look with Florian. *They drove us right toward them.*

In the blaze of light from the lamps the leader took the satchel of supplies and searched Tremaine and Florian's pockets. Tremaine had a few men's handkerchiefs, a penknife and the latchkeys to Coldcourt's front door and her room at the conscripted hotel in Port Rel. Gerard, she remembered, had kept her compass. Florian had small embroidered handkerchiefs, an empty notebook, a pencil, some cough lozenges, her hotel latchkey and a letter. "It's from my mother," Florian murmured, reassuring Tremaine that it didn't contain any Institute secrets.

The leader barked another unintelligible order, which Tremaine supposed was Gardier for "shut up." She could see he had a bad burn on his face, with blisters on his cheek and reddened skin leading down his neck under his uniform collar. It certainly wasn't improving his temper. The burn had been slathered with some kind of medical cream, but it seemed odd that a wounded man would be sent to search for them.

As she watched he suddenly flinched and grabbed for another device on his belt. The other two Gardier backed up uneasily, their weapons still trained on the prisoners. The leader looked from Florian to Tremaine, then back to Florian. With an angry comment, he stepped up to loom threateningly over her.

"All right, all right," Florian said, wincing away from him.

"What happened?" Tremaine asked, baffled.

"I tried an illusion charm," Florian admitted, giving the patrol leader a rebellious look as she backed away. The man again barked the order that probably meant "shut up."

Tremaine pressed her lips together, annoyed. It had happened so quickly she couldn't tell now which device had warned him. She wished Florian hadn't played that card just yet; now the Gardier were wary. *And now they know she's a witch.*

She heard angry shouting and scuffling from the tunnel behind them and looked to see five Gardier dragging a fighting, yelling figure. Florian gasped in dismay and Tremaine winced as she recognized the mud-splattered man who had helped them escape the hunter-things. *They caught him too, dammit. This is not going well.*

There were manacles on his wrists, connected with a length of chain, but it was still taking three Gardier to force him along. He was shorter than the men who were struggling with him, but under the mud she could see he had a muscular build. He was ignoring both their weapons and their shouting. *He doesn't care if they shoot him,* she thought, impressed. Maybe he was even hoping they would.

They had almost wrestled their prisoner to the ground when suddenly he was on his feet again, knocking two Gardier sprawling. The prisoner whipped his chains around the neck of a third, driving the Gardier to his knees. The others surged forward, but the man put his back against the cave wall, bracing a knee against his hostage's back as the trapped Gardier choked and struggled.

The leader barked an order that the prisoner ignored and the other Gardier were too occupied to follow. Then the leader grabbed Florian's arm and jerked her toward him, drawing his pistol and pressing it to her head.

Florian yelped involuntarily and Tremaine took a half step toward her, with no idea what she meant to do. Her brain caught up to her a moment later and told her there was no hope; they were unarmed, outnumbered. She turned, yelling, "Hey! This isn't helping!"

Maybe it was the female voice that caught the prisoner's attention. He looked up, blue eyes startled, furious. He saw the threat to Florian and for a long heartbeat no one moved.

Tremaine held her breath; he had no reason to help Florian. He had distracted the hunter-things away from them, but this might be different. Then the man made a succinct but unintelligible comment. He pulled the chains off the Gardier's neck and shoved him away, then spit on him.

Two of the Gardier grabbed the prisoner, flinging him down at base of the wall. The leader shoved Florian down next to him and then, apparently out of a sense of fairness, grabbed Tremaine's arm and threw her down too.

"Ow," Tremaine muttered, sitting up cautiously. The Gardier had gathered in front of them, the leader asking angry questions, the disheveled and bloody ones who had captured the man making defensive explanations. "Are you all right?" she whispered to Florian.

Florian nodded, eyeing the Gardier resentfully. "Yes, I'm fine." She looked at their new ally, slumped against the wall and watching the Gardier with wary contempt.

He glanced at them with a quizzical expression, very at

odds with the earlier violence of his demeanor. Tremaine gave Florian an encouraging nudge and the girl edged closer to whisper, "Hello. Who are you?"

As the man listened to her his shoulders slumped a little and he shook his head slightly, then replied softly in a language Tremaine didn't know. This close she saw he did seem to be wearing clothes under the mud, except on his bare arms and mostly bare chest: low boots and dark-colored trousers, a jerkin of braided leather over a faded, frayed shirt that was so torn it was barely intact. She saw the mud-plastered mane of hair fell past his shoulders and he had a thick queue that hung to midway down his back. He also had a cut on his forehead under the fringe of mud-coated hair; the Gardier must have knocked him senseless just long enough to get the chains on him.

It didn't sound like he was speaking the same language as the Gardier, unless he just had a completely different accent. His speech wasn't as hard and guttural as theirs and it sounded a bit like Aderassi, but Tremaine could speak Aderassi and this wasn't it. She looked at Florian hopefully, but the other girl shook her head to show she was stumped too.

Tremaine felt obligated to say something, though it didn't look like he expected much. "We don't understand," she told him, keeping her voice low, miming a baffled shrug.

He said something, looking away with a glum expression. Tremaine had the feeling what he had said was "no kidding."

She reached across Florian to pick up the lock on his chains, examining it speculatively. It was a squarish pad-lock with an oddly shaped keyhole. When Tremaine had been traveling with her father she had carried a set of handcuff keys that fit all the standard restraints used by the Prefecture of Ile-Rien, but this lock looked far too large for any of those keys even if she had still owned them. She didn't carry her picks anymore either. The man watched her curiously, lifting his brows. There was quick intelligence in those eyes, as well as humor and kindness. *We're lucky he has a more developed sense of chivalry than the Gardier,* she thought ruefully.

Florian glanced at their captors. They were still arguing and checking various devices. Keeping her voice to a bare whisper, she said, "I hope Gerard is all right. I think all of those things chased us." She gingerly touched a bruise on her forehead. "What did the sphere do?"

Tremaine bit her lip, trying to remember exactly what had happened. "I think it was trying to drive them off, but it got me and Gerard too. Maybe it was because I touched it. I thought I had to so Gerard could use it for whatever spell he was about to try."

"That's how it's always worked before." Florian read Tremaine's expression and added sharply, "Isn't it?"

"Well, the night I first came to the Institute it destroyed a ward all by itself," Tremaine admitted reluctantly. "I was holding it but I didn't tell it to do anything."

"So maybe it was already reacting to the danger at the same time Gerard tried to use it for a defensive spell, and it just . . . backfired?" Florian frowned. "I don't think any of the test spheres ever just did things on their own."

Arisilde's first sphere had acted on its own whenever it had the urge, needing only to be held by someone with a little magical talent. Fortunately, the urge had moved it only when it was confronted by a magical force acting in a hostile manner. Tremaine wasn't sure if Gerard had mentioned that little fact about Arisilde's spheres to the other Institute sorcerers or not.

The Gardier leader shouted again, making all three of them jump. Their new friend recovered by baring his teeth at the Gardier and saying something that Tremaine was fairly sure wasn't complimentary.

The leader backed up a step but motioned sharply for them to get to their feet.

Tremaine tried to keep track of where they were but she had never been good at directions and all the tunnels were uniformly dark, slimy and full of sharp rocks and debris. All she could tell was that they were going up. It did give her time to get used to her fear and focus on her overwhelming feeling of embarrassment at being caught. The Gardier didn't insist on making her and Florian keep their hands on their heads; most of their attention was focused on the male prisoner. It was doubly humiliating not only to be caught but to be obviously filed away as harmless. *If you could think faster, we wouldn't be in this mess,* she told herself bitterly.

Finally, they came to a tunnel where electric bulbs had been haphazardly strung along the rough walls. Tremaine exchanged a look with Florian. This had to mean they were almost there, wherever there was.

The tunnel opened into a huge cavern, lit with buzzing arc lights, the smell of burned oil hanging in the damp air. As they drew closer she could see the floor had been roughly leveled and was crisscrossed with electric cables and hoses. The thrum of a massive generator, or several massive generators, made the air hum like it was itself electrified and Tremaine's head started to pound in sympathy. She saw their new friend wince away from the lights.

As they came out from behind the last tumble of rocks, they saw the center of the cavern was filled with an enormous jumbled mess of latticework girders and wires. For a moment Tremaine's brain insisted this was a modern sculpture, a larger version of the sort that the Palace of Arts had been exhibiting before the start of the war. But then her eyes found the conical shape of the nose and she realized it was a half-completed dirigible, some of its giant ring frames lying flat atop scaffolds for construction. *Great, we're at their base,* she thought. *If I knew what I was doing, this could actually be a good thing.* She wished Ander or Gerard were here to help. The rest of the cavern curved away out of sight, lost in darkness past the range of the arc lights.

There were people in brown uniform coveralls, some moving around near the scaffolds, but the place looked . . . *understaffed,* Tremaine decided after a moment. Maybe that was why the wounded man was still on duty. Only a few people were working on the new airship's frame, surely not enough to finish it anytime this century.

The Gardier led them toward the side of the cave. There were a couple of tunnel entrances there under an over-hang, separated from the rest of the cave by a wire mesh fence that looked as if it had been hastily erected. There were other, smaller tunnels opening higher up in the wall. Metal scaffolds with steps and catwalks had been erected to reach them.

The patrol leader called to two more armed Gardier sta-tioned at the stairs to come over. The group of Gardier tightened around them suddenly and Tremaine hesitated, confused. Their new friend muttered something, throwing the two women a rueful look. The leader grabbed Tremaine and Florian by their jackets, dragging them out of the way as the circle closed around the man.

He slammed his shoulder into the nearest Gardier, send-ing him staggering away, but three others hit him from the side, grabbing him by his chained arms and hauling him forward. He planted his feet, throwing his weight back-ward, but one of them caught his hair, yanking him off-balance. The others moved in, and despite his struggles, they dragged him into the tunnel entrance next to the wire mesh. The next moment the whole group had vanished around the bend.

Tremaine felt her flesh creep. They hadn't treated him like a prisoner. They had acted as if he was a dangerous an-imal they were hauling off to slaughter. "That didn't look good," she said under her breath.

Florian looked bleak. "Surely they wouldn't just kill him. . . . If they were going to do that, why bring him all the way back here?"

Tremaine just shook her head. *I bet we find out, but I'm not looking forward to it.* Their remaining guards held a brief discussion, then the leader went up a set of metal steps to one of the smaller tunnels, leaving the other two behind to watch Tremaine and Florian.

Ilias knew he was dead when the wizards wrestled him through the tunnel entrance, but he made them fight for every step. Then they shoved him forward and for a moment he was standing alone, the wizards gathered around him at a wary distance. *This can't be good,* Ilias thought, twisting around, trying to keep an eye on all of them at once. He saw they were in a small cave-room, hollowed out of the rock, lit by wizard lights strung across the ceiling and empty except for a long metal table and metal cabinets against the wall. His head was pounding and his shoulder hurt like fire, but it didn't matter; soon he would either be dead or wish he was. Past the men surrounding him he had a brief glimpse of another wizard, this one thin and spare, with a narrow grim face. This new one pulled something glassy and metallic off his belt and gestured sharply with it.

Ilias felt the ground snatched out from under him then struck it hard, the breath knocked out of him. He tried to scramble up and realized his legs were numb, that he couldn't move them at all. *Another damned curse.* He spit at the wizard, trying to push himself up with his chained arms, angry and terrified.

Two of the men grabbed his arms, dragging him up and slamming him down facefirst onto the metal table. He struggled to push himself up but two of them bore down on him, shoving him against the cold surface. He twisted his head, managing to get a breath, then someone grabbed his hair again, pinning his head down and putting a painful pressure on his neck.

Ilias waited for death but they just stood over him, talking angrily. *They're arguing,* he realized. He would have liked to know if it was about when to kill him or just how. He squinted, pushing up against the bodies holding him down. He could just see the leader of the group who had captured him confronting the new wizard. The leader was holding a folded water-damaged paper packet.

Oh, Ilias thought, nonplussed, *the maps.* They had searched him when they had caught him running from the howlers. One of them had tackled him, slamming him into the rock wall, and he had been half conscious for a few moments. Long enough for them to find his hunting knife, the smaller spare blade tucked into his boot and the maps Giliead had found on the flying whale and stuffed under his belt.

So it was the maps that were causing all the angry arguing. Maybe he should have cached them somewhere but he couldn't see how it mattered. They were wizards; they were already going to kill him just for existing. Burning their flying whale and stealing from them couldn't make it any worse. At least he hoped it couldn't.

The leader suddenly reached across him, pulling roughly at his shirt and jerkin, ripping it down to bare his wounded shoulder. Ilias flinched and involuntarily tried to writhe away, thinking they had finally gotten to the torture part. But the leader didn't touch him again. The arguing continued and he wondered if the man had bared the wound as proof that Ilias had been near the flying whale when it burned. *Of course I was,* he thought in exasperation. *How many other people are running around these caves trying to kill wizards?*

Then the men pinning him suddenly wrenched him up off the table and threw him against the wall. He collapsed at the base of it, pushing himself up into an awkward sitting position with his chained hands. He shook the hair out of his face, looking up as the leader knelt in front of him. The man held up the maps, asking an urgent question. The other wizard stood behind him, shaking his head, his narrow face disgusted.

Ilias looked from one to the other, half wishing they would just kill him and get it over with. If the curse making his legs useless was permanent, he couldn't escape anyway and he didn't want Giliead risking himself trying to come after him. If Giliead was even still alive and not a prisoner here somewhere.

The leader gripped his chin, forcing his head around to face him, and said carefully, "Rien. Rien?"

Ilias stared at him, truly baffled, too startled to wrench his head away or try to bite the man. He realized he had heard the wizards say the word before, all during their argument, but it meant nothing to him.

His belief that they were out of their minds, or at least his complete incomprehension, must have shown on his face. The other wizard made a derisive snort and turned away. The leader let go of him and stood, his face frustrated, rubbing his hand on his pants as if it had been contaminated by the physical contact. He gestured at the other men. Ilias squirmed to avoid them, swinging his chain and managing to catch one in the face. But they grabbed his arms, dragging him upright, and hauled him back toward the tunnel.

He fought as best he could but with his legs mostly useless there wasn't much he could do except annoy them. They dragged him to a large, shadowy high-ceilinged room with heavy doors in the rusted metal walls. Opening one, they hauled him into a small cell, dumping him against the stone that formed the back of it. Two of them sat on him while the third attached his chains to a ring anchored into the rock at waist height. The same one kicked him in the stomach as they left, slamming the door behind them.

Panting, Ilias curled around the pain as best he could, his arms stretched back and over his head by the chains, his legs still paralyzed. He was glad there wasn't anything in his stomach to throw up. When he could finally lift his head, he saw just a small bare room, the walls scarred stained metal except for the rocky one behind him, the sickly yellow light coming from a single wizard lamp set high in the ceiling. He eyed it nervously, but at least it wasn't anywhere near him. There was a narrow grille in the door, but too small and too high to see out of. The dirty stone floor smelled of piss and vomit.

Ilias leaned against the wall gingerly, shifting to hold his injured shoulder away from the rock. The struggle had reopened the wound and he could feel blood trickle down his back. Now that more urgent pains were fading, he realized his legs were starting to hurt, prickling with sharp needle pricks, but it was better than that frightening numbness. Gritting his teeth and putting all his effort into it, he managed to wriggle his toes. Relief made him slump back against the rock, taking a deep breath. *The curse isn't permanent.*

He wasn't sure how long it had been since he had come to dazed and bleeding in the impenetrable dark of the underground city or how long he had searched for Giliead. The river had swept him down one of the small passages and washed him aground while he was still half conscious. The metal that had struck him had sliced through his baldric; his sword and scabbard had ended up somewhere on the river bottom. He had been lucky to land where he had; if the water had carried him further along into the lower caves, he would have been eaten by something before he woke.

When he had recovered enough to walk he had worked his way back up to the wizards' tunnels, searching for Gil, hoping his friend had made it out of the flying whale's cave. Chances were the curse that had knocked Ilias into the river wouldn't have affected Giliead; Ilias just hoped he hadn't gotten himself captured while searching the river for him.

If the wizards did have Gil, he might be in one of the other cells. Ilias sat up, spit to clear his throat, and yelled, "Gil! Are you here?"

No answer.

Frustrated, he leaned back against the rock. It didn't tell him anything; Giliead could still be here, held in another area. But if he had been here and the wizards had already killed him . . . Trying to put that uncomfortable thought aside, he wondered about the two women captured with him.

When he had first seen the howlers hunting them he had thought they were escaped slaves, but after getting a good look at them he decided that couldn't be possible. Their clothes were different from what the slaves and wizards wore and they just hadn't acted like cowed captives. Especially the one with the light brown hair, the one who had looked more annoyed by the wizards than frightened. He let his breath out, shifting uncomfortably as his shoulder burned and his bruises ached. *Whoever they are, I hope they're better off than I am.*

Looking around the cavern, Tremaine weighed their options and decided they didn't have any. It was too far to any of the tunnels even to contemplate making a break for it. Then Florian nudged her and she looked around to see people coming out of an opening under the overhang, gathering in the area on the other side of the wire mesh. They moved slowly, the brown coveralls they wore stained with sweat and greasy dirt, many of them carrying welding goggles or wearing baggy caps covering their hair. Men, women, young, old. Tremaine's eyes narrowed as she realized none of them were armed. Were they Gardier? The older man with the dark skin and the hooked nose looked distinctly Parscian. Then a man leaned on the mesh and spoke to a woman with him. Tremaine didn't catch the words but his accent sounded Lowlands.

Florian nudged her more urgently. Tremaine nodded, motioning her to stop, and sneaked a look at their two guards. They were talking together, most of their attention on the half-completed dirigible. She sidled a couple of steps closer to the mesh near the couple and said in a low voice, "Where are you from?"

The man looked up at her, startled, then darted a look at the guards. "We can't help you," he whispered.

She had been right, his accent was Lowlands, but that covered a lot of territory. More, if you counted colonies and independent ex-colonies. "We don't need help," Tremaine said firmly, keeping her voice low. That was anything but the truth, but what the hell. "Just tell us where you're from, how they captured you, how you got here."

The man just stared but the woman with him flicked a glance from Tremaine's face to Florian's and wet her lips. "You're Ile-Rien." Her accent was thicker than his.

Florian nodded. "Yes." The others were beginning to notice, some turning to look and some just edging close to listen. Nobody seemed to think it was a good idea to alert the guards.

The woman leaned forward. "We live on Maiuta, we're missionaries of the Benevolent Order of Dane." The man caught her arm but she shook him off impatiently.

Tremaine nodded rapidly. Maiuta was in the Southern Seas, a large island that was mostly jungle with only a few ports and towns, but with a substantial population of warring tribes who had long been the target of exploitation by more modern nations. Aberdon, a Lowland state to the north of Ile-Rien, had a colony there.

The woman whispered rapidly, "The Gardier came, captured the ports and killed anyone who tried to resist. We were in the interior and had some warning. Most of the villages in our area escaped up into the hills, but we stayed at our infirmary with some of the older people who were too sick to move. We didn't think . . . But they took us to the port and put us on a ship with some of the townspeople and many others." She nodded around at the people clustered nearby, watching anxiously. "We had only gone a little distance when we felt— Ah, I don't know how to explain—a great crash—"

Florian gave Tremaine a grave look and supplied, "Like the ship suddenly dropped a few feet and hit the water again."

"Yes, yes. We didn't see it, but some of the others were chained up on deck because there was no more room below, and they said they saw a circle of light appear just above the waves and the ship sailed into it. They said the land disappeared and the sky turned more blue, and it was morning instead of evening. We sailed for many days, then they unloaded us in these caves and they make us work for them. There are others here from the south islands, from Venais and Khiatu." The woman shifted closer. "Something went wrong here a few days ago. There was an explosion in one of the caves they use as a hangar—"

Someone on the other side hissed a warning and they sprang away from each other like guilty children talking out of turn in a schoolroom. On the other side of the mesh two Gardier came out of a tunnel entrance and moved through the group, gesturing with short clubs, forcing the prisoners to move along.

Tremaine saw their two guards suddenly look alert again and glanced up to see the leader coming down the steps near the wire mesh fence with another man. The new Gardier wore the same sort of uniform as the others, except that he had a small silver medallion with an inset crystal around his neck. His features were thin and hard, his dark hair cut so close it was barely a fuzz over his skull.

He walked up to them, eyeing them with a cold familiarity, fiddling with his medallion. Tremaine dropped her eyes, trying to look helpless and pathetic. *Stalling,* she thought, *stalling is an option.* It might give Gerard more time to get away.

"Who are you?" he demanded in accented Rienish.

Tremaine threw a tremulous, uncertain look at Florian and said softly, "We're missionaries, from Maiuta."

Florian's eyes widened, but she managed to suppress any other response.

He let go of the medallion and addressed a couple of sharp comments to the patrol leader in their language. Tremaine hadn't had any plan in mind, but it looked as if she had derailed any prepared questions. The patrol leader planted his hands on his hips and replied tartly. Tremaine sensed dissension in the ranks.

The interrogator turned back, grasped the medallion again and said, "When did you come here?"

The medallion is the key to some kind of translator spell. Tremaine hadn't heard of anything like it before. She said earnestly, "We don't know. We've been underground, we can't tell how many days and nights it's been."

The interrogator turned back to the patrol leader, saying with exasperation, "We recovered all the labor who escaped yesterday. They can't be—" before he dropped the medallion.

The discussion continued for a moment more, with both men appearing increasingly annoyed with each other, then the interrogator touched the medallion briefly to say, "Come with me."

He started back up the stairs to the tunnels above. As the patrol leader turned to call the two guards to follow, Tremaine exchanged a brief glance with Florian. The other girl looked somewhat taken aback, but this was the best chance they had. If the Gardier hadn't found the Pilot Boat yet, or had found it after it had drifted further off the rocks, they might think the entire crew had drowned. That was good for Gerard, at least.

The door opened onto a catwalk overlooking a larger chamber, lit by a few bare electric bulbs suspended from a network of wires crossing the ceiling. The far wall was raw stone, cracked and pitted, and the other two were stained metal partitions fixed against it. In the partitions there were heavy metal doors with small barred grates to look through. *Cells,* Tremaine thought. *Uh oh.* There wouldn't be any options once they were in a cell. As the interrogator led the way along the catwalk, a door banged open in the room below. She glanced down to see two disheveled Gardier crossing the floor; she was sure they had been in the group who had hauled off the other prisoner.

The interrogator said, "You were with a native, one of the dangerous primitives that infest the mainland."

Tremaine saw Florian lift a brow at that comment and privately agreed. *If anybody's doing the infesting here, it's the Gardier.* But it was odd that the man had said "native." *So the Gardier must come from some other part of this world.* They must have invaded this area because the island made such a good staging ground for their attacks on the coast of Ile-Rien.

Without glancing back, the interrogator said, "If you aren't truthful with me, perhaps we'll put you in the same cage with him."

The words *better him than you* came to mind and Tremaine managed to lock her throat against them. It sounded like the man was still alive, at least for now. Like they were still alive, at least for now.

Tremaine had read in one of the government pamphlets

that not speaking at all if captured was the only sure way to avoid revealing any information. That was undoubtedly true; she also remembered her father's late-night lecture to Gerard and some of his other cronies, about how it was possible to tell one simple lie and stick to it at all costs; it was the unnecessary elaboration that would ruin you. It didn't apply to Nicholas, of course, who had been able to tell very elaborate lies by adopting other personas. Tremaine already knew she couldn't pull that off.

The interrogator opened the door at the far end of the catwalk and led them into a bare room with two more doors and a table. At a comment from him the guard who had been carrying their satchel dumped it out on the table and began to sift through the contents. The interrogator gave them a cold smile, touched the medallion and said, "I am Gervas. I command here." Tremaine saw the patrol leader's eyes go hooded. *Dissension, oh yes.* She wondered if the explosion the Lowlands woman had mentioned had taken out part of the command structure. He continued, "Where do you get these things?"

Tremaine looked up at him, trying to hold the mental image of a meek little missionary woman. She knew she couldn't stall much longer but every moment of delay counted. "We've been hiding them," she said.

Gervas dropped the medallion and lifted his hand. Tremaine had time to see it was going to be an open-handed slap before the blow spun her around into the table. She caught herself awkwardly, heard Florian give an involuntary cry of protest. Blinking, carefully putting a hand to her aching jaw, she looked up. Florian must have started forward because one of the guards had her by the arm, twisting it painfully. Gervas's expression hadn't changed. He lifted the medallion again and said calmly, "You lie."

"About what?" Tremaine asked, still trying to look innocent and wishing she had thought of a different plan.

"You—" Gervas caught himself. He stared at her, eyes narrowing thoughtfully. "You are not a missionary."

Stalling is over, Tremaine thought. *Oh, well.* "Give me a chance to prove it." She carefully wiped blood away from her mouth, trying to ignore the fact that her hand was shaking, and grinned at him. "Why don't you ask me some questions about religion?"

Gervas smiled thinly, dropped the medallion and turned to speak in his own language to the patrol leader. *This is over and we're dead, whatever happens,* Tremaine thought, sick. She found herself staring at the holstered pistol of the guard standing near her, almost within her reach. *Might as well go out with a bang.* She had actually swayed toward the weapon when running footsteps sounded outside one of the other doors. It banged open and another Gardier leaned in, speaking urgently.

The patrol leader tensed, looking toward Gervas, who muttered in frustration and snapped an order to one of the guards. The man strode over to the other door and opened it.

Gervas turned to them. Touching the medallion around his neck, he said, "Get in there," punctuating the order with a shove to Florian's shoulder. Florian turned, glaring at him, but moved into the room. Tremaine got a shove too and stumbled after her.

He slammed the door shut and Tremaine heard the lock click. She turned around to see another bare room with a long metal table and chairs, lit by three bulbs suspended from the ceiling. There was a large sheet of paper tacked to the wall, covered with writing in an incomprehensible script. Florian shoved her hair back and started to speak but Tremaine hastily motioned her to be silent.

She stepped to the door to press her ear against it, listening. She heard the men speaking in their own language again in some urgency, then their boots on the stone as they walked away.

Tremaine turned to ask in a whisper, "They have a translator spell; have you ever heard of a translator spell before?"

Florian shook her head. "I've seen one that translates documents; you can make the writing appear in a mirror in another language. But it only works when the person casting it knows both the languages so there's really not much point to it."

Tremaine nodded. The translator was something else

Gerard and Niles and the others at the Institute would give a great deal to know about. She frowned. "And the Gardier are capturing civilians as slave labor. Did we know that?" She could see why the government would have concealed that little detail; people were panicked enough already.

"I didn't." Florian grimaced. "If we can just get home, the invasion troop can rescue them." She looked over the room. "Strange. There's no switches or pull cords for the lights. We can't turn them off."

Tremaine's face was going numb and to distract herself she moved to the far wall to study the paper tacked there. It was mounted on a wooden board, with long pins topped with different-colored beads stuck in it to mark various paragraphs. It was obviously a checklist or an agenda or something similar. "Why do you want to turn the lights out?"

"So we could lure them in and . . ." Florian's brows drew together as she considered the variables in that plan.

"Get beaten up?"

"Something like that." She added abruptly, "You didn't flinch."

Busy working one of the long pins out of the wall, Tremaine glanced up, confused. "What?"

Florian pushed her hair back, looking confused too. "When he was about to hit you. You just . . . watched him. It was creepy."

"Well, yes," Tremaine had to admit. "I should have flinched. It made him more suspicious when I didn't." Thinking that hindsight was a wonderful thing, she stepped back to the door to listen at it again. Still nothing. All four men must have left in response to whatever the urgent summons had been.

"And we got that poor man caught, whoever he is," Florian added, pacing back and forth in agitation. "I wouldn't mind so much if it was just us. I don't mean exactly that but—"

"I know." Tremaine nodded glumly. "Did you catch it when Gervas called him a native?"

"Yes! He said he came from the mainland."

Now they knew there were people in this world fighting the Gardier, potential allies for Ile-Rien. More information they should take back home. "If he hadn't stopped to help us, they would never have caught him." Tremaine tried the handle carefully, then stooped to look through the keyhole. If they were caught trying to escape, could the Gardier possibly do anything worse to them than they undoubtedly already planned to do? *Sure,* she answered her own question. *Lots worse.*

"It's a metal door—we can't break it down," Florian said from behind her. She hesitated. "Can we?"

Tremaine looked at her. The other girl was trembling, her arms folded tightly and her hands tucked into her jacket. Tremaine thought of the contempt in Gervas's eyes, the scorn evident in locking them in here like a couple of truant children. *We should do this.* She turned, looking around the room. "I think . . ." She stepped past Florian to the papers tacked onto the wall and plucked another one of the pins out. ". . . this might work."

Florian stared as Tremaine knelt by the door. "You can—" She lowered her voice even further. "You can pick the lock?"

"Maybe. I'm out of practice." Tremaine held her breath, probing at the lock and trying to visualize the tumblers. It had been a long time.

The moment stretched until her lungs started to hurt. Then the lock clicked and she felt the door move.

Florian gave an excited bounce. Heart pounding, Tremaine edged the door open enough to peer out. The room was empty.

"Yes," Tremaine breathed. She pushed the door open, shoving the pins into her pocket and climbing awkwardly to her feet. Florian stepped out behind her, carefully pushing the door to again and turning the lock. Tremaine nodded approval and looked around. She saw their bag on the table, the contents spread around, some of the ration packages torn open. *At least we didn't have the sphere,* she thought, grabbing the satchel and holding it as Florian hastily scooped in the remaining rations, medical kit, boxes of matches and the other intact supplies.

"I want to check that room that looked like it had cells." Tremaine jerked her chin at the door that led to the larger prison chamber. Gervas had made his comments about natives when they passed through there, as if he was reminded of the other prisoner. She slung the satchel over her shoulder as Florian turned to the door.

Breathless with fear and excitement, she listened at it briefly, then tried the handle. "Locked," she whispered.

Tremaine was still reeling over being able to get them out of their makeshift prison; she just hoped she didn't fail now. She stepped past her to peer into the keyhole and thought, *Oh yes.* The key was still in it. She looked down and saw the door wasn't flush with the floor; there was a nearly half-inch gap. *Good thing this place is jury-rigged.* She glanced up at Florian, holding her hands about a foot apart. "I need a piece of paper, about this big."

Florian bolted back to the other room and reappeared a moment later with a large square torn from the papers on the wall. Tremaine slid it under the door, then used a pin to poke the key out. It fell onto the paper with a faint clink and she carefully drew it back under the door and into reach.

With Florian performing an abbreviated victory dance behind her, she quickly unlocked the door and peered through. What she could see of the large room below the catwalk appeared to be unoccupied. As she opened it further a voice just on the other side of the far wall turned Tremaine's blood to ice. She froze for an instant but Florian's frantic pounding on her shoulder galvanized her.

Tremaine stepped hastily out onto the catwalk. Florian slipped after her and they both pushed the door shut. Tremaine leaned over the railing to look down into the lower part of the room and saw with relief that it really was empty.

They both stood frozen as the voices grew louder. After an endless moment when Tremaine was ready to throw herself off the catwalk just to bring it to an end one way or another, they heard the voices fade as the speakers moved away. Florian leaned against the door in relief. Tremaine made herself breathe and turned to walk softly toward the ladder at the far end of the cat-walk. She winced as the metal creaked with each step. Her palms leaving sweaty marks on the metal ladder, she started down, Florian right behind her.

At the bottom Tremaine got her bearings. There were three cell doors in one metal wall, two in the other, and one solid door under the catwalk. *I bet that leads to a guardroom.* If they got caught now, not only would they look stupid, they would have simply saved the Gardier a few steps.

Tremaine peered through the grates on the first two doors, seeing empty cells, bare except for the usual electric bulb set high in the ceiling. From the other side of the chamber Florian whispered her name and waved urgently. Tremaine hurried over.

Florian was looking through the grate and Tremaine stood on tiptoe to see over her head. He was sitting back against the wall on the far side of the cell, his hands pulled above his head and the heavy manacles encircling his wrists fastened to a ring set in the stone. He looked star-tled, then delighted to see them. Florian waved at him.

"All right," Tremaine muttered, stepping back to look over the door. "So far so good." There was a wheel instead of a handle and it was set low in the door, so there was no possibility of an occupant reaching it through the grate, even if he had hands small enough to work through the nar-row mesh of bars. *So therefore* . . . She tugged on it exper-imentally. It turned sluggishly and Florian glanced at her, saying ruefully, "I could have done that."

A door banged nearby and Tremaine flinched. "Oh no," Florian whispered. Muffled shouts sounded from some-where through the metal walls, then running feet.

Tremaine swore as she pulled the cell door open and they slipped inside, dragging it hastily shut. There was an inside handle but the heavy door didn't want to stay closed without the outside wheel being turned. Tremaine swore and crouched as low as she could, clinging to the handle to keep it shut. Florian dropped down beside her and they both flattened themselves against the door.

The prisoner stared at them, his expression torn between admiration and severe doubt, probably of their sanity. Tremaine couldn't blame him for the latter; she didn't feel very sane at the best of times and the circumstances of the moment weren't helping. Heavy boots thudded on the catwalk, Gardier voices called to each other, the ladder creaked. If there was some way to look at those wheel handles and see they were unlocked this was all over. Tremaine's heart pounded painfully and her own breathing sounded loud in her ears; her stomach tried to lurch and the unpleasant odor of the cell floor wasn't helping. She clutched the satchel to her chest with her free hand though it made a very inadequate object to hide behind. She heard footsteps cross the lower level of the chamber toward the cell door. *This could be really, really humiliating.*

The footsteps stopped just at the door. The prisoner glared murderously at whoever was looking in through the grate, his eyes carefully not straying down to his new cellmates. A voice commented harshly in Gardier, then the footsteps receded.

Tremaine let out a slow breath, her knees weak. She looked at Florian, who slumped against the wall, and the man, who shook his head in amazed relief at their escape.

Tremaine waited until she heard a door slam again, then listened to the quiet in the chamber for another few moments, just to make sure. "All right, let's get him loose so we can get the hell out of here." Tremaine pushed away from the wall, thinking, *God, I'm turning into an optimist.* She advanced cautiously toward him, stopping about a pace away. "I'm going to try to get you out of there," she told him, trying to convey what she was saying with pointing and gestures.

"We came to rescue you," Florian seconded, stepping up beside her and gesturing too. The man lifted a brow inquiringly, his expression bemused, his blue eyes warm and unwavering. *No, he doesn't mean us any harm,* Tremaine thought.

More confidently, she took the last step, digging the pins out of her pocket and managing to stab herself in the thumb in the process. She tugged on the lock that fastened his chains to the wall. The man twisted around to try to see what she was doing, hopeful curiosity on his face. Close enough to feel his body heat, Tremaine realized she couldn't smell anything but the bitter odor of the mud he was covered with. Telling herself *all right, don't mess up now,* she braced the lock against the wall with the heel of her hand and poked the pins into it, feeling for the tumblers. Florian leaned over to help her hold the lock and Tremaine forgot to be self-conscious in her concentration.

Florian touched the man's arm and when he glanced at her she pointed to Tremaine. "Tremaine." Indicating herself, she said, "I'm Florian. Florian," then pointed to him. "You . . . ?"

He held her gaze, smiling a little, and said, "Ilias."

She smiled back and repeated. "Ilias."

Tremaine couldn't tell if the tumblers were moving just a touch or if it was her imagination. Then one of the pins snapped. Tremaine swore, then looked down at the man in guilt.

He jerked his head toward the doors, speaking rapidly. Telling them to go. This made Tremaine even more determined not to leave him and it evidently had the same effect on Florian, who said in frustration, "We have to think of something."

With no warning the cell door flung open. All three of them yelped, Tremaine and Florian swinging around. Tremaine found herself staring at a Gardier. "Shit," she said, mildly surprised at how calm her voice sounded.

The Gardier stared at them in blank surprise, then smiled. He looked bigger than the others but maybe that was just her nerves. He wore one of the plain brown uniform coveralls and had a pair of goggles pushed up on his forehead. He started toward them, still smiling, pulling something that looked an awful lot like a billy club off his belt.

Tremaine struggled to think of something clever to do, but her body was already pulling the satchel off her shoulder and flinging it into his face.

He batted it away, shouting angrily, and she dived for his knees, trying to tackle him. He staggered backward and lifted the club but Florian flung herself on that arm, sending him staggering around.

He shoved Florian away, the other girl slamming into the wall, but the club went flying too. He dragged Tremaine to her feet to throttle her and she twisted, instinctively clawing for his eyes. All she could think was that if he killed her, first she had to make damn sure he didn't walk away from it. Her fingers stabbed into his goggles and she grabbed them, yanking back with all her strength before letting go. He yelled as the goggles smacked him painfully in the eyes, stumbling backward and dragging her along. Suddenly he dropped, Tremaine falling with him. He landed heavily on top, knocking the breath out of her. He yelled, twisting around and trying to struggle up, but something prevented him.

Tremaine managed to lift her head and saw Ilias had tripped the Gardier, that his chains were stretched taut as he had one leg hooked around the other man's knee. His face feral in fury, he slammed a second kick into the Gardier's chest.

The Gardier snarled in rage and tried to roll away from him. Tremaine grabbed a fistful of his uniform collar, throwing her weight the other way to drag him further into Ilias's range, pummeling his head with her free hand. She didn't have the leverage to do much damage but it must have annoyed him because he turned from his struggle long enough to try to slam her head into the floor. Tremaine ducked and tried to bite him, knowing she was about to get a cracked skull. The Gardier sat up to get a better grip on her and she saw Ilias's bootheel slam into the side of his head.

The Gardier fell back. Before Tremaine could move,

Florian loomed up behind him, clutching the club stick. She lifted it high, bringing it down to strike the Gardier's head with a loud crack. He slumped on the floor, motionless.

Tremaine stared up at Florian and Florian stared down at her, both breathing hard. Ilias said something urgently, nudging Tremaine with his knee when she didn't respond. She looked at him blankly and he repeated it more forcefully, jerking his chin toward the open door again.

He still wants us to go. "Not without you," she muttered, lurching forward on her hands and knees toward the fallen Gardier. The uniform didn't have any pockets but she tore open the pouches on his belt. She found cartridges for a pistol the man wasn't wearing and knew that if he had been armed, she and Florian would be dead or locked into another cell by now. He didn't seem to have any of the little square devices that the patrol leader had carried. Then she found a heavy oddly shaped key and pushed to her feet.

Florian still stood there and Tremaine gave her a push to get her moving. She blinked, shook her head, then hurried to collect the satchel and their scattered supplies.

"This is it." Tremaine turned to Ilias, who was watching her intently. "I hope this is it," she told him, stepping over to grab the lock and insert the key.

The lock turned.

"It worked!" Tremaine said, then was too startled to react when Ilias jumped to his feet and grabbed her around the waist, swung her around and kissed her on the mouth, then released her. She staggered; it had happened too fast for her to take in any sensory information and her jaw was still too numb to feel anything. Florian had just enough warning to drop the satchel before he repeated the process with her.

All right, now that we're all better acquainted, Tremaine thought, as a red-faced Florian fumbled to collect the satchel again and their new friend bolted for the cell door. He gave the outer chamber a quick assessing look before motioning for them to follow him. He rapidly checked the other cells, looking through the grates, though Florian waved and whispered, "There's nobody else here."

The door under the catwalk was open, revealing what was surely only a temporarily unoccupied room and corridor. Tremaine started for it but Ilias caught her arm, shaking his head and pointing toward the ladder.

"Back up?" Florian asked, watching him dubiously.

"I guess." Tremaine was just glad at the moment that somebody knew where they were going.

They followed him back up the ladder, where he paused on the catwalk, looking up intently at the rocky ceiling of the cave. There were openings in it, Tremaine realized, following his gaze. She hadn't noticed that before, but they were too high up to reach and too small. Surely they didn't go anywhere. She looked at Florian who shrugged, equally puzzled.

He stepped to the door that led back into the room where Gervas had started to question them, easing it open carefully. The room was still empty, and without pausing to look around, he jumped to catch the top of the door. Using the knob as a foothold, he boosted himself up to reach the wooden panels in the ceiling. He pushed the nearest one up, revealing a dark crawl space. Cool damp air flowed down. *Of course.* Tremaine smacked herself in the forehead. *This whole place is just jury-rigged walls and panels blocking off the tunnels and caves.* The darkness and damp foul odor of the air was almost homey and welcoming.

Florian nudged her with an elbow. "We should have thought of that."

"Next time we'll know," Tremaine told her.

"You mean the next time we're captured, because I'd rather not—"

Ilias leaned down, holding out his hand. Tremaine made a stirrup with her hands for Florian. "Time to go."

Boosting Florian up, Tremaine staggered because the other girl was heavier than she looked. But the man hauled her up until she could steady herself on top of the door, handling her as if she didn't weigh an ounce. Florian awkwardly scrambled up into the crawl space, reporting, "There's a ceiling beam up here you can step on."

"Careful," Tremaine whispered back, with visions of the entire ceiling coming down and alerting every Gardier within earshot. The man leaned back down and Tremaine took a deep breath and grabbed his arm. He swung her up just as easily, until she could get a purchase on the door and push herself through.

The light from below revealed furrowed rock stretching up over her head. Florian was perched precariously on an outcrop, grinning in nervous triumph. Tremaine grinned back. *We did it. Screw the Gardier.* She got hold of another outcrop and dragged herself up onto the slimy stone.

The man climbed up after them, crouching on the beam to nudge the ceiling panel back into place, leaving them in darkness.

Chapter 8

Gervas cursed as he looked down at the dead man sprawled on the floor of the cell. The other guards still searched the surrounding passages and chambers but there was no sign of the escaped prisoners. He spent a moment considering if the summons that had caused him to leave the women alone had been a diversion of some kind. The message had been from one of the perimeter patrols reporting signs of the Rien spies they were searching for. Surely not. The Rien would have needed magic to coordinate such a trick and the alarm device at his belt would have detected it.

"I told you they weren't labor," Verim said as he came back into the cell. He grimaced at the dead man, shaking his head. "They were the Rien spies. And now we know they're in league with the natives."

"Those women weren't strong enough to do this," Gervas argued. He nudged the dead guard with the toe of his boot, his lip curling in contempt. "It was the native. We know they're little better than animals." They weren't even useful as a potential labor pool, since they spoke no civilized language and the translators wouldn't work on their speech. Once Command had the resources available, the plan was simply to eliminate them. The airships were already under orders to destroy any shipping or coastal habitations they encountered. He wished he had had the option to eliminate this one, but Command had ordered any potential saboteurs be held for examination. And Verim, damn him, had argued that the creature was a saboteur.

Verim strode to the chains that still hung from the wall and lifted the lock, shaking it at Gervas. "This was opened with the key, the guard's key. After his skull was broken." He dropped the chains in disgust. "First the sabotage, then this. If the natives aren't in the service of the Rien, how do you explain it?"

Gervas couldn't explain it and that fact made him even angrier. "If your men had found their boat sooner, we would have known where the Rien came ashore."

Verim glared. "We were lucky we found it at all, as shorthanded as we are."

Gervas grunted, looking away. The supply vessel from the main base wasn't due for another seven days and there was no chance of reinforcement until then. And more important, no chance to replace the dead Command personnel and the Scientists who should be in charge of all contact with the Rien, or the avatar that had been destroyed in the airship explosion. Gervas had ordered the other two avatars removed from their airships and stored in different secure locations on the base when not in use aboard the craft, but he knew Command wouldn't appreciate that hindsight.

The sabotage had caught them at the worst time. The base had only recently been established and was still being stocked with supplies and personnel. They had been warned that the Rien had managed to create a portal nearby and had set the storm to catch any craft that came through, but the loss of one airship and so many personnel had badly hampered their effort.

If Gervas was to stop the attack that would come through the Rien portal, he needed more information. He would have liked to blame Verim for some part of this, but the man had still gone out on patrol, despite the burns he had received fighting the fire, despite the fact that he was Command too and should stay back at base while the Service risked themselves in the tunnels. He said, "They will go to the east quadrant to meet the other spies the patrol detected there. Recapture them."

"That quadrant is inhabited by creatures that make the

howlers look like domesticated cattle." Verim hesitated, eyeing Gervas. "If we had a way to control them as well . . ."

Gervas's eyes narrowed. It was a good idea and he wished he had thought of it. "Very well. I'll question our informant. Get your men ready to leave."

Gervas left the cell, going down the corridor past the guardroom, taking the turn that led further back into the rock. The lights were spaced more widely here, allowing the darkness of the caves to creep in, and moisture ran continually down the walls. He hated to have to do this, but Harman, the Scientist who had first discovered the thing and insisted it would benefit them to communicate with it, had been one of those killed in the fire. The Scientists' directives took precedence over Command orders, so Gervas was bound by Harman's decision, even now that he was dead.

A man stood guard at the door that had been fixed across the entrance to the cave. They could ill afford to waste anyone in guard duty right now, but Gervas didn't trust the thing that lived behind that door.

As he approached, the Service man unlocked it for him and moved aside. Gervas drew a deep breath and stepped in. It was a small chamber carved from the solid rock, poorly lit. When they had first discovered the thing here, it had lived in pitch darkness; even now the lights were only for the convenience of Gervas and the Scientists who had to speak to it. The equipment it lived in was primitive and all apparently of the thing's own design. The vat that bubbled with milky white liquid in the center of the room was a large cast-iron cauldron; the pipes that connected it with the clay pots and other cauldrons around the edges of the chamber were wooden, secured with twine or linen wrappings. The whole slapdash affair leaked, making the chamber echo with the constant sound of dripping liquids. Gervas grimaced at the odor of corruption; if it had been up to him, he would have tipped the thing into a rubbish bin and set it afire. But it wasn't up to him.

He made his way to the central cauldron, careful not to

step in the glistening puddles. "Are you there?" he said impatiently. "I need to speak with you."

The fluid splashed as the thing in the cauldron undulated, arranging itself so the orifice that served as its mouth was near the surface. "Where exactly do you think I would go in this state?" it said, its voice thick and raspy.

Gervas grimaced and reined in his temper. The thing had taught itself civilized speech with amazing rapidity; the sarcasm was evidently an innate talent. Whatever it was now, it considered itself a man, even a Scientist of sorts. He knew Command had been right to let it live, if only for the information it had supplied that allowed control of the howlers and the other creatures of these caves. But once its usefulness had ended he meant to see the foul thing destroyed as soon as possible.

Pretending patience, Gervas said, "We have a report of spies in the upper east quadrant of these caves. Tell me how to control the creatures there to assist us in finding them."

"Oh, that's where the grend are. I did love the grend." It choked, cleared its air passage with a sickening noise. "Did you catch the men who set your flying contraption on fire?"

Gervas's jaw tightened. "How did you know about that?"

"Oh, I hear things. Chat with people who stop by, that sort of thing." Its voice hardened. "Did you catch them?"

Gervas pretended to hesitate, considering. "We caught one native. He escaped with two Rien spies. The spies will attempt to make contact with the others in the east quadrant." He lifted his brows and added, apparently carelessly, "If you tell me what I need to know, we will recapture—"

"Yes, yes, I got that already, thank you." It sloshed in the vat and Gervas caught sight of a long white limb and a very human-looking eye. His stomach tried to turn and he was glad he hadn't had time to eat today. It said, "I'll tell you what you need to know; in fact, I'll do better than that. I'll show you. If you save any natives you catch for me."

Gervas laughed sharply. "Save them for you? What exactly would you do with them?"

Fluid splashed out of the cauldron, then suddenly long-fingered, spidery hands clutched the sides. Gervas stepped back, his gorge rising, as the thing heaved itself out of the vat. "I'll think of something," it said, the thick white liquid running down out of the orifices in the round face. "And as we've become such good friends now, you can call me Ixion."

They climbed through narrow crevices, struggled through passages that were barely larger than their own bodies. Crossing a long stretch where dim light leaked up through chinks in the rock below, Tremaine heard shouts and running footsteps. *Well, they know we escaped,* she thought, surprising herself with a tight grin.

Then she heard a low hungry howl. It echoed off the rock and ahead of her Ilias stopped abruptly, muttering what had to be a curse.

Oh, no, Tremaine thought in disgust. Of course the Gardier would use their hunter-creatures as bloodhounds again. Those things made the ghouls she had encountered in the bombed-out buildings of Vienne look positively civilized.

Ilias changed direction, leading them in a long scramble down a dark narrow cleft that gradually flowed into a wider passage. The keening gained volume and was joined by another voice howling in a different key. Then another, and another. *This is how we got into this,* Tremaine thought in annoyance, ducking a low thrust of rock.

They rounded a sharp bend and suddenly the tunnel dropped off into complete darkness. Ilias leapt down the sloping rock into the lower passage without hesitation, but Tremaine stumbled to a halt. A vicious cacophony of howling and snarling echoed from behind, reminding her there was no other option. Florian grabbed her arm with an urgent look and Tremaine nodded grimly. They slid down the gritty stone together.

A few more steps and they were blind. Tremaine forged on, stumbling over the uneven ground, glad for Florian's firm hold on her shoulder. For a bad moment she thought Ilias had left them but an instant later she just managed to bite back a yelp as he grabbed her outstretched arm. He took her hand and hooked it through his belt. That was reassuring. *He's not going to leave us,* Tremaine thought, profoundly relieved. The hand that had gripped hers briefly had been rough with callus and hard as a rock.

They stumbled along in the dark, Tremaine bouncing off the rough stone surface he was evidently using as a guide. He stopped abruptly and she bumped into him. It was like running into a wall except that his hair tickled her nose. He started moving again and she heard the chuckle and splash of running water and was jerked forward as he jumped down. A moment later she almost fell as she staggered knee deep into a running stream. It was lukewarm and the scent rising off it was sulfurous. Florian lurched in after her and they sloshed downstream.

Tremaine stumbled along the uneven gravelly bottom, Florian gripping her shoulder. The water soaked through her boots and stockings, and into the heavy tweed of her knickers. Ilias stopped suddenly with a whispered warning, half turning back. Tremaine froze and Florian bumped into her. His words had been unintelligible but the tone conveyed everything she needed to know. From back the way they had come she heard a low yowl, sending a chill through her. It was very near. Ilias reached around to grasp Florian's arm and pull them both close behind him.

High-pitched growls and furious splashing erupted from somewhere nearby, the echoes making it impossible to tell how close, how far. The urge to run was overwhelming. Willing herself not to move, Tremaine bit her lip until she tasted blood. She felt Florian tremble as the other girl's fingers knotted in her jacket. Pressed against Ilias's back she could feel his heart pounding.

It was forever until she could tell the sound was moving away, until the cacophony of their pursuers' disappointment gradually faded. Finally he whispered a relieved comment and tugged lightly on Tremaine's arm, signaling they should move forward again. Tremaine took a deep breath and reached up to squeeze Florian's hand. She wasn't sure if her own hand was numb or if the other girl's fingers were ice-cold.

They continued down the stream. Still reeling from the narrowness of their escape, Tremaine just hoped she didn't fall; wet underwear would definitely not improve the situation. Finally, after her feet were waterlogged and her head ached from the sulfur smell, they staggered back up onto the rocky bank. Tremaine bumped into Ilias again when he stopped and she fell back a step and tromped on Florian's foot. He said something softly and detached her fingers from his belt.

Her hand was cramped from holding on so hard. Shaking her fingers to get the blood moving again, she whispered to Florian, "Those things must hunt by scent and that's why he's got that mud all over him."

"I hope we don't have to roll in it to get out of here," Florian replied, her voice hushed. "Of course, if it's a choice between that and being torn apart or captured again, I'll do it and like it."

They crept along the wall after that. After what seemed a long time with no further sound of pursuit, Tremaine called a halt and dug the matches out of the satchel. She lit one carefully, shielding the flame behind a rock, to show Ilias that they had a source of light.

He looked relieved and turned to search energetically along the edge of the stream until he found something that looked very like a femur bone to use for a makeshift torch. Florian sacrificed a wad of her handkerchiefs to tie onto the top for fuel. It wouldn't last long, but it was nice while they had it.

The light revealed the passage to be fairly wide, with the water running in a dark channel down the center. They made quicker progress with light and after a time of navigating the twists and turns of the tunnel, Ilias stopped and pointed at a narrow opening about ten feet up the wall ahead. He glanced at them, saying something urgently.

Tremaine nodded, hoping that was the right response. It seemed to be, since he handed her the torch and turned to climb lightly up to vanish into the crevice.

Florian followed his progress with lifted brows, then turned worriedly to Tremaine. "Where's he going?"

"Ah . . . I don't know." Tremaine awkwardly fumbled with the makeshift torch. Even with its smoky light the cave seemed much darker than when they had first come down into this warren; maybe night was falling outside. Or maybe knowing now what was down here just made the shadows press closer. She peered at Florian and wondered if she looked that owl-eyed, hollow-cheeked and exhausted, with dark smudges under her eyes. *Probably worse.*

Ilias scrambled out of the crevice and dropped to the ground next to them. He gave them both an encouraging smile and pointed up at the opening.

Florian sighed wearily. "Here we go again." She leaned against the wall, fumbling to reach the first ledge, feeling for hand- or footholds.

Tremaine handed Ilias back the torch and followed her, self-consciously stretching for a handhold, annoyingly unsure whether she wanted him to help her or not. She faltered at the top when her hand slipped on the lip of the crevice and a sudden boost from behind pushed her forward. She scrambled the rest of the way in, cursing herself.

Now she could see the crevice wound back for a short distance into the rock and dim light came from the far end. It was only about four feet at its widest and not quite high enough for Tremaine to stand up in. As she awkwardly crawled further in, Florian turned back to report, "There's another tunnel back here and it looks like there's an opening to the surface too. That must be moonlight we can see."

"Good." Tremaine felt her stomach unclench a little. She moved on up to where Florian had settled in the widest part of the little cave and sat back against the opposite wall, pulling the satchel off. She thought they badly needed to rest and hoped Ilias thought so too. Her jaw throbbed, the strap felt as if it had left a permanent groove in her shoulder, her feet squelched in her sodden boots and she was acutely conscious of every bruise and ache.

Ilias scrambled into the crevice and crouched near the entrance, digging into a cranny in the wall. After a moment he fished out a sheathed knife, a couple of wooden stakes, a little leather bag and a fat yellow candle. Lighting it from the dying torch, he fixed the base down onto a flat rock.

"That's a relief," Florian commented and Tremaine nodded. Their makeshift torch wouldn't have lasted much longer. She continued, "He must have stayed here before."

Tremaine leaned over, glancing up at him to make sure he didn't mind. At his "be my guest" gesture, she picked up one of the stakes. She saw the knobby end was covered with pitch and realized it was a prepared torch. She looked in the bag and found flint chips, an odd-sized bit of metal and some straw. She told Florian, "It's a tinderbox. No wonder he thought the matches were so nifty."

Florian peered past her, watching Ilias. In the candle-light he was examining some marks roughly carved on the rock above the niche, brushing the dirt away as if hoping against hope to find more. Then he sighed, drew the knife and used the point to begin a new set of marks next to the older ones. Tremaine edged closer, craning her neck to see the figure he was carving into the stone. It looked like the others already there, but with a couple of extra symbols. She wondered if it was a ward.

Ilias twitched aside the tangled muddy curtain of his hair, caught Tremaine looking at him and grinned, then went back to his task. This close she could see there was a faint scar on his forehead, mostly hidden by his hair and the mud, and his nose looked like it had been broken a time or two. The knuckles of his hands were thickened from fighting, like a prizefighter's. Like the men who used to come at odd hours of the day and night to deliver mysterious messages for her father and receive even more mysterious orders. Except his expression was more open, the faint lines at the corners of his eyes and mouth from laughter. He shifted a little, leaning down over the markings, his hair shielding his face.

"You're making him shy," Florian said, smiling.

"What?" Tremaine asked blankly.

"Staring at him. He's using his hair to hide. But he likes it too, because he's smiling. I can see from this angle."

"Oh." Tremaine hadn't realized she was staring. She moved back to lean against the wall. "I should probably stop, then."

"Probably." Florian blinked. "I'm doing it too, now."

"All right, all right." Tremaine deliberately moved around to face Florian. "Let's look at each other."

Florian shifted too, folding her hands in her lap. "I hope Gerard has a place like this to hide out. I hope the Gardier didn't—" She broke off, shaking her head.

Tremaine hugged her knees. She didn't want to say it aloud either, but she hoped Gerard was still alive to hide out.

Florian must have read Tremaine's expression, because she said, "I'm sure he's all right." She added a little wanly, "I just wish we could look for him now. He probably thinks we're dead." She looked away, her expression turning bleak. "I just . . . That man I hit. Maybe he wasn't dead?"

"What?" Tremaine stared at her blankly. "Oh, the Gardier. No, he was dead."

"Oh." Florian took a deep breath.

Tremaine hesitated. She realized belatedly that what Florian had really wanted her to say was that maybe the Gardier wasn't dead after all, no matter if neither of them believed it. She could pretend to be upset about it too and probably convince herself as well as Florian. She was good at that. There had never been anything wrong with her imagination. But it would be just pretense. And in this place, it just didn't seem worth it.

And you haven't thought once about killing yourself since you've been here.

"Tremaine?" She looked up to see Florian watching her worriedly. "You all right?" she asked.

Maybe nothing had changed. But she couldn't leave the other girl here alone. "Uh, yes, just thinking of something." She shook her head, putting it aside.

Florian stole a quick glance to the right. "He's staring at you now."

"He is?" To her annoyance, Tremaine realized she was tucking back her hair. It had never looked that good even under the best of conditions and after the past day it had to be hopeless.

"He's not looking anymore." Florian absently dug in her coat pockets, pulling out one of the wax-paper-wrapped ration packages hastily collected from the mess the Gardier had made of their supplies. "I'm not really hungry, but I feel like we should eat."

Tremaine pulled the satchel around to root through it. She felt a little sick, but maybe that was hunger. She pulled out a water flask and a couple of ration packages. *I hope Gerard has something with him.* Suddenly the idea of being solely responsible for their remaining supplies was too much for her. "We should divide this up in case we get separated." She pulled out some waterproof packets of matches to give to Florian. "Here, put these in your pockets."

Florian obediently accepted the matches, but said, "Don't even say that. We're not getting separated." She scooted closer and tore open the ration package, shaking out some dried fruit.

Tremaine glanced up from sorting out items to stuff into Florian's pockets and found herself looking at Ilias. He was staring at the food like he was having a religious experience. He saw she had noticed and looked away abruptly, taking a sharp breath.

Tremaine and Florian exchanged a horrified look. Florian handed her the open package of fruit and turned back to the satchel, digging through it for more. "I can't believe we didn't think of this earlier," she said, contrite.

"I know. I feel like an idiot." Tremaine scooted over to Ilias. "Hey, look, we'll share." She pressed the open package into his hands. He looked uncertain and she nodded rapidly. "No, really, we've got plenty. Well, sort of plenty. Enough. Go on."

With another quick glance at her to make sure she was serious, he tore into it like a starving wolf.

Tremaine sat back. "I wonder how long he's been here, avoiding the Gardier."

Florian watched him sympathetically. "I wonder if he knows what happened on their base, what that explosion was that poor woman mentioned. If we could just ask him— Oh, get the wrapper!"

"No," Tremaine told him firmly, rescuing the wax paper. "That's for later, when we get desperate." If they were here long enough, eating the paper wrappers might become a last resort.

She turned back to the satchel, studying the ration packets without enthusiasm. There were crackers, chocolate bars, dried fruit and some unappealing tinned meats, plus two water flasks. It didn't look like it would last them very long; they had to find a way home or reach some more hospitable place, safe from the Gardier. If there was anyplace that was safe from the Gardier. She looked at Ilias, watching Florian show him how to open a tin that the label claimed was beef. Noticing his intrigued expression, Tremaine said, "I don't think he's ever seen one of those before."

Florian frowned. "You mean one of these where you roll back the lid with the key or seen a can ever?"

"A can ever." She noticed there was leather lacing down the sides of his pants and the stitching she could see looked rough and uneven, not machine-made. That didn't necessarily mean anything; there were plenty of places where people still wore homespun clothes in Ile-Rien. But he had never seen matches or cans. It was more evidence that his people hadn't had much contact with the Gardier, anyway.

Florian was looking thoughtful. "You know, we've made contact with a new civilization."

"A whole new world." Like the explorers who had been the first to cross the continent of Capidara and meet the native peoples there, or voyage to the Maiutan islands. It was a little hard to realize. *They're not like fay either, they're real people.* It was still possible in some remote parts of Ile-Rien to encounter fayre creatures or hidden entrances to fayre realms. But then poor Tiamarc had proved pretty conclusively, at least to himself, that this wasn't a fayre world. And now she and Florian seemed to have confirmed that theory. A creature of fayre wouldn't have helped them. And when fay took human form they looked eerily perfect. They wouldn't have scars or torn clothes. *Or,* she thought, watching Ilias vigorously scratch his head, *do that.* Not to mention using a knife with a cold iron blade and needing human food. It still didn't tell them what the Gardier's place in this world was.

After two tins of meat, crackers and another package of dried fruit, Ilias was licking his fingers and looking a lot less desperate. Bits of mud had flaked off his hair, revealing straw-colored strands. Tremaine was getting an image of a seagoing people, short and compactly built, with bright blond hair.

Frowning at Ilias, Florian said, "We should do something about that cut. It's still bleeding." She shifted forward to point.

Tremaine leaned closer to study the matted hair above his temple. The mud and the flicker of candlelight made it hard to tell. She touched it tentatively and he pulled away, giving her an indignant look.

Tremaine wiped at the blood on her fingers and reached back for the satchel, taking out the small medical kit. Ilias eyed the white enamel box warily. She opened it and he shifted away from them, grimacing at the smell of the alcohol. The look he gave her suggested that the food had been a nice gesture and all that but there was no way she was getting near him with whatever that was.

Tremaine sat back, thinking. She didn't want him leaving their shelter to get away from her. She asked Florian, "Can you break off a little piece of one of those chocolate bars?"

Florian found a bar among the litter of ration packages and tore open the wrapping, capturing Ilias's attention instantly. He might never have seen a can before, but he had learned immediately what waxpaper meant. Florian broke off a little piece and offered it to him. He edged closer to take it, sniffing it dubiously.

Florian took another piece and nibbled it in demonstration. He tasted it and Tremaine saw his mud-coated brows lift. She said, "And there's more where that came from if you let me look at your head."

He hesitated, though she could tell he knew what she meant. After a moment he grudgingly gave in, moving forward so Tremaine could reach him. She put the medical kit in her lap and scooted closer, motioning for him to lean down a little so she could reach better. She used the wet handkerchief Florian handed her to clean away the worst of the mud and dried blood around the cut on his temple, while Ilias shifted impatiently.

Her hand brushed against his cheek, gritty from mud and beard stubble, and she felt him flinch slightly. Her hands were still cold and his skin felt hot and flushed. She hoped he didn't have a fever. She didn't want to risk giving him any of the sulfa drugs in the kit and she didn't know what else to do about it. "All done," Tremaine told him finally, giving him an awkward pat on the arm as she shifted back.

He sat up, probing cautiously at the wound. He must have been satisfied with the result, because he twisted around and pulled the braided leather jerkin and the tattered rag under it off his shoulder. There was a nasty discolored gash on his back, just to the inside of his shoulder blade, sluggishly leaking blood. It was about three inches long and looked infected.

"Ouch," Tremaine murmured, leaning closer to examine it. She could see the spot where something had cut and charred the leather cords, the blood matted in them. There was mud all down his back under it and in the wound. Feeling in over her head, Tremaine turned worriedly to Florian. "Can you do anything about this?"

Biting her lip, Florian picked up the medical kit and sorted through the packets of dried herbs. "A healing stone is really what we need, but I've never done one. Here's mandrake." She opened the paper packet, frowning furiously in thought. "I can do a general healing charm while you clean it."

Tremaine started to nod, then hesitated as a thought struck. "You don't think the Gardier will hear it?"

Florian thought about it, stirring the dried herbs with a finger. "It's a charm, not a spell. It . . . should be all right." She nodded, and said more firmly, "I think we should do it."

"All right." Tremaine looked up to see Ilias watching them both alertly. He couldn't see the wound but it must hurt like hell, and he would be able to feel the swelling and the heat of the infection. She found some gauze in the kit and used alcohol on it, ruthlessly ignoring the strangled gasp Ilias made when she cleaned away the dried blood and dirt. He had other scars on his back, two nearly identical broad stripes that ran from the insides of his shoulder blades to down further than she felt she could go on such short acquaintance. Someone had inflicted that damage deliberately; they were far too straight, too uniform to be the product of accident. *Earlier encounter with the Gardier, maybe,* she thought, distracted.

Trying to get all the mud out she found a small fragment of sharp metal and gently began to prize it free. He didn't make a sound, though he twitched with relief when she removed it. Muttering, "That wasn't comfortable," she leaned over to the candle to study it.

She rubbed the blood off on her fingers. "That's odd." It looked like aluminum shrapnel. *Or duralumin.* She had seen enough of it in the bombed areas. *He must have been involved in that explosion in the Gardier base.* "There was a big fire, an explosion? A big boom?" she asked, showing the fragment to Ilias. He poked it with a finger and grimaced. Tremaine glanced at Florian to see what she thought. The other woman held the crushed mandrake between her cupped hands, her eyes closed in concentration as she mouthed the words of the charm. Tremaine wiped her fingers off on her coat sleeve and went back to work.

Finally Tremaine blinked sweat out of her eyes and said, "I think that's it." Ilias straightened up, craning his neck to try to see the results. The wound was mostly clean and the sluggish blood flow had no dark fragments in it. She wasn't sure how good a job she had done but hopefully the charm would take care of anything she had missed. Just then Florian whispered a last phrase under her breath, then made a ritual gesture of casting the mandrake away.

Ilias turned sharply toward her, then he blinked and started to slump forward. Tremaine caught him and eased him down into her lap, supporting his head on her arm. "Is he all right?" she asked Florian anxiously. "You didn't do something wrong?"

"No, no," Florian assured her, leaning over to smooth his hair back from his forehead. "If you hurt someone with magic, you know." She brushed a few more flakes of mud away and carefully lifted his eyelids to check his pupils. "I think he was so exhausted the charm just put him under."

"Oh." Relieved, Tremaine leaned back against the wall. It was darker in the crevice despite the candle and she realized the light wasn't coming from the far end anymore. *Clouds must have covered the moon.* The passages around the cave harbor and the wrecked ships would be locked in utter darkness. She thought about what Florian had said about being trapped down here alone. *Gerard. God, we've got to find him before the Gardier do.* She hoped Ilias wouldn't be out too long.

He was a warm heavy weight in her lap. Even unconscious, his presence was comforting. The mud had worn off in enough patches to show that his skin was a warm bronze color from long exposure to the sun and there were more streaks of blond visible in the mud-coated hair. She realized there was an odd mark on his cheek just below the bone, visible now that the mud was flaking away. It was a small silver half-moon that had somehow been impressed into his skin. *That's different.* He was also wearing copper-colored rings in both ears.

Florian picked up the knife that had been stored in the cranny with the candle and the other supplies, examining it curiously. The long blade was leaf-shaped, the handle a flat hourglass of bone or horn. She set it aside and said suddenly, "With the Gardier, you weren't afraid."

"No." Tremaine took a deep breath. "I was terrified. I thought I was going to wet myself."

"But you acted like we were spies, like we were supposed to get captured all along." Florian prompted hopefully, "I was actually hoping that was part of a plan I just didn't know about."

"If there was a plan like that, they wouldn't have picked me to pull it off." Tremaine shook her head, absently drawing her fingers through Ilias's hair. Without waking, he snuggled a little. "My family . . . I had a lot of training in the theater. Sort of."

Florian nodded. "Was that where you learned to pick locks?"

"Yes . . . No." *What the hell,* Tremaine thought. She might as well tell Florian the whole truth. It was doubtful they would make it out of here alive anyway, so it seemed foolish to prevaricate. "My father taught me how to pick locks. Before he started the Viller Institute, he used to do things that weren't quite legal."

"Oh." Florian was struggling not to look shocked and almost managing it. "Really? Like . . . what?"

Tremaine hesitated. *You are going to wish you hadn't done this.* Maybe Florian's life had been too normal to give her any basis for understanding. Maybe Tremaine didn't care. Maybe it was time for her to talk. "Steal things, kill people. It's a long story."

Ilias drifted in and out, too wrapped in heavy sleep to make a serious effort toward consciousness. He wasn't comfortable; there was a sharp rock grinding against his hip and the warm surface his head rested on kept moving. Two feminine voices in anxious conversation right above him was reassuring if confusing. He kept trying to hear them as Amari and Irisa. *No, that can't be right.* Amari and Irisa were dead.

Finally, the odor of decay penetrated the haze around his thoughts and everything abruptly connected. The caves, the wizards, the flying whale on fire. *Giliead.* He awkwardly pushed himself up and rubbed his stiff neck, grimacing at the feel of the gritty dried mud. He blinked blearily at the two women who were watching him. They looked worried. "Right, I remember. Hello," he said, trying to sound reassuring.

They glanced at each other and resumed their conversation. Ilias cleared his throat, shoving his hair out of his eyes. Surprised at the lack of pain from his wound, he worked his arm and shoulder, then reached around awkwardly to probe it with his fingers. What he could feel seemed to be scabbed over. *Huh. Maybe it was just the piece that was still stuck in there.*

He worked his shoulder again cautiously. Maybe he had just needed the rest. And the food. *I don't even remember falling asleep.*

Then Ilias saw how far down the candle had burned. Swearing, he turned to scramble down the crevice. He hadn't meant to sleep at all, just to let the women rest and give the howlers time to take their hunt out of this area.

He reached the end of the crevice where it overlooked the passage leading into the bottom well of the surface shaft. All he could see was a faint glow of moonlight falling down the opening from above. It was still night at least. Relieved, he turned back to see the two girls watching him curiously. He took a deep breath. *Right.*

He ruthlessly chivvied them along as they got their belongings together, then lit one of the torches from the candle. He took the knife since without it they were unarmed, but left the candle, the tinder bag and the remaining torch behind. If Giliead was still somewhere down here and stopped to check this cache, he might need them. Ilias hadn't found a trace of him in any of the other spots they had camped on previous forays to the island and this place had been his last hope. But there were no new trail marks here and no one had disturbed the cache of supplies.

The two women did their best to hurry, though they kept making little alarmed noises, then shushing each other. Shooing them to the end of the crevice, he helped them climb down, knowing this would be much easier if he could talk to them and explain the need for haste.

Whatever language they spoke was just as impossible to understand as the wizards' speech, though it sounded less abrupt and harsh, more like the way people spoke in Cirenai or Tanais. Their clothes were strangely cut, the bulky heavy fabrics obviously meant for colder weather and the dull colors an odd choice for two pretty girls. And with the strange provisions and the clever little metal boxes for food and the flint-sticks, they had to be traders from somewhere, maybe the far south. Very far south, since neither of them seemed to know what his curse mark was. If they did know, they had both been expert at concealing their reactions to it.

If there were any more survivors from their ship . . . *Hopefully the* Swift *picked them up,* he thought, absently catching Florian's arm when she stumbled in the dimness. She murmured something shyly and ducked her head. Tremaine, glancing back at the other girl, tripped, and Ilias just managed to catch her too.

He would have to get them out to Dead Tree Point. If Giliead wasn't there, then hopefully the *Swift* would still be waiting and he could hand them over to Halian's care. Then go back for Giliead. *He'll be there,* he told himself firmly. *And if he isn't, I'll find him.*

The first snag in this plan came almost immediately. They reached the surface well, dimly lit by moonlight from above. It was square-cut like the air passages and went up at an angle, the chinks and cracks in the walls bristling with ugly little plants and trailing vines. Fresh air flowed down it, carrying the clean scent of the sea. Ilias breathed deeply; he had been down here so long he had almost forgotten what real air smelled like. Both women looked relieved, pointing up the shaft and commenting to each other. But when he tried to get them to climb, they plopped down on the ground and started drawing something in the dirt.

Ilias gritted his teeth in frustration, planted the torch and sat on his heels to try to figure out what they wanted. After a lot of extensive gesturing he finally realized the

drawing was a very bad map of the way back to where he
had found them, that they wanted to go back to the harbor
cave, or at least to a tunnel that branched off from there.
He shook his head emphatically and tried to explain,
"That's not a good place to go." He drew a line in the opposite direction, toward the surface shaft above their
heads and tapped it. "There, that's the way out."

They both shook their heads just as emphatically.
Tremaine wiped out his line and drew another back toward
the half circle that indicated the harbor. Holding on to his
patience with both hands, Ilias shook his head again. "No,
we can't do that."

Tremaine just stared at him and Florian bit her lip. Ilias
took a deep breath and tapped the circle in the dirt that rep-
resented the surface shaft again. Surely they knew what
would happen if the wizards caught them all again. He was
considering performing a pantomime of what exactly
would occur if the howlers cornered them when Tremaine
sat up straight with a thoughtful expression. Ilias tensed in
hope; maybe she had finally gotten the point.

Moving deliberately, Tremaine pointed to Florian, to
herself, to the empty space next to her, then held up three
fingers. Florian nodded urgently.

Ilias drew a sharp breath. Now he understood. "Three of
you." He looked away and rubbed his forehead. "Oh, no."
So they had lost somebody down here too. He looked up to
see them watching him expectantly. He pointed to himself
and the empty space next to him and held up two fingers.

Tremaine blinked as Florian nodded in sudden understanding. As the two women discussed this revelation, Ilias
stared at the makeshift map, not really seeing the crudely
drawn image. He had to help them. Even if they hadn't
saved his life and shared their food and tended his wounds,
even if they had been openly hostile instead of friendly, he
wouldn't have left the two of them alone here. He couldn't.

Ilias took a deep breath, formulating and discarding alternate plans. The best option would be to get them to the
meeting point on the surface and have them wait there
while he went back to search for Gil and their friend. *And*

you're thinking as if you know Gil's not there waiting for you. One step closer to thinking of him as dead. *No, stop that,* he told himself bleakly. It wouldn't do any good. Giliead was either dead, at the meeting point, or down here somewhere following Ilias's trail signs and trying to find him. And if it was the third option, then doubling back this way would only mean Ilias would find him sooner.

I could move faster alone. He looked up, wondering if he could trust the women to stay where they were put, to wait for him while he went back after the others. He eyed them, noting the patient way Tremaine sat there waiting for him to give in and how Florian kept casting little glances at her for guidance. He thought in resignation, *No.* He couldn't chance it. Not without being able to explain coherently and extract promises not to follow or go searching on their own.

Ilias took a deep breath. "All right, let's see." He tapped his chin thoughtfully, looking at the dirt map again. There was another surface shaft at the opposite end of the city near where their friend had been lost. It wasn't as easy to reach as this one but it would put them on the surface at about the same distance from the meeting point. He just didn't like it; it hadn't exactly been a lucky spot for him before. Ixion had set a family of grend to guard it too but maybe after so long they had wandered off or killed each other for lack of better prey. It didn't matter, it was still the best option. The only option.

He rubbed the map out briskly, then drew his knife to make a quick trail sign giving the direction he meant to take on the rock wall. Tremaine and Florian watched with interest, then hurriedly got to their feet when he stood up. "We'll probably all regret it," he told them, "but let's do it your way."

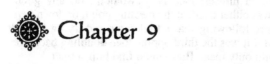

Chapter 9

I'm beginning to take all this too personally, Tremaine told herself, trying to be philosophical though she was gritting her teeth with impatience. She, Florian and Ilias were crouched in the concealment of a fold of rock, their feet in another sulfur-laden puddle, as a Gardier patrol moved through the rocky passage just below them. *They want to kill you because you're from Ile-Rien. There's nothing personal about it.*

Tremaine was pressed against Ilias with Florian wedged in behind her. She could sense the tension in the hard muscles of his back as he watched the Gardier pick their way through the cave below them, their handlights drawing sparkles of reflected light out of the rough walls slick with purplish moss. The alliance with Ilias seemed to be working well and they were getting better at communicating. They had learned each other's words for *yes* and *no* and a handful of others. Fortunately, most common gestures seemed to be the same since there wasn't much time or scope for language lessons down here; the only sort of words they could teach each other readily were *rock*, *water*, and *ick*, which were all self-evident. But gestures and their limited vocabulary had carried them through the incident earlier when Tremaine had had to explain that he needed to turn his back while she and Florian answered the call of nature. If they could manage that with a minimum of embarrassment, they could accomplish anything.

They were near the spot where she and Florian had lost Gerard, and she was impatient to get moving. She didn't think he would be there waiting for them—at least she hoped not. If he was, it would have to be because he was dead or badly injured. But there would surely be some clue to which direction he had gone.

They had made their way here by following a narrow tunnel that branched off the sulfur stream and on the way Florian had tried to continue their conversation about Tremaine's father. "Wasn't it hard for you to be that different?" Florian had asked her thoughtfully.

Tremaine was starting to regret those confidences. She still wasn't quite sure how Florian had taken it. Not that she had had many options. *This isn't exactly the best place to run off screaming.* "Not at first," she had admitted. "Or I didn't notice it at first. I think I was proud of it, for a while. That we were different."

"But it must have been dangerous. Going after powerful criminals, when he was a powerful criminal himself. He couldn't just go to the Magistrates for help when things went wrong."

"When my mother was killed, I started to realize it wasn't a game. And it wasn't something I could ever really get away from." Tremaine hadn't mentioned her stint in the asylum. Honesty was all well and good, but she was willing to take it only so far. Maybe that was when Nicholas had realized it too. That he couldn't retire, not as himself. If he had ever really wanted to. She had envied him his ability to put on a new persona with the ease of putting on a different set of clothes and just walking away into the night. Free and unencumbered by physical or emotional ties. She couldn't imagine giving that up. *Except he always came back.*

Below, the last of the Gardier disappeared down the tunnel that curved away into darkness; she nudged Ilias with her elbow. He nudged her back, harassed, but eased to his feet, keeping a watchful eye on the opening the patrol had disappeared through. Tremaine crawled out after him, her bones creaking, and Florian unfolded herself with a smothered groan.

Ilias made them wait on the ledge until the last hollow

echoes of footsteps and quiet voices faded. Then they got the torch lit again and he leapt down into the passage. Tremaine and Florian followed more awkwardly and they hastened into the cross tunnel.

After only a short distance it opened abruptly into a larger chamber and Ilias motioned urgently for them to hang back. As she and Florian trailed behind him, the torchlight revealed two other tunnel openings in this side and one bigger one directly in front of them.

"This looks familiar," Florian said softly, lifting the torch higher to look around.

"How can you tell?" Tremaine demanded. Everything looked the same to her. She had realized earlier that must be one of the reasons Ilias stopped to scratch signs on the stones every so often.

A puzzled-sounding remark from Ilias sent them hurrying to catch up with him. He had gone a short distance down the larger passage and was sitting on his heels to poke cautiously at something on the ground. The torchlight danced as Florian leaned down to see. "That's our lamp!" She grabbed the handle and lifted it. The glass was smashed and the slide bent and twisted, as if something large had stepped on it.

"You're right, this is the place." This was the spot where the hunter-creatures had attacked them. Encouraged, Tremaine moved forward, fumbling along the wall in the dark. She passed the remains of the two creatures Gerard's spell had killed, just heaps of stripped bones and dark blotches in the sandy dirt. "That other tunnel has to be right here." Her hand plunged into empty space just as Florian caught up to her with the torch. They found themselves looking down the tunnel that led off from the main passage, the one Gerard had been thrown into by the force of the sphere. Tremaine hadn't got much more than a glimpse of it before. It was wider, the ground sloping up and mostly dry, and it seemed to curve just before the limit of the torchlight. There was no sign of Gerard.

That's a relief, Tremaine thought. Despite everything, she had been half expecting to find his body. She bit her lip thoughtfully, looking around. The torch revealed no blood-stains on the rocky ground. "Even if those things caught him and ate him, there'd be something left," she said, trying to look on the bright side.

Florian took a sharp breath, wincing as if she didn't quite appreciate the image. "You're right, that's a good sign. Maybe we could—" She stopped, startled as Ilias caught her wrist and steadied the torch. "I think he wants me to hold it still."

Tremaine shouldered the satchel, watching as Ilias moved around, examining the ground. She followed him, trying to see what he was looking at. "There's a lot of scuff marks here," she reported to Florian, leaning to see around him.

Tremaine stepped back as Ilias turned suddenly and bumped into her. Muttering under his breath, he took her arm and steered her over to the wall. Tremaine took the hint and backed up out of his way.

He turned back to his examination of the ground, crouching to inspect an area of disturbed dirt more closely. "Does it look like Gerard escaped?" Florian started to step forward. "Sorry," she added, as he waved her back in exasperation.

After another moment of intense study, Ilias bounced back to his feet and started down the tunnel.

The passage wound back and forth, its upward slope becoming steadily more pronounced. Tremaine couldn't see any sign of Gerard but Ilias seemed confident. As Tremaine scrambled up a sloping turn, Florian halted suddenly in front of her, one hand on the wall. "What?" Tremaine asked impatiently. From Ilias's attitude she thought they were close and she wanted to keep moving.

"Somebody did an illusion here." Florian drew her hand back, studying her fingers intently in the torchlight. Tremaine leaned in to look but all she could see was the sickly moisture from the wall. "It's etheric residue, I can feel it. I wouldn't have found it unless I put my hand on it."

"If Gerard was using an illusion to keep those things off him, or maybe avoid the Gardier, would it leave those traces?" Tremaine was starting to get a picture of what must have happened. Forced to retreat down this passage, unable to use a more violent offensive spell because of the close presence of the Gardier, Gerard would have tried an illusion to keep them off his trail.

Florian nodded grimly. "They must have been right behind him."

Ilias retraced his steps with an impatient exclamation, wondering what the delay was, and they hurried to catch up.

Around the next upward bend in the passage he halted, hands planted on his hips, surveying the terrain ahead thoughtfully. As Tremaine drew even with him, she saw a wide crevasse cutting through the tunnel. It was bridged by one of the long stone logs with both ends wedged into the rocks on either side. Florian moved forward, holding the torch out. "Looks like somebody put that there to— Yow!"

Florian retreated hastily and Tremaine stepped around her to look. All she could see was a dark gap, just like the others they had stepped across or leapt. Cold air flowed up from it, a relief after the warm dampness in the close passages. Then Ilias took the torch away from Florian and held it up.

"Damn!" It was Tremaine's turn to start back. The shaft plunged deep into the caves below. Somewhere far down minute crystal outcrops caught the light and cast it back.

"This is the part where we toss a rock and we never hear it hit bottom," Florian said, giving Tremaine a tense glance.

She wiped her sweaty hands on her jacket. "Let's skip that part."

As she and Florian watched, Ilias stepped up onto the rocks that anchored the log. He eased one foot out onto it, then another, testing it cautiously with his weight. "Oh, don't fall," Florian breathed.

Evidently satisfied it was stable, he crossed it matter-of-factly, arms out for balance. On the far side he wedged the torch into a gap between the stones. Turning back, he smiled encouragingly and made coaxing motions indicating they should follow.

Tremaine and Florian exchanged a look. Florian did not appear happy. Tremaine took a deep breath. "Want me to go first?" *It's all in the head,* she told herself. *You'd cross a ditch on a log that wide without thinking twice.*

"No, I'd rather get it over with." Florian sounded gloomy but resigned, as if they were planning to jump headfirst instead of cross over.

Tremaine tossed the supply satchel across to Ilias, then stood by as Florian stepped up onto the rocks, ready to steady her if she had to.

"Here goes." Florian eased out onto the log bridge, her brows knitted in concentration. Tremaine bit her tongue to keep from uttering useless injunctions to be careful; if anybody knew to be careful right now, it was Florian. Time seemed to stretch but it was really only a moment before Ilias was able to lean out, catch her arm and guide her the rest of the way across.

Florian took a deep breath in relief as she stepped onto solid ground. "Right." Tremaine took a careful step onto the log and felt her stomach do a nervous internal dance. She took another, thought *so far so good,* then made the mistake of looking down.

The sight caught her like a moth in a candle flame. The way the shadows fell from the torch turned the planes and angles of the cliff wall into some sort of abstract sculpture, the depth vanishing into the jumble of disconnected images. The crystal fragments caught in the stone glittered like stars. It was intoxicating. Just one step and . . .

She came back to reality abruptly as Ilias caught her around the waist. The log creaked at the extra weight but he leapt back swiftly, yanking her with him.

In a heartbeat they were on the far side, on the stable rock, and she had her head buried in his chest. She clung to him for a moment, needing the warm solid anchor, no matter what he smelled like. *That . . . was close,* she thought. She hadn't meant to do it. She hadn't wanted to do it. They hadn't found Gerard yet and she couldn't

leave Florian in the lurch like that. The fact that she almost hadn't been able to stop herself was more frightening than the thought of the fall.

An anxious Florian patted her back. "Tremaine, are you
all right?"

Ilias tipped her chin up so he could see her face, asking
a soft worried question. Tremaine pulled away, shaking her
head. "No, I'm fine. Just got dizzy there for a second." She
added lamely, "ha ha."

"You did get hit in the head," Florian pointed out, sling-
ing the satchel over her shoulder and taking Tremaine's arm.
"Maybe that's it."

"It still hurts," Tremaine admitted truthfully enough.
She forced a smile. But Ilias was still studying her, his blue
eyes troubled and knowing; somehow she didn't think he
was fooled.

Only a short distance ahead the passage turned sharply.
Tremaine, still preoccupied, bumped into Florian before
she realized the other girl had halted abruptly. She looked
up, stared and whistled softly in appreciation.

They had found the underground city again.

The flicker of their torch caught dark columns, formed
of bundled masses of those long stones so like tree trunks.
A double row of them led away into a limitless dark space
that must be a large cavern; the pillars seemed to stretch up
and up. Between them was a walkway of cracked and broken paving stones.

Past the torchlight the darkness seemed less oppressive
and Tremaine realized light was filtering down through
cracks and crevices above, giving glimpses of more
shapes too regular to be natural. Ilias stepped back, taking the torch away from Florian and grinding it out
against the damp stone. They all stood still a moment as
their eyes adjusted.

Most of it was lost in shadow, but Tremaine could see
buildings: a pyramidal one with galleries spiraling
around the cracked slanted sides, square ones with pillars, like peristyle halls, some with collapsed bridges to
connect them. All were built of the same dark stones,

tumbled atop each other or sunk into the ground or half collapsed. It looked like an avalanche she had seen once, where a section of pine forest had plunged down a mountain in a shower of rocks and dust, leaving the denuded logs jammed at the bottom of the slope. Water trickled down from above, and moss and the purplish gray plants clung to cracks everywhere, thorny brush and vines draping the windows and doorways. Tremaine found herself twitching as she caught glimpses of imagined movement in the corners of her eyes. This half-light was almost as bad as pitch-dark.

Ilias started cautiously forward, handing the dead torch back to Florian, who tucked it into the outside pocket of the satchel. The still oppressive air was just as warm and damp as the tunnels, but there was something chilling about it, something that made the skin prickle on Tremaine's scalp. The odor that hung over this place was certainly worse. It smelled foul, like an exposed garbage midden. She started to say, "This is—"

Ilias glanced back at her urgently and held two fingers in front of his mouth, cautioning her to silence.

"Sorry," Tremaine whispered. She wasn't sure what she had been about to say anyway.

Between the broken paving stones the ground squished unpleasantly underfoot. It was covered with a thick carpet of dead leaves from the ugly little plants mixed with mud, and they had to step over chunks of wood, purplish, sickly palm fronds and other debris. There were little streams running between the toppled structures and small pools choked with leaves everywhere. Ilias was studying the ground, the set of his shoulders conveying tension. *It's not just Gerard,* Tremaine thought, concerned. He knew Gerard was their friend; but the sorcerer's track must have been crossed by something else.

Suddenly Ilias motioned them to wait. He moved between the columns to a building that lay at a crazy angle, its dark stone roof sloping up sharply. He scrambled agilely to the top. Squinting in the dimness, Tremaine saw his shoulders hunch as he flattened himself against it.

"He saw something," Florian murmured under her breath.

Ilias hesitated, then, looking down, pointed at Tremaine and motioned for her to come up.

The round stones the roof was composed of had grooves between them and she was able to wedge her feet in, concentrating on not losing her grip on the slippery stone. When she was close enough to reach up to him he grabbed her arm and pulled her up, catching her around the waist and tucking her securely against his side. Tremaine grabbed his shoulder to steady herself, mud-coated spikes of hair brushing her cheek. *Damn, he's solid.* It was a far cry from the languid artists she had known in Vienne café society. For a moment she found it hard to concentrate on the task at hand. But he was looking intently at something ahead in the darkness.

With her free hand Tremaine pushed away his hair and followed his gaze. After a moment her eyes caught movement against the lighter stone of the cave wall. Then she felt the skin on the back of her neck creep in earnest.

Ahead there was a kind of raised plaza formed by big stone blocks. Past it was a wide cleft in the collapsed buildings, then a ledge on the edge of a crevice, just visible under a heavy overhang of tangled vines. There was something standing on it.

Tremaine squinted, making out a large creature with a mottled brown hide. It turned its round head and she saw a wide mouth gleaming with fangs. Its body was long and thin and obviously female, with a small waist and pendulous, shriveled breasts. As she watched, it straightened up from its crouch and lifted large, webbed reptilian wings. *Oh, that's new,* Tremaine thought nervously. With one flap the creature leapt to the ground, sinking down among the broken walls.

Ilias leaned close to whisper almost voicelessly, "Grend."

"Wonderful," she replied under her breath.

Ilias glanced down at her, brow furrowed in frustration. Then he held up three fingers and pointed toward the crevice.

Ah, I get it. Tremaine nodded rapidly. He was telling her the third person in their party—Gerard—had gone that way. The grend was stalking the crevice because he must have taken shelter in it. *Now what do we do?*

Ilias started down, keeping an arm around her waist until she had her footing. She scrambled down to Florian, who whispered, "Well?"

"It's a grend," Tremaine explained, keeping her voice low. "It's got Gerard trapped."

"You saw him?" she demanded. "What's a grend?"

"A big . . . thing." Tremaine flapped her arms in a vague gesture. "We didn't see him, but he's got to be there. If it had already eaten him, surely it wouldn't still be hanging around."

Florian stared, taken aback. "You know, when you're optimistic you have a strange way of phrasing things." She shook her head, obviously putting it aside. "How are we going to get Gerard out?"

"Don't know." Tremaine looked around to see Ilias rooting in a dark pile of leaves and detritus at the base of a column. He came up with a heavy stick of wood a few feet long and weighed it thoughtfully, slapping it against his palm. "You're going after it with that?" she asked, aghast.

He glanced up at her tone, one brow quirked, his expression admitting that it wasn't a great idea. He dropped the stick and looked around with a frustrated frown.

"What do you need?" Florian asked him.

Ilias started to gesture but all Tremaine could get out of it was "something big." "We don't have anything big," she said helplessly.

Florian set the satchel down and held it open to let him go through it. "At least he's got a plan."

"If beating that thing with a stick is part of it, I'm not sure it's better than no plan at all," Tremaine replied. Rummaging in the bag, Ilias pulled out a folded square of tarpaulin. He stood up and shook it out, nodding thoughtfully to himself.

"That?" Tremaine asked, baffled.

He looked from her to Florian, came to a decision, then squatted to make a drawing in the dirt on a flat paving stone. Tremaine leaned down to look as he drew a rough diagram of the cave wall and the buildings, with dots indicating the grend, herself and Florian, then himself.

"*Caertah*," he said, tapping himself in the chest and looking at them inquiringly.

Florian lifted her brows. "What do we think that means?"

Tremaine looked down at the drawing again, studying the group of figures. " 'Bait,' " she said slowly. "We think it means 'bait.' "

Ilias flattened himself against the stone, easing forward carefully, the heavy cloth tucked under his arm. *It would have to be a grend,* he thought grimly. He should have known they were too stubborn to just die or leave; the damn things had always been Ixion's favorites and they were probably still hoping the wizard would return.

His nose wrinkled at the heavy musky stink of the creature, detectable even over the mud. There was grend shit on all the walls and pillars, the rotted offal of their kills in every crack and cranny in this cave. Fortunately, they weren't scent hunters like the howlers and they were too big to get down into the smaller lower passages. The odd thing was that they had seen only the one so far.

From the spoor down in the tunnel Ilias could tell two howlers had chased a man up here, a man wearing boots of the same odd make as Tremaine and Florian's. They should have found his body by now, or what was left of it after the grend had their fun. It was lucky for the stranger, but the absence of more grend here made Ilias think of the wizards' captive howlers. If the wizards had spooked the grend away, he just hoped they weren't here still.

Ilias reached the edge of the wall and glanced back at the two women. He could just see them in the wan light, crouched against the tumbled stone a short distance away.

He held two fingers to his mouth, cautioning them to be quiet, and their heads bobbed emphatically in agreement.

After their escape, he knew they could both be counted on to act, but he was worried about Tremaine. From the way she had attacked that wizard, he wouldn't be surprised if she had killed before. She had gone for him without any hesitation, as if she knew what it was to fight for her life. But when she had frozen on the bridge over the chasm, he had recognized that fey look in her eyes immediately. Giliead had lived with that same look for a long time. All through that dangerous period after they had returned from killing Ixion, when the reality had begun to set in that Amari and Irisa and the others were dead.

No help for it now, Ilias thought, *so let's get this over with.* Grend preferred male victims since they liked to mate with their prey before they ate it; if this went wrong, the creature was unlikely to chase the two women. He just hoped he had been able to explain the plan coherently.

He leaned around the wall until he could see the grend, perched at the mouth of the narrow crevice. Her wings were tightly furled as she rocked back and forth, frustrated by her inability to reach her prey.

He took a deep breath. This wasn't the first time he had faced a curseling since Ixion had tried to turn him into one. *So it should be easy,* he thought with a rueful bitterness that surprised him.

When Ixion had captured Ilias, he had used him in one of his transformation curses. He had been trying to make something like a male grend; Ilias had returned to consciousness to find himself a malformed winged travesty. Whether Ixion really expected Ilias to do his bidding afterward or just wanted to torture Giliead with the sight, Ilias wasn't certain. His memories of it were confused, but he knew he hadn't felt any compulsion to obey Ixion; what he had had was an urge to tear the wizard apart and the claws to do it. The scars that it had left behind were as much a reminder as the curse mark.

Ilias realized he was stalling and stepped out into the

grend's view. She shot to her feet, flaring her wings, her head cocked toward him.

"Come on, you've been waiting for him a long time," Ilias told her in a coaxing tone. He sidestepped cautiously further out into the open plaza between the buildings and the cave wall, the cloth wadded in one hand, his knife in the other. She couldn't understand the words but the challenging air would get across. "What's better, one you can see or one you can't?"

She leaned forward and suddenly she was swooping down at him, landing only a dozen paces away. Ilias dodged backward, bouncing lightly on the balls of his feet. He had forgotten how fast they were. Their hollow bones were light and delicate but the creatures were deceptively strong.

The grend hesitated, casting a glance back at the mouth of the crevice. "No, not him, me!" Ilias needed her attention on him; if she saw Tremaine and Florian, she might spook and retreat; they couldn't afford to have her stalking them. "Come on, you know you want me."

The grend snarled, crouching. Air rushed overhead as she suddenly pounced, her claws scraping on the paving stones only a few paces away. The gust from her wings sent him tumbling in a whirlwind of dead leaves and dirt.

Ilias slammed into the base of a broken pillar and scrambled back to his feet. The creature's head tilted as she looked down at him, her yellow eyes gleaming with malice. Suddenly she jerked back, hissing angrily and flailing one arm behind her head.

Ilias caught a glimpse of Florian behind the grend, hefting another rock. The grend twisted her head around to look for them, but didn't pounce. As he had hoped, she was distracted by the two women but too eager for her favorite prey to attack them. *Lucky Ixion never had time to finish breeding these things for brains,* he thought grimly, ducking backward as she swiped at him with a long clawed hand. He shook out the cloth, rocking on the balls of his feet, ready to move.

Another rock sailed over the grend's shoulder from the

other direction and she turned at bay, snarling and flaring her wings to drive the women off. As Ilias moved to circle her, she whipped around suddenly, reaching for him. Ilias dived under a clawed hand and rolled away. He dropped the cloth rather than be tangled in it himself and scrambled under the thorny branches of the sickly brush at the edge of the plaza. In her eagerness to get her claws in him, the grend pushed forward, ignoring the branches that tore at her wings. He heard Tremaine calling his name but couldn't see her past the grend's bulk.

Suddenly Tremaine ducked around the creature's wing. Ilias felt his heart freeze, thinking she was fey again, trying to get herself killed. But the expression on her face was a mix of determination and alarm. She pitched a rock, striking the grend right in the head, then bolted away as it reached for her. A hail of smaller stones from Florian peppered the creature's back and the grend twisted away in furious confusion.

Ilias whooped in approval and rolled out from under the brush, grabbing up the cloth where it lay in the mud. He whipped it around and lunged at the grend, shouting. She snarled, turning on him again. Ilias tossed the cloth over her head and she reared back, shrieking and tearing at the heavy material. He dived under her lifted wing, rolling back to his feet to ram his knife between her ribs.

The grend shrieked in rage and pain and her wing struck Ilias across the back, knocking him flat. He rolled over to see her leap into the air. She landed near the columns, blood streaming from the wound in her side. Shrieking again, she leapt up to vanish in the darkness of the cave.

Ilias pushed himself up, feeling his ribs ache. He got to his feet, grinning, as the two girls ran up. "Now let's find your friend."

Gervas waited impatiently up the tunnel, watching the creature that called itself Ixion, his stomach churning with disgust. He could barely see the pale form crouched on a rock a short distance down the tunnel passage. The loose coverall it now wore didn't fully conceal the dead white limbs, the waxy texture of its skin, the sleek shape of the malformed skull. It was a terrible thing to call ally, even for a short time.

He suspected the thing Ixion was speaking to was even more terrible.

They had gone a little distance from the base perimeter into the open caves, Gervas, Ixion and a squad of four guards. Ixion had demanded that their handlights be dimmed so that the creature he spoke to would be more comfortable. Gervas could tell it was small, barely a foot high, and the dim lamplight reflected off a glistening silver-gray hide. Its high voice trilled and sang as Ixion nodded, occasionally murmuring what sounded like endearments to it. Finally he waved the creature away and got to his feet.

"What did it tell you?" Gervas demanded. As Ixion limped toward him, Gervas gestured to the guard with the lamp to turn up the light. The electric blaze just caught the creature vanishing into a crevice, its small body another grotesque parody of the human form.

"It suspects they've gone toward the grend caves." Ixion stared into the light, his lidless eyes thoughtful. "A risky move, but a bold one," he added, half to himself.

Gervas suspected Ixion said such things to pretend he had some secret knowledge of the Rien spies, to make himself appear more useful. It was impossible, of course. With a dismissive expression he said, "That's all? I heard as much from my own patrols."

"I gave you the spell to keep the grend from attacking your men, you should be grateful for that." Ixion turned to the lamp, using its light to study his half-formed fingernails. The blue and red of veins and arteries were clearly visible now under his translucent white skin. The Service man holding the lamp looked away.

Verim and his search team had been unable to trace the escaped prisoners and had gone to join the east quadrant patrol. From their last report, having the search area free of the large winged predators—the "grend," as Ixion called them—had allowed them to cover more ground. This was fortunate, as the howlers had refused to go down into that section of the caves, no matter how much force was used. Ixion had claimed that their fear of the grend's territory was responsible. "I am grateful," Gervas managed to say, though the words nearly choked him. "It is a pity your other creatures, the howlers, could not hunt the spies down for us."

"Oh, they know how to avoid the howlers, you won't catch them that way." The lipless mouth drew up into a smile. "They know a great deal about the grend, too."

"They?" Gervas stared. The Rien couldn't know of the misbegotten inhabitants of these caves. "Who do you mean?"

The lidless eyes gave him a guileless look. "I meant a generic 'they.' They, our enemies, that sort of thing."

Gervas's mouth twisted in annoyance. If Ixion did have some sort of special knowledge, prying it out of him in time to be of any use could be difficult. He was very much looking forward to the moment when he could pronounce Ixion's usefulness over and have him shipped to Command to undergo conversion. Even with the coming invasion of Ile-Rien, Command was always desperate for more sorcerers and Gervas would win a commendation for providing another one.

"By the way," Ixion said, "when are you going to show me that fascinating device you've installed in the west passages?"

Gervas pressed his lips together. "Who spoke to you of that?" If the guards had been speaking foolishly with this creature he would feed them to the howlers, no matter how short of personnel they were.

"No one." Ixion sighed. "Oh, don't look like that. I'm a wizard. I can hear it, I can smell it. I know you have something of great power back there."

Before Gervas could pursue it, a shout from the other end of the tunnel made him turn. He recognized the man as the communications room runner and hurriedly waved him forward. Concealing his relief, he listened to the message, then turned to Ixion and smiled. "We've caught one of the Rien spies. Perhaps we don't need your help after all."

"Better safe than sorry," Ixion told him, unperturbed. "You never know what you could run into down here."

 **Chapter 10**

Florian struck matches for Ilias and they got the torch lit while Tremaine jittered impatiently. Then Tremaine tried to charge ahead but Ilias caught her jacket and hauled her back, handing her the torch to slow her down and starting up the crevice himself. She followed, Florian close behind, both of them stumbling on the slick stone and loose rock.

The folds of stone that formed the crevice loomed up on either side as they climbed toward the spot the grend hadn't been able to squeeze past. Ilias had just reached the narrowest part of the fold when a dark form exploded out of the opening. Tremaine yelped and stumbled back, her feet catching on the loose rock and sliding out from under her. She caught herself awkwardly on the slope, nearly falling on the flaring torch, Florian stumbling into her.

Tremaine saw Ilias duck under a dim shape that swung at his head and dive forward, tackling the figure and pinning it against the wall of the crevice. It twisted and threw Ilias off. He slipped on the loose scree and slid back, catching himself against the rock.

Florian managed to push herself up off Tremaine, who surged to her feet and swung the torch wildly to distract whatever it was. In the flare of firelight she got her first clear look at their opponent. She stopped abruptly. "Ander!"

"Tremaine?" Ander stared at her, blank with surprise, poised to swing a heavy branch. Still blinking, trying to adjust to the sudden light, his eyes widened and he shouted, "Behind you!"

Tremaine whipped around. Ilias ducked away from the torch as it swung perilously near his head. "Oh, sorry!"

"No, no, he's our friend!" Florian explained hastily, stumbling up the slope toward them.

"What?" Baffled, Ander looked from Florian to Tremaine, his makeshift club still ready. In the flickering torchlight he looked half-wild. He was missing his jacket and his shirt was torn and bloodstained. There was a large bruise on his temple. "Are you out of your minds?"

Tremaine rolled her eyes, relief at seeing Ander alive beginning to fade into annoyance. "Ander, you scared me out of my—" It was pointless. She pushed the sweat-soaked hair out of her eyes. "Is Gerard with you?"

Ander glared at her but finally lowered the branch. "No, he isn't! But who the hell is that?" he demanded.

Tremaine turned to Ilias. He had his hands planted on his hips and an expression that said that if this was the friend they had been searching so hard for, there was obviously something wrong with them. Mud was still smeared on his bare chest and arms, clotted in the rough material of his clothes. The patches of it left on his face looked like a tribal marking and wild streaks of blond showed through the coating of mud and dried blood in his tangled hair. And he needed a shave. She said, "He's not as . . . as he looks."

"That's Ilias," Florian said more practically, digging the water flask out of their satchel to hand to Ander. "He saved us, and then we saved him when we were captured by the Gardier, and he's been helping us since."

"You were captured by the Gardier?" Ander repeated blankly, accepting the flask without noticing he had. "How—? What—?"

"It's a long story," Tremaine said brusquely. She had been sure it was Gerard that the grend had cornered and felt the disappointment keenly. "Have you seen Gerard at all? He was with us and we got separated. We think the Gardier are tracking him through here."

Eyeing Ilias warily, Ander said, "I heard a party of Gardier a couple of times, and I could tell there was someone ahead of me but I wasn't sure if it was one of you, so

I hung back. Once I followed him down into this cavern I thought I heard Gerard's voice. Before I could catch up to him, this big winged thing came after me." Ander took a quick drink and wiped his mouth on his torn sleeve. "Did you see it?"

"We chased it off," Florian told him, screwing the cap back on the flask and tucking it back in the satchel. "We've been trying to find Gerard before the Gardier did. We thought you were dead."

"So did I, for a while there," Ander admitted, pressing a hand to his side. "What did you mean when you said you were captured by the Gardier?"

While Florian tried to explain, Tremaine turned to Ilias, who was still watching the conversation with a disgruntled air. He caught her eye and one brow quirked as his lips twitched in a smile. He knew Ander wasn't happy to see him. Guiltily, she avoided his eyes, rubbing her forehead. "God, he's not going to like this. All right." Smiling apologetically at Ilias, she pointed to herself, Florian and Ander in turn, then held up four fingers.

His jaw dropped. His expression eloquently said *You've got to be kidding me.*

"I know, I know," Tremaine said hurriedly, trying to convey what she was saying by shrugs, gestures and expressions. She pointed to Ander and mimed her head flopping over, tongue hanging out, staring eyes. "We thought he was dead. But our other friend, Gerard, is still down here somewhere." She tugged her ear, wondering if Ilias was getting any of this or just thought she was insane. "He, Ander, heard him before the grend came."

Ilias made a gesture half in appeal, half in frustration, then shook his head, muttering under his breath. He turned and scrambled down the crevice.

"Where's he going?" Ander demanded, stepping forward to watch him.

"To look for Gerard's tracks." Tremaine ran a hand through her hair, still feeling guilty. "Or he's leaving us. If he does, we're dead."

Her face etched with concern, Florian told Ander, "He

has a friend lost down here. He put off looking for him to help us." She took the medical kit out of the bag, gesturing for Ander to sit. "Are you hurt? And how did you get here? We thought you'd drowned."

Ander shook his head vaguely as he eased down to sit on the rock. "I was washed off the deck— I got swept into a kind of cave harbor, full of old wrecks." He gasped as Florian pulled back his shirt, tears in his singlet revealing bloody scrapes along his ribs.

"Sorry." Florian glanced up at him, biting her lip.

"It's all right." Ander looked toward Tremaine, then shook his head. Whether the incredulity was at her naïveté in trusting a stranger or just at her in general, she couldn't tell. "He lives on this island? Why is he helping you?"

"We don't know where he lives." Tremaine rubbed the bridge of her nose. Her eyes hurt from the bad light and her back ached from all the walking. *If the grend got Gerard . . .* Ilias hadn't taken the torch with him. *God, I hope he doesn't need it. I hope—* She shook her head. It would be better if he left; if they were caught again, the Gardier would surely kill him this time.

"He was helping us before we helped him," Florian said pointedly.

"So he just showed up?" Ander snorted, then grimaced, his hand going to his ribs again. He looked urgently from Florian to Tremaine. "You can't trust him. He could be a Gardier spy."

"He's not," Tremaine said shortly. She could go into detail about why this was unlikely but she felt like being disagreeable.

"The Gardier caught all three of us, Ander, we know he's not a spy," Florian told him, frowning.

A faint scrape on stone made Tremaine's head whip around. Ilias scrambled up the crevice, grabbed the torch from her and ground it out against the rock. Tremaine, opening her mouth to say something, snapped it shut. She heard Florian draw breath to speak and a muffled snort as Ander must have clapped a hand over her mouth. In the sudden darkness in the crevice Ilias took

Tremaine's arm and tugged her back toward the spot where the rock dropped away and the faint light allowed a view down on the ruins of the city. For a moment she thought she was seeing things. There was a light moving along the walkway between the double row of dark columns. She could just make out that it was carried by a human figure, with others trailing in its wake. Her imagination conjured a ritual procession, the old owners of this city or their ghosts making a tour of inspection of their ruined homes. Then the group turned off the walkway and made their way through the collapsed buildings, nearing the plaza where they had fought the grend. Then she saw the color of their uniforms in their lamplight.

Gardier again. She ducked reflexively, though there was no way they could see up here in the shadows.

The group paused in the plaza and the Gardier in the lead held what looked like field glasses to his eyes, studying the cave wall. *What is he doing?* she wondered. Field glasses wouldn't help in this dim light and the wall wasn't that far. *Not field glasses, aether-glasses, you idiot.* He was looking for spells.

Then she stopped breathing, grabbing Ilias's arm in reflex. The leader wore a makeshift sling over one shoulder. It was the sling Gerard had carried the sphere in and she could tell it held something the right size. "Dammit," she said under her breath. The sight of the Gardier with the sphere made her sick with rage. "Oh, I can't believe this."

"What is it?" Florian whispered at the same time Ander demanded, low-voiced, "What's down there?"

"Gardier, they've got the sphere," she reported. "They must have Gerard too." *We should have moved faster, caught up sooner. This is all my fault.* "Goddammit."

"No. Oh no." Florian scrambled forward over the loose scree, putting her hands on Ilias's shoulders to peer past him.

Ander followed her, crouching behind the rock on the other side of the opening. "They're Gardier, all right. What is that he's . . . Those have got to be aether-glasses."

Tremaine grimaced, glancing at him. "And he's not using them to look for the local grend sorcerer."

Ilias nudged Tremaine with his elbow, pointed down at the Gardier and held up four fingers. Tremaine stared. "What? Yes, there's four of them."

"No, wait, four," Florian interrupted, thumping her on the arm. "The fourth person. He means Gerard."

"Oh, right! Yes." Tremaine nodded rapidly. "Yes, they have something of ours, that bag." She shook the satchel hanging over Florian's shoulder and pointed at the Gardier leader to explain. "They must have him too."

"Where is he?" Florian muttered. "They'd want to question him." The leader seemed to be staring right at them, the etheric lenses pointing directly at their hiding spot as the man scanned the cave wall. She sank down behind Ilias, who shifted uneasily.

"They can't see us," Tremaine said, more hopeful than certain. The shadows under the heavy shelf of rock were too dark. They were just lucky Ilias had seen them in time to douse the torch. "They must have found Gerard and the sphere using those lenses, and they're looking for more."

"We can't let them have the sphere," Ander said with grim purpose.

"No kidding," Tremaine snarled. *We can't let them have Gerard either.* The Gardier leader lowered the lenses, staring up at the cave wall. The moment stretched as Tremaine's nerves jittered. Then he motioned for the others to follow and the group moved off, working their way through the tumbled remains of the buildings.

Ilias shifted impatiently and spoke, jerking his head down toward the retreating Gardier. Tremaine nodded sharply, not bothering to consult Ander. He was the Intelligence expert and probably better at this but some stubborn voice in her head didn't want him running the show. "Yes, we're going after them."

Ilias was able to track the Gardier's passage through the leaf loam and decay collected on the paving stones and this let them hang back far enough to avoid being seen. The Gardier took a path that wound deeper into the sunken city, past another curving colonnade of stone-log pillars and a fantastic screen of stalagmites and stalactites that looked as if it would be at home in some elaborate cathedral. Ilias paused to make quick marks on the stone a couple of times, though Ander eyed this process with suspicion. "Why is he doing that?"

Ilias might not understand the words but he correctly interpreted the tone, and the look he cast back at Ander as he stood up and tucked his knife away was definitely piqued. Tremaine rolled her eyes. The last thing they needed was to insult Ilias. After all this she didn't think he would abandon them down here, but he didn't have to help them find Gerard, either. "He does that so we can find our way back," Tremaine said, picking a possibility at random. Florian nodded helpfully. Faced with this logic, Ander let it drop.

Peering cautiously over the rocks, they glimpsed the Gardier climbing an uneven set of steps up to a large plaza elevated atop bundled piles of the long stones. Tremaine snarled under her breath, knowing there was no way they could follow them across the plaza without being spotted. But Ilias led them to one side of it, around a ruined structure where the shadows were deep. A narrow channel ran between the plaza and the rough rock of the cave wall and they traversed this cavity with difficulty, slipping in the dark. Tremaine had many bruising encounters with sharp rocks. At one point Ilias stopped abruptly and gestured for them to climb along the rock wall to avoid an apparently innocuous muddy flat.

"Why does he want us to go that way?" Ander objected. Tremaine suspected he was still smarting over the encounter in the crevice. "What does—"

With a gasp, Florian tugged his sleeve and pointed. Tremaine leaned to look and saw the ground was rippling. She edged back hurriedly. Whatever was digging there just below the surface, it was much larger than a badger.

"Never mind," Ander said, low-voiced.

Already climbing the rock to avoid whatever it was, Ilias glanced back with a disgusted snort.

Not far past the danger spot, Ilias motioned for them

to wait and scrambled up the ruins of a stone staircase that cut upward through the base of the plaza. They waited impatiently until he reappeared and gestured for them to follow.

Tremaine managed to shove in ahead of Ander and climbed up the narrow rocky trench after Ilias. He stopped at a spot where a gap between the stones revealed the glow of electric lamplight, crouching down to look through. Tremaine eased in beside him, looked, and felt her stomach clench in a knot.

The four Gardier they had followed had joined two others at what had to be their temporary base camp, set up in an open area ringed by the remains of a large building, tumbled and broken pillars marking the boundaries. And they had Gerard.

The sorcerer sat on the ground, cross-legged, his hands bound behind him. Tremaine could make out his disgruntled expression from here. He didn't seem to be injured. His shirt and vest were open at the throat and his coat was missing. "Right," she muttered, keeping her voice low. *Now what?* Ander crouched beside her and swore softly under his breath and she heard Florian scramble up behind her.

Two of the Gardier held rifles and stood guard on either side of the little camp. They had a few large battery lamps to light the area and what looked like a portable wireless stood on a handy flat rock. Tremaine could hear the squeal of static occasionally as one of the Gardier fiddled with the dials. Ander leaned over to whisper, "They can't be using ordinary radio signals in these caves; that set's got to have some kind of magical booster."

"I knew that," she whispered back, annoyed.

The one with the sphere sat on a rock a few feet away from Gerard. Tossing the sling away, he examined the sphere curiously, occasionally addressing a question to Gerard, which the sorcerer stolidly ignored.

"He's got one of those translator crystals," Florian leaned over Tremaine's shoulder to whisper. "See, he touches it when he tries to talk to Gerard."

"What?" Ander frowned.

Tremaine shook her head impatiently. "They have some kind of magical translators for our language. They don't work that well."

Ilias nudged her and motioned for them all to move back from the opening. "You've got an idea?" Tremaine asked him hopefully.

"How can you tell?" Ander murmured as he shifted back to make room.

"He's got that look." Tremaine watched as Ilias found a patch of damp earth in the light from the opening and started to draw. She studied the diagram thoughtfully. *Communication would be much more difficult if we didn't have one plan: distract it/them and then throw rocks.* "That's where we are now, that's the Gardier . . . but what's that?"

Ilias sighed, rubbed his forehead wearily as if tired of pantomiming every sentence, and then mimed digging, and pointed vigorously back down the way they had come.

"The digging thing," Florian guessed, thumping Tremaine's arm excitedly. "He means we get the digging thing to come out and attack the Gardier. *Caertah*, that was the word he used with the grend."

"Bait." Tremaine nodded thoughtfully. "All right, but not you," she told Ilias. She tapped herself in the chest. "Me."

Nobody else liked the idea.

They retired further back down the broken stair to have the argument, with Ilias torn between returning to the opening to watch the Gardier and coming back to use various sign language techniques to tell Tremaine she was crazy.

"Tremaine, it's ridiculous, you can't," Ander told her firmly, in as no-nonsense a tone as he could manage in a whisper.

"Look, there's six of them, you have to be ready to jump them," she replied in a hushed voice, adding an aside to Ilias, "And don't think I don't know exactly what you're saying because there are some attitudes that don't need translation."

He planted his hands on his hips and glared, but the effect was ruined by the fringe of fluffy hair where the mud had washed off. Ander's glare was perfectly functional. He said, "You are going to get yourself killed."

Tremaine pressed her lips together. That was unfair, considering for once that wasn't what she was planning at all. Telling him that wouldn't exactly help her case.

"All right, I see why one of them can't do it," Florian put in with some asperity, ignoring Ander, "but why not me?"

"You fall down a lot," Tremaine told her.

"So do you!" she protested.

"Not as much as you."

This stymied Florian, who obviously hadn't been keeping track. Tremaine hadn't been keeping track either but Florian didn't know that.

"You can't do this," Ander told her, shifting from no-nonsense-let's-be-reasonable to anger. "I'm not going to let you."

"Sure you are," Tremaine said, in a deliberately maddening tone. She knew Ander couldn't argue worth a damn when he was angry. "We're wasting time." She stood up, turning to climb back down the jumbled steps.

Ander swore, pushing to his feet to block her way. "Dammit, Tremaine, you are not—"

Ilias shouldered in and forced Ander back a step. Annoyed, Ander shoved him in the chest but Ilias didn't move. Ander was a few inches taller but Ilias suddenly seemed to be taking up a lot more room in the narrow passage.

While Tremaine stood there stupidly, wondering who was going to win, Florian stepped forward, saying in a sharp whisper, "Don't fight!" She clouted Ander in the ear and aimed a blow at Ilias. With faster reflexes Ilias ducked, giving her a reproachful glare.

"Dammit, Florian." Ander clutched his ear, glaring at her incredulously. Finding one thing they could agree on, he and Ilias exchanged mutually outraged expressions.

"It was a reflex," Florian explained, still ruffled. "I've got four younger brothers."

"We don't have time to argue." Seizing the opportunity, Tremaine pushed past everybody, leading the way down.

"Wait." Ander caught up with her, carefully not touching her arm. He glanced warily back at Ilias. "Let's talk this over."

Frustrated, Tremaine let him draw her a little further down the crevice, just out of earshot of the others. Ilias watched this suspiciously and Florian put a restraining hand on his shoulder.

It was hard to make out any expression in the dim light, but Ander asked softly, "Are you sure you know what you're doing?"

Tremaine let out an exasperated breath. "Are you?"

"You know what I mean." He shook his head. "I know Gerard knows all about it, so I didn't tell Averi about the asylum, but—"

Tremaine just stared at him. It was so unfair to bring that up right now. "I am not crazy."

"I know that. But—"

"But—" *There's always a "but" when it comes to my sanity.* It was taking a great deal of effort to keep her voice low and not explode. "You want to know the truth? I was kidnapped by an old enemy of my father's and locked up in a mental asylum. My father found out about it and pieces of the people responsible were found floating in the river for a month. Only the Prefecture never could figure out how many people it was, because there were more right parts than left. That's an old Valiarde family joke. But it ended up in the society column that Tremaine Valiarde spent a week in a nuthouse and that's all the family enemies really wanted anyway, though they didn't expect to have to give their lives for it. That's the story of Tremaine and the asylum."

Ander stared at her. He shook his head, caught somewhere between fascination and shock. "If that's true—I thought your father was—"

"I'll tell you what he was later." Tremaine gestured helplessly. She hadn't meant to get into this just at the moment. "If it's not true, so what? I used to be crazy. You used to be a playboy that everybody thought would run as far from the war as possible, and you didn't. You ran toward it. So why can't I?"

"All right, all right." Ander looked away, shaking his head. "Your new friend doesn't need to protect you from me."

She knew he didn't mean Florian. "Why don't you convince him of that?" She motioned for the others to come on and started back down the crevice herself.

Behind her, Ander muttered under his breath, "Who put you in charge?"

Tremaine was pretty certain it was a rhetorical question.

Yes, I know the way. Yes, I know what to do. Now go on, go, shoo." Tremaine and Ilias were crouched down in the shadowy lower passage, near where the ground still rippled with the digging creature's efforts. Ander and Florian had already gone to take their positions for the ambush.

Ilias hesitated, watching her closely, obviously worried. She realized he might be thinking about her little moment above the chasm and felt her cheeks redden. "I'll be fine," she said emphatically, making go-away gestures again. He sighed, squeezed her shoulder and stood, vanishing in the shadows of the passage.

Tremaine let out her breath and rubbed her face. Besides making sense logistically, it was just better for her to do this. Maybe she was getting some odd idea that risking her life was making her value it more. *Worry about it later,* she told herself.

When she thought Ilias had had enough time to get into position, she got to her feet and cautiously eased up on the spot of rippling ground, gripping a rock. *I can't believe they're going along with this,* she thought, both baffled and terrified by the phenomenon. *Even Ander. He should know better than to listen to me.* She swallowed in a dry throat, braced herself to run, and tossed the rock.

Whatever it was, it exploded out of the ground with a roar. Tremaine bolted back up the passage.

She tore down the narrow alley between the stone walls that Ilias had shown her. She hadn't thought then how the thing would follow her through it; there was only a few feet of clearance between the looming walls and the creature had to be much wider than that. She looked back.

She had imagined something like a bear. This thing was large and dark and didn't seem to have a head at all. It had turned sideways to follow her through the narrow passage and it towered over her, its lower part tearing through the dirt and gravel and sending a plume high in the air above it. Tremaine ran faster.

The rock fell away and she bolted between two pillars and across open ground, still casting frantic looks back. She slammed into something that staggered back a step and grabbed her arm. Looking up she saw the pale startled face of a Gardier. He stared past her, his eyes going wide with horror. He slung her away from him, bringing up his rifle.

Tremaine fell, skinning her elbow on the gravelly ground, seeing the other Gardier in the open area turning, jumping to their feet, yelling in alarm. Gerard stared at her incredulously, shouting her name. She looked back and saw the thing looming up, the electric lamplight revealing something like the little round squidlike creatures that washed up on the beaches at Chaire, with hundreds of small white tentacles bristling along its underside. Except that it was a good ten feet tall and nearly that broad and a mouth filled with concentric rows of sharp teeth leered out of its underside.

The Gardier managed to get off one shot before the thing fell atop him.

The other rifleman pounded across the camp, sliding to a halt to fire into the rippling dark surface of the creature's hide. Another man dragged out his sidearm and fired, but it moved swiftly toward him, rearing up again.

Tremaine recalled the rest of the plan and pushed to her feet, stumbling for the nearest lamp. Someone shouted at her as she shoved it off its rock base. It smashed and that half of the camp plunged into darkness. She turned to see Ilias leap down out of the rocks and land on one of the Gardier. Tremaine ran for the other lamp.

Another man grabbed her arm but Ander tackled him from behind. Tremaine tore free and saw Florian smash the other lamp. She turned to see the leader shouting angrily and lifting his pistol but Gerard rammed into him with his shoulder, sending the man staggering before he could shoot. The other Gardier clubbed Gerard down just before Ilias reached him, tackling him around the waist. They fell over the rock where the last lamp stood and it crashed to the ground and went out. In the sudden darkness Tremaine halted, confused. She heard Gerard shout a warning.

Tremaine started toward his voice but as her eyes adjusted she saw Gerard drop like a dead man, collapsing onto the stone floor. The Gardier leader was just a few steps away from him but she hadn't heard a shot. *Dammit, he's a sorcerer,* she thought frantically. She looked around, hoping someone had dropped a pistol. The Gardier leader was a sorcerer and they were all dead.

The leader turned to her and in the darkness she saw him lift his hand in a ritual gesture. Then Ilias leapt on him from behind, one strong arm wrapping around the man's neck as his knife came up to his throat.

Tremaine winced away from the dark wash of blood and saw two shadowy figures on the ground, Ander still struggling with his Gardier. Florian hovered over them with a rock, waiting for a chance. Ander rolled suddenly, bringing the man up on top of him, and Florian swung with frantic strength. The Gardier went limp and Tremaine swore in relief. She looked for the digging creature, realizing she couldn't hear it anymore but in the shadows she couldn't tell if it was still here or not.

"Stop where you are!"

Tremaine stumbled to a halt automatically, staring at the two Gardier who had suddenly appeared out of the rocks, not six paces in front of her. Their lamp blinded her and she winced away. She didn't dare look back at the others; Ander and Florian were too far away to do anything and in another moment the Gardier would shine their lamp on Ilias, crouched over the bloody corpse of the leader. The first Gardier's pistol was just now moving to point at her and Tremaine realized she shouldn't have stopped, she should have kept moving, that she could have thrown herself at him and given Ilias the chance to jump him or Ander time to find one of the discarded weapons. If the man shot her now, she would fall where she stood, useless.

"Put up your hands!" he snapped roughly, his eyes moving nervously from her to the shadows behind her. "Now!" She heard the odd tone of the translator in his voice and saw he had one hand against his chest.

Paralyzed with indecision, Tremaine saw a shape move in the shadows behind him and realized it was another person, someone trying to edge up on the two men from behind. It had to be Ander or Ilias, though she could have sworn both were behind her and unable to circle around behind the newly arrived Gardier. Whichever one it was, he couldn't do anything while she was in the line of fire. "We're just lost here, we're shipwrecked," Tremaine said and thought, *Now, before they have a chance to think.* She lifted her hands, starting forward. "You have to help us," she said, her voice coming out high and shaky and hysterical. "We're going to die here!" *Try for pathetic, not crazy,* she reminded herself. Crazy meant dangerous. If he shot her, this would still work but she had to be close.

The lamp showed her the Gardier was young, his round face under the tightly fitting cap lacking definition, any clues to character. He looked startled and wary and confused. The man with him held another set of aetherglasses, his pistol still holstered. He was looking past her, squinting to see into the darkness, fumbling to shove the lenses back in their case and reach for his weapon.

The one facing Tremaine tried to say something that began with "Stop—" but she talked over his words without any idea of what she said. She could have been reciting the alphabet for all she knew. She wrung her hands, lifted them to her hair, making herself shake. It wasn't hard. One more step and he started to lift the gun, shouting, and she faked a stumble and fell on him. He tried to catch her and was almost as surprised as she was when she grabbed the revolver barrel and twisted it down. The report as it went off was shattering, stunning her, and she didn't see the punch that came at her jaw.

Tremaine was lying on the muddy ground blinking up dazedly before she realized she hadn't been shot. She rolled over, her ears ringing. The lamp was on the ground now, its light showing her both Gardier sprawled not far away. And there was a dark figure standing over them.

Tremaine struggled to sit up, then saw he was dressed in faded dirty clothes and had patches of mud on his face and arms. He also had a sword, a big one with a broad flat blade and a curved horn handle. A moment later Ilias flung himself on him, staggering him back a few steps. Tremaine stared, confused, then saw it was a wildly exuberant greeting, not an attack. That was probably for the best; Ilias was almost a head shorter than the other man. Watching them hug and pound each other on the shoulders, she realized this had to be the missing friend their difficulties had kept Ilias from searching for. *At least I don't have to feel guilty about that anymore,* she thought in relief. Ilias was apparently filling his friend in on what had happened, in detail and with excited gestures.

Tremaine took a deep breath, realizing she was trembling. *We did it.* It was hard to believe. And her jaw hurt. A lot. "Ow. Ow, ow, ow." She touched it gingerly. *Why do they always have to hit me in the face?* Then Ilias was pulling her to her feet, turning her head gently to see the injury.

"Tremaine?" Florian called sharply.

"Yes," she answered vaguely, dizzy and swaying a bit. His friend loomed over both of them, touching her arm lightly. She looked up at him blankly and he smiled down at her. She realized she had been imagining Ilias's people to all be about his size; this man was bigger and physically more intimidating. It was hard to see much detail in this light, but his hair was darker and less wild and he had a few extra braids.

Apparently satisfied the wound wasn't lethal, Ilias released her to poke his friend in the chest in a proprietary manner and say, "Giliead."

"Hello," Tremaine managed. He was taller even than Gerard. *Gerard.*

Tremaine pulled away and headed into the shadows where she could vaguely see Florian. Light blossomed as Ander managed to get their torch lit and she saw Gerard still lay on the ground, Florian busy untying his hands. Ander eyed Giliead narrowly and asked, "Not that I'm ungrateful for the help, but who the hell is that? Another friend of yours?"

"Right, I've got them stashed all over the place." Tremaine crouched next to Florian, too worried about Gerard to explain further. Between them they managed to roll him over. "Is he all right?" she demanded, too flustered to check for herself. She didn't want to look for a pulse and not find one, she just wanted someone to tell her and get it over with. Ander jammed the torch between two rocks and she saw Gerard didn't seem wounded, except for the dried blood around the cut on the temple he had gotten in the boat wreck.

"I think so, he's breathing. They used some kind of spell on him," Florian said, glancing worriedly at her. She was trembling too but didn't seem to notice. "The survivors of the attack on Duncanny reported that something similar happened to the sorcerers there." Ilias and his friend followed Tremaine over and Florian's eyes widened as she looked up, taking in Giliead's appearance at close range. He had sheathed the sword in a scabbard hung across his back, but he still looked intimidating.

"That's right, they were struck with spells that caused unconsciousness," Ander said, then added, sounding exasperated, "A little forewarning might have been nice."

"What?" Tremaine looked up, realizing he meant Giliead. "We knew Ilias was looking for someone. We couldn't really discuss it in depth or anything."

Ilias dropped to his knees beside Tremaine, speaking

and pointing urgently toward the dead Gardier. She nodded, pushing her hair back in distraction and trying to get her brain started again. At least the digging creature had disappeared, leaving a broad trail of dark blood or ichor and three badly mangled Gardier. *I vote somebody else make all the decisions now,* she thought, but pushed to her feet and said, "Yes, the noise, there'll be more of them. We need to get out of here."

Ander took one last uneasy look at Giliead, nodded sharply and turned back toward the rocks. "I'll get our supplies."

Tremaine went to where the leader lay sprawled. The small wireless box crackled at her, barking a command in the Gardier language. It was different from any wireless she had ever seen before, with odd-sized dials and unintelligible symbols printed on the gray case. She absently pushed it off the rock, smashing it with a satisfying crunch.

She found the sphere where it had rolled into a hollow in the dirt. It clicked at her when she picked it up and she brushed the dirt off, saying, "I'm glad to see you, too."

She looked up to see Ilias watching her dubiously, one brow lifted. She considered trying to explain the sphere by gesture, but since she would have been hard-pressed to explain it in words, disregarded the notion. "This is ours," she explained, tapping the sphere, then herself in the chest. "The Gardier stole it."

He nodded understanding. She looked down at the leader and saw it was the man who had first captured them, the one with the burns on his neck. *Well, you should have stayed back at the base with Gervas.* A translator medallion lay on his chest and she picked it delicately out of the blood, then jerked it to break the chain. The man still had three of those devices on his belt, the intriguing little metal boxes with triggers. One was in his hand. She leaned closer, wondering if she should take them too. The sphere's gears started to spin as it drew near the devices and it clicked anxiously. Tremaine shifted the sphere to the other arm, pried the box from the dead man's hand and unsnapped the others from his belt, stuffing them into her pockets.

Gerard's belongings, his notebook, aether-glasses and spectacles, a pocketknife and her compass lay on the rock where the wireless had stood and she hastily scooped them up as well. Florian stepped up with the sling, helping her tuck the sphere back into it. "You got his translator?" she asked.

Tremaine shouldered the sphere and found the translator medallion in her pocket. She wiped the blood off on her coat before handing it to Florian.

"Can we make it work?" the other girl wondered. Holding it, she turned to Ilias, who was watching her quizzically. "Do you understand me now?"

He lifted a brow and threw the equally puzzled Giliead a "they act like this occasionally and I have no idea why" look.

Florian grimaced, studying the disk. "Guess not. Maybe it only works for Rienish. Or maybe there's a way to activate it—" She tapped it thoughtfully on a rock.

"I don't think that's going to work," Tremaine told her, distracted. She lifted one of the Gardier's lamps, but it jangled with broken glass, useless, and she dropped it again. "The Gardier are going to be able to find the sphere with those glasses—"

Florian looked up. "If we get a chance, we could put it in water. That would block any etheric vibrations."

Ander scrambled down out of the rocks with their satchel slung over his shoulder. He paused to pick up one of the fallen rifles, then turned and almost ran into Giliead. The big man stood with his hands planted on his hips, his expression forbidding.

Ander eyed him aggressively, then tried to go around him. Giliead shifted slightly to block him. Ander stepped back. "Any idea what he wants?" he said, still watching him carefully.

Ilias stood near Tremaine, surveying the scene with a thoughtful expression but no hostility. Tremaine looked at Ilias inquiringly. He glanced around, found one of the fallen pistols, poked it with his boot, then looked back at her and said clearly, "No."

"No?"

He looked apologetic but repeated firmly, "No."

"Tremaine?" Ander prompted tensely.

"Leave the rifle. They don't want you to take it," she explained.

Ander swore in annoyance, watching the big man who blocked his path. "Can we explain that it could be useful?"

Tremaine looked at Ilias again. He looked back at her. She told Ander, "It doesn't appear to be a negotiable point." She let out her breath, wincing as her jaw throbbed. "We have a vocabulary of maybe six words, Ander, I don't think we can discuss this."

A sharp report echoed off the rock around them. Everyone flinched. "That was a shot," Florian whispered, "and it was close." Giliead and Ilias exchanged an uneasy glance, but Giliead didn't move.

"We don't have time for this, Ander, just leave the damn gun," Tremaine said urgently.

Ander swore again and dropped the rifle. Giliead stepped back, letting him pass.

"Good." Tremaine looked down at Gerard again. He was still deeply unconscious. Ander and Florian hadn't said how long those other incidents of sorcerous catatonia had lasted and she didn't feel like asking at the moment. She squatted down to grab his arms. "Somebody come help me with—" Giliead took her shoulders and shifted her gently aside, then lifted Gerard's arm and hauled him up over his shoulder. "Never mind."

While Giliead carried the unconscious man, Ilias shouldered his friend's sword. "I wish you'd found mine. That was a good blade," he said regretfully. They had reached the end of the ruined city and found the passage in the wall that curved sharply up through the rock toward the surface shaft. Water trickled continuously down the walls and the torch threw red reflections onto the slick stone.

There were rough-cut steps that made the going somewhat faster, but it would also make it easier for their pursuers.

"I was too busy looking for your dead body," Giliead retorted sharply, earning a nervous glance from Florian.

Giliead had already told Ilias that he gone into the river after him and been swept down it as the flying whale burned, fetching up on the bank in a lower cave. He had had to take the long way back through the upper passages to get down to the harbor cave and search the lower city before he found Ilias's trail signs.

It was too much like what Giliead had gone through on their last trip here, when Ilias had fallen into Ixion's hands. Ilias knew just how hard that search must have been, but there was no point in dwelling on it.

The man Ander walked between them, carrying the torch. He and Tremaine had continued to exchange argumentative-sounding remarks and Ilias had the feeling it was about the wizards' weapons. It was odd; most people were leery of anything that had to do with curses. Wizards could put an evil touch on objects and cause whoever had them to fall ill and die, let alone the danger of handling curse weapons. He put it aside; maybe they had come from so far away that there were no wizards there, which would explain their strange clothes and traveling gear.

Scrambling up a gravelly incline, Ilias heard a wordless shout echo from the cavern. He paused at the top, reaching down to take the torch from Ander as Florian climbed past him. "You hear that?" he asked Giliead. The girls were good company but it was a relief to be able to talk without sign language.

"They're on our trail now," Giliead said grimly. He helped Tremaine with a hand under her arm, then climbed after her.

Ilias gave him a wolfish grin. There was another reason besides grend and burrowers that this surface shaft was dangerous. "They're in for a surprise."

A few more moments of scrambling progress up the passage and they reached the bend Ilias remembered. A big stone pipe, large enough for a couple of men to crawl through abreast, stuck out of the rock at an angle, pointing down the rough steps. It was dripping with slime and had strange white parasitic vines growing along it. The end was closed off with a heavy iron cap and there was a lever to release it along the top. Ilias found handholds in the slippery rock and pulled himself up, saying over his shoulder, "Go, go, I'll take care of it."

Giliead managed to get the girls to move past but Ander shoved the torch at Tremaine and climbed up onto the rocks. Ilias grabbed the lever, glancing back to make sure the others were clear, then tried to swing it over. It creaked but barely shifted. He swore, bracing his feet on the mossy stone, and threw all his weight into it. Ander leaned in to help and Ilias shifted position so he could pull while the other man pushed.

Ixion had used this ancient waterflow so he could periodically drown the burrowers when they got too numerous. The valve that controlled the flow hadn't been opened since Ixion had used it to trap Ilias inside the cave last year; if some important part of the mechanism was rusted through, they were dead.

The lever gradually began to move, the metal groaning from the effort, and foul-smelling liquid gushed from the pipe. Then white wizard light blazed from the passage below and Ander yelled a warning. Throwing his weight on the lever for all he was worth, Ilias glanced down and got a confused image of figures in brown, and one white face. For a heartbeat he froze and that might have been the end, but Ander was still pushing and the lever gave suddenly, releasing a torrent of foul-smelling water that burst down the passage with the force of an avalanche. The loud bang of a wizard weapon blasted off the rocks and chips of stone rained down on his head. Ilias flinched and Ander grabbed his arm and they both leapt off the pipe.

The fluid gushing down the tunnel forced the wizards back, but it wouldn't last forever. Ander made a relieved comment and turned back up the passage, following the wavering light of the torch to where the others waited. Ilias had to stand there a moment and get control of himself. *It was your imagination,* he thought. *It couldn't have been him. Gil cut the bastard's head off and no wizard comes back from that.*

"Ilias," Giliead called from above, his voice barely audible over the growing roar of the pipe. "What's wrong?"

"Nothing," he said hurriedly, climbing up toward him. "I'll tell you later."

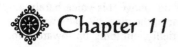 **Chapter 11**

Tremaine's jaw throbbed and she was so tired she was stumbling. She followed Ilias with Florian and Ander behind her and Giliead bringing up the rear, carrying the still unconscious Gerard. Ilias and his friend would call comments or questions to each other occasionally, but Tremaine, Florian and Ander were too occupied with trying to keep up to talk much.

Tremaine scrambled over a rock wedged across the way and looked up to find herself facing a dead end. It was a good-sized chamber, a relief after the narrowness of the last passage, and the walls reached up to the open air only twenty feet above. It was a shock to see the soft gray daylight framed by dark leaves and vines clustered along the edge of the shaft. *It's day again*, she thought blankly, not sure how long they had been down here.

"That's a relief," Florian said, sounding heartfelt as she stumbled to a halt.

"I didn't think I was nervous of enclosed spaces until I came here," Ander agreed. He shifted the strap of their satchel on his shoulder and studied the open air above. "Do we know where we're going?"

"Away from here?" Tremaine suggested. At the moment she just didn't care.

Ilias and Giliead held a quick consultation in which they seemed to hold opposite opinions. Ilias won and started to climb, using the thick vines and chinks in the rough stone face, while Giliead watched with a disgruntled expression.

Ander grabbed a vine to follow but Giliead motioned for

him to stay back. Accustomed to the exploring technique they had used so far, of waiting for Ilias to conduct a reconnaissance every time they entered a new place, Florian caught Ander's sleeve, explaining, "Wait, they want to make sure nothing is up there."

At the top Ilias scrambled over the edge, then appeared again to call back down. With a muttered comment, Giliead started up, Gerard still slung over his shoulder.

They all made it to the top with a minimum of injury and aggravation, crawling out onto a flat rocky surface in the shadow of a fifty-foot cliff. Stunted trees and thick green-black vegetation clung stubbornly to the rock all around. The sky was still heavy with gray clouds and mist drifted among the branches. Tremaine just sat on the ground for a moment, wiping the sweat off her forehead with her sleeve, her shoulders aching and her arms trembling from the strain. She hoped there wasn't much further to go; she knew she had just about reached her limit. Florian didn't look any better and even Ander was worn from his injuries and the long scramble through the cave passages.

Nearby was a canal like the one they had seen at the entrance. The opposite side was bordered by a high wall of more long black stones. Beyond it were wind-twisted trees, smothered with choking vines.

Standing up, Tremaine discovered that the foul odor of the vines they had climbed had transferred itself to any skin and clothing coming in contact with their sickly green surfaces. She groaned, wiping her hands on her muddy jacket. Ander noticed and wiped his own hands, commenting, "Everything on this island smells bad."

They couldn't afford a rest stop. The Gardier had been temporarily blocked by the water pipe, but Ilias had indicated that the flow wouldn't last forever. As he led the way down to the edge of the canal, Tremaine moved behind Giliead, trying to get a look at Gerard. Giliead obligingly stopped so she could check the unconscious man. Peering past her, Florian asked, "Is he any better? Can you tell?"

Tremaine brushed Gerard's hair out of his face and carefully lifted one eyelid. He was still deeply unconscious. "No," she said, then clarified hastily, "I mean, 'no, I can't tell.'" She patted Giliead on the back. "Thanks, we can go now."

He glanced over his shoulder to see what she meant, then moved on. She had noticed he seemed more reticent than Ilias, though she had the feeling he was just shyer with strangers than his friend. Ilias was the more animated of the pair, making broader gestures, and it was easier for her to understand what he was trying to say.

In the gray daylight she could see Giliead was not only built on a bigger scale, his skin had a dark olive tone under the tan, though that might be ground-in dirt. About the only physical resemblance between the two men was that they both had kind eyes. He was dressed like Ilias in mud-spattered cloth and leather though there was enough of his shirt left to tell it had been dark green. He wore earrings too, but didn't have the silver mark on his face. She frowned, noticing he had red streaks on his upper arm and the tattered sleeve of his leather jerkin looked charred. That, and the possibly duralumin debris Ilias had had in his wound, meant they both must have been nearby during the explosion in the Gardier hangar. She shook her head, making a mental note to see what Florian and Ander thought later.

Ilias picked a path for them along the side of the canal. The surface was thick with green scum and weeds and it smelled worse than the vines. After only a few yards the walls rose up on either side, covered with lichens and small plants growing determinedly in every niche, and they had to pick their way along the edge. Gripping the rock as best she could for balance, Tremaine looked at the scummy surface and winced. "I might as well go in headfirst now and get it over with."

From behind her, Ander said, "Don't be such a pessimist. You've been wonderful so far."

Tremaine glanced back to give him a weak smile, uncomfortable with the praise. Mostly because she didn't believe that it was particularly true or that Ander meant it as anything other than an attempt to assuage her feelings.

He added regretfully, "I just wish we'd been able to collect some more information."

"Maybe we still can," Florian put in. She nodded to Ilias and Giliead. "If this place has been a Gardier base for any length of time, then their people might know all about them."

Ander conceded that reluctantly. "We'll have to learn their language before we can get any facts out of them. I was hoping for something faster."

Because we don't know how much time we have left at home, Tremaine finished the unspoken thought. She sighed. Daring escapes aside, they weren't exactly doing a great job at assisting the attack. A random thought occurred and she asked, "If that Gardier was a sorcerer, why didn't he do something about the burns?"

"That is odd." Florian frowned thoughtfully.

Ander asked, "What are you talking about?"

"The leader of that patrol, the one who put the spell on Gerard," Tremaine explained, looking back at him. "He had recent burns on his face. Why didn't he heal himself?"

Ander stared into the distance, his brow creased. "Good question," he said finally.

Ilias crawled up the embankment and over the roots of the gnarled dead tree. The clouds were low and heavy and mist rose off the sea, the view of the water stretching out around the headlands obscured by the roiling white vapors. The thicker than usual mist would be an advantage in leaving the island unnoticed. If the *Swift* was still there. Ilias was too relieved at finding Giliead alive to worry much; if Halian had followed their plan and left, it just meant a few more days of hiding out from the wizards while they built a boat to sail to the mainland.

Ilias reached the bluff and pushed himself up to look over the tufts of grass clinging to the edge. Below, the mist hung in shroudlike shreds and streamers. Waves lapped on the tumbled black rocks that protected the cove, and in the shadow of the bluff, the *Swift* lay at anchor. Ilias let out his breath in relief.

The *Swift* wasn't the biggest ship ever to leave Cineth's harbor but at the moment she was the most beautiful. She was high in the stern with a fore and aft rig and the bow had a stylized eye painted on it so she could always find her way home. Her purple sails were furled and he couldn't see any movement on the deck. Getting to his feet, Ilias picked up a loose stone and threw it at the ship.

It bounced off the roof of the small aft cabin. For a heart-beat the ship was silent, then Arites exploded out of cover behind the water barrels like a flushed quail, holding a bow. Ilias waved and grinned while Arites slowly lowered the weapon, staring, then waved wildly back.

Halian and the rest of the crew appeared from conceal-ment belowdeck. Ilias signaled for them to drop the gig, waited for Halian's acknowledging wave, then climbed back down the embankment to where the others were waiting.

They crouched among the rocks at the base of rise, near the edge of the canal. All their new friends jumped in alarm when Ilias slid through the brush. Giliead, who would have heard and recognized his footsteps, looked up in mild inquiry.

"Halian's sending the gig," Ilias told him.

"Good." Giliead nodded, relieved. "Let's get them down there."

As Giliead got to his feet, Ilias leaned down to look over Tremaine's shoulder at the unconscious man. "He's still breathing strong, that's something. Maybe it'll wear off on its own."

"Maybe." Giliead spared the man a concerned glance. "I've never seen a sleeping curse before." His hands on his hips, he looked around blankly, as if wondering how best to move the others along.

Ilias tapped Tremaine on the shoulder and pointed toward the cleft in the rocks that led down the rise to the beach. She blinked and looked up at him, so weary she could hardly keep her eyes open. "It's not far," he promised sympathetically, helping her to her feet. The trip down the canal hadn't been easy either; everyone but Giliead had fallen in at least once.

Ilias watched Tremaine's face as they emerged from the rocks and was rewarded by seeing her perk up at the sight of the ship. The mist curled up around the *Swift*'s painted hull and Arites and Elanin were just lowering the gig. Halian was leaning over the rail and Ilias waved at him.

All the travelers exclaimed over the *Swift* as if they had never seen anything like her before. Elanin jumped over the side to swim the gig out to them and they got the unconscious man, Giliead's sword and the strangers' gear into it. Then Ilias swam out to the *Swift* and climbed the net Gyan threw over the side. Hanging on with one hand, he slung his wet hair out of his eyes and looked back. On the beach, Giliead tied the gig's rope to his waist so he could tow it while the others paddled toward the ship.

"Who are they?" Gyan leaned over the rail to ask. He was getting on in years and girth for a sailor, but he had been with Halian since the early days fighting the Chaeans.

"Shipwrecked travelers," Ilias said as Florian reached him. He caught her arm and steadied her as she climbed the net, bracing himself to catch her if she fell. "They don't speak a word of Syrnaic or anything else recognizable so we don't know where they come from."

Tremaine was next and she was obviously having trouble. Ilias caught her around the waist and lifted her until the others waiting above could help her over the rail. "How many women have you got on this island?" Gyan asked, his brows quirking.

"Just the two so far," Ilias told him with a grin. "Want me to ask if they have a sister for you?" He kept an eye on Ander as he climbed, but knew better than to offer the stubborn young man a hand. Then Giliead arrived with the gig.

They used the net to haul the unconscious man up with a little difficulty and Gyan and Arites carried him back to the aft cabin, the women and Ander following. Ilias and Giliead got the gig back aboard as the rest of the crew scrambled down to unship the oars.

As they finished tying it off, Halian arrived, slapping Giliead on the back and catching Ilias around the shoulders in a one-armed hug. "I didn't think I'd see you two again," he said, grinning and ruffling Ilias's hair.

"I didn't think you'd see us again either," Ilias told him honestly. Halian looked so relieved, as if a huge weight had been lifted off his shoulders. Ilias hated to think that the news he and Giliead brought was going to put that weight right back, with more besides.

Giliead smiled at Halian, clapping a hand on his shoulder, but his eyes were shadowed. "We need to talk as soon as we're under way."

Halian's face stilled. He knew Giliead well enough to read the look in his eyes. "All right. As soon as we leave the mist, I'll give Gyan the helm." He nodded to Giliead and gave Ilias another affectionate shake as he released him.

Halian gave the order to haul up the sleeping stones; released from her mooring, the *Swift* began to drift. As the rest of the crew unshipped the oars, Ilias stayed on deck, leaning on the rail next to Giliead as the ship plowed through the mist. Gyan was in the bow, watching for rocks and signaling back to Halian at the tiller. No flying whales appeared out of the clouds to menace them and after a time he let himself relax a little. The familiar thump and splash as the oars stroked the water made him feel like they were home already. To his relief the brief swim had washed off much of the remaining mud and canal ooze; it was like washing off the caves with their distorted creatures and lingering memories. He glanced at Giliead to say something to that effect and saw the grim expression on his friend's face. "It'll be all right," he said instead, trying to sound certain.

Giliead cocked a brow at him and smiled faintly, but didn't comment.

They watched until the *Swift* left the unnatural mist and the wind came up. Halian gave the order to ship oars and raise sail and Ilias headed back toward the aft cabin, leaning in the doorway. The girls had taken off their wet boots and Florian was sitting on the bunk next to the unconscious man.

Dyani appeared from below with a bucket of water and

an armload of blankets. She deposited the bucket pointedly next to Ilias with the succinct comment, "You stink."

Dyani was another fosterling like Ilias. Her father had been a navigator for Halian, killed during the battle with the Eastern Islands Wizard. Halian had brought her home knowing Karima would love having another girl to raise, but shortly after that, Ixion's curse had made it too dangerous for Dyani to live in the house. She had gone to live with Gyan down in the village and now she wanted nothing more than to be a ship's captain and go venturing out past the Salamin Sea.

Ilias lay in wait at the doorway while Dyani stepped in to give the blankets to Florian. With a shy smile she turned to leave and as she passed him he caught her in a big hug, managing to transfer much of the remaining mud dripping from him to her shirt and pants during the brief struggle. She clouted him in the ear and escaped, laughing and making disgusted noises. "Oh come on," he called after her, "you've been at sea for days, you don't smell like flowers either."

He turned back in time to see Tremaine and Florian exchanging an enigmatic look. Then Tremaine started to wave agitatedly, digging in her bag.

Giliead passed Dyani, saying dryly, "We've got guests, don't you think you could clean up a little?"

Ilias watched Tremaine take the metal ball out of her pack. She gestured urgently, pointing to the bucket of water. With a shrug, he handed it to her. She shoved the metal ball into it, then pushed her already sodden jacket down on it, apparently to keep it from floating to the top. Then she took some other metal boxes from her pockets and dropped those in too. "Right," he muttered, scratching his head.

Giliead watched this performance with a frown, puzzled. "What's that?"

"Don't know." Ilias shrugged. "They have a lot of strange things, like for lighting fires and keeping food good. Maybe that's just something that . . ."—he gestured vaguely—". . . needs to be wet." He asked Tremaine hopefully, "That should do it?"

She and Florian talked for a moment, then Florian dug a crystal out of her pocket and handed it over. Tremaine shoved that under the jacket in the bucket too.

Giliead shook his head, still baffled. "But . . . what is it?"

"I don't know." Ilias shrugged matter-of-factly. Metal things that needed to be kept in water were a new one on him. "We're going to have to learn their language so we can ask them."

Florian carefully covered the unconscious Gerard with a blanket, then passed the others out to Tremaine and Ander. Tremaine promptly wrapped herself up in hers with an expression of relief, settling on the floor next to the bucket. Ander sat back in the corner, still watching them warily.

Ilias caught Giliead's eye and inclined his chin slightly toward the young man. "Maybe he thinks we're raiders."

"Maybe." Giliead smiled faintly, though he still looked thoughtful. "I wish we knew where they came from."

"Do you know how long they were on the island? Their ship could have gone aground in the storm yesterday." Halian stepped into the cabin, leaning against the doorway. "We were almost swamped. It was definitely wizard-stirred."

"Huh. Maybe they knew you were out here." Giliead tapped his fingers on his belt.

Halian looked at the travelers, giving the two women a reassuring smile. "We're taking them home?" he asked Giliead.

"Where else?"

"What about the curse?" Halian frowned. "It isn't right, since we can't explain the danger and give them a choice."

Ilias had been wondering that himself. Giliead hesitated, then shook his head. "They're only staying until they can travel. It should be all right. And," he added with a trace of bitterness, "their friend's been cursed; no one else would take them in."

Halian's mouth twisted ruefully but he didn't deny it. "Well, your mother will certainly appreciate the company." He eyed Giliead for a moment. "You said 'wizards.' So there was more than one?" He read Giliead's expression and his face went still. "What did you find?"

Giliead exchanged an uncomfortable glance with Ilias. "Nothing good," he said. He nodded out toward the deck where they could see Barias checking the set of the ropes. "Shut the door."

"Nothing good" is putting it mildly, Ilias thought as Giliead began to tell Halian all they had seen, the wizards and their flying whales and weapons. He sat on the floor at the foot of the bunk, next to Tremaine and her bucket, resting his aching shoulders against the wall. Halian's face grew ashen as he heard the story.

Halian said finally, "They have to be getting ready to attack Cineth, and maybe the whole Syrnai. That's the only reason to take the island." He shook his head. "Flying whales. That explains a lot about the ships that have gone missing and the attacks on the villages along the coast. You know, in that storm that nearly swamped us, I thought I saw something in the sky, but I put it down to imagination." He looked up, his expression drawn in concern. "How many do they have?"

"One less than they had before. We saw docks for at least three." Giliead pulled the folded maps out from under his shirt, leaning forward to spread them on the cabin floor.

Ilias shifted forward to help him. "This paper has wax on it or something. It all went into the river but the ink only smeared a little, see?"

Exhausted and with nothing to keep them awake but a conversation they couldn't understand, the three travelers had started to doze off. But as they spread out the maps, Ander made a startled exclamation and scooted forward to look. Florian almost fell off the bunk and Tremaine sat up, half asleep and blinking.

Brows quirking, Halian pushed one of the maps over to Ander. "Maybe they can make some kind of sense of this. Is that writing?"

"It has to be." Giliead leaned forward, tracing a line.

"Knowing where they mean to attack first would be nice." Ilias propped his chin in his hand. "At least we know those flying whales burn like oilpaper." He lifted his brows at Giliead, who nodded, frowning thoughtfully.

Halian watched them both. "You're thinking Fireliquid?"

"We've got maybe twenty pots left at home from the last time," Giliead said, leaning back against the wall. His mouth twisted ruefully. "I hate that stuff."

Ilias had to agree. They had used it on the ships Ixion had sent against the Andrien village and Cineth. But those ships had been packed with his curse-spawned creatures, not people. Not even wizards.

"Everybody hates it, everybody with any feeling," Halian told him gravely. "But we won't have a choice."

Giliead looked at Ander, who was avidly studying the foreign map while the two women watched with interest. "I know."

Tremaine shifted to see the map, feeling her wet clothes squish unpleasantly. Ilias and Giliead were still dripping dirty water onto the deck but they had lost much of their mud covering. The man they called Halian was older, with a weather-beaten face and cropped graying hair. He was big like Giliead and dressed in a dark brown shirt, pants trimmed with braided leather, and stout leather boots. The fabric seemed finely woven and it was interesting to see how the native clothing looked when it hadn't been burned, drenched and stained with stinking mud.

"What is it?" Tremaine asked Ander, who was studying the maps as if they held Ile-Rien's salvation. "You can't read those, can you?"

"No, but these are routes, air routes." Ander was breathing hard from excitement. He twisted the map around, leaning down over it and tracing one of the dotted lines. "This shows . . . Here." He turned it so Tremaine and Florian could see. "These here, these have got to be Gardier airship bases, like the island. And look at this! It's much bigger than the others, it's obviously some kind of main hub." He frowned, pulling the other map forward. "I don't understand what these other lines are, not longitude. . . ."

His eyes widened and he whistled softly. "These lines, superimposed here, that's the western coastline of Ile-Rien, Chaire, Port Erafin, Port Rel. And this is the island, and the mainland—"

Florian leaned forward, fascinated. "You mean it's a map of both worlds, together?"

"Yes, this one superimposed over Ile-Rien. I just wish I could figure out what these other symbols and lines are."

Florian tugged the larger map out of the pile, looking it over intently. "Is the island on this one, in relation to the other Gardier bases?"

Ander studied it for a long moment, then frowned, shaking his head. He turned the map around again. "No, this doesn't show any island bases that match this one, or anyplace else I recognize." He sat back with a grimace. "Damn."

Tremaine didn't know if she was just tired or getting stupid. "Now what?"

"Our only point of reference for this world is the island and our coastline," Florian explained, sitting back crosslegged against the wall with a glum expression. "If it's not on the big map, then we don't know where those other bases are."

Ander nodded, still thoughtfully tracing air routes. "You said that Gervas joker called these people 'natives,' as if the Gardier came from somewhere else? This map might show their home continent."

"Oh." Tremaine sighed. She caught Giliead's eye, who was watching them all intently, and shrugged. "I think I'm going to take a nap," she told the others.

L ater Tremaine woke with no idea where she was. She lay on a hard surface that swooped and dived with relentless regularity and her nose was full of the odor of wet wool. *The Pilot Boat . . . No, it sank.* She pushed herself up, shoving lank hair out of her eyes and looking around. *Oh, right.* They were in the little cabin on the boat with purple sails. She had fallen asleep on the deck not long after Ilias, Giliead and Halian had finished their conference. Next to her Florian had curled up around their satchel, sound asleep. Ander was against the wall, an arm flung over his eyes. Gerard still lay unconscious in the bunk.

Bright sunlight fell through the open hatch. She smoothed out the beautifully woven blanket she had wadded up as a pillow. The wool was dyed with a multitude of shades of blue and green, forming patterns that made her think of sea foam and ocean deeps.

Tremaine climbed to her feet, one hand on the wall to steady herself, and looked outside. They had left the mist behind and the sky was deep blue, a few fleecy clouds overhead, the wind clean and warm. She took a deep breath and her head didn't feel quite so foggy anymore. The crew moved around the deck messing with the ropes and doing the other incomprehensible things one did on sailing boats.

Now that she was awake enough to notice, she saw they were all dressed in pants and loose open shirts, the leather or cloth dyed in soft colors, and many wore their hair long or pulled back into braids. Some of them were shorter and light-haired like Ilias and others were tall with dark complexions like Giliead and Halian, while most seemed to be a combination of both physical types. She saw the girl who had brought the blankets earlier— had Ilias called her Dyani?—climbing the rigging. She was shorter than Tremaine and slight, with dark brown hair tied back in a loose ponytail. Past the railing Tremaine saw land ahead and she stepped outside for a better look.

The water was incredibly blue and clear. A coastline of low green hills and forest was near and the boat seemed to be heading toward a small town or village spread out on the terraced slopes above a white crescent of beach. There were little houses of wood or stone with tiled roofs. Wooden racks held large fishing nets hung up to dry and smaller boats, some without sailing rigs, were drawn up on the beach. She could see people moving among the houses

and on the stone breakwater that extended out into the bay.
It was a vast improvement over the island.

Suddenly, not far away, a huge fish leapt into the air. It
was bright yellow with black stripes and easily the size of
a cow. Impressed, Tremaine eased back from the railing.
*I'm glad I didn't know about those when Gerard and I
were treading water.*

She looked around the deck and saw a platform above
the cabin, where Halian steered by holding on to a big
tiller. Ilias was up there with him, shading his eyes to look
toward the coast.

Tremaine wandered back into the cabin, stepping over
Florian for a closer look at Gerard. He lay on the bunk, his
face pale and gaunt, his breathing shallow but steady. She
had seen the Gardier sorcerer cast the spell. *All he did was
point.* Tremaine's layman's education in the magical arts
had been mostly from a defensive perspective, but she
knew that anyone who cast a spell this powerful with just
a gesture was an accomplished sorcerer. But he hadn't
known the healing spells to cure the burns on his own face.

Wait. He was holding one of those little devices. She remembered taking it out of his hand. *Did he point that at
Gerard?* He must have.

Gerard made a faint sound, startling her out of her
thoughts. Tremaine sat up on her knees to lean over the
bunk. "Gerard?" This was the first sign of life he had
demonstrated since falling under the spell. Wondering if
she had imagined it, she shook his shoulder gently. He
murmured and turned his head. "Finally," she breathed,
reaching to thump Florian on the back.

Florian stirred, shoving hair out of her eyes and looking
around sleepily. "What?"

"I think Gerard's coming around." Impatient, Tremaine
shook him again, less gently, as Florian struggled to sit up.
"Gerard, wake up!"

"Tremaine, please lower your voice," Gerard muttered.
He lifted one hand to press against his temple. "God, my
head's splitting."

"He's awake!" Florian called happily.

Ander started, sitting up. "Gerard?"

Tremaine helped Gerard sit up and he leaned forward, clutching his head. "What— Are we moving?"

"We're on a boat," she told him as Ander came over, standing back against the cabin wall by the bunk.

"Oh." Gerard looked up, blinking owlishly. "What happened?"

"We escaped," Tremaine said, deciding to stick with the short version for the moment. She remembered his spectacles and hastily dug them out of her coat pocket.

"Thank you." Gerard got his spectacles on and looked around at the spare little cabin, the tumbled blankets on the bunk, an uncertain expression on his face. "Where's the sphere?"

"It's right over there," Florian told him, her tone reassuring. "We put it in a bucket of water so the Gardier wouldn't be able to follow it."

"You put it . . ." He rubbed his face, then stared, startled, at something past them.

"Are you all right?" Florian asked anxiously, catching his arm.

"Yes, yes, I'm fine." Gerard shook his head slightly, as if he thought he was seeing things. "Tremaine, who is that?"

Tremaine glanced back to see Ilias standing in the doorway. "Oh, um." She scratched her head. Ilias grinned at her, gesturing to Gerard. She smiled back, nodding. "Yes, he's better."

Giliead leaned in with a question, then his brows lifted in surprise when he saw Gerard awake. He spoke to Ilias, who replied, jerking his head toward them.

She turned back to see Gerard staring at her, baffled. "We ah . . . made contact with another civilization," she explained. It had sounded better when Florian said it.

"I see that." Gerard rubbed his brow, eyeing both men warily. "They're . . . natives of this world?"

"We think so," Florian admitted as the two men stepped back out. "We're still having problems talking to them in that we don't have a clue what language they speak." She nodded toward the doorway. "That was Ilias and Giliead."

"All right, well . . ." Gerard was obviously having trouble keeping up. "Now that introductions are out of the way, where are we going?"

"We don't know," Ander told him grimly. "Somehow, they've got Gardier maps from that base. We have to get those back to the Institute."

"Ander thinks they're kidnapping us," Florian explained to Gerard.

"I didn't say that." Ander glanced at her impatiently. "I said we don't seem to have much choice about where we're going."

Tremaine rolled her eyes. "We're going to that little village."

All three of them stared at her this time. "What village?" Florian asked, startled.

Tremaine gestured vaguely at the cabin door. "The one the boat is pointed at."

"Help me up," Gerard said firmly. Ander and Tremaine helped him stand and they went out on deck.

The warm sun and fresh air seemed to perk everyone up, Tremaine noticed. She went to lean on the rail again, pointing out the village.

"Oh." Florian stood next to her. "It's beautiful."

"Isn't it?" Tremaine nodded. They were close enough now to see the boats on the beach all had painted designs along the hulls, leaping fish or swirls or eyes. The little collection of houses on the terraced slope had carved and painted eaves and even the tumbledown shacks had colored hangings in the windows. Tall trees shaded the dirt pathways between the houses.

Ander took a deep breath. "They're not going to be able to help us."

Tremaine looked sharply at him. He sounded grimly resigned. "How do you know?" she asked.

"That sailing rig, this fishing village. These people are primitives." Ander shook his head regretfully. "The Gardier are going to sweep right through them."

Gerard leaned on the railing and rubbed his eyes. "I'm afraid you're right. We have to find a way to ask them to take us back to the target area. Or perhaps we could—"

An alarmed shout made Tremaine turn. The girl Dyani was standing in the bow, pointing up. At first Tremaine saw nothing, then Florian grabbed her arm. Her eyes found the dark familiar shape against the sky then, growing larger as it dropped toward them. "Oh no," Tremaine groaned. "Not again."

All over the deck the sailors pointed, yelled and scrambled into action. Tremaine saw Giliead tear off in one direction and Ilias in the other.

"Gardier," Ander said grimly.

"They followed us?" Florian asked, dismayed. "How?"

"Where's the sphere?" Gerard demanded.

Tremaine bolted for the cabin, found the bucket and dragged her sodden jacket out. Water sloshed as she pulled out the sphere, disentangling it from the Gardier translator. Remembering the other Gardier devices, she fished for them and pulled out only a handful of broken metal pieces and crystal fragments. There wasn't a single one left intact.

Thinking the devices must have been enspelled to destroy themselves if stolen and cursing Gardier ingenuity, she shoved the medallion in her pocket and scooped up the sphere. It hummed eagerly as she hurried back out on deck.

The boat seemed to leap forward, skimming over the water for the shore. She saw Halian leaning on the tiller up on the steering platform but most of the crew seemed to have vanished, except for two men hauling on the ropes, changing the position of the sails. Realizing the deck was vibrating rhythmically beneath her feet, she held tightly to the sphere and leaned over the rail. Below she saw the oars scooping rapidly at the water, driving the ship straight in toward the beach at a faster pace than she would have believed possible. "What are we doing?"

"The Gardier chose their moment well," Gerard told her, watching the approaching airship narrowly. It was much lower already, the dark predator outlined against the brilliant blue sky. "The ship has to go ashore or it will be dead in the water."

"Why?"

"With that sailing rig, it would take them forever to turn this bucket," Ander clarified. He struck his fist on the railing. "Dammit, if they'd let me bring those firearms—"

"They won't work against an airship." Florian stared at him, uncomprehending. "Even Gardier guns—"

Ander shook his head. "They're going to land and take us alive. There's nothing to stop them."

Tremaine heard a bang and looked wildly around. She knew that noise too well; the airship had just fired its artillery. Florian pointed wordlessly and she saw two of the other big boats pulled up on the beach burst into flame.

A vibration ran through the deck and Tremaine heard a weird hollow booming noise. She thought, *We've been hit,* but realized an instant later it was the oars being shipped.

Ander dragged her back and Gerard grabbed Florian to steady her as the bow struck the sloping sand beneath the waves. Tremaine staggered, the jolt nearly throwing her to the deck despite Ander's support. Wood groaned as the ship shuddered to a halt. More of the crew boiled out from down below, leaping over the sides and landing in the surf. Ilias saw them and motioned wildly, shouting, then vaulted the rail himself.

Gerard began, "We'd better—"

"Jump!" Ander yelled.

Gerard helped Florian over the rail and Ander grabbed for Tremaine again. She wrenched away from him as he reached for her arm. "Go," she told him, hefting the sphere, "I can't risk dropping this."

Ander hesitated, but then swung himself over the side and dropped. Leaning over the railing, Tremaine waited until Gerard had his balance again. She dropped the sphere into his outstretched hands, then clambered over the rail herself.

She landed awkwardly and the next wave knocked her

flat. She dragged herself to her feet, spitting out salt water, and staggered after the others.

Up on the beach, Ander pulled Florian into cover behind a large flat-topped rock and Gerard paused to wait for Tremaine, motioning urgently for her. "I'm coming," she gasped as she waded up onto the beach, her feet slipping on the loose sand. She saw the village's inhabitants scattering in all directions; women grabbed children and hared off into the woods, men ran into the houses and came out with clubs, spears, swords, shields. Tremaine reached Gerard and he pulled her into the shelter of the rocks.

The airship fired again, this time into the ramshackle houses along the beach. They ducked back behind the rock as wood and debris rained down briefly and flames leapt up from the tumbled ruins. *Ander's right, they want us alive,* Tremaine thought as she took the sphere back from Gerard. The Gardier were firing to cause confusion and panic, not to kill people. Not yet.

She saw Ilias and Giliead bolt across the beach, running toward a structure that stood on the flat ground above the high-tide line. It was covered with tarred leather cloth secured by ropes and they started to tear the wrappings off. Men she recognized from the ship's crew ran to help and in moments the coverings fell down to reveal a large wooden apparatus.

"Is that a weapon?" Florian asked hopefully, peering cautiously over the top of the rock.

Tremaine nodded. It looked like some kind of catapult. There was a heavy wooden arm with a long lever to each side and it was strung with twisted skeins of rope. The whole thing was on some sort of revolving base that allowed them to turn it to aim. There was a sturdy rack in front with a thick pad of hay tied to it. As Giliead and the others pulled ropes and wrestled the firing arm into position, Ilias and two other men came out of a nearby shed lugging clay pots. Giliead steadied the sling as Ilias lifted in the first pot and Dyani ran up to stand ready with a torch. Halian stepped behind the apparatus, shading his eyes, then waved for them to move it to the left a little.

"It's an onager," Gerard said in startled realization, as everyone put their shoulders to the platform and forced it to turn. Tremaine heard the grating creak of stiff wooden gears. Gerard squinted up at the airship, a heavy dark shape looming even lower over the beach. "It's low enough, but its wards will protect it."

Tremaine shifted the sphere to her other hand, realizing it was getting hot. Smoke from the burning houses drifted over the beach and a burst of gunfire tore through the buildings above the shoreline. She shook her head, not understanding what Gerard had called the thing. Two men cranked the levers back as others hurried to pile rocks on the platform, apparently to help stabilize the rotating base. Giliead stuffed a rag into the top of the pot and lit it with the torch. "I thought that was a kind of horse."

Gerard shook his head. "No, it's like a catapult, only more—" There was a thunk as the arm slammed forward hard enough to stop a train, releasing the clay jug so fast she could spot it only by the trail of smoke. "Powerful," Gerard finished.

Tremaine held her breath but as the missile neared the airship's side it dissolved abruptly in a burst of white light. There was a shout of dismay from the crew. She saw Ilias and Giliead exchange an anguished look. *It's not fair,* she thought. *It's never fair.* Giliead shook his head grimly but motioned for the others to lift a second pot into the sling.

"They got the range on the first try, that's impressive. But it is a pretty big target," Ander was muttering to himself. "If it wasn't for the damn wards, we'd have a fighting chance."

Gunfire from the airship peppered the beach in response and two men near the catapult went down.

Tremaine swore under her breath. It was the same problem they had back home. If they could just find a way to disarm those wards, then spells, gunfire, artillery, catapults with funny names would all have a real chance against the Gardier. The sphere trembled suddenly and Gerard yelled in pain, jerking back away from the rock and clutching his side. "What is it?" Florian cried. "Are you shot?"

A dull metal clunk made Tremaine look back toward the

catapult. Halian studied the base of the contraption, exchanged a shrug with Giliead, and motioned for the others to keep cranking. "It was the spell," Tremaine guessed, "the spell they use to wreck mechanical things."

"She's right," Gerard assured them hurriedly. He dug in his pocket and pulled out a handful of steaming metal fragments. "The spell destroyed my watch." He sat up on his knees and looked toward the catapult, frowning. "But it missed the intended target."

"Too much wood." Ander swore bitterly. "If it could just get past the wards, we'd have a chance."

The sphere trembled again, more violently. Tremaine looked down to see it sparkling with blue light, spitting and humming as if it had been stuffed with fireworks. *It wants to do something, it wants to do a spell.* "Gerard, help," Tremaine breathed.

He turned toward her, stared down at the sphere in consternation. "What?"

"It's doing a spell. Put your hand on my shoulder."

He grasped her shoulder and she held up the sphere. The light boiled over and shot upward in one great pulse. It crackled through the air like lightning, striking the airship and streaming over it. The light blazed, forming or revealing a network of lines that made a patchwork pattern over the black hull's entire surface.

"It's mapping the wards," Gerard said softly. "It knows the spell, the Gardier warding spell. It can't possibly . . . but it does."

Ander stared from the sphere up to the airship in growing amazement. "How the hell—"

"I just wish it would hurry." Tremaine's hands were starting to burn. Her grip on the sphere faltered and Florian edged up behind her, grabbing her arms to steady her. Tremaine felt the sphere reach out to touch her too. Florian gasped in alarm but didn't let go.

"Try again!" Ander called to the men around the catapult. They were staring at the sphere, at Tremaine, at the light, transfixed in amazement. He pointed urgently at the catapult, trying to make them understand.

God, this would be easier if we could talk to them.
Tremaine felt the sphere surge again and bit her lip, feeling
light-headed. She heard a distant report and felt a vibration
travel down the power connecting the sphere to the wards.
The airship was firing again, the flash of the guns from the
gondola hidden by the maze of blue light. Surely it was too
close to the ground now to risk dropping its bombs, even to
escape.

"Try again!" Gerard shouted, pointing urgently
toward the catapult.

Giliead started, looking around for the next clay pot.
Ilias scrambled to grab it, which galvanized the other men
into motion, cranking the levers and shifting the device to
take account of the airship's lower elevation.

Giliead touched the torch to the clay missile and ducked
out of the way. Halian released the catapult and the arm
slammed forward again. Tremaine felt the sphere release
the spell and the light vanished, an instant before the pot
struck the airship's hull.

Tremaine had expected it to puncture the skin but it
broke across the surface, splashing its contents over the
black hull. The men watching cheered wildly and scrambled to ready another missile.

"It didn't go through," Florian said, not understanding.
"Did the wards stop it?"

The substance was still burning, crawling across the
black surface of the hull like a living creature. "What is
that?" Tremaine demanded. Not pitch, not oil, it burned too
fast, too bright.

"It's naphtha," Ander said, laughing suddenly. He shook
Gerard's shoulder in delight. "It's got to be." He turned to
the catapult crew and shouted, "Give 'em another one!"

The airship's engines buzzed as it tried to turn, heading
back out to sea. It gained altitude but the next missile
struck the underside of the hull. The third fell short, but the
airship tipped suddenly, going nose down as flame leapt
above the surface of the hull. Tremaine couldn't hear the
engines anymore and it was the wind driving the enormous
bulk further out to sea. Fire raced along the length of it,

trailing off the spiny fins as the ship drifted down toward
the water.

"What's naphtha?" Florian asked, looking up at Gerard.

Gerard began, "It's a highly flammable substance composed of—"

Then they were all on the ground, scrambling to get behind the shelter of the rocks as noise, smoke and fire con-
sumed the space the airship occupied. Tremaine cautiously
lifted her head to look and saw the crew around the catapult had hit the sand too, some of them trying to burrow
under it. She saw Ilias had tackled Dyani and pulled her
behind the weapon's base. Giliead was the only one half
sitting up, watching the airship's death throes.

"Must have reached the fuel tanks," Ander said, stumbling to his feet. He wiped grime and sand off his forehead
and grinned.

Tremaine climbed to her feet, shifting the sphere to her
other arm and shading her eyes. Burning debris floating on
the waves sent up columns of smoke. Down by the catapult, people were stirring, warily lifting their heads to look.

Ilias ran up to them, breathing hard. He looked at the
doomed airship again as it drifted down toward the sea, then
back to Tremaine. "How did you do that?" he demanded.

"I don't—" Tremaine stared at him. "What?"

✦ Chapter 12

"I understood you just then, how—" Tremaine halted in confusion. She wasn't speaking Rienish. She shifted the sphere absently to her other arm, nonplussed.

"You're speaking Syrnaic now," Ilias said, as bewildered as she was. "You know our language?"

"No, but I do now." The words were there in her head, in both languages. She knew it like she knew Aderassi and Bisran. She knew it better than she knew Aderassi and Bisran.

"Me too." Equally perplexed, Florian tapped her ear and looked from Tremaine to Ilias. "I'm hearing . . . I mean, I'm speaking . . ."

Ilias looked more upset than baffled. Tremaine felt that she was mostly baffled. She turned to Gerard and Ander for help. They were watching the villagers beating out the fires on the huts just above the beach. "Umm, we've had a development."

"What?" Gerard asked, he and Ander both turning to her just as Giliead and Halian arrived.

The rest of the crew still gathered around the catapult, torn between watching the airship burn as it collapsed into the water and staring at the strangers. Like Ilias, Giliead and Halian seemed more shocked than puzzled. Halian threw a dismayed look at Giliead and demanded, "How did they do that?"

Still a good question, Tremaine thought. "We don't know," she told him. The foreign words were still sorting themselves out in her head.

Wearing the same baffled expression that was beginning to appear on everyone's face, Ander said, "I understood that. How . . ." He looked helplessly at Gerard. "I'm
speaking . . ."

"Syrnaic," Tremaine supplied.

"I know." He turned to her impatiently, then stopped as
he realized what he had said.

Gerard shook his head wonderingly. "I don't . . . Am I
speaking . . . ? My God."

Tremaine decided they couldn't do worse than to start
with the most basic piece of information. She turned back
to Ilias and said, "It's magic. I think. I mean, I know it was
magic, but . . . You see, Gerard's a sorcerer and . . ." She let
the sentence trail, unnerved by the reaction.

Ilias's expression said he badly wanted to unhear what
he had just heard. Giliead's face had gone as still as if she
had struck him. Halian looked at her as if he couldn't understand her, as if she were speaking gibberish again. Ilias
looked up at Giliead in appeal, obviously hoping he would
respond. Seeing an answer wasn't forthcoming, he turned
back to her and said, "But he . . . can't be."

Uh oh, Tremaine thought. She glanced at Gerard, who
had an expression of dawning apprehension that didn't in-
spire confidence. He nodded for her to go on. She asked
Ilias carefully, "Why not?"

Ilias threw another helpless look at Giliead, whose face
had darkened with some strong emotion. Halian was hanging on every word, his brows drawn together in consternation. Ilias took a sharp breath. "Because wizards are evil."

"Oh, that's all we need," Ander muttered, throwing a
worried look at Gerard.

That's not good, Tremaine thought. If the only sorcerers
they had had any experience with were Gardier, they
couldn't have a good opinion of magic. Somebody else
definitely needed to handle diplomatic relations right now
before she messed things up even worse. She leaned over
to Florian. "All right, you talk now because I don't think
I'm doing a very good job."

"All right, I'll try." Florian took a deep breath and

pointed toward the burning remains of the dirigible. "Those wizards are evil. We're not."

Ilias looked at her, aghast. "You're a wizard too?"

Florian hesitated. "No, but I'm studying to be one."

Halian looked a little sick. Ilias covered his eyes for a moment, apparently trying to get a grip on himself.

Trying to help, Tremaine said, "I'm not a wizard."

"Tremaine!" Gerard said sharply.

"Well, I'm not!" she protested, turning to him. "This is not my fault."

Gerard took a calming breath, rubbed his brow and turned to the three men. "Where we come from, sorcerers help people," he explained carefully. "They protect people from things like that." He nodded toward the surf and the growing cloud of smoke above the airship.

Halian's frown deepened and Ilias stared at Gerard as if he couldn't quite get his mind around this idea, though his expression said he was trying. He looked up at Giliead for help again and, frustrated at the lack of response, thumped him in the shoulder.

Giliead twitched. His voice tight with tension, he asked, "Why are you here?"

Deliberately, Gerard said, "We came here from our home, by magic, to fight those wizards. That island is only one of their bases, the places they use to attack the land we come from, which is called Ile-Rien."

"There's more of them?" Halian glanced sharply at Giliead. "More than on the island already?"

"Thousands more," Ander put in, eyeing them warily.

Halian swore softly, exchanging an appalled look with Ilias. Giliead looked out at the column of smoke rising from the sea. The breeze off the water carried the stink of burning oil, mingling with the woodsmoke from the smoldering wrecks of the boats on the beach and the huts under the trees.

"We're not like them," Gerard repeated, watching him intently. "Where we come from sorcerers are healers, scholars . . ."

"Healers . . . ?" Ilias repeated blankly.

"We fixed your shoulder," Florian admitted with a wince. "In the caves, when we were hiding, you had that big gash in it and I did a charm to make it heal faster. We didn't think you'd mind. Nobody would, where we come from."

Ilias stared at her, startled. Giliead grabbed his arm and turned him, yanking down his tattered shirt to look at the wound. Ilias craned his neck to see, telling him, "It doesn't hurt."

Ander swore under his breath and shook his head. Tremaine knew he thought Florian shouldn't have said anything, but even she realized this was a time when nothing but the truth would do; leaving anything out would just look like deliberate deception. She folded her arms and waited, her shoulders tight with tension. They had all gotten along fine when they couldn't talk to each other; it seemed absurd that they couldn't manage it now.

Giliead shook his head slightly. "This looks more than a week old." He fingered the bloody rip in Ilias's shirt. Ilias pulled free, trying to reach back to probe at the wound. His eyes met Giliead's and they just looked at each other. Ilias's face was serious and determined and Giliead's deeply troubled. They were making a decision.

The moment seemed to stretch, then Giliead let out his breath and turned to them. His expression was still wary but had lost some of that high color and unnerving intensity. He said, "Those other wizards will be back."

"Yes." Gerard nodded, his expression grave. "They know where this village is now; you should evacuate it immediately."

"How will they know?" Halian demanded. He jerked his head toward the wreck. "No one survived that."

"Before they began their attack, they would have used wireless—" Gerard hesitated. He had spoken the word "wireless" in Rienish; it didn't exist in Syrnaic. "They would have communicated with their base and described their position. Another airship or a boat will come searching for them."

Halian nodded slowly, seeing the sense of this. "I'll tell

Agis." He looked at Giliead and Ilias. "You two . . . sort this out."

He walked away, calling to the villagers poking through the smoking ruins of the burned huts. Giliead stared after him incredulously, muttering, "Thanks, Halian, we'll get right on that."

Ilias rolled his eyes in annoyance and gave Giliead another thump. "Talk."

"All right, all right." Giliead turned to Gerard again and asked carefully, "There's just the four of you? And you came here to fight them?"

"Yes, and we need your help," Gerard told him.

"Those maps you have—" Ander added, "they show details of the Gardier's operations, the locations of their other bases."

Ilias's brows lifted. "You need our help?"

"Badly," Tremaine said. Florian nodded in earnest agreement.

Gerard began, "We came here to help our people get information—"

"Gerard!" Ander interrupted sharply.

Florian finished, "But the Gardier wrecked our boat and now we can't get back to tell them how to attack the island." She saw Ander staring incredulously at her and demanded, "What? It's not a secret. Is it?"

Giliead hesitated, turning all this over thoughtfully. "Why can we understand you now?"

Another good basic starting point, Tremaine thought. Feeling on safer ground and wanting back into the conversation, she answered, "We don't know."

Gerard ignored her, saying, "I don't know. The Gardier—that's what we call those sorcerers—don't speak our language either. They had a magical translator device, but I wasn't aware . . ."

Tremaine fished in her pocket for the medallion, drawing it out. Surely it had something to do with this. "Here it is. Maybe it's decided to work."

"It didn't work this well for the Gardier." Florian took it and examined it with a worried frown. "The crystal's cracked and the color's gone funny, all yellow and dull." She glanced at Tremaine, frowning. "Did the sphere do that?"

Glad someone was still speaking to her, Tremaine leaned over to look at it. "Maybe when it was in the bucket with it. Those other things I took off the Gardier were in pieces— I thought they self-destructed or something, but maybe the sphere—"

Gerard stared at them. "You put that in the bucket of water with the sphere?" he demanded.

Tremaine shifted uncomfortably. "Yes."

Gerard swore. "Water conducts electricity and etheric potency!"

She glared at him. "I know that!"

"But it's a barrier to magic," Florian protested. "We thought the Gardier would follow it if we didn't block it off from them somehow."

"What she said!"

Gerard looked upward as if trying to gather the strength not to shout, then managed, "The water is a barrier between the sphere and the air, but if a second magical object is in contact with the water—"

"Oh." Tremaine looked at Florian for help. "Um."

Florian took a breath to speak, bit her lip as she reconsidered, and finished, "Oh."

"What does that mean?" Giliead asked, cutting in before Gerard could add any further recriminations. He nodded to the sphere. "What is that thing?"

Tremaine turned to him. "Our magical thing killed the Gardier's magical things, and now ours knows everything theirs used to know. But we didn't know that was going to happen. Well, Gerard would have, but he was unconscious."

"God." Gerard rubbed his brow and winced. "It must have, but I don't see how. The original spheres were defensive, reactive only. They couldn't initiate spells without some human guidance, let alone create an entirely new one."

"That thing"—Giliead pointed at the sphere, his expression dubious—"killed something that belonged to the wizards— The other wizards, like it killed the flying whale?"

"What? Oh, the airship. Yes." Tremaine nodded rapidly.

"But without the fire," Florian added.

"But that translator wouldn't work with their language," Ander pointed out, exasperated. "You tried it before. How is it doing this?"

Tremaine shook her head, wishing he hadn't brought that up. "When I was holding the sphere earlier I just wished we knew how to talk to each other, it would make this so much easier. . . ." She trailed off as she realized they were all looking at her again. "I'm still not a wizard."

"Tremaine!" Gerard stared at her.

Someone shouted and she turned to see a party of horsemen emerging from the trees above the village. They rode down the main path between the houses, the horses' hooves sending up a cloud of dust. Some of the men were dressed in dyed leather jerkins, all of them armed with swords or long spears with a curved blade on the end. The horses were unusual too, with rough, dun-colored coats with patterns of small spots along their backs and down their hindquarters.

"This is like something out of a book," Florian murmured.

Tremaine nodded. The villagers waved and called and pointed, greeting the new arrivals with relief. She noticed Ilias didn't seem so glad and that Giliead appeared positively grim.

"Who is that?" Gerard asked, turning worriedly to the other men.

Giliead pressed his lips together, then said, "It's Nicanor, Halian's son." He exchanged a troubled look with Ilias, then his eyes met Tremaine's. He said, "It'll be all right."

Tremaine found herself nodding. She looked away, suddenly self-conscious, but she believed him.

Halian strode back down the beach to stand with them as the man in the lead reined in nearby. As the other men pointed and exclaimed at the burning remains of the airship, he swung down off his horse and came toward them, star-

ing off toward it in consternation. Tremaine saw he did look
like Halian, though he wasn't quite as tall. He had long dark
hair and the family resemblance showed in his eyes and the
shape of his face. He looked around at everyone, frowning
as he noticed the strangers and their odd attire. "What happened?" he demanded.

Ilias shifted uncomfortably and rubbed the back of his
neck, looking like someone who badly wanted to answer
"nothing" but didn't think he could get away with it. Giliead
started to speak, then just stopped, taking a sharp breath.

"We're not sure quite yet." Halian stepped in smoothly.
"Our new friends here were helping us defend against a
wizard attack and uh . . ." He scratched his chin and
shrugged, smiling. "Something happened, and we haven't
quite sorted it out yet." He spoke easily, reassuringly, and
Tremaine thought he was doing a damn good job of pretending he knew that everything was all right and would
soon be settled by being reasonable. He added, "We need
to talk in private."

Nicanor shook his head, obviously unconvinced. "What
do you mean, 'defend against an attack'? I saw fire shoot
up from the ground all the way up on the road." He stared
at the four of them, his dark brows drawing together, a variety of expressions crossing his face, alarm, suspicion, be-
wilderment. Tremaine sympathized. Then he said, "Are
those . . . wizards?"

"No," Ilias said immediately. "Not like that."

"Not like what?" Nicanor said, looking at him in growing incredulity. "Are they wizards?"

Tremaine felt Florian stir anxiously beside her.

Giliead said, "They were on the island. They're fighting
the wizards there. They can tell us about them—"

"They *are* wizards." His eyes went to Tremaine and Florian and flicked away again. "You should have killed them
already."

Tremaine stopped sympathizing. Ander tensed and Gerard caught his arm, silently cautioning him not to interrupt.

"They saved my life," Ilias said. "It's my fault they're
here—"

"They saved this village," Giliead interrupted. "We owe them guest-right."

"We?" Nicanor stared at him, his face darkening with anger. "You were taking them home? Once wasn't enough, you had to do this to your family again?"

Ilias looked away, his jaw tightening. Watching Nicanor grimly, Giliead said, "It's none of your concern."

"Stop that," Halian interrupted sharply. "Nicanor, they saved everyone in the village. You don't think that thing"—he pointed at the airship—"wouldn't have slaughtered all of us? You owe them more than guest-right, you owe them family-right."

Nicanor stared at him, his jaw locked against an angry reply.

Halian stepped up to put a hand on his son's shoulder. "Let's sit down and talk about it," he said again.

They were going to use Gyan's home to talk, Dyani hurrying in first to warn the old woman who kept the house. As Halian and Nicanor went inside, Giliead stopped Ilias on the porch. Gyan's house was up under the trees, near the center of the village. The breeze carried the acrid scent of the flying whale's pyre and people scattered out along the paths, helping the wounded away from the beach, rounding up livestock and children. "Are you sure?" Giliead demanded, keeping his voice low.

"Yes. I know it sounds insane, but yes." Ilias pushed his hair back, frustrated, and looked back at their guests. They were gathered in an uneasy group near the corner of the house, with an equally uneasy Gyan standing by. The decision was simple in Tremaine and Florian's case; even if Ilias hadn't grown to trust them through shared danger, they had saved his life and he was obligated to defend them. Ander he trusted less, but then the young man wasn't a wizard. And Gerard . . . They had never met a wizard who behaved in such a civilized fashion; even if he hadn't obligated them by saving the village, it would have been an

impossible decision. Ilias looked up at Giliead in appeal.
"Are you?"

Giliead nodded with a grimace, his expression saying
that he wished he wasn't. "Yes, I'm sure. We don't just
owe them hospitality, we owe them our lives; it doesn't
matter what the rest of their people are like in— How did
they say it? Rien?"

"Rien," Ilias repeated thoughtfully. "One of the
Gardier"—that name was an awkward mouthful—"said it
to me." He nodded to himself. "They must have thought we
were Rien's allies because we burned that flying whale."

Giliead rubbed his forehead as if trying to chase away an
incipient headache. "We'll worry about that later. Let's just
concentrate on trying to keep Nicanor from killing them."

They went on into the small main room of Gyan's home,
Ilias stepping aside to lean against the wall and fold his
arms. Nicanor was ignoring him, something that most people might have attributed to Ilias bearing a curse mark. But
Nicanor had avoided speaking directly to Ilias for years,
mostly in retaliation for slights delivered by Giliead,
whom he couldn't afford to ignore. Ilias took a deep
breath, reminding himself *just keep your mouth shut and
let Halian handle it*.

"Where did these people come from?" Nicanor demanded, taking a seat at the carefully scrubbed table. He
was obviously still fuming. He had grown up in Cineth
with his mother's family while Halian was at sea or at war
and was as different from his father as he could be. His
younger sister Delphi had fled to Halian as soon as she had
been able to manage it.

Halian sat on the bench across from him. "They were
shipwrecked on the island, by the other wizards. That's the
simple part of the story. The rest is . . ." He glanced at
Giliead. "Complicated."

Giliead stopped at the far end of the table, as if he was
going to stand instead of taking the other seat. Ilias knew
Giliead didn't want to make it look as if he was putting
himself forward as Nicanor's equal, a guilty reflex after the
way he had spoken to him in front of everybody. But he

also knew after that little altercation Nicanor would take it as Giliead refusing to sit down with his brother by marriage. Ilias caught Giliead's eye and glared, jerking his head slightly toward the table. After a moment of stubborn refusal, Giliead sighed faintly, hooked a stool out from under the table, and sat.

The stiff set of Nicanor's shoulders eased a little and he said dryly, "Complicated? That's an interesting word to use. I take it that flying thing was what's been attacking our villages and the trade ships?"

"Yes, but it's not the only one," Halian told him.

"There's an army of wizards on the island," Giliead said bluntly, and started to explain.

While Nicanor, Halian, Giliead and Ilias went into a house to talk in private, Tremaine and the others waited outside with the owner Gyan, one of the men who had helped them aboard the ship.

Tremaine rubbed the sweat off her forehead and looked around. The air was fresher here, up off the beach and away from the smoking ruins. The little tile-roofed houses were all close together, separated only by small gardens or goat pens and muddy pathways. The place was shaded by large trees that had been left to stand between the buildings. There was painting and carving everywhere, around the windows and doors, under the eaves. They liked variety, as evidenced by the different geometric patterns, leaves and flowers, animals, sun and moon designs. Florian nudged her with an elbow and pointed between the houses. Tremaine leaned to look and saw a fountain under a wooden pavilion not far away, the water falling from spouts carved into the shape of spritelike faces. She wondered if they had fay here too.

The armed men who had come with Nicanor were gathered loosely around this part of the village, leaning on their long spears, staring at the newcomers and talking in low voices. The rest of the place's inhabitants were too occupied with tending the wounded or rounding up goats and chickens and hauling bundles out of their homes in preparation for the evacuation to pay much attention. Though Tremaine caught sight of eyes peering at them through the cracks in the carved shutters of the nearby houses.

Like the crew of the ship, many people were tall, with brown or reddish hair and olive skin, though there were enough shorter blondes and dark brunettes mixed in to show the population was fairly cosmopolitan. She saw quite a few young men wearing their hair in long braids too, so that must be the current fashion, though many of the older men seemed to cut it off at the shoulders or crop it short. The women seemed to wear whatever they wanted, loose comfortable skirts or dresses dyed in colorful swirls or block-printed with designs, or cotton pants and shirts like the men. Some people, maybe those who had been interrupted while at work on the boats or the fishing nets, weren't wearing much more than a twist of cloth wrapped around their waists. *And a lot of them are injured, or were injured,* she realized suddenly. She saw old scars, limps, a patch covering an eye, an occasional missing limb. Granted she wasn't seeing everybody in the village parade by, but a disproportionate number seemed to have old injuries, especially considering most of them seemed in good health otherwise. *And they had that catapult all ready to go. They've had practice with sudden attacks. Not from airships maybe, but something.*

"Those devices you found," Gerard was saying thoughtfully, "must work something like the sphere, but perhaps in a more limited fashion. We know the Gardier can detect the presence of magic with them, but if they can also cast certain predetermined spells like the one that was used on me—"

"Never mind that now." Ander swore. Speaking Rienish, he told Gerard in a low voice, "We should make a break for it—"

"No," Gerard said, his voice sharp but quiet. "Let them try to handle it first."

"Gerard—"

"Ander, we need their help to get back to the target area. At the moment they don't seem hostile toward us. Just . . . give them some time to work it out."

Ander pressed his lips together, looking mutinous. Florian glanced worriedly at Tremaine, who rolled her eyes. The sphere's activity and all the arguing had left her tired and cranky. She looked at Gyan, who stood politely just out of earshot, pretending he was interested in a crack in the corner of the house's stone foundation. She remembered he had been the one to help them into the boat and that he had seemed fairly friendly. She cleared her throat, remembering to speak Syrnaic. "Excuse me?"

He looked up, startled. He was an older man with a heavy build and a good-humored face, balding with a long fringe of gray hair.

"Is there someplace we could sit down?" Tremaine nudged Florian, who immediately assumed a wan and pitiful expression.

"Oh." Gyan blinked. Tremaine hadn't planned this, at least not consciously, but she could practically see his attitude change. Suddenly they were people again and he was their host. "Oh, yes, right back here in the garden." He motioned around the side of the house.

It was a little area of cropped grass surrounded by ferns and flowering bushes and clay pots of herbs. Tremaine took a seat on one of the rough wooden benches and put the sphere at her feet. Florian sank down gratefully beside her and began to work her boot off. Ander, tense as an overwound watch, stayed on his feet.

Gyan sat on the little stone wall opposite them. "Ah . . . You folks been here long?" he asked, with a game effort at polite conversation. Dyani slipped in through the gate and sat next to him, apparently to offer moral support.

"Not really," Gerard replied with a smile, taking the other bench. He asked carefully, "Nicanor is a figure of authority here?"

"He's lawgiver of Cineth," Gyan explained, looking relieved to have an easy topic. "He's Halian's son from his first household, before he married into Andrien. Halian was lawgiver for a while, then warleader, last time we had a war."

"I see." Gerard nodded encouragingly.

Gyan warmed to the topic. "When the war was over—under Cineth's law once you've been warleader, you can't go back to being lawgiver—Halian retired and married Karima, Giliead's mother, of the house of Andrien. This was all a few years ago."

Tremaine tried to look like she was following this. She had enough trouble trying to keep track of her own relatives.

"Giliead's the god's Chosen Vessel," Dyani volunteered, looking as if she was trying to be helpful.

Someone else Tremaine recognized from the boat, a young man with wild brown hair, hurried up and stepped over the garden wall, plopping down on the ground. He pulled out a pen that was little more than a sharpened stick with a groove in it, a little clay pot of ink and a handful of scraps of rough brown paper. Pulling over an overturned wooden bucket to use as a desk, he set up his materials and demanded without preamble, "What color was the fire that destroyed the flying whale?"

As they stared at him in blank surprise Gyan explained hastily, "That's Arites. He's a poet."

"Oh, right." Tremaine turned to Florian for help. "Sort of a reddish yellow, wasn't it?"

"I think so." Florian nodded, shaking out her stocking.

"Ah . . ." Gerard must have seen the quelling look Gyan was trying to give Dyani because his voice was cautious as he asked, "What does it mean to be the god's Chosen Vessel?"

"Well, he, uh . . ." Dyani hesitated, uncertain.

"He kills wizards," Arites supplied helpfully, still scribbling away.

Florian, trying to get her wet stocking back on, froze and stared at him, eyes wide.

"Oh." Gerard sat back, frowning.

Ander folded his arms, muttering, "Wonderful."

Gyan rolled his eyes in annoyance and cleared his throat

significantly. Arites looked up, suddenly recalling his audience. "No offense," he added brightly.

Tremaine propped her chin on her hand and yawned. Giliead had told her it would be all right and now she knew what he meant. All the noise Nicanor had made aside, it was Giliead's job to kill them and his decision whether to do it or not, and she knew he wouldn't. He would help them because they had helped Ilias.

A little desperately, Dyani asked, "How did you meet Giliead and Ilias on the island?"

"Oh, yes," Florian said, relieved to have a less controversial topic. "We—Tremaine and I—were captured by the Gardier and—"

"You were what?" Gerard stared at them.

"That's right, we didn't tell you that part." Tremaine shifted to face him and her foot knocked against the sphere, which clanked. She picked it up, wondering what to do with it. She didn't want it to go off accidentally again and frighten their hosts or attract more Gardier. She glanced up at Gyan. "Can I borrow that bucket?"

"Consider it a gift," Gyan assured her hastily. "Arites, give her the bucket."

"The Gardier shouldn't be able to detect the sphere as long as it's quiescent," Gerard told her, brows drawing together in annoyance. "Besides, putting it in a bucket of water, where it's in contact with the wooden side, doesn't help block all the etheric vibrations."

"Yes, but it blocks it from me, and I'm not making etheric vibrations," Tremaine told him with some asperity, getting up to collect the bucket from Arites. "Sometimes I do things for a reason. Not often, but sometimes."

As he listened to Giliead tell the story, Nicanor's expression grew dark with worry and he interrupted only a few times with questions. Ilias kept out of it, speaking only when Giliead asked him to tell his part of what had happened after they were separated.

Finally, Nicanor shook his head and said, "We've lost

this village. If you're right and there are more of those flying things on the island, they'll be back."

"There's more." Giliead said, watching him narrowly. Ilias knew what he was thinking; there were those in Cineth who wouldn't care that this village lived or died. Out of deference to Ranior's memory, the headman Agis had always permitted people with curse marks to live here. There were three here now, living in the outskirts further up the hill.

"Better the village than the people." Halian was absently rubbing an old scar on his forearm, a memento from the last time Ixion had attacked the coast in force. "And you know who we have to thank for it."

Nicanor kneaded his forehead, reluctantly accepting that. He said grudgingly, "I see now why you owe them guest-right, but how do you know they understand what that means?"

"We don't." Halian folded his hands on the table. "But they know far more about these Gardier wizards than we do. You saw how they killed that flying whale. And by our own sea treaties, if they're fighting wizards, we owe them our help."

Nicanor shook his head. "Still . . ." He looked at Giliead and took a deep breath.

Giliead's eyes narrowed in anticipation of being reasoned with. Ilias pinched the bridge of his nose, thinking, *Please be sensible, just the once.* He wasn't sure who he was thinking it at, maybe just the world in general.

Nicanor said, "You don't know that you can trust these people. It could be another trick."

Ilias gritted his teeth. *Yes, it was a big mistake. But didn't we pay for it?* He caught the sour glint in Giliead's eye and thought for a moment he was about to say just that. But Giliead said, "There is a way. We can go to the god."

Nicanor hesitated. Whatever problems he had with Giliead, he knew the god was to be trusted. Nicanor said finally, "It will know if they're lying?"

"If they are what they say they are, it will know."

"It didn't know Ixion," Nicanor pointed out.

Gilead nodded. "It would have—if I had had the sense to ask it."

Nicanor watched him for a long moment, then looked away. "All right. It will depend on what Visolela decides, but if the god says they aren't a danger, she will have to agree."

Ilias let out his breath in relief. Halian tapped the table thoughtfully and said, "So then. Let's go tell them."

Tremaine eased the sphere into the full bucket and sat down next to Gerard. Arites, sitting at her feet, was rapidly taking notes on the sphere's appearance, bracing his parchments on a flat piece of stone. "This is going to make a great ballad," he told Tremaine earnestly.

She leaned over to look at what he was writing. The marks didn't make any sense to her and she wished the spell had included being able to read Syrnaic as well as speak it.

"You're saying there are different groups of these Gardier wizards and they attack your land from here?" Gyan was asking with a troubled frown.

"Yes." Gerard nodded. "They launch airship attacks from at least seven distinct points, from every direction except the east. They have their foothold in Adera for that."

"Here that would be—" Ander looked thoughtful. "That way." He pointed. Ander had done his best to stay suspicious, but the conversation, once it had shifted back to the Gardier, had drawn him in. "What's in that direction?"

"Cineth," Gyan told him. "The port city."

"Past that?"

"The sea." He looked up and Tremaine realized Ilias, Gilead, Nicanor and Halian were back. Tremaine's eyes went to Ilias. One corner of his mouth twitched in a smile and she sat back, relieved.

Nicanor studied them for a moment, his expression still forbidding, then asked Gerard, "Would you be willing to go to our local god, to prove you are what you say you are?"

Tremaine looked at Ilias. He inclined his head slightly and she said, "Sure."

Gerard, who had his mouth open to reply, turned to stare at her. She nodded and gave him a nudge on the arm. He sighed, turned back to Nicanor, and said, "Of course we will."

"Sorry about all this," Tremaine told Ilias, feeling inadequate. The path they took led up the forested hills behind the village. The trail itself was barely visible in the tall grass and Tremaine had lost sight of it several times; apparently the god didn't get many visitors. It was cool in the shade of the tall birches and pines; the green scent of damp earth and foliage came from the bracken and waist-high ferns covering the forest floor.

"It's all right," Ilias said with a distracted shrug. His eyes were on Giliead where he walked ahead with Gerard and Ander. Halian had stayed behind to help organize the evacuation of the village and to sail the *Swift* to the port of Cineth. Then he glanced at her and laughed. "You can stop apologizing. It's not your fault."

"Well . . ." She thought about the sphere and exchanged a rueful look with Florian. "Yes it is, actually."

Ander glanced back at them, brows drawn, as if he suspected Tremaine and Florian of telling Ilias all about Ile-Rien's secrets, as if they knew any to tell. He was carrying the bucket with the sphere, as they had all agreed it was probably safer if Tremaine had as little contact with it as possible.

"Is Ander your husband?" Ilias asked suddenly, eyeing the byplay.

"God, no." Tremaine startled herself with her own vehemence. Florian made a choking noise she managed to turn into a cough and Ander glanced suspiciously back at them again. Tremaine lowered her voice. "He's not married. I'm not married. None of us are married."

Just ahead Gerard had asked about the island and Giliead was replying, "It's been used by wizards for a long time."

"Did the wizards construct the harbor cave and the city? It looked very old."

"The stories say that it was all there before the wizards came. That people who lived here long before we came built it. At low tide, you can see pillars and walls in the sea around it."

"Fascinating. I wonder how the Gardier knew about it," Gerard murmured, half to himself.

"Why were you there on the island if you didn't know about the Gardier?" Ander asked, eyeing Giliead with skepticism. He shifted the sphere's bucket to his other hand.

Giliead looked thoughtfully into the distance. "When ships started to disappear again, we knew another wizard had taken Ixion's place."

"It started out with missing ships in our world also," Gerard said. "Tremaine's father . . . often looked into mysterious occurrences and he was intrigued by the disappearances when others were still attributing them to accident or unusually bad weather. He investigated and uncovered a Gardier group operating in Adera, a small country on our eastern border. At first he thought he was dealing with a scheme for profit, not an invasion. Now we believe that when they started by attacking commercial shipping, they were feeling us out, testing for weakness." He glanced at Ander, who was maintaining a stone-faced expression. "Perhaps testing to see how effective their offensive spells were."

"And taking slaves," Giliead added bluntly. "Those were your people imprisoned on the island, then?"

"From Maiuta and the other Southern Seas islands," Tremaine put in. "Did the government know about that, Ander?"

Ander confirmed that supposition by refusing to answer it. Instead, he asked Giliead, "Who's Ixion?"

Giliead flicked a glance at him. "The wizard who used to live on the island."

Ander didn't look satisfied with this elliptical reply and Gerard was too lost in thought to pursue it.

"What did Nicanor mean when he said you'd done it again?" Florian asked Ilias tentatively.

Tremaine watched Ilias look away into the green shadows of the woods. She hadn't thought to ask the question.

Finally he said, "Ixion . . . We didn't know what he looked like. We fought him for years, but we'd never seen him, just the people he paid or forced to work for him, or the curselings he made. Then two years ago we met a man who called himself Licias. One of Ixion's curselings was attacking his village and he was trying to fight it. We helped him drive it away, then he came with us to where it had laired, up in the mountains, to finish it off. He was wounded and he said his family had been killed by the curseling, so we brought him back home with us."

Tremaine had an odd feeling about this. "And it was Ixion," she said.

Florian frowned in surprise. "Was it?" she asked Ilias.

He nodded, glancing sideways at Tremaine. Lost in thought, she stared at the ground, her hands shoved into her pockets. She said, "He hid what he was and became your friend, part of your family. He made it last for months before he struck. Because it was the worst thing he could think of to do to you."

Ilias watched her with a troubled expression. "How did you know?"

She lifted her shoulders in a slight shrug. "I guessed. Something similar happened in one of my plays."

"Your what?"

Florian explained, "Her stories. She's a writer, like Arites. Where we come from they take stories and act them out, and call them 'plays.' " She glanced thoughtfully at Tremaine. "Now that I think of it, that's awfully close to what happened to the characters in *Varnecia*, isn't it?"

"So . . ." Ilias said slowly, "you made up a poet's tale about something that happened to us before you ever came here, or knew that here was here?"

Tremaine's brows quirked as she considered it. "It looks that way."

"That's strange," Florian commented, frowning.

"No kidding," Ilias muttered.

They walked a while in mutual nonplussed silence,

while birds sang in the trees and the breeze stirred the high grasses. Florian kept saying "Well . . ." as if she was arriving at and then discarding possible explanations. Giliead glanced back once and gave them an odd look, probably puzzled by the similar expressions of bafflement they must all be wearing.

Tremaine was expecting some sort of temple, but as they passed through a grove of trees with fernlike fronds, Giliead said, "That's it."

They walked out into a grassy clearing drenched in afternoon sun. On the edge of the open area was a rocky outcrop and at its base the dark hole of a cave.

There was nothing to indicate it was a special place until they drew near. There was a small carving in the rock above the entrance, just a ring of intertwined circles, very crudely done in comparison to the artwork Tremaine had noticed at the village. On the packed dirt around the cave mouth were little piles of fruit and nuts, pieces of bread and cooked meat. It was all in various stages of rot and flies buzzed over it.

Giliead eyed the collection with annoyance before saying, "I'm going to see if it's home." He handed Ilias his scabbarded sword and ducked under the low-hanging rock, stepping down into the cave.

Ilias waited with them, scuffing one boot in the dirt. Gerard looked around at the piles of food. "Are these offerings for the god?" he asked, puzzled.

Ilias nodded. "People leave food for it." He shrugged. "But it doesn't eat."

Gerard lifted his brows. "I see. How long has the god been here?"

Ilias looked at the cave entrance, his brow furrowed thoughtfully as if he had never considered the question before. "Forever, I guess."

"Are there many gods?"

"This is the only one in Cineth. Most places have just one but Teypria, to the south, has two." With another shrug he added, "They have two Chosen Vessels too; I'm not sure how that works."

From inside Giliead called, "It's here. You can come in now."

Ilias smiled at them and stepped down into the cave. With the muttered comment, "Casual attitude toward religion here," Gerard followed him.

"Well, after you, ladies," Ander said with a sweeping gesture and an ironic expression. Tremaine and Florian trailed after Gerard, Ander following.

After the bright afternoon sun, the dark seemed impenetrable and Tremaine thought, *Not again.* But this cave smelled dry and clean and after a moment her eyes adjusted and she saw it was lit through rents in the rock overhead. It wasn't very big, not much more than twenty or thirty feet across. Vines and tree roots from the forest above grew down the walls from the cracks and it was cool and pleasant. It was quiet also, the sound of the birdsong and breeze deadened by the thick stone.

Giliead stood in the center of the chamber, hands on his hips, just waiting. Ilias stood back against the wall, shifting the sword off his shoulder and leaning on it.

Nothing happened. A warm breeze moved over the rocks above, bringing the scent of greenery and wet loam into the cave. Giliead blew out a breath and gave Ilias a wry glance.

"Is something wrong?" Gerard asked carefully.

Giliead gave him a faint smile and explained, "Sometimes it's shy."

Gerard and Ander exchanged a guarded look and Tremaine knew they were both thinking the god was going to be imaginary, or swamp gas, whatever swamp gas was, or something else natural. She looked at Ilias; he winked at her and she smiled. *I bet it's real.*

Something sparked against the cave roof above Giliead's head, moving among the vines trailing in from the cracks and making the leaves rustle. *Firefly,* Tremaine thought, then *firefly?*

More fireflies appeared among the leaves, each surrounded by a blue-tinged mist. Ander swore softly and

Gerard studied it in amazement. Florian drew in a breath in admiration.

The blue light grew, sparkling and dancing over the rough cracks in the ceiling. It darted down to Ilias, a light touch that sent a spark through his hair and made him shake his head and sneeze.

"What do you think that is?" Ander asked Gerard, his voice hushed.

"Some sort of fay, a localized elemental perhaps or . . ." Gerard blinked, shaking his head. "Or I haven't a clue."

"It's not very big," Ilias said apologetically. "The Chaeans have a god that can make the whole roof of a big cave turn gold."

Giliead turned to regard him with lowered brows. "What?" Ilias demanded. "It's true."

The light played down the wall, toward the bucket. "It's going to want to look at the sphere," Tremaine said thoughtfully.

Ander stared at her. "How do you know?"

"If I was whatever that is, I would," Florian put in, watching the light get closer to the bucket. She glanced worriedly at Tremaine. "You think it'll be all right?"

Tremaine shook her head. *Good question.* "Don't know."

"But the sphere's not sentient," Ander said, looking at them in confusion. "That . . . god . . . is something alive. How does that work?"

"Yes, well . . ." Gerard watched the light play across the rock. "The spheres Riardin and the others created aren't what we'd consider sentient, but this one . . . It isn't supposed to be able to instigate spells but that's exactly what it's done today." His expression was troubled. "It certainly isn't supposed to be able to extract a spell from a foreign object like the Gardier translator, modify it and cast it, all the while stripping the protective wards off a Gardier airship."

Giliead and Ilias were both listening intently, though Tremaine wasn't sure the translation spell was giving them the right words. *Sentient* seemed to want to be translated as *souled.*

Ander eyed Gerard for a moment, not happily. "I'm not sure that was made clear to the Intelligence division."

Gerard said deliberately, "This is an Arisilde Damal sphere, Ander. It's the closest we can come to the destroyed Viller spheres. There's very little about it that can be made clear to anyone."

The light was playing over the lip of the bucket now. Tremaine watched, half hypnotized by the coruscating play of it. She looked up to realize Giliead was standing next to her. He said, "You're right, it wants to see what's under the water."

"Tremaine . . ." Gerard said worriedly.

Tremaine wasn't sure what prompted her to act. Before anybody else could argue or voice any objections, she leaned down and scooped the sphere out of the bucket. The water streamed out of it, dripping down onto her mud-encrusted boots. From the bucket rim the light leapt up to it, the firefly motion playing gently over the metal. The sphere hummed and throbbed in her hands as it started to spin, the wheels inside spitting out more water. Giliead blinked at the sudden spray and Tremaine said, "It's all right, it's supposed to do that."

Ilias eased forward to Giliead's side, watching the sphere curiously. The light clung to Tremaine's hands, faintly warm and tickling a little. She had expected it to be like the illusory fayre light the sphere had produced before, but this had substance, life. It was like being brushed gently by feathers and she could see why it had made Ilias sneeze.

Giliead shook his head a little, frowning. "I can't see the curses."

Not understanding, Tremaine looked up at him and he explained, "It's part of being the god's Chosen Vessel. I can tell where curses are. Some of them don't work on me."

"The sphere doesn't often react to magic unless its wielder is attacked," Gerard said quietly, watching them. "Perhaps your ability works along the same lines, and you can't detect adjurations that aren't hostile to you."

Giliead and Ilias looked at each other, both turning over

that piece of information. Tremaine realized that Gerard had used the Rienish word for *adjuration* or *spell*. The only Syrnaic word available was *curse*, with everything that implied.

The light drifted away from the sphere back up toward the cave roof. It twined among the vines, fading back to vanish in the cracks and crevices, the firefly glimmers going out one by one.

Ander let out a relieved breath. "Is that it?"

Giliead looked quietly vindicated. Not so quietly, Ilias grinned up at him and said, "I like being right."

Giliead smiled and gave his shoulder a shake. He looked at Gerard and asked, "So how can we help you?"

Chapter 13

The afternoon sun was hot but it was still cool under the shadows of the trees as they walked back from the god's cave. Despite the aches and bruises, Tremaine realized she was enjoying herself; the air was filled with the scents of pine and damp earth and the countryside was lovely.

They took a slightly different path, winding further up the gentle hills, heading toward a spot further inland from the village. Gerard and Ander had explained about their need to reach the point at sea near where the Pilot Boat had been attacked so they could return to their world. Giliead had agreed to take them in the *Swift* tomorrow morning when the tide went out. During this explanation Gerard had tried to describe the concept of different worlds and traveling between them, stopping to draw diagrams in the dirt of the path as illustrations. Both men had listened with interest but Tremaine really couldn't tell if this was comprehension or just courtesy; Gerard's diagrams weren't terribly illuminating even for her and she knew what he was talking about. Finally Giliead had stopped him, saying, "As long as you know how to get there."

Tremaine noticed that Giliead had relaxed considerably once the god had approved them. Ilias hadn't seemed to ever think the outcome was in doubt, but then he knew them a little better. Now they were talking of more immediate concerns: the airships and how to fight them and the likelihood of an attack tonight.

"It's best if we try to conceal our presence from the

Gardier now, rather than using the sphere to fight them again," Gerard pointed out. "If they perceive your people as a threat, the island base could summon more airships and attack the entire undefended coast."

Florian grimaced and Tremaine muttered, "Ouch." The image Gerard's words had conjured wasn't a pleasant one.

Gilead frowned thoughtfully, digesting the uncomfortable thought. "You said even with all your people's curses, you couldn't defend your cities."

"We tried everything." Ander looked off into the woods. Tremaine remembered he had done his first work as an Intelligence officer on the Aderassi front; he would have seen more of those failures than most.

Gilead watched him a moment, perhaps reading the same thing from Ander's expression, then glanced at Gerard. "Halian and some others will be watching the village from a distance, to see what happens when the Gardier come after their flying whale." He still hesitated a little over the word *Gardier* and Tremaine realized it wasn't particularly easy for a speaker of Syrnaic to pronounce.

Ilias walked along ahead of her, his thumbs hooked in his belt. "Why do the flying whales burn so easily?" he asked Gerard. "They go up like straw."

"The hydrogen gas . . . the air inside the flying whales is very flammable. Like oil."

"Oh." Ilias looked at Gilead, brows lifted.

The larger man pursed his lips thoughtfully. "That explains it."

"Explains what?" Ander asked, just a touch sharply. He still didn't seem to trust their new allies. Tremaine supposed it was his job.

"We set one on fire, in their caves," Gilead admitted.

"We heard about that from the people who are prisoners there." Florian nodded rapidly. "And their base was still disorganized. That's why we were able to get away."

"You set one on fire?" Ander asked, stopping to stare at the two men.

"It was an accident," Ilias explained. "Killed some wizards, though." Gilead nudged him and he glanced around at them, suddenly recalling his audience. "Present company excepted," he added with an apologetic smile.

"So they lost two airships." Ander whistled appreciatively as they started to walk again. "That base could only have had four at most, we knew that from the attacks it launched on Chaire."

"How did you set one on fire?" Gerard asked, casting an intent glance at the two men. "The Gardier airships should be protected from fire by spells, though the sphere appears to have learned a way around that."

As Giliead described his and Ilias's earlier adventure with the Gardier, Tremaine was impressed. They hadn't had a clue what the airship was, whether it was alive or not, and yet they had had the courage to explore it. Even knowing it was surrounded by dangerous wizards. *And we know how they feel about wizards,* she thought. The fact that they were able to overcome those prejudices, at least in the case of their Rienish visitors, said a lot for them as well.

"I'd swear that one burned much bigger than the one we got today," Ilias commented as Giliead finished the story.

"Those metal cylinders you found on the dock, those were bombs," Gerard said thoughtfully. "At least one of them must have exploded when the burning hull fell on them."

Giliead shook his head, giving Gerard a quizzical smile. "Some of those words didn't mean anything."

"Bombs. They're like those pots you threw at the airship with the catapult," Tremaine explained. "Except they do a lot more damage."

"Oh." Giliead threw a wry look at Ilias. "Good thing we didn't find a way to open them."

Ilias snorted. "No kidding."

"It seems very odd," Gerard said, frowning. "The . . . There doesn't seem to be a word in Syrnaic for 'electrical,' though I suppose that's to be expected. The system that provides the power . . . well, it shouldn't be that vulnerable. Perhaps their spells to prevent sparks focus on the outside of the craft."

Giliead listened to this with drawn brows. Tremaine

thought he hadn't followed what Gerard was trying to say until he pointed out, "They were afraid of fire, even outside the whale."

"They went crazy when the wizard lights made a fire," Ilias added.

Looking up at the two men thoughtfully, Florian put in, "In Ile-Rien we've got regulations that say even if a building has charms on it to prevent fire, it's still against the law to pile up oily rags in the stairwell or do other stupid things. Maybe the Gardier just rely on their magic and don't take other precautions."

"It's a possibility," Gerard admitted, not sounding satisfied with the explanation. "Spells used to prevent fire are rather difficult to construct. Most of our magic is designed to assist natural processes, or to manipulate the ether in ways not adverse to those processes. But considering the Gardier's other abilities, it shouldn't be beyond them."

They came out of the forest and stopped at the top of a low hill. Nestled in the shallow valley below was a rambling flat-roofed two-story stone house, shaded by big trees. Tremaine could see it was built in a square with a central atrium, but it didn't look as if it was meant for defense; there were windows in the outside walls, just openings without even shutters to close. To one side there were outbuildings and animal pens and she could see a large garden plot with grape arbors and smaller trees with soft purple blossoms. On the far side of the garden were the ruins of another building almost the size of the big house, the remains of the foundation and tumbled roof beams outlined in the tall grass.

Figures moved in the woods at the edge of the fields below and Tremaine caught a glimpse of men pushing a two-wheeled cart through a clearing. Giliead glanced back at them, explaining, "Those are people from Agis's village. They'll be passing the word to evacuate to all the villages close to the beach and telling people not to light fires tonight."

"Good." Ander nodded, watching the movement below. "That will buy you some time."

Tremaine winced. *It would have happened anyway,* she told herself. *The Gardier wouldn't leave them alone for long.*

Giliead still hesitated and Tremaine saw Ilias watching him with worried expectation. Then Giliead faced them and took a deep breath. With obvious reluctance, he said, "We have to tell you, this house is under a curse. The curse makes things happen to women and children who belong to our family." He looked deliberately at Tremaine and Florian. "I don't know if it would affect people who weren't related to us, but if you'd rather stay elsewhere . . ."

Her mind still on the imminent Gardier attack, Tremaine shrugged. "I'll take the chance."

Gerard threw her an odd look but said to Giliead, "Would you accept our help with this curse? I could try to remove it."

"Remove it?" Ilias repeated, startled.

Giliead shook his head, puzzled. "It's Ixion's curse," he said, as if he wasn't quite sure what Gerard meant.

With a thoughtful frown, Gerard looked down at the house. "Even though a different sorcerer cast it, magical methods . . . it's still a matter of patterns of etheric energy." He frowned in frustration, perhaps realizing that the words were coming out in Rienish and meant nothing in Syrnaic. "Of course, I can't promise anything."

"But you could try?" Ilias asked, casting a pensive look at Giliead.

Gerard lifted his brows. "Considering what little you've said of Ixion, I would be delighted to try," he said dryly.

A s they came out of the woods again and up the path toward the house, they saw people herding cattle—big, red-coated cattle with shaggy manes and huge horns—and others carrying baskets and bales up toward another broad path into the woods. As Halian had said, they had been attacked by wizards before. Fading back into the hills was something they knew how to do. Tremaine saw familiar faces from the crew of the *Swift* among the men who seemed to be organizing the exodus.

The large trees surrounding the house shaded the bleached stone from the afternoon sun. Tremaine noticed they were oaks, one of the few trees she could positively identify with any degree of accuracy, and knew the house must have been here for many years.

There was a woman on the porch speaking to Gyan. When she saw them coming up the path she hurried down the steps. She was an older woman, with long graying brown hair, wearing a sleeveless gown of dark green, the hem printed with blue and gold designs, and a rich maroon silk stole. The expression of delighted relief that lit up her face made her look years younger.

She greeted Giliead with a hug, then held out a hand to Ilias, pulling him to her to kiss his cheek. Gyan remained on the porch, watching them with a smile.

Giliead turned back to explain, "This is my mother, Karima." Tremaine saw Ander's startled look and hid a smile. He might find it a little hard to support his "they're secretly planning to kill us" theory now. You didn't bring people you meant to kill home to meet your mother, not in Ile-Rien at least. Probably not even in Bisra.

Giliead introduced them all around, then hesitated, saying, "Mother, they're—"

"Gyan told me what happened," Karima interposed swiftly, letting him know they could skip discussion of the touchy wizard issue.

Giliead nodded, relieved. "Halian took the *Swift* to Cineth?"

"Yes, and Agis sent the fishing boats down the coast to Vela." She stepped to Florian, smiling at her and giving her shoulders a reassuring squeeze. "You've been walking this poor child all over the country. Don't stand out here, come into the house."

As the others followed her, Ilias stopped Tremaine on the porch, asking softly, "Can Gerard really take the curse away?"

Tremaine hesitated, thinking about it, trying to give him an honest answer. "Gerard's a very good sorcerer. When he worked for my father he had a lot of experience with keeping sorcerers from spying on us or trying to kill us." She glanced up and saw Ander standing in the doorway, staring at them suspiciously. She glared at him, waving at him to move along. Ilias observed this with a lifted brow, his lips twitching in a smile, and it took Tremaine a moment to get her train of thought back. "Gerard comes from the kind of magical training where there's a big emphasis on knowing how things work and why, and looking for subtle ways to do things instead of just throwing a lot of powerful spells around."

Ilias nodded. "He's a scholar."

"Exactly. And I think he's thinking of Ixion as one of these types that are all flash and no foundation but I'm not sure that's the case. If you could tell him more about Ixion, that might help."

Ilias scratched his chin, looking toward the house but with such a distant expression she knew he wasn't seeing it as she was. Then he shook his head slightly. "I'll try."

They went inside to a large airy room where Giliead was explaining to Karima that Gerard was going to attempt to remove the curse. She was listening with a faint worried frown but didn't voice any objections. Tremaine looked around, taking in the big doors looking out into the garden atrium and the dull red walls with borders of decorative figures along the cornices. The floor was a mosaic of tiny chips of stone, forming a stylized seascape with islands and galleys like the *Swift*. For all the color it had the comfortable-shabby feel of an old house where the inhabitants like it as it is and don't bother with new paint and plaster. Tremaine was getting the feeling that this family hadn't worried about what their neighbors thought for a long time.

Gerard patted his pants pockets, frowning. "The Gardier took my aether-glasses."

"Oh, I've got them." Tremaine fished in her jacket pocket, pulling out the lenses.

"Ah, thank you." Gerard fitted them on over his spectacles, a process the Syprians watched with a kind of wary bemusement, then he wandered toward the atrium archway. "These allow me to see the etheric traces left by the curse."

Karima turned to Tremaine and Florian. "Let me take you to a room where you can clean up and get some fresh clothes."

"Really?" Florian said wistfully.

Tremaine wanted to see Gerard find the curse, but she wanted to scrape the muck off herself too. And her feet hurt. "All right."

About to go after Gerard, Ander paused, trying to give her a "be careful and keep your mouth shut" look. Even less in a mood to accommodate him than ever, Tremaine gave him a sarcastically cheerful salute as she followed Karima.

Gerard stopped in the open double doorway that led into the atrium. Under the bright sunshine, the garden looked like an unlikely place for a curse, but he knew how deceptive appearances could be. Vines climbed the wooden pillars that supported the gallery along the second floor and fragrant flowering bushes with purple and pink flowers or tiny blue blossoms wandered in and out of the orderly beds. Some of the plants were familiar, some might be unique to this world. In the far end was a domed clay bread oven next to a firewood stack and a large stone cistern surrounded by an herb garden.

As Gerard studied the air for etheric disturbances, Ander stepped to his side, asking softly in Rienish, "Gerard, do you trust Tremaine?"

"To do what?" Startled, Gerard turned to him, lifting the aether-glasses so he could see the younger man's face clearly.

Ander's expression went bland. "Never mind."

Gerard stared at him, suddenly realizing what the question meant. *I know he's an Intelligence officer, but Tremaine? Good God. The girl would make an excellent spy, but do the Gardier have that much imagination? Or did Ander think she might share too much information* with the Syprians? He was conscious of Giliead and Ilias standing nearby and he didn't want to prolong this moment; deliberately speaking in a language they couldn't understand was no way to reciprocate the trust the men had extended by bringing them here. Giliead's face had already turned closed and enigmatic and Ilias was watching Ander with a kind of thoughtful patience, like a cat trying to decide if something was prey or not. Gerard said shortly, "I've known her most of her life, I may be the wrong person to ask."

Ander shrugged, smiling affably, reassuming his feckless playboy role. "Just curious."

Gerard turned away, stepping out into the garden and replacing the aether-glasses. Tiny green lizards basking on the sun-warmed stone skittered away from his feet. He would have to warn Tremaine, of course. God knew how she would take it. The one thing he knew for certain about Tremaine was that she never reacted to anything the way you thought she would. He wasn't worried that she might retaliate, the way her father Nicholas surely would have, but still . . .

As the others trailed after him, Giliead asked cautiously, "What do you mean by 'etheric traces'?"

He had done a good job of pronouncing the unfamiliar words. Gerard explained, "To put it simply, the disturbance that a spell makes when it travels through the air. They're invisible to the naked eye." He paused by the cistern, an ideal spot for a disease-causing element, but the glasses showed no traces in the air above the water's surface. "The most common method of cursing a house is to enspell an object and hide it somewhere on the premises. The etheric disturbances would be stronger near the spot where the object was hidden." He paused, head cocked back toward the other men. "Were the deaths associated with any particular part of the house?"

"No. There was sickness, then a fire," Giliead explained, with a quick glance toward Ilias. "The fire was in the new house, across the field, but there were deaths here too."

"I see." Anything that virulent would surely have affected the growth of the plants, but Gerard couldn't see any evidence of it. "The etheric tendrils should spread throughout the area of influence like a spider's web."

He looked back to see Ilias and Giliead exchange a dubious expression. "They should?" Giliead echoed.

"But they aren't." Gerard pivoted slowly, frowning. He could see indistinct spots of congealed ether here and there, near the stone floor of the walk, hovering above a climbing rose in the corner. But no clear pointers to their source. He began to wonder if they were talking about an actual curse in the Rienish sense of the word; from the description of its effects he had assumed so. "There are traces, but they're very faint. I think there's been some sort of protective influence at work."

"Maybe it's the god," Ilias said.

Giliead, arms folded, didn't venture an opinion.

"Perhaps." Gerard removed the aether-glasses, checked the lenses and put them back on again. He wondered if Giliead's reluctance to comment was policy or just reticence. Moving slowly down the atrium, studying the rafters of the second-level gallery, he asked, "Does the god have a name?"

"No." Giliead's tone didn't change, so it was hard to tell if the laconic answer was because he found the subject objectionable.

"But there are other gods in other areas, correct?" Gerard paused at an open doorway into what must be the kitchen. There was a big open hearth in one corner with a smoke-stained plastered chimney above it and tall blue pottery jars lined the far wall. Dried herbs and bundles of root vegetables hung overhead and the room smelled pleasantly of olive oil. Gerard turned to look at the two Syprians, the glasses distorting their images. "How do you tell the difference between gods?"

Ilias leaned in the doorway, not much concerned by the question. "If we were somewhere else, it wouldn't be this god, it would be that one."

"You can tell the difference," Giliead said, looking absently around the room.

It wasn't much of an answer, but Gerard supposed that was all he was going to get. He stepped into the kitchen, checking carefully over the battered wooden table and the jars. Again, he saw small blots of ether, but nothing that could cause any foreign substances to be introduced into the food. If the local god was protecting this place, it was doing a good job of it.

He caught a glimpse into a small larder, where three things that looked and smelled like blue sea crabs, but were the size of small sheep, hung from hooks. *Better warn the girls to take care if they walk on the beach,* he noted absently. A young man with a bewildered expression stepped into the doorway, wiping his hands on a rag. Gerard turned away, moving out onto the walk again.

Ander had remained outside and was waiting there with folded arms. Gerard paused, considering the problem. He had an idea, but he wasn't certain Giliead would accept it.

"There's a possibility I could draw the curse out of hiding." He turned to Giliead, taking the aether-glasses off. "I can produce a generalized Manifestation that causes most common curses to respond."

Giliead's enigmatic expression became more enigmatic. His face troubled, Ilias leaned back in the doorway and looked at his friend. Gerard didn't blame them for their caution; this wasn't a method anyone, even Rienish who were used to the benefits of magic, liked. "It antagonizes the curse, causes it to perceive that the object of its focus is present. But the curse attacks the Manifestation rather than the actual object."

Giliead's opaque expression was much harder to penetrate than Ander's. He looked at Ilias, who shrugged one shoulder, a gesture of indecision. Giliead sighed, as if he had been hoping for more help than that. Gerard persisted gently. "It would allow us to see the curse's actual form. Have you ever seen it?"

Giliead shook his head. "No."

"Would you like to?"

There was a flicker of something in Giliead's eyes. *Yes,* Gerard thought, *he wants to see it.* After living with a

faceless enemy in your own home, who wouldn't?
Giliead nodded.

Ander lifted a brow as if he thought this a dubious exercise, but didn't make any comment.

Gerard stepped out into the garden, feeling the wet grass
sink under his boots. This was a delicate piece of scholarly
sorcery developed at Lodun University less than twenty
years ago and needed no preparations. No matter who did
the casting, curses were all built on the same framework of
hate; this spell would weave its way into that framework to
read the bitter heart at the center.

He cleared his mind, putting aside tiredness, worry, the
pain of various bruises and the persistent ache in his back,
and sank into the words of the adjuration. The spellform
took shape, growing, drawing substance from the light, the
water, the living breath of the green plants. Gerard sealed
the spell and gently pushed it away from him.

"Something's over there." Giliead's voice was sharp.
"Did you do that?"

Gerard opened his eyes. The Manifestation was invisible to normal sight but he could feel it not far away, hovering over the flowering brush on the opposite side of the
garden. It wouldn't have appeared if the curse didn't
exist; this certainly wasn't a case of people imagining a
single cause for unrelated tragic occurrences. "Yes, that's
it." He blinked, still a little distanced from casting the
spell. "Can you see it?"

Giliead took a couple of slow paces toward the Manifestation, frowning. "Sort of. A cloudy gray shape?" Ilias
was trying to follow Giliead's gaze but it was obvious he
couldn't tell what his friend was looking at.

"Close enough," Gerard said under his breath. *So Chosen Vessels can see etheric traces.* Doubtless Ixion had
known that when he had constructed this spell. *If it isn't
moving through the ether . . . we may be looking for something far more substantial than I was expecting.*

Ander stepped up to Gerard to ask softly, "How can he
do that?"

Gerard shook his head, answering him in Rienish, "It

could be latent magical talent—I certainly wouldn't suggest it to them, though. Or it could be as they say, it's a gift that comes from the god." He hesitated, turning back to face the garden. Was the sunlight a little darker? He hastily put the aether-glasses back on.

He saw the Manifestation but nothing else. It was a cloudy shape as Giliead had said, but the glasses allowed Gerard to make out the forms roiling within it Those images were etheric illusions, created by the spell to antagonize the curse and force it to react as if its quarry were present. The sunlit air appeared just as undisturbed as it had before and Gerard frowned, afraid this curse of Ixion's was simply too different to be affected. He didn't have much of a sense for Ixion's craft yet; all he had to work with was a strong feeling that he would be damned if he let the bastard get away with this.

The ground trembled under his feet, just the slightest tremor; if he had been at home, he would have thought a heavy truck had passed in the street outside. Then the earth under the Manifestation erupted upward.

Gerard flinched back in surprise as Ander shouted a warning. Dirt, roots, leaves, gravel boiled up in a gush and out exploded something the size of a large dog. He had a confused impression of spiky black fur, wildly flailing claws and nothing that looked like a head.

The Manifestation dissolved and Gerard snatched the aether-glasses off but the creature remained, solid as the ground under his feet. Silently it rounded on them just as Giliead got his sword drawn and swung at it. It avoided the blow with unnerving speed and darted toward the house. Gerard saw, impossibly, that part of its body was still under the surface, that a plume of dirt fountained up behind it as it furrowed through the ground. Ilias dodged in front of it, blocking its path. It turned at bay, then suddenly leapt at Gerard.

He barely had time to throw his arms up to protect his face when it struck, bowling him over. He fell back into a bush and hit the ground hard, the foul-smelling weight crashing down on his chest. An instant later the weight lifted and he saw Ander crouched over him, gripping the creature by the fur and wrenching it away. Ilias leapt in to help him and together they wrestled the thing down as Giliead stepped in and rammed his sword through it. It gave one sharp cry, an animal squeal, then went limp.

Shaken, Gerard got to his feet, absently brushed the dirt from his already ruined trousers. Grimacing with disgust, Ander was wiping his hands on the tail of his shirt.

Gerard took a step forward for a closer look, but the creature's body was disintegrating. He caught a glimpse of six legs ending in paddle-shaped feet and a flat hole of a fanged mouth before it dissolved back into black dirt.

Ilias stared down at the fading remains, his mouth set in a thin line. "That's why we never saw it."

Giliead gave him a grim nod. He looked up as Karima appeared in a doorway across the court, calling, "What was that?"

"I'll tell her." Ilias hurriedly crossed the garden toward her.

Ander leaned over the disturbed ground as if tempted to prod it with a boot but not quite daring. "It only moved underground?" He glanced up at Gerard. "Have you ever seen anything like that before?"

Gerard nodded slowly. "Yes. It's not . . . usual." It was an ability that only fay and other elemental creatures possessed. Creating a creature that could pass through solid ground wasn't something that should be possible in human sorcery at all, especially not as a by-product of a curse. *So like the Gardier, Ixion and the other sorcerers here have abilities that we don't understand and can't match.*

Giliead sheathed his sword, eyeing Gerard thoughtfully. "It's not over."

"No," he answered, though it hadn't been a question. "After dark I can do a spell to make the etheric disturbances in the ground move to the surface so we can track the curse back to its heart." He looked up to meet the man's eyes. "Then it will be over."

K arima led Tremaine and Florian away from the atrium to a room on the outside wall of the house. It had been a children's room, a fact Tremaine had deduced by noting the wall behind the low carved table had been scribbled on at about knee height with the universally recognized figures of horsies and doggies. The bed was beneath the windows, big and low, piled with a thick feather-stuffed mattress, pillows and more of the gorgeously woven and dyed blankets. Tremaine ran a hand over them wistfully. The figures of leaves and vines were precisely picked out and the colors soft. If the Valiarde Galleries hadn't closed for the war, these would have made a wonderful exhibit.

A very bashful young boy brought a basket of clothing and Karima took it and shooed him away. "These should be more comfortable," she said, eyeing their torn and mud-splattered tweed. She pulled out a couple of long-sleeved shirts of tough cotton. "Try that for size."

Tremaine picked out a shirt and held it up. The hems and open neckline were decorated with block-printed geometric designs. No buttons, just lacings. She bet they were hand-me-downs from the young men in the household.

As Karima turned out the rest of the basket onto the bed, she said, "Your people are really wizards?" She was carefully not looking up at them.

Florian glanced at Tremaine, then plunged in, "They are. But we're not like the ones here. We don't treat people like that."

"I know Giliead—and the god—wouldn't have brought you here if you did." Karima nodded slowly, then looked up and gave them a rueful smile. "It's just very strange."

Deciding this was a good time for a change of subject, Tremaine asked, "Is Ilias your son too?"

"No, he came to us when he was very young." She countered with, "Is Gerard your father?"

"No, none of us are related. Gerard was my guardian when I was younger." At Karima's questioning look Tremaine found herself explaining awkwardly, "My father disappeared—he was fighting the Gardier—and he appointed Gerard to take care of me and the estate in case anything happened."

"In Syrnaic cities women own the property." Karima

cocked her head. "I know it's not that way among the Chaeans and the Argoti."

Florian sat down on the bed, curiously poking through the colorful clothes. "It's not like that with us."

Karima frowned. "It's not?"

"No, it's both. I mean, anybody can own it," Florian explained hastily. Tremaine knew she must have realized that Karima had wanted to make sure they weren't oppressed. *This is a matriarchy.* Men could still hold positions of authority, like Nicanor did now and Halian had before his retirement, but if they couldn't own property that still left the women with a great deal of power. It gave her an insight into why Ilias had objected so immediately to Ander's tone of voice when he had been arguing with her on the island.

"Ah, I see." Karima held up a shirt, measured it against Florian, ascertained that it would fit her like a three-man survival tent, and tossed it back in the basket. "I wish it was that way with us, then I wouldn't have to worry about what happens to my family when I die." She paused, absently smoothing the fabric under her hands. "Chosen Vessels don't marry. People are afraid of wizards and curses and they're afraid of the ones who have to fight them too, and that's just the way it is. But I had a daughter called Irisa and she wasn't the kind of girl to turn her brothers out, so I wasn't worried about the boys. But Ixion's curse killed my Irisa and Ilias's cousin Amari, then it killed Halian's daughter Delphi."

Despite her matter-of-fact tone the pain that crossed Karima's face aged her. Tremaine, who never knew what to say in such situations, stood tongue-tied, but Florian winced in sympathy and said, "I'm sorry."

Karima sighed and patted Florian's shoulder. "So if your friend can make the curse leave, you'll have our gratitude."

Tremaine found herself running a rapid calculation. She wondered if they were certain Ixion had cast the curse. It wasn't as if they could verify the curse's origin. And it was suspicious that it had apparently eliminated Karima's direct heirs, since Giliead couldn't inherit anything. This house and land had to be worth quite a lot. Holding a pair of pants up to her waist to check the length and lost in thought, she said, "Who does the house go to now?"

"It will all belong to Nicanor's wife Visolela, Halian's daughter by marriage, which is not her fault, but there it is." Karima regarded Tremaine thoughtfully for a moment, her hands planted on her hips, the sparkle coming back into her hazel eyes. Her lips twitched in a rueful smile and she said softly, "I thought of that too."

Tremaine felt her cheeks go hot. It probably wasn't a good idea to introduce herself to the family by hinting that even a distant relative was a murderer. "Sorry. I can't help it."

"Don't be sorry." Karima stepped up to her and put her hands on Tremaine's shoulders. "It doesn't hurt to be clever and careful and have eyes in the back of your head. Now hurry with your baths so you can come and eat."

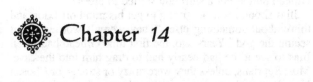

Chapter 14

Finally getting rid of the last remnants of the mud and the stink of the caves was a relief, but Ilias was too preoccupied to enjoy it. He sat in the window embrasure that looked into the atrium, rebraiding his queue and trying to gather his thoughts.

Maybe the curse's dramatic appearance had brought it back to him, but he kept seeing that image, that heartbeat's flash of Ixion's face among the Gardier in the tunnel. He couldn't put it out of his mind. *It was just your imagination. That was where he caught you before, so it's natural you'd imagine . . . all right, that's not working.* He let his breath out, frustrated.

Giliead wandered in from the bathing room, saying, "I talked to Mother about the village."

Ilias glanced up, his mouth twisted ruefully. He meant what was about to happen to it, that the wizards would destroy it tonight when they came to find out what had happened to their other flying whale. "How did she take it?"

Giliead shrugged one shoulder, looking away. "She understands."

That there was nothing they could do about it. At least not now. Ilias looked out the window again. It hadn't been so long since Ixion; they had all thought the big battles were over.

"Ander's asked for the maps we found, or at least two of them," Giliead added as he leaned down to dig through the clothes chest. "He can't read them either, except for the part that looks like the coast of their country, but he thinks his people can figure them out."

Ilias nodded absently. "They're useless to us."

"I just have to see if Nicanor and Visolela will agree." Giliead pulled out a shirt and started to dress.

Ilias shook his head, trying to get his mind off Ixion and think about something else. "They weren't worried about seeing the god." Years ago, the first time Giliead had taken Ilias to see it, he had nearly had to drag him into the cave. Most Syprians, unless they were crazy or strange or Chosen Vessels, would have been equally reluctant. It wasn't exactly fear, just a combination of respect and a reluctance to be noticed by something so undefinable and so important. People of other lands looked at it differently, but Ilias didn't know of anybody he had ever met who would have walked into that cave with such unconcern, not for a first-time encounter with a god. "They didn't think it was real, did they?"

Giliead straightened up, thinking it over. He had been taken to the cave when he was only a few years old so the god could confirm him as a Chosen Vessel, so Ilias knew it was hard for him to understand others' fear of it. "I'm trying to imagine a world without gods." With a rueful smile, he added, "It's strange enough to have wizards as allies, though they're much easier to deal with than the Chaeans."

"Gil—" Ilias hesitated, sitting back against the window frame. His expression would betray him and he didn't like to say it was nothing. Giliead wouldn't believe it, for one thing. *Of course, he's not going to believe this either.* He said reluctantly, "I thought I saw Ixion." He looked up to see Giliead staring at him blankly. He shook his head with a grimace. "I knew I shouldn't have told you. I knew you'd look at me like that."

"When?" Giliead demanded, taking a step forward.

"The way you're looking at me right now."

Giliead took a sharp breath and planted his hands on his hips, staring at the ceiling and obviously striving for calm. Speaking deliberately, he clarified, "When did you think you saw Ixion?"

"Oh." Ilias shook his head. Maybe he wasn't as calm about this as he thought. "On the island, right before we flooded the tunnel. He was with the wizards, the Gardier."

He chewed his lip, trying to think of the right words to describe it. "They were coming up the passage and I saw his face in a flash of light from one of those curse lamps." He shrugged helplessly, annoyed at himself. "Something about him wasn't the same, so maybe it was just a wizard who looked like him."

Giliead was silent, thinking, still absently holding the shirt he was about to put on. Ilias felt a flush of relief and realized he had been half expecting to be told he was crazy, with the strong implication that the last encounter with Ixion had marked his mind worse than it had marked his body. But Gil was Gil and he would consider it calmly and carefully, like he did everything. It might have been a tendency he had gotten from the god, but that was the way Ilias remembered Ranior, Karima's first husband.

Still, they had never talked about that last encounter with Ixion. Ilias had tried not to think about it, but returning to the caves had brought it back. They had both seen a lot of strange things over the years and Giliead had read all the journals with the accumulated knowledge of the other Chosen Vessels. Ilias was the only person they knew of who had been transformed into something else and come back to what he was before. Of course, the journals didn't know everything; they had found that out the hard way. In the end Giliead had come to the conclusion that Ixion's death, coming not long after he had cast the curse, had caused it to fail. *I don't feel any different,* Ilias had told him at the time, and it was still true. As far as he could tell.

Finally Giliead shrugged on the shirt and said slowly, "If you think it was just someone who looked like him, why did you feel you should tell me about it?"

That was a hard question. But Ilias knew a couple of harder ones. "If Ixion's not dead, why did the curse he put on me go away? And for that matter, how'd he grow his head back?"

There had been some kind of commotion about the curse, and Tremaine had gone out into the hall and found Ander on the way to a bath. He had told her only that everything was all right. Tremaine had given up on him and resolved to ask Gerard later.

After Karima had left, she and Florian had explored the room, finding a little cubby next to the fireplace with a hip bath set into the stone-flagged floor, a chamber pot, and a second smaller hearth built into the wall for heating water. "It's not as bad as a cold-water flat," Florian pointed out.

Tremaine thought about Coldcourt, with gas and noisy but efficient plumbing and the newly installed electricity. Every modern convenience. But lonely. And cold. She looked around the bedchamber, where the windows were open to a warm breeze and a view of the fields and the forested hills beyond. A blooming wisteria had draped itself around the supports of the porch on this side. "It's much better than a cold-water flat."

The same extremely bashful young man brought several buckets of water for them, then fled. Tremaine helped Florian fill the cauldron to heat it and then the bath; the fact that they enjoyed this process like a couple of little girls playing house Tremaine put down to shock and exhaustion.

While Florian was finishing her bath Tremaine took the wooden comb they had found and wandered across the hall and out onto the atrium's portico. Down at this end there were several carved couches piled with cushions, but she sat on the stone flags to try to restore her wet hair to some sort of order. The water hadn't been very hot but it had helped soothe the aches and scrapes and bruises. She was wearing a loose blue tunic printed along the hem with green and gold curlicues and pants of a thicker tanned material so soft it was hard to tell if it was doeskin or some kind of woven cloth. She was barefoot but had washed out her stockings and planned to wear her own boots. There was no mirror in the bathing room, but that was just as well; Tremaine had taken so many punches she knew she looked like a retired prizefighter.

The scent of the flowers was heavy in the late afternoon sun. Through the open doors into the main foyer, she could see the men outside the front of the house herding a last few red cows to the safety of the pens under the trees. Some of the women from the village were standing near them talking, bundles of belongings piled around their feet. The place had a "still before the storm" feel though she was surprised everyone was taking it all so calmly. *The Gardier are going to bomb that village,* she thought, *and maybe others besides.* It hurt to think that the little houses with the painted shutters and Gyan's garden wouldn't be there tomorrow. It had happened so often in Ile-Rien, she should be immune to it by now.

Tremaine paused, the comb caught in a tangle. The old house surrounded by fields of flowers and shade trees should have felt unreal; it didn't. It felt vividly real while the horrors of the island, and even the horrors of what the Gardier had done to Ile-Rien, faded away into hazy memory.

She heard Ilias's voice and looked up. He was sitting on a windowsill across the atrium, talking to someone in the room behind him. She almost didn't recognize him. He had just knocked the mud off his old pants and boots, but he wore a sleeveless blue shirt trimmed with leather braid and leather armbands set with copper disks. He was occupied with tying his hair back, giving the queue a practiced twist with a leather thong then tossing it back over his shoulder and shaking his head vigorously to make sure it held. Tremaine wished the camera wasn't with the Pilot Boat at the bottom of the bay. His hair was still a mane but with the queue rebraided and the long loose curls clean and free of mats, the effect was exotic rather than savage.

She found herself wondering if a Syprian wizard-killer would be interested in a dowdy ex-playwright with a past. The enforced closeness down in the caves made it hard to tell. A little observation today had told her that Syprian body language included casual touching; they made even the fairly relaxed Rienish look as stiff as Bisrans. But surely Florian, younger, prettier and less peculiar, had the ingenue role in this story. *Though they really don't like sorcerers,* she reminded herself. Had Ilias touched Florian since he had found out she was learning to be a sorcerer? Tremaine didn't think so. Karima had, but Karima was different too.

Giliead stepped up to the opposite side of the window and leaned against the sill, a thoughtful expression on his face that probably meant he was deeply worried. Without the mud, his hair was chestnut-colored. Another man walked up the portico to speak to them and Tremaine did a double take as she realized it was Gerard. He wore dark-colored pants tucked into his own boots and a light-colored shirt open across the chest, with a dark green printed sash. She grinned, momentarily diverted; he looked ten years younger at least. She got up to join them, picking her way down the stone-lined path across the garden.

As she approached she heard Gerard asking more questions about the god. With a thoughtful expression, he was saying, "So the people who founded Cineth actually chose to settle here because of the proximity of the god?"

"That, and it's a natural harbor," Ilias told him, "but you can't have a city anywhere there isn't a god."

"Why?"

"The wizards." Giliead looked a little reluctant to bring the subject up again. "There was a city in the Inari Mountain pass, built there for the gold mines. It was out of reach of the nearest god but the man who was lawgiver convinced everyone that it wouldn't matter as long as they were careful. It was a very rich city because of the mines, but they must have gotten careless. One month the supply caravan arrived and it was empty except for the guls."

"What are guls?" Tremaine asked, thinking she probably didn't want to know but it was better to get it over with now.

"Shape-changers. They lure travelers away to eat them." Giliead's expression hardened, as if the image recalled an unpleasant memory.

Ilias shook his head. "They couldn't have killed everyone in the city though, there weren't that many of them. And there were no bodies, no signs of fighting. There was food left on the tables, like the people had just gotten up and left. The animals—cattle, mules, chickens, every-thing—were all alive, untouched, unhurt except for being hungry."

Tremaine froze, the comb caught in a tangle. Not notic-ing, Gerard shook his head a little, deep in thought. "Was this reported to you by a reliable source? There's no chance the story simply grew in the telling?"

Gilead smiled suddenly, looking down at Ilias and cocking an eyebrow. Ilias grinned back and said, "We saw it ourselves." He looked at Gerard. "We went there, back when we were younger and more stupid."

Oh, God, Tremaine thought wearily. It was happening again. They were describing a story from one of her plays. Of course the culprits had been fay in her script and there had been no guls and nothing about the lack of sufficient godly protection, but the detail about the animals was exact. She couldn't explain it and she didn't want to think about it. Changing the subject firmly, she asked, "Did you ever meet any wizards who weren't evil?"

Gerard gave her a look of mild consternation and she re-alized he must have been purposefully avoiding the topic.

"There was that old man in Kani." Ilias looked thought-ful. "He kept saying he was cursing people, but nothing ever happened."

"What did you do?" Tremaine persisted, ignoring Gerard.

Gilead shrugged and smiled faintly. "Told them to send for me if he ever actually managed to curse anybody." He fixed his eyes on a bright-plumaged bird that was bathing in the cistern and said, apparently absently, "I like to know for certain."

A s the other men retired to finish dressing, Gerard led Tremaine off the portico and a few paces into the gar-den. "Did you find the curse?" she asked, looking around. Someone had been digging violently in the flower beds.

"I'll explain about that in a moment." He stopped, fac-ing her. "Right now I want to talk to you about Ander."

Tremaine looked up at him, blinking innocently. "Who?"

"Yes, very humorous." Gerard folded his arms, regarding her seriously. "He thinks you're a spy. Have you done anything, perhaps intentionally, to give him that false impression?"

"He doesn't think I'm a spy. Are you out of your mind? He thinks I'm a . . ." Lunatic, useless idiot, something along those lines. "Never mind, but he doesn't think I'm a spy. And why the hell would I do something like that intentionally?"

"I know your sense of humor. Granted you've been so . . ."—Gerard fumbled for a word—"out of sorts for the past few years that you haven't been your usual self, but you've been improving rapidly." He sighed, contemplating the blue sky. "If he came up with that idea on his own, I don't know why."

Tremaine stared at him. *Out of sorts?* She had thought she had kept her feelings from Gerard, mostly by avoiding him. She shook it off and tried to focus on what he was trying to tell her. "We escaped from the Gardier base, Florian and I. Maybe he thinks . . ." *That we're lying, that it was too easy.* She was willing to admit to lucky but not easy. If the base hadn't been still reeling from the airship explosion in the hangar, if the Gardier hadn't dismissed then as little better than children, they would never have gotten out of that first locked room. But no, that couldn't be what Ander was on about. She shook her head, baffled. "He said I was a spy?"

"Nothing so overt. He asked me if I trusted you."

"There you go, he thinks I'm crazy." She didn't want to bring it up but she had to correct Gerard's mistaken impression. Uncomfortable, she admitted, "He knows about the asylum."

Gerard pushed his glasses down to rub the bridge of his nose. He knew she didn't like to talk about it. For the first time it occurred to her to wonder just who had helped her father wreak so much havoc on that place. It hadn't been Arisilde; he had been with her that night. Nicholas had

had any number of people he could call on for assistance in such things. But in the different clothes, Gerard looked less like a scholarly sorcerer and more like someone who would cast a glamour to distract guards while someone else burnt a building down. And Nicholas had made him her guardian. He adjusted his glasses and let out his breath, saying finally, "Just take care."

D usk was falling as they sat out on the atrium portico and had a dinner of round loaves of flat dark bread, fruit and nuts, and grilled fish with little bowls of spicy sauces. During and afterward Ander continued to interrogate Giliead and Ilias for details of the Gardier base. After only a little of this Tremaine stopped paying attention; she was comfortably full and having trouble staying awake.

She sat on the stone porch looking out at the dark garden, hugging her knees. The stars were coming out and the sky was still glowing a deep purple from the last remnants of sunset; because of the Gardier threat, only two small bowl-shaped oil lamps had been lit in the sitting area, attracting suicidal moths. A chorus of insects sang in the trees around the house, a counterpoint to the distant roar of the surf. The evening breeze was pleasantly cool and perfumed with pine and cedar and an occasional whiff of goat from the pens. Karima had gone back inside to supervise the two young men who did the cleaning up. Tremaine could hear other voices occasionally from the front of the house; people had been coming and going most of the evening. They were all evacuees from the village who had questions or needed help or just wanted reassurance.

Ander, sitting forward on one of the low couches, asked, "And you didn't see any markings on the bomb canisters?" He had changed into a loose dark brown shirt and trousers and looked even more rakish than Gerard.

Giliead was half lying on one of the couches, Ilias sitting on the floor and leaning back against the side. "It was dark," Ilias pointed out, unconcerned. He stretched extravagantly. "And how would we know it was writing if we couldn't read it?"

Ander, caught in the middle of drawing breath to pursue the point, hesitated, stymied by this logic. Gerard cleared his throat significantly, as if he thought Ander was pressing their hosts too hard. Tremaine wasn't concerned; she had the feeling that when they were tired of answering questions they would just stop.

While Ander was trying to regroup, Giliead led the conversation back to the topic he had been pursuing just as relentlessly as Ander had the Gardier base: how sorcerers were treated, or how they treated everyone else, in Ile-Rien.

Listening to Gerard talk about instances of criminal sorcerers and how they were dealt with, one name stirred Tremaine's interest enough for her to say, "Wasn't Urbain Grandier a Bisran?"

Sitting on the other couch with Gerard, Florian corrected around a yawn, "I think he was half Rienish. Or was that half Aderassi?"

"It hardly matters," Gerard put in, forestalling the tangent. "And if it does, it's certainly outweighed by Constant Macob, who had a fine Rienish pedigree and was a murderous lunatic." He shrugged slightly. "There is the occasional mad or criminal sorcerer, and has been all through Ile-Rien's history. But for the most part a demonstrable magical talent means, at the very least, the guarantee of a lifelong profession. Even for the mercenary-minded, there isn't much motivation to injure people when helping them is so much more profitable. Also, it's a self-policing profession. There's always someone more powerful—or more cunning—to watch out for."

"What happened to Constant Macob?" Giliead asked, leaning forward, intently interested.

"Tremaine's father—" Gerard hesitated, searching for the right word. "Disposed of him."

Ander, mouth open to wedge an interruption in at the first opportunity, turned to stare at Tremaine, brows drawing together. Florian, apprised of Valiarde family history, widened her eyes in surprise, then nodded thoughtfully to herself. Giliead turned his enigmatic look on Tremaine, but it was tinged with approval. Ilias nudged her with a foot and gave her a smile. Suddenly self-conscious and feeling undeserving, Tremaine shifted uneasily. "Uncle Ari and my mother helped."

Before Giliead could ask another question or Ander seize control of the floor again, Ilias said suddenly, "Gerard, do you know about curses to turn people into other things?"

Giliead's head turned sharply toward him; Tremaine couldn't read his closed expression, but the sudden tension in the set of his shoulders was obvious. Ilias sounded, if anything, just curious.

"I know about them," Gerard said mildly. He was looking off into the dark garden and she didn't think he had noticed Giliead's reaction. "It's not something I could do myself."

Still sounding as if he was just making conversation, Ilias asked, "Why?"

"That kind of transformation is a very powerful act. It's also a violation against nature." Gerard shifted to face him, warming to the subject. "In our world, it's a power the fay have, but the fay aren't human; they aren't composed of the same sort of material as we are. It would take a human sorcerer an enormous amount of power to alter the state of an object—even something like turning a pebble into a bit of wood. And the transformation wouldn't be permanent; the sorcerer would have to keep the spell active to maintain the bit of wood. The effort would be incredible."

Florian didn't add anything but was nodding along with the explanation. Ilias cocked his head thoughtfully. "So . . . If a wizard did curse somebody to turn into something, they might just turn back all on their own."

"Yes, that's exactly what could happen, if it could even be managed in the first place," Gerard answered. "And the backlash against the sorcerer who tried to keep the transformation spell active would be intense, possibly fatal."

Ilias's expression was distant as he listened. Giliead stirred uneasily, but said nothing.

Gerard continued, "This is all hypothetical, you understand, since I'm not sure such an action would be at all possible for a . . ." He hesitated, perhaps recalling that in this world the physical laws governing magic might be different. "For a human sorcerer in our world, at any rate."

Watching them thoughtfully, Ander said, "Why do you ask?"

Ilias rubbed the back of his neck, looking as if he was still turning over Gerard's words. "Ixion could do it."

"He could?" Gerard sounded mortally offended. "You're certain?"

Ilias glanced up with a slightly twisted smile. "Very," he assured him.

It was Giliead's turn to clear his throat. "Is it dark enough now to look for the rest of the curse?" Tremaine lifted a brow as private commentary to herself, thinking that it couldn't be more obvious if he had simply said that he wanted them to drop the subject.

Gerard stood, taking a step to the edge of the portico to examine the darkening sky. Tremaine looked up at him as he nodded to himself and said, "Yes, the stars are—" He hesitated, glancing down and frowning, and Tremaine realized the sphere was clicking, the gears inside beginning to spin.

A distant rumble rolled over the little valley like thunder. Tremaine sat bolt upright, suddenly wide-awake. That sound was all too familiar.

They were all on their feet. "What was that?" Giliead demanded.

"The village." Ander said grimly. "The Gardier are back."

Giliead and Ilias exchanged a bleak look, then Giliead said, "We can see it from the roof."

They started away down the portico, Ander and Gerard right behind them. Karima stepped out of the doorway, her face drawn in concern. "Was that— Was that it?"

Giliead stopped to speak to her as Tremaine grabbed the sphere and turned to follow. "You coming?" she asked Florian.

The other girl was standing, hugging herself and rubbing her arms as if she was cold. "No, I've seen enough bombings." She nodded toward the sphere. "You want me to hold that for you?"

"No, I'll take it with me." *Just in case.*

They went up the outside stairs to the second floor of the house, from there taking a narrow ladder up to the flat tile roof.

Giliead and Ilias had made it up first and were both crouched tensely near the edge. From there they could see the airship as it drifted away from the ruined village, playing its searchlight over the beach, a silent deadly shape that caught the reflected glow of the fire it left behind. Everybody had agreed that they had to sacrifice the village to keep the Gardier from designating the entire coast as a target, but it still wasn't easy to watch.

"Odd," Gerard commented, keeping his voice low as he sat down near Giliead and Ilias. "The sphere seems to be getting more sensitive to the presence of the Gardier. It obviously felt that bomb blast before we did."

Tremaine settled cross-legged on the clay tiles; still warm from the day's sun, they felt good against her aching legs. She said, "It must know the airships pretty well now, after destroying the wards around that other one."

Ilias glanced back at her but it was too dark to read his expression. Ander sat next to Gerard, saying, "You mean it has the airship's scent?" His voice sounded thoughtful.

She nodded. "To attack something that big, with so many powerful spells and counterspells and who knows what else involved; that must have been a real treat after it was locked up alone in a cabinet for so long." She turned the sphere over thoughtfully, looking at the play of light deep inside. "No wonder it wants to do it again."

It was quiet while everyone thought that over. "Good," Giliead said softly.

Abruptly the airship's spot and running lights went out. There was just enough light left in the sky to see it turn south toward the forested hills. Tremaine shifted uneasily, but the house and the outbuildings were safely dark. Word had been passed to the inland villages and Nicanor had taken the information back with him to Cineth; the Gardier up in the airship might have been passing over uninhabited desert for all the signs of life they would see.

The Gardier might be reluctant to employ that search-light again; they would know that something had destroyed their other airship. As if tracking its movements, the sphere rattled on the tiles like it was filled with angry bees.

"Where did Ixion come from?" Tremaine asked, sud-denly wanting a distraction from the burning village she could see in her mind's eye. She shook her head slightly. "I mean, who taught him? How did he become a wizard?"

Giliead shifted back to face her and she thought for a moment he was going to avoid the subject again, but he an-swered, "People who want to be wizards usually swear themselves to another wizard as a slave. When they learn enough, they break free and kill the master. Or die in the process. We weren't sure where Ixion came from. He told us it was a village outside Renaie, but . . ." He shrugged, looking back toward the airship.

Ilias added, "He had three other wizards slaved to him that we killed."

Ander and Gerard were quiet for a moment, absorbing that piece of information. It did explain why all the practic-ing wizards here seemed to be homicidal madmen. Tremaine thought you would have to be some sort of nut to want to participate in such an arrangement in the first place, and cunning and vicious to survive it. She nudged Gerard with her foot. "And you said the entrance examinations for the College of Etheric Philosophy at Lodun were harsh."

He resolutely ignored her. He looked from Giliead to Ilias, saying, "Perhaps you should tell us as much about the wizards of this world as you can."

The Gardier flew a search pattern over the hills and val-leys, then came back to the village to drop two more bombs. After that the airship turned back out to sea.

Everyone else seemed to want to stay up and continue

the conference, but Tremaine found Florian asleep on a couch on the portico, woke her and shepherded her back to their room.

Stumbling with weariness, they changed into their borrowed shifts in the bathing room beside the hearth, then climbed into the big soft bed. Tremaine burrowed into blankets that smelled like summer grasses, ready to stop thinking for the day, but Florian woke up enough to want a report on what they had talked about up on the roof. As Tremaine told her about the conversation, Florian sat up in bed, frowning. She said, "The way Ilias was asking about transformation spells. The evil fay sorcerer Rogero casts a spell like that in your story in *Boulevard*. It reversed all by itself too."

Tremaine sighed. "No."

"No?"

"That story was in the *Bonicea Weekly Journal*."

"Oh." Florian was silent for a moment. Sounding worried, she said, "But that's the second time something happened here that was very like one of your stories."

"Third. There was another one while you were taking a bath. *The Vanishing Island,* the play that ran for two seasons at the Excelsior."

"That's . . . strange."

Tremaine wiggled further under the covers and said, voice muffled, "That's putting it mildly."

"It's like Ilias said on the way to the god's cave today. You've had some kind of connection to this place, even before we knew it was here."

"Six impossible things before breakfast."

"What?"

"That's all I can handle today. Good night, Florian."

Florian sighed and reluctantly said, "Good night, Tremaine."

Tremaine woke suddenly from a dream of antiaircraft batteries firing along the city wall. She reluctantly dragged herself out of sleep, feeling as if she was packed in cotton wool. The bed was warm and the mattress stuffed with feathers; it seemed to be trying to pull her back down and she wasn't convinced of the need to fight it. Sitting up with a groan, she looked around vaguely, blinking, trying to see what had woken her. The room was dark except for the red glow of dying coals in the hearth and dim moonlight falling through the window. The air was just cool enough to make the clinging mattress and the heavy cover comfortable. In the other half of the bed Florian was an unmoving lump buried under the blanket.

On the low table near the wall something emitted a metallic cluck. *Oh, wonderful.* Tremaine rubbed her forehead and sighed. It was the sphere.

Damn Gardier. She climbed reluctantly out of bed. Stumbling, she found her clothes draped over a stool and pulled the cotton shirt on over her shift. Picking her way across the dark room, the tiles cool under her feet, she found the sphere on the table. It clucked more rapidly as she picked it up.

"All right, all right," she whispered to it. "I hear you." While she was trying to make her sleep-muddled brain work, she thought she heard Gerard's voice. She went to the window and peered out.

Past the shade trees the field was silver in the moonlight. The ruins of the other house were just dark lumps under the trees at the far end. She couldn't see any movement but after a moment she thought she heard Ilias's voice, then Gerard again.

Shoes, shoes. Tremaine pulled her boots on without her stockings and stepped over the low windowsill. Crunching across the dry grasses and a scatter of acorn shells, she became very aware of all the sore spots and new calluses on her feet. She didn't see a Gardier airship overhead anywhere but caution made her keep to the shadows under the trees, making her way from one to the other as she followed the voices.

She found the men in a stand of pines, the last cover before an open area that surrounded the tumbled foundation of the other house. "—no one's done anything with it since the fire," Ilias was saying. "Hello, Tremaine."

"Hello." Tremaine hadn't thought she was sneaking up on them; they would have heard her swishing through the grass and crushing acorns all the way from the window. But he must be able to practically see in the dark to know who it was. "Gardier back?"

"The airship hasn't returned," the dark shape that was Gerard said, keeping his voice low. "Ander's on the roof, keeping watch."

"Gerard thinks he found where the curse lives," Ilias told her.

"Oh." The tree trunk next to her moved suddenly and Tremaine yelped.

"Sorry," Giliead's voice said.

"That's all right." Tremaine stumbled, clutching the sphere to her chest. She supposed it would have warned her if she had been standing next to something dangerous. At least she hoped so.

As the men moved off, Gerard said in annoyance, "Tremaine, try to be quiet."

Picking her way after him, she said, "Is the curse going to hear me and hide?"

Sounding exasperated, he replied, "It might."

"Are you sure it's there?" Giliead asked, preoccupied. "I still don't understand how we could have missed it."

Gerard answered, "It probably goes dormant for long periods of time to avoid discovery. Also, it may have had difficulty manifesting in the presence of the protective influence—the god, as it were."

"So the god kept it from doing anything worse?" Ilias asked, moving noiselessly through the grass somewhere ahead.

"Apparently so."

Tremaine stumbled on a stone block and recovered with difficulty, clutching the sphere. She picked her way more carefully forward, knowing she would have broken toes now if not for her stout boots. The tumbled blocks of masonry were sun-bleached white and in the silver moonlight they were almost invisible against the tawny grass. She caught up with the men at the remnants of a knee-high wall and stepped over it. "What are we looking for?" she asked. Gerard had told her about the curse traveling underground, more like a fay than a product of human sorcery. "I thought Ixion cast it before this house burned down." The fire would have eliminated most run-of-the-mill cursable objects, unless Ixion had tied his spell to a building block or a beam.

Gerard turned toward her and the moonlight flashed off the bulky aether-glasses. "I think we're looking for a solid object, not just an etheric focal point. Whatever it is, it's somewhere in these ruins." He paused in front of a lump that resolved into the remains of a hearth as Tremaine caught up with him. "Once the moon rose, I was able to bring up the tracks in the ground, crossing the field toward the main house."

"Is that it?" Giliead asked from somewhere to the left.

Gerard was silent a moment and Tremaine knew he must be staring at the whitened stone. It was barely visible in the night's soft coat of moonlight and shadow. Just the sad, innocuous remains of what had once been the center of a home. "Yes," Gerard said softly, his voice taking on an almost trancelike quality. "It's under the hearthstone, in some kind of clay container. When the conditions are right it creates the creature we saw and sends it out to spread disease. I can also make out sparks around it which must be indications of the salamander characteristics that allowed it to cause the fire."

The sphere clucked rapidly, as if it was antagonized by Gerard's description of the thing under the hearth. "Stop that," Tremaine muttered to it. *You got me out of bed so you could have a midnight snack? I don't think so.*

Gerard stepped back and finished briskly, "You were fortunate that the protective influence kept it from causing even more damage."

The shape that was Giliead knelt beside the white oblong of the hearthstone. Ilias slipped past Tremaine to lean over his shoulder. "I can't see a thing," Giliead confessed.

"If I understand your abilities, you wouldn't, not while the curse is dormant. Ixion probably chose this method specifically to circumvent you," Gerard explained, blunt but kind.

Ilias snorted. "I could have told you that— Ow." He backed out of elbow range.

Giliead blames himself for everything, Tremaine thought, and this curse had been like a wound that wouldn't heal. Ilias, more practical and without the onus of being the Chosen Vessel, was less affected by it, but it still had to hurt. Ixion had left a legacy of guilt and pain as well as death. Gerard was doing more here than rooting out a particularly nasty curse and he knew it.

Gerard rubbed his hands together. "We need to lift the stone and destroy the container. Then a sharp implement with a high percentage of iron—" Tremaine heard the snick of a sword clearing leather. "Like that. That should do the trick."

Chapter 15

"When you drove off the grend, how did— Wait." Arites, trying to ride while scribbling on a fragment of parchment with his thigh as a desk, wasn't having much luck at either. He had his ink bottle tucked into a pocket of his jerkin, but his horse kept veering off the trail toward the trees.

"It's really all a blur," Tremaine put in while she had the opportunity. "We don't really remember that much."

"That's right," Florian seconded from her seat behind Tremaine. Fortunately one of the sturdy dun-coated horses provided for them was a calm even-tempered beast both large and placid enough that both women could ride together. This was just as well, as Tremaine hadn't ridden in ages and Florian's experience had been confined to ponies that could be rented for a turn around the park. Gerard had confessed to being an adequate rider and Ander, of course, was an expert. "You could just make up the exciting details."

Ilias laughed and Giliead, riding ahead with Gerard and Ander, glanced back with a smile, saying, "Arites, enough."

After waking at an appallingly early hour and eating a breakfast of a thick grainy porridge sweetened with honeycomb, they had started on the trail across the hills for Cineth. Scratchy tweed and wool would have been hard to face after the soft simple native garments, so Tremaine was just as glad to stick with those. Karima had found an old battered leather bag with a shoulder strap that was perfect for the sphere. It was lined with pale silk that had been treated with oil, so they could even fill it with water temporarily if they had to. Gerard was carrying it now.

Gyan and Dyani had come along also and would be going out on the *Swift* with them once they rendezvoused with Halian and the rest of the crew in the city. Neither had gone back to the village yet to see what remained of their house. No one had commented on that at all, at least not in her hearing; perhaps they were too used to wizards appearing to wreak havoc. Or they were just too courteous to talk about it in front of their guests, who had brought all this trouble down on them.

The ride through the forested hills was actually pleasant, though Tremaine knew she at least would be paying for the unaccustomed activity with sore muscles tomorrow. Especially since the saddle, while made of beautifully dyed and detailed leatherwork, had no padding whatsoever.

It was lovely country, the rich green hills carpeted with pines and fern trees, mountain streams trickling down the rocks and turning into small waterfalls. Dyani and Ilias took turns pointing out the best views and Gyan swatted Arites whenever he tried to press for more details about the Isle of Storms for the epic he was writing.

It was almost too soon before gaps in the trees allowed them to glimpse the city ahead. Not terribly large by Ile-Rien standards, it sprawled across a series of low hills that overlooked the sea. The landward side was protected by a stone wall studded with square towers. As they followed the dirt path that wound down from the hill, Tremaine could see the houses were mostly white stone, with red clay tile roofs. Like the village, there were lots of trees, planted in the little yards or climbing the sides of the small hills that dotted the plain, most of which were surmounted by round stone buildings. *Temples,* she wondered, then remembered, *No, they don't have temples, do they?* Maybe they were forts.

As the path flattened out to approach the city, Giliead reined in and turned toward them to say, "They'll know about you by now, that you're wizards." He sounded fairly pessimistic about the prospect. "People from Agis's village will have talked about what happened during the first attack."

Ander's horse tossed her head impatiently and he settled her, asking, "You think there could be trouble?"

"No more than usual when we're there," Ilias said, with a wry look at Giliead.

Giliead regarded him with a lifted brow for a moment, then smiled back and admitted, "That's true."

As Giliead turned his horse to continue down the path, Ander shook his head wearily and Gerard frowned.

"I'm too old for this," Tremaine heard Gyan mutter behind her.

They rode through a gate in the white stone wall, past guards who leaned on long spears and watched them curiously. Then up a long straight street of hard-packed dirt, lined with white clay houses with fruit trees leaning over the walled yards.

There were people out, men and women, walking or riding along the street, hauling the little two-wheeled wagons, or talking in front of open gates. Children played in fountain courts, but Tremaine sensed some agitation in the air and in the wary glances that were thrown at them. Though if word had spread about the Gardier, that made sense.

The street opened up into a large common area with stands of trees shading little markets where awnings and small tents were pitched. Around the outskirts of it there were larger, more elegant buildings, with columns and brightly painted pediments that formed a ribbon of color just under their rooflines. None was taller than two stories but they were impressive enough for public buildings. The goat herd grazing on the grass just complemented the pastoral ambience and the simple elegance of the architecture. Tremaine wished again for the pocket folding camera that had gone down with the Pilot Boat.

While Ilias helped Florian down, Tremaine noticed the market wasn't occupied with merchants and customers. No one seemed to have any wares out and while groups gathered under the tents here and there, they had the look of uneasy people who had come for gossip and news.

"They've spread the word admirably quick," Gerard commented, reining in nearby. "That will help."

"Nicanor probably called an assembly last night," Giliead said, dismounting.

Tremaine, who felt she deserved a treat after not falling off the whole way, let Ilias help her off the horse. "That's the Assembly, where the town meets," he said, pointing to the long building with the pillared portico. "And that's the mint." A round building with a domed roof. "That's the lawgiver's house." A two-story house more imposing than Andrien, with a forbidding square façade. "And that's the Fountain House." A low square structure with what looked like sea serpents carved into its pediment.

Arites and Dyani led the horses away to the shade of a stand of pines. Brushing off her pants and glancing around, Tremaine noticed more people were staring at them. A group of older men standing near the portico of the council building looked in their direction and frowned. At the nearest market tent, a couple of women and another man were all but doing the classic "talking behind their hands" pose. It gave her the exposed feeling of being out during an air raid. She noticed that while Ilias and Giliead weren't acknowledging the stares, they both suddenly seemed to be taking up more room, as if daring anyone to come over to object to their presence.

"Well, they were right about people being unfriendly," Florian said under her breath.

Tremaine was frankly glad to see Halian appear on the portico and come toward them, passing the disapproving group of elders without an acknowledgment. He greeted Giliead with a slap on the shoulder and nodded to the others. Turning to Gerard, he said, "You were right, they came ashore first to look the place over. A ship, moving fast with no sail or oars."

She saw Gerard and Ander exchange a look. It was probably an ordinary skiff with an engine. At least Tremaine hoped it was.

Halian continued, "They landed small boats—they looked metal, but it was hard to tell with those wizard lights they use—and about twenty of them searched the place, tearing things up. Then they went back out to sea, and the flying whale appeared."

Giliead folded his arms, his expression grim. "We saw the fire."

Halian nodded, taking a deep breath, and Tremaine realized that for all his calm acceptance, the sight had affected him deeply. "Think of all the fireliquid we used on Ixion's ships, all going up together." He looked at Gerard again, his face grave. "That's what they're doing to your cities?"

Gerard was staring off toward the city wall, lost in thought. He said absently, "Yes. For three years."

"You're lucky it didn't find any other targets," Ander put in. "They can carry up to twelve canisters of explosive."

There was a moment of silence as the Syprians digested that. Ilias swore softly under his breath and exchanged a worried look with Giliead. Gyan made a shocked noise and even Arites looked bleak at the thought. Halian shook his head. Then he glanced up, his expression clearing. "Here's Nicanor."

They looked around to see the lawgiver standing on the portico of the council building, speaking to a beautiful dark-haired woman dressed in a deep red gown. *Arantha*, Tremaine said to herself, thinking of the doomed heroine of the classic play. It had been her mother's favorite. This woman certainly looked like someone who would burn down a Great House for love. Nicanor was holding her hand with casual affection but she glanced toward Halian and the others and spoke, her heart-shaped face turned up to his appealingly. Tremaine just caught the words "wish you wouldn't speak to them in public."

Tremaine glanced at Halian in time to see his eyes go hooded. Ilias sighed and looked down, scuffing his boot in the dirt. Giliead just rolled his eyes. Gerard was pretending he hadn't heard, Ander's deceptively innocuous expression meant he had seen it and filed it away for future consideration, and Florian kept nudging Tremaine with her elbow to make sure she was aware of it. Dyani, who had either missed the moment or was so accustomed to similar slights that she simply hadn't remarked it, said innocently, "That's Visolela, Nicanor's wife." Everyone stared at her and she blinked, startled at the sudden attention, and added defensively, "Well, it is."

As Giliead dropped an arm around Dyani's shoulders, Nicanor frowned down at Visolela and shook his head sharply. He left her, stepping out from under the portico and walking briskly toward them. There was something very decided about that walk to join his father and the others, as if he was making a statement by it. And after his wife's admonishment not to speak to them in public, it might very well be. If that was true, it made Tremaine like him more. It was one thing to yell at Giliead and Ilias in front of family and friends and strangers who weren't quite people yet, but it was another to show disrespect in the main plaza in front of everyone important in the city.

Nicanor nodded a greeting, which sort of almost managed to include the wizard strangers. Tremaine still gave him credit for doing it in front of everyone. He said to Giliead, "I need to talk to you in private."

Giliead nodded. "One thing first." He met Nicanor's eyes, saying deliberately, "Last night, Gerard found Ixion's curse."

Nicanor frowned and Halian shook his head slightly, not understanding. He asked, "What do you mean, 'found'?" He glanced at Tremaine and Florian, confused. "It didn't hurt anyone . . . ?"

"No, no." Giliead cleared his throat. Tremaine got the distinct impression it was hard for him to speak of this and he had been hoping to have to give as few details as possible. "He found what was causing it. It was in the new house, under the hearthstone. It's gone now."

"You mean . . ." Nicanor said slowly, "There's no more curse?"

Giliead smiled suddenly. "No more curse."

Halian stared at Gerard, hopeful and incredulous all at once. "You can do that? You did that?"

"It's done fairly often in Ile-Rien," Gerard said with a faint smile. He added hastily, "Of course, it's illegal to put curses on people there and it really doesn't happen very often. The consequences—"

"You saw this?" Nicanor demanded, speaking to Giliead.

"Ilias and I were both there." Giliead took a sharp breath. "Ander has asked to take two of the maps we took from the island back to their people. I've told him yes—" Ilias cleared his throat and Giliead added belatedly, "with your permission."

Nicanor still pressed his lips together, obviously well aware he was being pressured. He said nothing for a moment and Halian scratched the back of his head and offered carefully, "They're no good to us—we can't make anything out of them."

Nicanor looked at Ander and unbent enough to ask, "You can read them?"

"I can't." Ander faced him, practically radiating "stalwart scion of nobility," but Tremaine was willing to admit to being cynical. He said, "But there are others in Ile-Rien who might be able to in time."

Nicanor eyed him a moment, then nodded sharply. "Very well."

The others went to wait under the trees as Nicanor took Giliead aside. Giliead had signaled for Ilias to come with him and he had gone reluctantly, not sure it was a good idea to antagonize the lawgiver just now. But Nicanor didn't give any indication that he was annoyed. He faced Giliead, saying without preamble, "There's trouble with the council."

Giliead's expression remained noncommittal, but he flicked a glance at Ilias. Ilias's mouth twisted ruefully. That explained why Nicanor had been hanging around out here on the porch; they couldn't start the council until the lawgiver was seated in the chamber. Giliead asked, "What kind of trouble?"

Nicanor looked past them, where the others stood talking with Halian. "Your new friends. You gave them guest-right?"

"You know I did."

Nicanor's eyes came back to Giliead's. "And it's as Halian said, the god accepted them?"

Giliead folded his arms, his expression stony. "Do you think your father would lie to you?"

Nicanor just pressed his lips together and waited. He was speaking as the lawgiver now and wouldn't argue.

"Gil," Ilias said through gritted teeth. They didn't have time for this.

Without looking at him, Giliead stopped, took a breath. "Yes, it's as he said."

Nicanor acknowledged that with a lifted brow. "And you set the law aside for some better reason than that they helped Ilias when he got himself captured by the new wizards."

Ilias let his breath out and stared at the sky, squinting. It wasn't as if that hadn't been asked for. Giliead set his jaw, then said tightly, "Yes."

Nicanor nodded, keeping his face neutral. "Then I'll take care of it. I'll need you to speak for the god."

"Of course."

As Nicanor walked back to the lawgiver's house, Visolela gathered her skirts and disappeared inside.

"Do we trust him?" Ilias asked, suddenly feeling uncertain. He knew Giliead wasn't good at taking the mood of the council and the god knew neither of them had too many friends in town. Especially among the heads of families. Ilias hadn't spent much time in Cineth since getting the curse mark. He didn't want to force the friends he had had there, especially the women, into repudiating him. And Giliead had always been set apart by his status as Chosen Vessel.

"Yes. No." Giliead absently rested a hand on his shoulder, thinking. Then he looked down at him grimly. "Ask Halian to take them on down to the docks."

Ilias gave him a sharp nod. Nobody would try to stop Halian; he had too much clout from his former tenure as warleader and too many family alliances. And if things went very wrong, it would be best for their friends to be close to the *Swift* and a quick departure.

Giliead started for the council house and Ilias turned back to the others. He drew Halian aside and explained briefly. Halian swore in annoyance, running a hand through his graying hair. "Idiots," he added. It was probably a good thing that as warleader Halian hadn't had to deal much with the council. "I knew I should have brought your mother." He also couldn't speak as head of the Andrien family without Karima present.

"Somebody had to run things at home," Ilias pointed out. He had given up reminding Halian that Karima wasn't his mother.

"That's true enough. Still . . ." Halian eyed the lawgiver's house regretfully, obviously wishing he could harangue the council himself. Sometimes it was easy to tell he was Nicanor's father. Then Halian shook his head and went back to the others, saying, "We're going on to the docks."

"Is there anything wrong?" Gerard asked, concerned.

"No, just some things Giliead has to attend to," Halian told him, managing to hide his irritation with the council and sound reassuring. He gestured for them to move off toward the harbor road.

Somehow Ilias wasn't surprised that it was Tremaine who ducked the attempt to shepherd her away, detoured around Arites to avoid Halian, and asked Ilias, "What's wrong?"

As the others moved away, Ilias looked at her and gave up on trying to invent a polite lie. In normal clothes she and Florian looked more like the pretty girls they were, but Tremaine's gaze still had that hard edge. "We've got to talk to the council; they don't like the idea of you all."

Tremaine looked at the lawgiver's house, at the group of townsmen that were still watching them narrowly. One of them tried to stare her down and she coldly met his gaze, holding it until he looked away. She turned back to Ilias almost absently, as if the moment had been of such little concern to her that she hadn't really noticed the man's hostility. "Are you in trouble?"

"We're always in trouble." He added with a shrug, "It'll be all right. They'll believe Gil."

Tremaine gave him the penetrating stare. It was every bit as daunting as those Giliead was capable of; Ilias grinned at her. "Really."

"What happens if they decide they don't like their Chosen Vessel anymore?"

What if they kill him? she meant. Ilias planted his hands on his hips and looked at the market stalls under the trees. It was a serious question, so he answered it seriously. "That's only happened once before, many years ago and not here." It had been in the Vessels' Histories; thinking about it brought back long-ago memories of those nights sitting by the fire, Ilias curiously looking over the faded scrolls while Giliead learned what his life was likely to hold. How to kill wizards, how the other Vessels had died. "They killed their Chosen Vessel and their god left." He shook his head. "No one here is willing to risk that."

Tremaine frowned. "Where did it go?"

Ilias looked at her, his lips quirking. Only she would have asked that question. "Nobody knows. Back where gods come from, I guess." He nodded toward the others, who were past the trees and had reached the beginning of the harbor road. "You'd better go too."

She pressed her lips together, not happy, but she went.

Ilias watched until she caught up, then headed up the steps to the lawgiver's house to walk along the portico to the council house entrance.

The round high-ceilinged room was crowded, all the tiers of benches up to the roof occupied with the male heads of household and the younger sons and daughters. The female heads of the household sat up on the top tier, where the best view was and the little square windows just under the roof let in air. Across the dome itself was Ilias's favorite of all the murals in the lawgiver's house, the one that told the story of Elea's voyage to Thrice Cumae, with the Ocean of Snakes, the Walls of the World and all her other adventures picked out in delicate little tiles.

They were still talking among themselves in soft worried voices, shuffling for room, trying to get comfortable. The heads of household who meant to speak were standing and there was a depressingly large number of them. Giliead, his arms folded, was on his feet in a place on the lowest tier, wearing a stolid expression. Nicanor's place on the opposite tier was still empty, but he was up at the top, helping Visolela settle herself in her own seat, both exchanging comments with the other women. Despite the breeze the room smelled of sun-warmed dust and too many people.

As Ilias started forward, an older man stepped down from his seat, a preoccupied expression on his face. It was Pella, the lawgiver's deputy. He glanced up, saw Ilias, and his eyes narrowed. He would have liked to keep Ilias out, but he wouldn't speak to anyone with a curse mark, even to order him away. Ilias deliberately met his gaze as he shouldered past him.

Ilias crossed the tiled floor and sat down on the step at Giliead's feet. Ferias, a husky red-faced man with a perpetually angry expression, was one of the speakers already standing, waiting impatiently for Nicanor to sit down. Ferias's family had been enemies of Andrien so long no one could remember why and it was no surprise that he was leading the opposition.

As Nicanor stepped down the tiers and leisurely took his seat, the hushed conversations began to die down. Impatient to begin, Ferias faced Giliead, saying, "You brought those people into the city. Why?" His loud voice startled everyone into silence. Ilias could hear birdsong from the trees outside.

Giliead gave Ferias a hard stare. "They are travelers, with guest-right. They earned that guest-right defending Agis's village from the wizards that later destroyed it. We're taking them back to . . . a place they can reach their home from."

There was a low murmur of comment throughout the

room. Ilias hoped nobody asked how exactly that was going to happen. Gerard had tried earnestly to explain it, but the only point Ilias was clear on was that it required curses. Hopefully most here would just assume the *Swift* was taking them somewhere they could meet another ship.

Ferias looked around at his audience. "They are wizards themselves," he announced, as if everyone hadn't been talking about it all morning.

"They are at war with the Gardier wizards on the island. The lawgiver has already explained this and I'm not going to repeat his words." Giliead let his gaze travel around the room too. "They want to be our allies."

Ferias slammed his fist into his palm. "Bringing those people here is why the wizards attacked in force—"

"The wizards had already attacked," Nicanor interrupted suddenly. He fixed Ferias with a cold eye. "Unless you think the gleaners' villages and the missing ships were a coincidence?"

Gibelin, who spoke for the gleaners and was always a hothead, surged to his feet and angrily demanded, "Or perhaps the dead gleaners weren't worth your notice, Ferias?"

Ferias just stood there, breathing hard. Ilias looked at the ground to conceal his expression. Ferias had started out with the wrong argument; few here would believe the Gardier wizards would have just let the Syrnai alone. Everyone would know they would have attacked the coast eventually, provoked or not. Then Ferias fixed his eye on Giliead again. He said deliberately, "How can we trust your judgment? After Ixion. You let him into your house, led your own sister to her death." He turned away to appeal to the whole room. "How can we trust him after that?"

Everyone burst into talk. Some were agreeing, some disagreeing, some objecting on religious principles, and some agreeing but protesting the outright rudeness of Ferias's declaration. Mouth twisted, Ilias exchanged an annoyed look with Giliead. Ferias couldn't say anything they hadn't already said to themselves or each other.

Nicanor contemplated the ceiling mosaic, letting the

clamor continue, then said loudly, "Ferias. Do you trust the god?"

An uneasy silence fell. Ilias sensed Giliead tense. Lawgivers couldn't give orders to Chosen Vessels, but if Nicanor wanted to pursue this argument, he had far more stones to throw than Ferias. Even if Nicanor was on their side, Ilias wasn't sure he wanted to hear this.

Ferias looked as tense as Giliead. He was speaker enough to know that Nicanor was a canny opponent and that the question was a trap, but how to avoid it eluded him. "Of course I trust the god," he snapped, adding irrelevantly, "Didn't it cure my cows of the hoofblight last year?"

Up on the top tier, Ilias saw Ferias's wife cover her eyes with her shawl.

"Whatever its view of the events of last year, the god has not repudiated Giliead." Nicanor's impenetrable gaze went to Giliead. "His judgment is its judgment."

It was unfair but effective. The other heads of household started to argue among themselves and Ilias saw Ferias's wife motioning for him to sit down.

They tramped down the road that led to the harbor, Tremaine occupied with her thoughts. She hoped this council turned out to be nothing, but Halian looked worried. Along the way people stared at them from windows, from under the shade trees in the little yards or from groups gathered around the fountains, but nobody seemed to want to stop them.

The road turned at the top of a rise and they suddenly had a view of the harbor. It was sheltered by a high promontory, which boasted a pyramidal stone tower for a lighthouse on one side and a long breakwater of tumbled blocks on the other. Along the waterfront there were stalls with stone walls and wooden roofs, where a number of merchants presided over lots of raw materials like bars of copper and tin and sacks of grain. Short stone piers extended out into the water for the ships to dock at, though many were stored in long wooden sheds along the far bank.

The *Swift* was tied up decorously near the top of one of the stone piers, which was something of a relief; Tremaine had been afraid they would have to push it out into the water again and that seemed a far more difficult process than beaching it. Various crew members were climbing the mast and pulling on the ropes, getting the ship ready.

Gyan, who had gone ahead, waved at them as he came back along the dock, stopping to talk with Halian. Gerard, Ander and Arites gathered around to listen. Tremaine was already starting to feel sore from the ride and went to take a seat on a stone bench near one of the big wooden posts where the ship was tied off. Despite the bright sunlight the breeze coming off the water was pleasantly cool.

Florian and Dyani followed her, Florian plopping down with a sigh suggesting the ride had tired her too.

It was a busy place, with men hauling barrels, casks and big rust-colored pottery jars, traders hawking their wares. Tremaine caught snatches of conversation, most of which concerned the "wizards on the island." Fortunately no one on the crowded dock seemed to realize there were wizards right here, too.

As she watched, she saw a short, burly man with light graying hair come out of a grain stall and stop and stare at the group around Halian. Tremaine sat up a little. There was something in that stare; it wasn't just curiosity to know who the strangers were. His eyes moved over the men as if he was looking for someone in particular. He reminded her of an unfriendly dog, looking for someone to bite. Then he turned and moved away down the dock.

Dyani nudged Tremaine with an elbow. "That was Ilias's brother," she said softly.

"His brother?" Tremaine repeated stupidly, but Dyani nodded, knowing what she meant.

"They don't look much alike, do they?" Dyani eyed the re-treating back of the other man without favor. "That's how Ilias came to Andrien."

"What do you mean?" Florian asked, sliding forward on the bench.

Dyani threw a look around to make sure there was no one in earshot, then leaned confidentially toward them. "When he was a boy, barely seven years old, his father decided that he didn't want him anymore, and he took him out to the hill where people leave babies."

Florian's eyes widened in shock. "That's sick," she murmured. "That doesn't happen a lot here, does it?"

Dyani nodded. "Not as much. Ranior, who was Karima's first husband, made a law against it when he was lawgiver, but that doesn't stop people like the Finan."

"That's Ilias's family?" Florian asked, who seemed to be having better luck at keeping it all straight than Tremaine.

"It was then. Now he's Andrien."

"How did he get to be Andrien?" Tremaine prompted.

"He tried to find his way home. He was going along the road in the dark and Ranior and his men came riding by— this was after Gil was born and Ranior wasn't lawgiver anymore—and he found Ilias and he took him home to Andrien. They found out who he was and what must have happened, but Ranior hadn't caught Ilias's father in the act, so he couldn't do anything about it."

"Ranior was Gil's father?" Tremaine asked, frowning a little as she tried to get everyone sorted out.

"No, the god is Gil's father," Dyani explained patiently. "Ranior was Karima's husband. He died a long time ago, before I was born," she added.

"So Ilias's family won't have anything to do with him because of all this?" Florian asked, disturbed. "That's really unfair, considering it was all his father's fault."

"Well, it's that and the curse mark." Dyani grimaced and added, "Of course, that's not fair either."

"The curse mark?" Tremaine felt she sounded like a parrot, but there were too many unfamiliar words, too many concepts that didn't seem to have any equivalent in Rienish.

Dyani touched her own face, just at the cheekbone. "The brand, here. It's given to anyone who's had a curse put on them and survived. My father would have one, if he'd lived."

Tremaine and Florian exchanged a startled look. *Damn,* Tremaine thought. She had taken it for an ornament. Dyani was right, it was unfair. Considering how often Ilias and Giliead had risked their lives fighting wizards, it was a mortal insult.

Dyani shrugged and looked down at the rough boards under their feet. "Gyan says we're lucky we all don't have matching sets, considering how Ixion hated everybody."

"Having a Chosen Vessel in the family isn't really considered a good thing, is it?" Tremaine said, suddenly putting two and two together. Karima had said people were almost as afraid of the men who had to kill wizards as they were of the wizards themselves. And if she understood what Dyani was telling them, Ranior had left an important and prestigious position as lawgiver after Gil was born. And years later Halian had left a similar position before he married Karima. Tremaine wondered if that was the source of the tension between Nicanor and the others, if he resented his father for risking the family fortunes and prestige merely for love.

The people in the Andrien village hadn't seemed to care much about it, but then they would have been used to seeing Giliead and Ilias every day, would have watched them grow up or played with them as children. It was probably hard to develop a good full-blown superstitious fear about someone you had known as a grubby two-year-old.

Dyani nodded, looking somber. "I don't know why. I guess so few people in the city know them and don't realize they're just like ordinary people." She glanced up, smiling a little tentatively. "Like you. You're around curses all the time, but you're not strange."

"I'm strange, she's not," Tremaine said, straight-faced.

Dyani's smile turned into a grin and she nudged Florian with an elbow, as the other girl chuckled. Tremaine was aware of another pang. She had been having them all morning and finally she realized why. She didn't want to leave.

People accustomed to Giliead's deadpan sense of humor didn't find hers obscure at all. People used to being thought odd themselves took her oddness for granted. After they got on the boat she might never see this place again. And she found, after all, that she did want to see it again.

"You know, this is one time we could have used some cloud cover and mist." Ilias studied the faultless blue sky overhead.

Giliead nodded, giving the sky an annoyed look, as if the day had dawned clear solely to harass them. "I hope the waterpeople know something."

The council had finally disintegrated into a disorganized jumble, with no one sure all the questions had been answered but with everyone certain there had been more than enough arguing. On the way to the *Swift*, Giliead had decided to see if the waterpeople knew anything about the Gardier's activities around the island and they were walking out along the tumbled stone of the jetty to consult them.

The wind was wet with spray as the waves crashed against the rocks almost under their feet. "That was interesting, what Gerard said about curses," Giliead said finally.

Knowing something else was coming, Ilias agreed, "It was."

Paying far more attention to his footing on the damp rock than could possibly be necessary, Giliead said, "Whatever Ixion did to you with that curse, you were still you."

"I know." Ilias stepped over a gap where foamy water rushed against the rock, trying to think what he wanted to say. "I just wasn't sure you did."

Giliead paused, one foot on the next block. He looked back at Ilias. They regarded each other for a moment in silence. Then Giliead said, "Well, I did."

There didn't seem anything else to say after that. They continued on to the end of the jetty, where the rocks were tumbled and scattered and the water foamed up between. Ilias could see sleek brown forms playing and diving in the waves not far off the end and he and Giliead whistled and shouted to get their attention.

A small group of waterpeople gathered just off the rocks, their blunt brown heads bobbing in the waves. "You see anybody we know?" Giliead wryly studied the nearly identical heads.

Ilias snorted. It was nearly impossible to tell waterpeople apart at any distance. Their thick fur made their features hard to distinguish and there wasn't that much difference between the men and the women. Waterpeople thought landpeople were indistinguishable too, so they had to wait until somebody recognized them.

Finally, a big male swam closer and heaved himself up onto the rocks. Waterpeople didn't have legs, just long tails with heavy fins on the end, making them awkward on the land but blindingly fast in the water. Their hands had blunt awkward fingers tipped with large claws, useful for breaking open clams and crabs. Ilias and Giliead climbed down closer to him, sitting on the rocks so their heads would be mostly level. As the waterman shifted closer, peering at them, Giliead asked, "Is that Tuvas?"

Waterpeople had their own names, but their speech was all whistles and clicks and squeals and impossible to duplicate. They called this one after a cousin of Ilias's who had had the same blunt features and flat ears. Ilias said, "I think so. Hello, Tuvas."

Tuvas whistled back whatever name he used for Ilias and made a gesture of greeting, the whiskers around his heavy muzzle pulling up in an attempt to mimic a human smile.

"We need to know about a place in the sea," Giliead told him, "if there are any strange ships sailing there."

It took both of them to make Tuvas understand the area they meant, mainly because all his landmarks were underwater. More blunt heads surfaced to watch and the young ones climbed up on the rocks, curious about the humans. The babies especially were all over Ilias, poking and tugging, but Giliead remained unmolested.

The waterpeople liked Gil, they spoke to him and smiled at him, but they didn't touch him. Even now one of the younger females crouched beside Tuvas, staring longingly at Giliead's gold earrings, obviously wanting to touch them. It had to be something about him being the Chosen Vessel, something that they could see or smell. Giliead had never mentioned it, but Ilias wondered if it didn't bother him.

Finally, Tuvas realized the area they meant and began to nod rapidly, using his entire upper body. "Things stir," he said, his rough voice slurring the words.

"What things?" Giliead asked patiently. Tuvas always tried to answer their questions to the best of his ability, he just didn't always know how.

Tuvas weaved back and forth for a moment before he answered, "Evil things of rock-that-isn't."

"You mean wood? Like that?" Ilias pointed back toward the ships tied up along the piers, ducking his head away from the baby that kept tugging on his queue.

"No." Tuvas leaned forward. "Like . . ." A long clawed finger hovered for a moment, then tapped Ilias's knife hilt. "That."

"Metal things?" Giliead exchanged a glance with Ilias. "Halian said the boats the Gardier landed at the village before they attacked looked metal."

"Boat." Tuvas nodded and put his hands together, miming something that cut through the water and made swishing noises. "Big boat."

Chapter 16

While the crew was bringing aboard and storing the last casks of water, Tremaine and Florian explored the ship a little, finding there wasn't much more to it than what they had already seen. Below the deck was just one big open area, with the banks of rowing benches, ten to a side, through the middle. There was a space at each end filled with rope, red-glazed pottery jars and other supplies. Woven rope hammocks festooned the ribs that supported the decking and it smelled strongly of tar and wet wood. Even in the calm waters of the harbor, the sea seemed awfully close to the ports for the oars.

Florian stood by the ladder, leaning down to look out a port. "Can you imagine taking a long voyage in this?"

"It wouldn't be so bad, as long as nobody was shooting at you," Tremaine replied, picking her way back down the central aisle, trying not to trip on the shipped oars. "And you weren't seasick. And there wasn't a storm—"

"Hey," Ander called, leaning down to look through the opening in the deck. "They're back!"

Tremaine hurried to the ladder, scrambling up after Florian to see Giliead and Ilias standing with Gerard, Halian, Ander and Gyan. As the two girls reached them, Giliead was telling the sorcerer, "They're expecting you, all right. The waterpeople said a metal ship is patrolling the seaward side of the island."

"Couldn't we use the sphere to attack them, like it did the airship?" Florian asked hopefully.

Tremaine nodded. "Yes, let's do that."

Gerard shook his head slightly, worried. "That's not entirely practical in this situation."

"Why?" Giliead asked, watching him.

Planting his hands on his hips and looking thoughtfully down the length of the *Swift*, Ander said, "That ship will have big guns—projectile weapons," he clarified as there wasn't a Syrnaic word for gun, "and one or two good hits will blow this hull to pieces. And the guns fire much faster than the sphere works. Also the Gardier know we've got a secret weapon now, they'll be prepared for an attack. They may not even mess about with trying to take us alive."

Gerard lifted his brows. "I think we're going to have to try a ward." He turned to the other men, explaining, "It wouldn't work with one of our ships. The Gardier use their spell that destroys mechanical and electrical devices as a blanket attack, casting it over large areas. Even if the ships are protected by illusion, the spell is still able to destroy their engines." He smiled faintly. "That spell won't have any effect on this ship, any more than it did on your catapult."

Ander nodded approval. "We could slip right past their patrol."

Gyan and Halian looked doubtful. Giliead just stood with arms folded and that blank expression that could mean anything. With a dubious look, Ilias asked, "What's a ward?"

"Ah." Gerard hesitated, suddenly recalling the difficulties. "It's a type of spell . . ."

"You want to cast a curse on the ship," Halian repeated. His tone was not encouraging.

Arites, sitting on a bundle of ropes nearby, whistled softly in astonishment. He started to dig in his bag for his writing materials.

"It's not a curse," Florian said persuasively. "Really, it's just a charm, and all it does is keep the Gardier from looking at the ship."

None of the Syprians looked convinced and Tremaine wasn't surprised; the word for *charm* in Rienish meant *curse* in Syrnaic, just as *spell* did.

"There are wards cast on the ships we still have in port," Ander elaborated. "The wards make the Gardier think they see empty water, or a wrecked hull."

"It's like what the guls do," Giliead said finally.

"Sort of," Tremaine said, fairly sure that wasn't the mental association Ander and Gerard had been hoping for. The guls were the shape-changers Giliead had mentioned before, the creatures that drew travelers to their deaths. "Only it's not a lure, it's the opposite. It's a go-away."

"Or a look-away, really," Florian put in, with what she obviously hoped was an innocent smile.

Giliead looked at Halian, who sighed, ran a hand through his hair, and stared unhappily off at the waves. Halian said finally, "You know a ship that's been cursed has to be burned."

Gerard let out his breath. "I didn't realize that." *Halian probably loves this boat,* Tremaine thought unhappily.

"That's just if anybody else finds out about it," Gyan said suddenly.

Tremaine saw Ilias's face go still. Giliead started to speak, then glanced worriedly at Ilias and said nothing. Ilias's reaction surprised her a little; if anyone had moral objections to the plan, she would have thought it was bound to be Giliead.

Halian stared at Gyan. "Well, it's true." Gyan shifted uneasily and folded his arms, his tone defensive, as he added, "If Gil thinks it's all right, I don't see why it's anybody else's business but ours."

Ilias abruptly turned and walked away, heading over to the far side of the deck. Giliead watched him go, his brows drawn together in concern.

Halian looked after Ilias too, then fixed a glare on Gyan. "We don't even know that the rest of the crew will agree to it."

Gyan shrugged. He looked guilty but determined to stick to his ground. "You know they'll go along with you and Gil."

Halian let out his breath. "We'll see." He threw Gyan a

quelling look and added, "And we'll worry about who we do or don't tell when we get back to port."

Giliead walked over to where Ilias was leaning on the starboard railing. The set of his friend's shoulders was a clear warning that he wanted to be left alone, but then it was Giliead's job to go places others didn't dare. He said, "You don't think we should do this."

Ilias looked at him, his expression carefully neutral. "There's no choice. It's stupid not to. Everybody saw what their curses can do to the Gardier wizards."

The neutral expression and mild tone were bad signs. Giliead said deliberately, "I meant, you don't think we should lie about it afterward." The law that mandated that anyone who had survived a wizard's curse should be marked forever had been born out of fear. Gods didn't have eyes to see the marks anyway; Giliead had never talked to one who gave a damn who had been cursed and who hadn't. The law did nothing but punish innocents for surviving.

A flicker of emotion crossed Ilias's face at the thought of the consequences of telling the truth. Giliead knew he didn't want to see the *Swift* burned any more than Halian did. But Ilias shrugged and said noncommittally, "Halian will leave it up to you. It's your choice."

Giliead took the last step and leaned on the railing next to Ilias. It had been his choice since the day they had told him he was a Chosen Vessel and he was weary beyond words of it. "But it wasn't your choice when it happened to you."

"The *Swift* doesn't have to live with herself afterward." Ilias shook his head, letting a little of his frustrated anger show. "I'm not arguing, I'm not saying we shouldn't do it, and I don't blame Gyan for suggesting it." Gyan's wife had died from a curse long ago; he had every reason to oppose the curse law. Ilias turned back to the railing. "I just . . . need some time, all right?"

There were a lot of things Giliead wanted to say, none

of which was the least bit relevant. *I never believed in it either; I told you you shouldn't do it; it's not my fault.* He still didn't understand why his friend had allowed himself to be marked. Why he didn't believe in the law for anybody except himself. He said finally, "I just wish I understood."

"I do too," Ilias said under his breath, but Giliead wasn't sure which one of them he meant.

They got under way, most of the crew going below to man the oars. The cloudless sky stretched forever and the sun was bright on the clear blue water. Tremaine hung over the railing with Florian, watching the golden cliffs along the shore, the wind and sea spray in her hair. *We'll be back in Ile-Rien soon*, she thought, not happily. It was probably a traitorous thought, that she would rather disappear into this world than go back to the problems of her own. After the ship left the harbor and the purple sails caught the wind, Ilias joined them, leaning on the railing next to her.

She considered him thoughtfully. She had seen his discussion with Giliead and it had made her uncomfortable. She couldn't help but feel responsible, even though the ward hadn't been her idea and she was contributing nothing toward it. Even the sphere wouldn't be needed. "You don't think the ward is a good idea?" she asked. She felt as if she was poking a beehive with a stick but couldn't help herself.

Ilias glanced up toward the helm where Halian stood holding the tiller. Ander was up there too, probably asking questions, because Halian was pointing off toward the coast as if describing the terrain. Gyan, apparently disagreeing with Halian's assessment, was shaking his head and pointing in the opposite direction. "It's not my decision." Ilias shrugged, refusing to be poked. "And cursing the ship is the only idea we've got."

Tremaine didn't think he was as immaterial to the process as he would like to think. It was easy to see Giliead consulted him in one way or another on every important point and most of the unimportant ones too.

"It's not a curse, it's a ward," Florian corrected gently, using the Rienish word, "And it won't hurt the ship."

"Halian knows that." Ilias shook his head, turning to look back out to sea again. The cliffs on the far side of the harbor might have been carved out of gold. Banners of cloud trailed overhead. Some children, barely stick figures at this distance, ran along the shore waving wildly at the ship.

Despite his easy expression, Tremaine scented trouble and couldn't help pursuing it. "So it's just the way your people are very uneasy around anything that's had a spell put on it?"

Florian looked a little anxious. "Was that why Giliead was so upset when he found out I used that charm to heal your shoulder?" She wet her lips uneasily. "I still feel bad about that. If we'd known how you felt about spells—"

"No, that was nothing," Ilias told her, smiling, but still gazing off toward the cliffs. "Don't worry about it."

Tremaine eyed him a moment. "You've been under a curse before," she said, remembering what Dyani had told them about the mark on his cheek.

He nodded, giving her a thoughtful sideways glance. "Once or twice."

Florian drew breath to ask more and Tremaine, suddenly guilty for prying, kicked her in the ankle.

When they were out past the headland, Halian ordered the crew to ship oars and come up on deck. There were some uneasy looks and shifting around as he explained the plan, but as Gyan had predicted, everyone seemed to find the fact that Giliead had agreed to it reassuring.

Creating a simple ward, not meant to last very long, was not a complicated process. They had salt in the supplies on board and some charred coal from a brazier. Before the ship cast off they had sent Dyani and Florian running down the dock, one to the house of an old sailor to borrow some sprigs of rosemary and the other to collect nettle from the scrubby grass patches between boat sheds.

Gerard prepared the ingredients in the privacy of the small cabin, Giliead sitting on his heels next to the sorcerer to watch and Ilias leaning in the doorway with Tremaine. Florian perched on the bunk so she could learn Gerard's method.

Gerard combined the herbs with the charcoal and salt in a pottery cup, using a simple incantation to activate the principles of all the ingredients. With the mixture he drew the operant characters on a piece of parchment, then sat back. "That should do it."

Giliead lifted his brows. "Is that all?"

"It's only a temporary ward and not a very complicated one." Gerard wiped sweat from his brow. It was damp and hot in the cabin. Tremaine could see he had written the characters in a square so that they read the same four ways, from top to bottom and left to right, then from bottom to top and right to left backward. "Indeed, a more elaborate ward would hardly serve the purpose, since it would be bound to draw their attention."

Ilias frowned, giving Tremaine an uncertain glance. "So when they look for the ship—"

Gerard carefully folded the paper, glancing up with a smile. "They can look all they want, but it simply won't occur to them that what they are looking at is anything other than a drift of fog or a trick of the light."

"We got away from the Gimora wizard once by setting a rowboat adrift with a lamp in it," Giliead said thoughtfully.

"Was that in one of your plays, Tremaine?" Florian asked, glancing up at her.

Tremaine shook her head. It didn't sound familiar. "I don't think so."

Gerard glanced up absently. "What?"

"Some of the things that they told us about, Ixion and the city that didn't have a god," Tremaine explained, "they're very close to things that happened in some of my plays."

Gerard stared at her as if she was mad. Perhaps feeling responsible, Florian said hurriedly, "It's very odd, but it's true. There's a part in *Varnecia,* and then some of the magazine stories . . ."

Gerard listened with an expression of growing incredulity as Florian outlined the similar incidents they had noticed. "Why didn't you say something?" he demanded finally.

"We said something to each other about it," Tremaine protested. "And Ilias."

"I told Gil," Ilias put in helpfully. Giliead, still keeping a thoughtful eye on Gerard's spell mixture, nodded confirmation.

Tremaine couldn't understand Gerard's dismay. "Why? It's just a series of coincidences."

"It could be highly significant!"

"Of what?" Ilias asked, listening with interest.

"I . . . don't know." Gerard shook his head, annoyed, and asked Tremaine, "When did you write that play and the serials? Before or after Nicholas and Arisilde disappeared?"

Tremaine blinked. She hadn't thought about that. "After."

"There was obviously some sort of connection established between you and this world." He looked suspiciously at the sphere, sitting next to Florian on the bunk, still in its bag. "Where were you when you wrote them? You were living at Coldcourt, with the sphere?"

"I wasn't living *with* the sphere. It was there in the house, but . . ." She stared at the device, disturbed. "So you think it had something to do with it? It had a connection with this world, because one like it sent my father and Arisilde here?"

"That's the only explanation I can think of," Gerard said slowly. He shook his head. "I just wish I knew what it meant."

Tremaine had to agree.

"There it is!" Standing atop the aft cabin, Arites was peering through a crude telescope. Tremaine got to her feet, trying to see what he was pointing at. Behind her

Ander climbed up from the tiller platform where he had been sitting with Halian. Arites handed him the device.

Tremaine shaded her eyes. She had been down below where Ilias and Giliead had been taking their turns on the rowing benches with the other men, until the heat had finally driven her back on deck. The late-afternoon sun was bright and the sky cloudless and she couldn't see a damn thing. She went to the cabin and hauled herself up the rope net that was draped over it to sit on the plank roof. Ander sat on his heels to hand her the telescope, saying, "Take a look."

Tremaine peered through the "seeing glass" as it was called in Syrnaic. The tube was intricately carved wood, but the lens was ground very roughly and it was difficult to make out anything. She finally saw what everybody was pointing at. There was a low gray shape out there on the water and she could discern the outlines of a deckhouse and funnel. She lowered the glass, glancing up at Ander uncertainly. "It's not coming this way. Is it?"

"No, she hasn't seen us." Ander took a sharp breath. "So far."

"Your curse must be working," a wary Halian said from the tiller, squinting toward the Gardier ship.

Ilias slung himself up beside Tremaine, perching on the roof, and she handed him the glass.

"You have those ships in your world?" Arites asked eagerly. "Ixion used black ships without sails and they moved by curses too."

"His were smaller than that," Ilias commented, sounding grim as he looked through the telescope.

Gerard, consulting the compass, waved at them from the deck. "Come on, we're just within the perimeter of the target area!"

Tremaine jumped down with Ander as Florian came hurrying up from the bow. Ilias handed the glass back to Arites and followed.

"Now how are we going to do this?" Ander asked as they gathered around the sorcerer. He checked the pouch at his belt, where the maps Giliead and Ilias had taken from the airship were folded and protected by an oiled silk cloth. "Without taking the whole ship across and scaring the hell out of our new friends, I mean."

"I think if we can borrow that small dinghy," Gerard said to Ilias, eyeing the little boat where it was lashed to the deck, "we could—"

"Leviathan!" Arites's voice slid up half an octave on the word.

Tremaine heard Florian gasp and turned in time to see a huge hump of mottled gray-green break the surface not twenty yards off the side. She gaped. The back was rimmed with spiny fins and the whole thing was at least half the size of the *Swift*. "And that's only one hump . . ." she said, not realizing she had spoken aloud until she heard her voice.

"But it can't see us, can it?" Ander whispered. The ship had gone oddly quiet. *Funny,* Tremaine thought, *you'd think people would scream.* She sure felt like screaming, though her throat couldn't seem to manage it just at the moment. Gyan and three other men were frantically hauling on ropes, changing the sail's position, and Halian was leaning on the tiller, throwing his whole weight against it. Giliead was standing up by the bow, staring intently into the water. Ilias had moved to the railing on this end, leaning over so far she was afraid he would overbalance.

Florian, staring rapt as the hump began to sink below the surface, shook her head. Gerard cursed softly and said, "The ward won't extend below the surface of the water. It can see the underside of the hull."

The boat was starting to turn, but with nerve-abrading slowness. The oars had been shipped already and no one was moving for them. *It'll hear the oars,* she realized. Dyani was crouched at the base of the mast and the rest of the crew stood frozen, waiting.

Gerard shrugged off the leather bag with the sphere and shoved it at Tremaine. She clutched it awkwardly as he spoke the words of the reverse adjuration. *Brilliant,* she thought frantically, *take the whole boat across, send the Syprians back later when it's safe. . . .*

But nothing happened.

"Dammit, when they turned the ship we moved out of the target area." Gerard grimaced and shoved the sphere's bag all the way into her arms. "You and Florian stay with Ander."

Tremaine clutched the bag, staring at him blankly. "What?"

"Gerard, the Gardier will hear any spells," Florian said desperately as the sorcerer went to the railing.

"We don't have a choice," Ander told her, taking her arm to keep her from following Gerard. "They probably sent that thing after us, the way they used the howlers in the caves."

God, he's right. Tremaine swallowed in a dry throat and hugged the sphere to her chest. Gerard lifted his hands, speaking softly, staring into the water. Tremaine felt the sphere shudder and click and behind Gerard dust stirred on the deck, spiraling up in the invisible current of whatever force he was summoning. Ilias threw him an uneasy glance but didn't move away.

"What's he doing?" Ander asked Florian quietly.

She shook her head, biting her lip in consternation. "I'm not sure, I've never heard . . ." She blinked in understanding. "That was the old speech for 'to reveal all, to cease enchantment, to pull the veil, to dissipate the energies—' He must think it's a construct."

"A what?" Ander asked sharply.

She explained hurriedly, "Not a natural creature, but something created by a sorcerer. If he can break the spell that created it . . . but that's got to be one powerful spell." She threw them a desperate look. "I don't think he can do it without the right preparations."

Giliead suddenly leapt back from the bow, yelling a warning. Before they could move the ship shuddered. Tremaine felt the deck lift under her feet. She grabbed Florian, feeling the other girl's fingers dig into her arm. People scrambled for handholds, cried out in alarm. Ilias swung back on the railing, clinging to it. Ander cursed, bracing his feet to keep from falling. *It's surfacing under us,* Tremaine thought, shaken, then she heard wood crunch. *No, it's got us in its teeth.*

The sphere jerked suddenly inside the leather case. "Uh oh," she muttered. She could hear it clicking, feel the trembling as it spun itself up into a frenzy. "I think it's going to—"

A flash like ball lightning flared between the sphere clutched in her arms and Gerard. Tremaine could almost feel it add its power to his. *It didn't even have to be in contact with him,* she thought, startled. *It's getting stronger.*

Gerard's voice rose to a shout and Tremaine's stomach lurched as the ship dropped. The sea sprayed up, soaking them, then fountained as if the ship had plowed into a waterfall.

A triangular head crested with spines surfaced suddenly, sending up another drenching spray. Tremaine stumbled back, getting a confused image of white staring eyes and scales the size of platters. It opened its jaw in a soundless screech, revealing huge teeth clotted with splintered wood. Then the eyes grew a gray film and the head wavered back and forth as it sank.

"He got it, Gerard got it!" Florian called excitedly. Then she froze in shock.

As the leviathan's head submerged they could see the Gardier ship, only a few hundred yards away. It must have come for them at full steam, alerted somehow by the creature. "We're done for," Tremaine said under her breath.

She saw a flash near the gray deckhouse and Ander yelled, "Get down!" He dragged Tremaine and Florian to the deck just as a booming crash announced an artillery shell.

Tremaine felt the deck shift under her feet, then suddenly the world turned upside down and planks smashed down on top of her and she slammed into the sea's surface.

Tremaine flailed underwater. She surfaced, gasping, and caught a wave in the face that almost drove her under again. She kicked and managed to get a breath, looking around in time to see half the bow roll over. A haze of smoke drifted over splintered wood, people clutching floating timbers. Something tugged at her arm and bumped her shoulder. Her mind on monsters and Gardier, Tremaine splashed wildly before realizing it was the leather bag with the sphere, still caught on her arm.

She heard Florian calling her name and twisted around to see the other girl clutching a floating spar, only a few yards away. She saw Ilias surface near it and realized he was holding on to an unconscious Ander. He shook the hair out of his eyes, trying to paddle awkwardly toward the spar, but something was wrong with his free arm. *He's hurt,* Tremaine thought, swimming toward him.

Her progress was awkward and furious but it got her there. She grabbed Ander's arm just as Ilias went under again. Without that burden he surfaced, managing to keep himself above water with his good arm. Florian, holding on to the spar and kicking, managed to bring the end of it within reach. Ilias grabbed it and Tremaine managed to push Ander up far enough that Ilias could hold on to him too. Tremaine treaded water, looking around as the sphere, still caught on her arm, bashed her in the head with each wave.

The damn Gardier boat was almost on top of them. Tremaine cursed under her breath. She wasn't seeing a ready way out of this one. Several people clung to the *Swift*'s largest remaining hull section, about twenty yards away. With relief Tremaine saw Dyani and Arites among them. Then Giliead surfaced, pulling Gerard up so he could get a grip on the wood. "Gerard!" she yelled, waving to catch his attention. The sorcerer was conscious, shaking his head and gasping.

He spotted her and shouted, "Try to go! We might be in the target area!"

"We can't!" she shouted back, appalled. They had discovered early in the experiments that the sphere could transport large numbers of people and objects, as long as they were connected by something etheric waves could travel through. It would have taken the entire *Swift* and everyone on it through the portal easily. But with the ship in disconnected pieces and most of the people floating on the water, it would leave them behind.

A hatch sprang open on the upper hull of the Gardier ship and a man carrying a large gun emerged, then another.

"Go, go! Get the sphere away!" Gerard shouted furiously.

"Shit." Tremaine gritted her teeth and swam toward Florian. She caught hold of the spar one-handed and held out the bag to the other girl.

Florian eyed it uncertainly and twitched her wet hair out of her face. "I don't know— Can I see it?"

"Sure." Tremaine pulled at the lacing and Florian helped her get the sphere out of the bag. She didn't know whether she wanted Florian to be able to do this or not. She didn't want to leave Gerard and the others, but they couldn't let the Gardier get the sphere either.

Ilias, keeping Ander's head above the surface and awkwardly gripping the spar, twisted around to shout desperately, "Gil!"

"Go with them!" Giliead shouted back.

Hating this, Tremaine told Florian, "Now."

Florian nodded, her expression torn between anguish and anxiety. She put her hand on the sphere, whispering the words of the reverse adjuration.

Tremaine felt the familiar lurch as the world changed. Something slammed into her legs and she collapsed, knocked flat by a heavy thump in the back. The light of a poisonously red sunset dazzled her. The surface beneath her was hard, warm and gritty.

She shook her head, dazed, trying to push herself up. She could see a dusty brown hill rising in front of her, with scrubby dark-colored grass poking up out of the sand. *Where the hell . . . ?*

Something heavy lay across her back and she twisted, shoved at it. It was the spar. Squinting against the brightness, she could see Ilias and Ander a few feet away, sprawled on the gravel-strewn ground. Ander stirred without waking, but Ilias sat up, shaking the dripping hair out of his eyes, wincing as he looked around. He was cradling one arm and she could see Ander's temple was bleeding.

Tremaine turned to see Florian, curled protectively

around the sphere, just lifting her head. She managed to say vaguely, "What . . . where?"

Florian shook her head, bewildered. Tremaine looked at Ilias hopefully, but he was staring past her, eyes narrowed incredulously.

She twisted to look. About fifty yards away a dark cliff face stretched up, curving away at the top. There was an oddly square cave entrance in it, nearly a good three stories high. The land around it was barren, empty, just dusty desert hills rolling away under the orange-red sky.

Aghast, Ilias shoved to his feet and said slowly, "Is this your world?"

"No, no, this isn't it." The impact of her own words hit and the bottom seemed to drop out of Tremaine's stomach. *This isn't it.* She wet her lips nervously. "We're in the wrong place."

"The wrong place?" he echoed, looking at her, his expression torn between relief and dawning horror.

"Oh, shit!" Florian dropped the sphere as if it had burned her. "I did something wrong!"

"Florian." Tremaine caught the other girl's shoulders, speaking calmly and deliberately. She felt she had gone beyond panic and into a state far more profound. "Just calm down, and try it again."

Florian's eyes were wide and she choked on the words, shaking her head rapidly. "I can't—"

Tremaine gave her a gentle shake and smiled. She didn't know where this strange calm person had come from, but she hoped Florian listened to her. "You can. You just . . . dropped a decimal point, that's all. Just try it again."

"Right, right, I have to." Florian pressed her palms to her forehead. She looked up at Tremaine, uncertain. "The return location sigil is very close to one of the other sigils that Niles and Tiamarc and Gerard never could figure out. But it was a constant, so we didn't have to manipulate it, so . . . Maybe I changed it by accident."

Ilias flicked a desperate look at them. Tremaine nodded reassuringly to Florian. She hadn't a clue what the other girl was talking about, but Florian needed encouragement, not questions. "That must be it."

"Right." Florian nodded to herself and rolled the sphere back between them. "Everybody hold on to the spar, we need that to connect us."

Tremaine nodded to Ilias and he crouched next to them again, between her and Ander.

Florian closed her eyes, wetting her lips. "Here goes," she whispered.

"Let it help you," Tremaine told her impulsively as she put her hands on the humming metal. "It just wants to help." *It better help. You hear me in there, sphere? You want to act on your own, then get us the fuck out of here.*

"All right. I'm calm. I'm taking a deep breath," Florian whispered.

The ground shook and they stared at each other. Then it did it again. And again. "What is that?" Florian muttered, distracted.

Warily watching the opening in the cliff, Ilias hissed, "Hurry!"

Tremaine shook her head slightly, baffled. "What is it?"

He looked at her as if she was crazy. "It's coming this way! The giant thing that lives in the . . . thing." He nodded toward the cliff face.

In the opening Tremaine suddenly saw a shadow, a moving shape, coming closer. . . . Her eyes widened as her perspective shifted and she realized what she was looking at. It wasn't a cliff, it was a wall, a stone wall, and that opening— "That's a door."

Florian swore as the realization struck her too. She grabbed the sphere and the world shifted again.

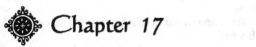

Chapter 17

Tremaine plunged into salt water again but this time it was freezing cold. She thrashed, her feet reaching unsuccessfully for the bottom and surfaced into pitch dark, treading water. *Oh no, we did it again.* Her voice harsh with panic, she called out, "Florian! Ilias!"

She heard splashing nearby and a gurgle and a gasp, and Ilias's voice called roughly, "I'm here! I've got Ander. Where's Florian?"

"Florian!" Tremaine bellowed, sweeping her arms around in the dark, the freezing water making her teeth chatter. No answer. That was a big spell for a barely trained witch like Florian. If she was unconscious she would be floating facedown. *She won't be far away, dammit.*

Her flailing hand encountered wet cloth and she grabbed and pulled, feeling hair slide over her hand. "I found her!" She hauled Florian's head out of the water. Having no recourse to better methods of resuscitation, she slapped her as hard as she could, almost submerging herself in the process.

She felt Florian twitch and gasp, then the girl started to cough up water, her body convulsing. Tremaine supported her head, paddling frantically to keep them both afloat.

A door banged open and a light split the darkness. She saw a silhouette poised in the illuminated doorway, hanging apparently in midair somewhere above them. She clutched Florian more tightly and sank lower in the water, wondering if this was the Gardier again or if they had fallen into some odd surrealist world, like something out of a bad modern painting. Doors floating in the air had to be worse than giants, or at least less explicable. Then the figure shouted, "Who's there?" in Rienish and flashed an electric torch.

"Here!" Tremaine called in relief, splashing so he would see her. "It's us!"

More figures appeared in the lighted doorway, then someone flicked on the overhead lights, revealing the bare wooden rafters of the old boathouse. Tremaine swore, her chattering teeth garbling the words. Florian had managed to bring them through right into the Pilot Boat's old slip.

Out of the shouting and confusion and familiar faces, Niles emerged, leaning over the edge of the dock as Tremaine struggled to hoist Florian up to the waiting hands. "Where's Gerard, Feraim, Stanis?" he demanded, looking past her into the water, as if expecting to see them surface at any moment.

A soldier and a man she vaguely recognized from the research group lifted Florian up onto the dock. The girl was trying to come around, choking on the water she had swallowed, but she still didn't seem aware of what was happening. "Feraim and Stanis are dead," Tremaine reported as someone caught her arm and hauled her up. She scrambled onto the wet wood on her hands and knees, looking around for Ilias and Ander. Ander lay on the far end of the platform, still unconscious, someone hurriedly covering him with a coat. Ilias crouched nearby, uneasily watching all the activity, his wet hair making him look like a drowned rat. She turned back to Niles, waiting impatiently. "Gerard was captured by the Gardier just before we did the reverse adjuration."

Niles, pale to begin with, went white. Tremaine felt a sinking sensation in the pit of her stomach. It was the right thing to do, she knew that. They could still pull this whole situation out of the fire with what they knew about the Gardier now. She meant to say that, but what came out was, "He told us to go back so we did. I didn't know what else—"

Niles shook his head, telling her it could wait. "Where's the sphere?"

"It's here." Tremaine looked around vaguely, realizing she didn't have it with her. The bag Karima had given them was still looped over her arm but it hung open, empty. She was shivering hard enough to make her bones rattle and it was getting difficult to focus on the conversation. "It's probably on the bottom. Do that calling charm thing. Gerard did it once before."

Niles turned immediately to stare at the still-choppy surface of the water, lifting a hand and muttering the ritual words. The sphere surfaced in a plume of spray and Niles waved wildly at the soldiers. "There it is! Get a net, a net!"

Colonel Averi, wearing an undress uniform jacket over a pajama shirt, pushed forward to take stock of the situation. He said briskly, "Call the infirmary. And get them out of the cold." Tremaine looked hopefully to see if he wore bedroom slippers, but he had managed to get his pants and half boots on. His eyes fell on Ilias and he asked, frowning, "Who the hell is that?"

"He's our friend," Tremaine said quickly. People turned to stare at her, startled, and she added, "We made contact with a new civilization."

There was a door under the stairs to the upper platform that Tremaine had never noticed before. Someone opened it and they were rapidly shepherded into a room that had been stripped down to stained plaster and worn water-damaged wainscoting. But it had a potbellied stove and several bunks with worn dusty mattresses.

In a thankfully short time, Florian and Ander lay on the bunks, heavily bundled in coats and blankets and under the care of the nurse who had hurried down from the infirmary. Both were still unconscious. Tremaine was sitting on a straight chair, wrapped in a heavy wool blanket that smelled of mildew and was stamped with *Property of the Royal Navy*. Many of their lower-ranking rescuers had been shooed away to wait in suspense for word of what had happened, but some intelligent person had got a fire going in the stove and Tremaine could smell coffee heating.

Niles stepped in, the sleeves of his coat dripping wet and

the sphere tucked under his arm. He gazed worriedly at Florian and Ander. "How are they?"

"I think the girl got a bit of water in her lungs, but she's breathing well now," the nurse reported, sounding weary. "The young man's had a bad knock on the head; he may need a healer."

Niles nodded and Tremaine saw he looked exhausted and older than when she had seen him last, only a few days ago. He said, "Is Doctor Divies on his way? I don't want to try an intrusive healing spell on a head injury without a physician present."

"He's on his way with the stretchers."

Niles glanced around and spotted Ilias, standing against the wall and trying to appear as much like a piece of furniture as a man dressed like he was could in this bare room. Someone had dropped a fatigue jacket over his shoulders and he was cradling his injured arm. "What about . . . ?" Niles touched Ilias's good shoulder lightly.

Ilias flinched, backing away along the wall, eyeing Niles warily. Suddenly he looked dangerous. Sharply he said, "No," one of the few Rienish words he knew. The two soldiers still in the room tensed, one of them dropping a hand to his sidearm. Niles just looked startled and mildly affronted.

"Hold it," Tremaine ordered, standing. Dumping her blanket, she stepped quickly over to Ilias. She put an arm around his waist and was relieved when he didn't pull away from her. The gesture reassured him, while keeping anyone from attacking anyone else.

"It's all right—" She realized she was speaking Rienish and shook her head in annoyance, switching hurriedly to Syrnaic. "It's all right, that's Niles. He is a sorcerer, but he's like Gerard. They're friends and they work here together." She realized that since Gerard had discovered the Syprians' feelings about magic, he hadn't done any of the little spells and charms that working sorcerers commonly used. No wisps of light, no calling charms. It was probably a mix of caution and Gerard's habitual good manners, but it hadn't prepared Ilias for a sudden visit to Ile-Rien.

He threw a dubious glance at Niles, still wary, but she felt his tense muscles relax a little. Of course he was edgy. All his friends had been captured by the Gardier and he was trapped in a strange world full of sorcerers, where he couldn't even understand the language. Switching back to Rienish, she told Niles, "They don't have real sorcerers where he comes from, just the Gardier and a few crazy wizards."

Niles's expression cleared. "I see. Can you explain to him that I can heal his arm?" He frowned suddenly. "And how do you know that language? I don't recognize it."

"Later, Niles, it's a long story." She told Ilias, "He just wants to fix your arm."

"It's fine," he assured her with a touch of earnestness that told her just how frightened he was. "It doesn't need fixed."

"Ilias, you're the only one here who knows the caves. When we go back for the others, you can't afford to be hurt."

He looked down at her, desperation warring with relief in his eyes. She realized he hadn't been sure if they meant to go back for the others or not. "Because we are going back," she added. *And I am, and I don't care what I have to do.* "We're going back to kill every Gardier we can catch. But I need your help to do it."

"Tell him it won't hurt," the nurse urged, glancing up from cleaning the cut on Ander's head.

I can handle this, thanks, Tremaine thought, annoyed. "That's not what he's concerned about."

Still watching her closely, Ilias said, "This is like what you and Florian did before, to my shoulder?"

"That was all Florian, but yes, like that," Tremaine assured him, adding honestly, "except Niles is much better at it."

Ilias hesitated, mouth twisted in reluctance. Then he nodded. Tremaine tugged on him, getting him to follow her back to a bunk and sit down. In Rienish she told Niles, "It's all right now, he'll let you do it."

"Ah, yes." Niles set the sphere aside on a table and approached, regarding his patient almost as warily as his patient was regarding him, but without the underlying layer of hostility.

"This is the first time I agreed to having a curse put on me," Ilias said, easing away from Niles as the sorcerer sat down to examine his arm.

"It's not a curse, it's a spell," she told him, having to use the Rienish word. "There's a difference, really." He was leaning against her, practically in her lap again, a situation the nurse was regarding with a startled eye. Tremaine wished the woman would pay more attention to Florian and Ander and mind her own damn business. To distract Ilias, she asked, "What curses were put on you? I promise not to put it in a play, unless it's already in one."

"It's a long story." He was trembling, either from nerves or cold or probably both. She tugged the borrowed coat back over his shoulders.

Niles probed his arm gently, frowning, watching Ilias for a reaction. "Tell your stoic friend he needs to let me know if it hurts."

"Tell him if it hurts," Tremaine urged.

"Ow," Ilias said stolidly, his eyes never leaving the other man's.

Tremaine wasn't going to apologize for him, but she explained to Niles, "They really hate sorcerers where he comes from."

"There are some I'm not particularly fond of either," Niles said grimly. He glanced up from his examination. "Good, it's a fracture; tell him I'm going to cause the bone to set and knit." Niles's face went still with concentration. "It's a relatively simple spell," he added, his voice going distant. "The bone wants to be whole. I just have to give it the ability."

Tremaine didn't think Ilias was interested in details right now. She knew Niles had started the healing already but she didn't think Ilias was aware of that. "He's about to fix it," she translated.

Ilias took a sharp breath, blinked and shook his head, making a valiant effort to hold on to consciousness. He wavered back and forth, then folded over. Tremaine grabbed him as he slumped. "Did you do that?" she asked Niles accusingly.

"Yes." The sorcerer kept him from falling forward and helped her ease him down on the bunk. "There are some ritual objects—just a bit of iron and a split reed—that have to be fixed to the injured area for a time to complete the spell, and I don't want to have to argue with him about it. And the bones will knit more quickly if he's not twitching around."

"That was very high-handed of you, Niles," Tremaine pointed out, deciding not to mention Florian had done the same thing by accident. Someone handed her a blanket and she tucked it around Ilias, brushing the damp hair off his face.

"Probably so," Niles agreed. He eyed her determinedly. "Now, Tremaine, you are going to tell me where you've been and exactly what's happened."

E xplain it again," Niles said firmly.

"No, Niles, no. I can't tell you anything else." Tremaine set the white china mug down on the table a little more firmly than necessary, raising a shaking hand to her brow. She was faking, but she was tired and she didn't want to talk anymore.

They were in the infirmary, which had been converted from one of the hotel's dining rooms and did double duty as the commissary. Standard-issue hospital cots and the smell of alcohol and ether contrasted oddly with the painted seascapes on the walls and the high figured ceiling. The parquet floor and the dark wood wainscoting were much the worse for water stains.

Ilias, Florian and Ander were in the part of the room closed off by white hospital screens. She knew Ilias was just sleeping off Niles's healing spell, and Florian the effects of working with the sphere and inhaling too much water, but Ander . . . *That was a hell of a knock on the head,* she thought, looking worriedly toward the screens. The nurse and the army surgeon and a physician were talking quietly just on the other side, but she couldn't tell how serious it was.

Besides the fact that she didn't want him to die, she had counted on Ander's help to go after the others. He had been in the caves, knew the situation, and his army intelligence background was perfect for this sort of thing. With some troops, Ilias's knowledge of the passages, and Niles or another army sorcerer to back up the sphere, it would have been easy to take the undermanned base. *Well, not easy. Easier.* She was counting on the use of the *Ravenna* too, to move the spell circle out into the bay, to allow them to cross back over to the other world closer to the island, in a place the Gardier wouldn't be waiting for them. Perhaps on the island itself if Niles could manage it. Ander would have been instrumental in gaining that advantage, too. Everyone would have listened to him.

Niles eyed her with dry skepticism. "It's fortunate for your theater career that you were a playwright rather than an actress."

Tremaine smiled thinly, but the fact that when he put his mind to it he was nobody's fool was one of the reasons she liked him. She saluted him with her mug. "Points for Niles."

Single-mindedly he ignored the tribute, persisting, "It's impossible for the sphere to construct that translation spell. It would have had to . . ." He gestured helplessly. "Record everything the natives—"

"Syprians."

"—Syprians said like a dictaphone, to build a dictionary and a grammar, to plant the information in your minds—"

"But the Gardier translator must have had spells that did similar things," Tremaine pointed out. "Like a dictionary of Rienish words and a grammar, and it took what we were saying and put it into the Gardier's mind in his language—"

Niles shook his head, emphatic. "But even if it could have learned the spell from another ensorceled object, it couldn't stitch a new spell together with bits of the old one just to answer a passing whim of yours—"

"It wasn't a passing whim— I'd been wishing we could talk to them since we got the sphere back," Tremaine interrupted, exasperated. "It must have been trying to work out that spell even before it got access to the translator. It just wasn't until it had the chance to tap into Gerard and Florian's magic that it could cast it."

"But even the original spheres were useful only for defense. They didn't originate actions."

"This one interprets 'defense' a little differently."

"But it couldn't—"

"It couldn't, but it did." She shoved her ragged hair back impatiently. She had changed back into a tweed jacket and skirt, leaving her Syprian clothes to drip dry in her room in the hotel. Her wool blouse was already starting to itch and she kept self-consciously touching the pancake makeup she had used to cover the bruises on her face. "It would be impossible for you or any other human sorcerer, but the sphere doesn't build spells from the outside. It does it from the inside out."

Niles sighed, shaking his head. "You're talking about it as if it's alive."

"It could be." He glared at her as if he thought she was being facetious, but she said seriously, "Think about it, Niles. The other spheres the Institute made all had flaws. Even the one you're working on isn't as capable as the others."

"I've finished it." Then he acknowledged reluctantly, "But you're right, it isn't as versatile as the Arisilde Damal sphere. And it's untested against the Gardier." He glanced at Arisilde's sphere where it sat on the next table. The brass was a little tarnished and it had leaked a pool of water from its recent dunking. As Niles looked at it, it clicked and sparked. He frowned slowly. "If we could discover how it defends itself against the Gardier's mechanical destruction spell and how it penetrated their wards . . ." He shook his head, his mouth twisting ruefully. "But I'm afraid it's too late."

Tremaine stared at him, startled. "What do you mean, 'too late'?"

From across the room someone said, "We've run out of time." It was Colonel Averi, standing in the archway to the other dining room. He had managed to find the rest of his uniform, though it was a little rumpled. His face might have been carved from granite. "We've lost the war."

"We were always losing the war," Tremaine countered, but she felt ill. She had never heard Averi talk like this before. She glanced at Niles in time to see a bleak look cross his face.

As Averi stepped into the electric light she saw his expression was so still and blank only because he was fighting to keep it that way. He hated to say it, to admit it, and that made it real. "The invasion from Adera has begun. Our military detachment was called back to defend the evacuation routes."

"It was the first step in shutting down the project," Niles explained. "No one thought you were coming back." He shook his head, turning to Averi in appeal. "But surely now that the situation has changed—"

Averi rubbed his forehead and said shortly, "I'll try."

"You don't have the men for the mission. To rescue Gerard and the others, or take the base." Tremaine looked from one man to the other. Niles avoided her eyes and Averi was stone-faced again, but a muscle jumped in his cheek. She slammed her hand on the table, fury overriding all concerns. "You can't leave the Syprians like this; some of those people died for us. You can't leave Gerard like this. And we can take that base, just like you planned. We still need that opening in the blockade and they're hurting, they lost two airships, they're undermanned . . . We'll never have a chance like this again—"

"Don't you think I realize that?" Averi cut her off sharply. "This war is about to end. The palace has issued an order for all civilians to evacuate. Sorcerers have been released from duty and told to flee, to go into hiding. The *Ravenna* will be used to try to evacuate the remaining military and Institute personnel and anyone else from Chaire and Rel who wants to take the risk of running the blockade to reach Capidara."

"She won't make it," Niles put in, sounding tired. He lifted his head from his hands and regarded them with grim humor. "I'm the only qualified sorcerer left in town and I can't defend her in the open sea from a Gardier attack. Even with my sphere. It would only take one Gardier craft getting close enough to use their mechanical disruption spell and she'd be done for." He rubbed his eyes. "We considered taking her to the other world, at least as a temporary measure, but with the Gardier base so near, we would be in the same situation. And then, we didn't know what had happened to the Pilot Boat."

"The *Ravenna*'s crew is still here then," Tremaine said, her brain starting to click over again. She thought Niles was underestimating the spheres, Arisilde's and his own. It was true that Arisilde's could only protect mechanical objects from the disruption spell if it was in close contact with them. Like the way it had shielded Gerard's pocket watch, but had been unable to defend the Pilot Boat's engines or wireless. But anyone who had witnessed the sphere's ferocity in battle knew it was a powerful advantage. Using it wasn't like being one sorcerer with augmented powers, it was like being two sorcerers, one of whom never hesitated, never forgot a spell, made snap decisions and acted on them with unbelievable speed. And she was sure its power and abilities were increasing with each use, even if Niles didn't want to admit it.

Niles shrugged. "Yes, it's a skeleton crew, but—"

"But that's all we need," Tremaine persisted. "We can use it to take the spell circle further out in the bay so we can change the target point and get through the portal without the Gardier knowing."

"I'd like to know how the Gardier discovered where the first target point was," Niles said under his breath. "That wasn't something an outside saboteur like the one who killed Tiamarc could learn."

"So would we all," Averi said tiredly. He leaned on the back of a chair. "But Miss Valiarde, without the troops—"

Tremaine hated being reasoned with and she hated it that Averi felt sorry enough for her to be polite. "We don't need troops— Well, yes, we do need troops, but I know a few of us could get into the Gardier tunnels and get the others out. Ilias knows—"

"I know! Tremaine— Miss Valiarde . . ." Averi pressed the heels of his hands against his eyes. "I will try to get the authorization. But you have to understand . . ." He looked at her bleakly. "The ship has been designated for evacuation. The Gardier have broken through the Aderassi border and in a matter of days will be inside Vienne." He let out his breath. "Even those maps Ander brought back are of no use to us. We can't even reach Kathbad, let alone mount an attack—"

"Kathbad?" Tremaine repeated, startled. It was a country west of Capidara.

"Yes, the *Ravenna*'s cartographer identified the superimposed coastline a little while ago. The map shows a large Gardier installation there—or at least, in that area of the other world."

Tremaine looked at Niles, who avoided her eyes, staring off toward the other end of the room. Maybe it was time to give up. Hadn't she wanted to give up, just a couple of weeks ago? Hadn't she wanted it more badly than her life? *I want to give up . . . I want to give up, but on my terms, not theirs.* Maybe that was the root of her problem.

It didn't matter, she didn't have time to think about it. Now she needed to stall Niles and Averi from doing anything that might prevent their return to the other world. She said, "Look, at least let me try too. I know some people in the Ministry who may still be in Vienne. If I can speak to one of them, get authorization, will you agree to let us use the ship to cross over?" It wasn't quite a lie, the Valiarde name did still have some pull in the Ministry. But it was the trustees of the Viller Institute who knew the right people and Tremaine wasn't sure if any of them were still in Vienne.

"Miss Valiarde . . ." Averi shook his head wearily. "I'll give you all the help I can." He turned and walked away, disappearing into the shadows of the other room.

Niles looked at her gravely. "Tremaine, if Averi doesn't

receive permission to use the *Ravenna*, I'm going to use my sphere to send your friend Ilias home. We can take one of the small sailboats from the hotel's boathouse; from what you've told me, he should be able to manage it alone." He leaned forward, regarding her seriously. "I think you should go with him. Florian too, if she agrees. And the Damal sphere should either be destroyed or go with you."

Tremaine lifted her brows, taking a sip of the cooling coffee to give herself a moment to think. She leaned back in her chair. "Why do I get the free ride?"

"If I could send everyone at the Institute with you, I would. The Syprians may find themselves under attack by the Gardier once they've finished with us, but at least there's a chance." Niles sat back, looking away, his face tired. "It's what Gerard would want. In his absence I feel an obligation— And surely it's what your father would have wanted."

Tremaine rubbed at a crack in the table's polished surface. *My father would have wanted me to think of a way to sabotage the Gardier base while I was there the first time, so we could have come back that first day with a huge victory and they wouldn't have given up hope.* She said only, "I'll think about it."

I lias woke all at once, freezing into immobility, trying to think where he was. He lay sprawled facedown on a little bed, covered with blankets that had a faint musty smell. He heard voices and lifted his head cautiously. He was in an area separated from a larger room by metal-framed fabric screens. There were wizard lights here too, a cluster of them set high in the ceiling, but colored glass shields made the light dim and soft and more natural. *Right, the other place,* he remembered. He heard Tremaine's voice, arguing with the other wizard in their own language. He took a relieved breath, relaxing a little. Tremaine sounded annoyed but not afraid. Of course, with her it was nearly impossible to tell.

He pushed himself into a sitting position, pulling the blanket around him, and digested the fact that the only thing he was wearing was a loose white shirt that hung down to his knees. *Well, that could be a problem.* His hair was still damp with seawater, so he hadn't been unconscious long. He worked his arm thoughtfully, rubbing his wrist. The skin was still bruised, but there was only a ghost of remnant pain. He shook his head a little. He should have known it was possible, since Florian had made the cut on his back heal faster. But this was the first time he had really believed curses could do something that wasn't destructive.

Sitting up on his knees, he leaned over the metal headboard, edging the rough white cloth aside to peek past the screen. Outside was a large room, parts of it sectioned off with more screens, with several tables and chairs and polished wood covering the walls and floor. One wall opened into a big dark room, with graceful carved wooden archways and elaborate glass shapes like clumps of icicles covering the wizard lights.

Shaking the hair out of his eyes, he looked around for his clothes and found himself staring at a captured sunset, blazing above the sea. He squinted in disbelief until he realized it was painted on the wall across from him.

Ilias climbed out of the bed, shivering as his feet touched the cold wood, and stepped cautiously toward the painted wall. Fascinated, he leaned close, but the waves weren't really rolling up the beach, they just looked like it. *That's just incredible. How do they do that?* He lifted a hand, tempted to touch, but decided against it.

He spotted his clothes draped over a straight-backed chair and his knife on the little table next to it. If that wasn't a gesture of good faith, he didn't know what was. The clothes were still damp and a puddle had formed on the floorboards beneath, so he grabbed a blanket off the bed and wrapped it around his shoulders. He hesitated over his knife, but if they had made the gesture of leaving it out for him, he could make the gesture of not carrying it.

Ilias shifted a screen aside and stepped out. The sphere, sitting on a table nearby, clicked at him. The wizard looked up, making a comment to Tremaine, and she glanced around with a worried look. "Are you all right?" she asked him in Syrnaic. "Do you want us to try to get the sphere to let you speak Rienish? Niles might be able to—"

"No," he interrupted, eyeing the wizard cautiously. "No more curses." He was willing to admit the healing had worked, but he really didn't want to take any more chances.

Niles stood up, gesturing for Ilias to take his chair. With another comment to Tremaine he took the sphere off the table and went out through the archway into the bigger room. Relieved, Ilias sat down, tugging the blanket around him. "Where are the others?"

"They're back there." Tremaine nodded to the screened-off part of the chamber. "With the healers. Florian is all right, she's just asleep." She frowned. "Ander is still unconscious."

"He'll be all right," Ilias told her, more hopeful than realistic. He knew how terrible head wounds could be. He reached across the table and took her hand.

She blinked suddenly, her eyes bleak, and for a heartbeat he could see she trembled on the edge of control. She took a sharp breath and squeezed his hand, her skin icy cold. Then she pulled away, her face shuttered again, all the walls back in place. Ilias watched her worriedly. She and Giliead were a lot alike.

He just hoped Giliead was still alive. Ilias looked away, rubbing his forehead. And Halian, Dyani, Gyan, Arites, all the others. *Karima will be alone.* He had said the *Swift* didn't have to live with herself afterward and maybe that had been tempting fate. The *Swift* was gone now, with no chance to save the part of the prow where her soul lived so they could build her again.

Tremaine glanced up and must have noticed his expression. She blinked and reached for the metal pot on the table and poured another cup of whatever was in it, pushing it across to him. "Try some of that."

He sniffed it cautiously, tasted it and winced. The smell was good but the liquid itself was incredibly bitter. At least it was warm, though. He looked around, noticing more of the wall paintings that seemed so real, trying to distract himself. There was a big one of a deep green forest that reminded him of home. The trees cascaded down rolling hills to a stretch of beach with a little village sprawled across it. He glanced at Tremaine. "What are those?"

It took her a moment to understand what he meant. "You mean, the paintings? Landscapes, mostly. You don't have paintings like that, do you?"

"No. It's curses?"

She shook her head. "Sorcerers can put magic into paintings, but those are just oil paint and canvas. Oh, here." She took a little white pitcher and added milk to both their cups. "This should help."

The trees in the painting looked real enough to touch. It was hard to believe it was just paint and skill. He felt better about this place now. This building was obviously old, but just as obviously it had been made by people who liked beautiful things. "This is better," Ilias said.

"The coffee?" Tremaine looked vague. "The milk did help."

"No, this." He made an uncertain gesture, indicating the room. "It looks like people live here."

"It does?" Tremaine looked around frowning, as if she hadn't noticed it before.

"It doesn't look like the Gardier," he clarified. He told himself the Gardier wouldn't understand what Giliead was, it wouldn't be the same as if he had been captured by a wizard like Ixion. *Unless you didn't just imagine you saw him.* . . . He shook his head determinedly. If he let his thoughts go that way, he wouldn't be able to think. "When can we go back?"

Tremaine stirred a little. "When we didn't return on the first day, they sent most of the men and the sorcerers who were here away to fight the Gardier."

He stared at her. "What does that mean?"

"Niles said he would send you back—and he wants me and Florian to go with you—but we wouldn't have any help to go after the others."

"But they will send us back?" Ilias said deliberately, wanting to be absolutely sure of it.

Tremaine nodded, still distracted. "Yes."

Ilias leaned back in relief, feeling his heart unclench a little. As long as they sent him back, he could find some way to get to the island for the others. It was just being stuck here he couldn't stand.

He had never been anywhere that he couldn't walk, swim or sail home from before. And if he died here where there was no one to perform the funeral rites . . . He had been in distant lands or isolated places where it was unlikely anyone would find his body, but that had been with Giliead. Then at least they had known that if they ended up as lost wandering shades, they would still have each other for company. And there was always the chance that someone would find their bones and put them to rest. Death in this strange faraway place seemed much more . . . final. *Don't think about it,* he reminded himself firmly.

Tremaine tapped her fingers on the table thoughtfully, and as he watched, the expression in her eyes went from vague to razor-sharp. Ilias sat up a little straighter, suddenly hopeful. Whatever it was, he was certain she had just had a great idea. She looked at him, one brow quirking, and said, "Want to go to Vienne with me?"

G erard blinked as the Gardier prodded him and the other surviving members of the *Swift*'s crew out of the patrol ship's hatchway. The hold had been pitch-dark and now even the watery sunlight that shone through the damp mist was too bright. As his eyes adjusted he saw the patrol ship was docked against a long stone shelf in a rocky cove. His hands were manacled; the Gardier had chained them all and dumped them into separate compartments.

A rifle butt prodded his back, reminding him to move. He stepped off the gangway onto the stone dock but apparently not fast enough; a second shove sent him staggering. He stumbled into Halian, who braced his feet until

Gerard could catch his balance. "Thank you," Gerard murmured, careful to speak in Syrnaic.

Halian gave him a tense nod. The Gardier shouted and made threatening gestures with their weapons and the two men moved along. Gerard saw Giliead was a few men ahead and a quick glance back showed him Dyani behind him, Gyan and Arites further back in the line.

While still in the water, Gerard had thrown away his spectacles and the pouch containing his aether-glasses and the rest of the contents of his pockets. He hadn't thought of removing his boots, the one article of clothing he was still wearing that would mark him as Rienish, until the Gardier had been about to fish him out of the sea. Several of the older men wore their hair cropped as short as his, but he knew he was unreasonably pale for a Syprian sailor.

At least Tremaine and the others got away—with the sphere, he thought in relief. He had felt its power join him to dissipate the spells that had created the sea creature. The sphere had become more precocious, more . . . aware each time it was used. The idea of the Gardier getting access to that kind of power was horrifying.

As they drew closer to the end of the dock he saw the Gardier were using a small harbor, a half circle constructed of bundles of the long log-shaped stones the island's original inhabitants had favored. It had been built up right out of the side of a sheer cliff face, the stones simply piled up in the sea until they rose high enough to provide breakwaters and a dock. Gerard would have liked to get a closer look at it, but the Gardier prodded them along the dock, giving them no time for observation. They passed under the high curved arch that led back into the caves, under the heavy dark vines that cascaded down the cliffs overhead, cutting out the misty daylight. *Oh, God,* Gerard thought wearily, *not the caves again.* It had been hard enough getting out of the place.

They passed into a large chamber lit with strings of electric bulbs, where crates and tanks of various supplies were stacked to one side. The Gardier were steering them into a narrower corridor, running them through a gauntlet of guards. Gerard saw several men with recent burns; it wouldn't incline the Gardier to be merciful toward the Syprians, but then he didn't suppose that had been an option anyway.

As Gerard passed the guard nearest the corridor entrance, he heard a yelp behind him. The guard had Dyani by the arm, hauling her out of the line as she kicked and struggled. Giliead turned back, slamming his shoulder into the man, sending him staggering. Another guard shoved forward to club him but Gerard used the distraction to catch Dyani's arm with his bound hands and pull her to his side. A guard took a swing at them with a rifle butt and Gerard twisted to take the blow on his shoulder. Dyani clung to him and Halian shoved forward to shield them with his body.

There was shoving, pushing, confusion. Giliead fought his way to their side, but Gerard knew it was useless; there were too many men with too many guns for them to make a successful break. Then he heard Halian curse, sounding as if the words had been forced out of him by pure shock. He saw Giliead freeze, staring.

The shock seemed to spread through all the Syprians like a ripple. Gerard looked past Halian and saw a man, obviously different from the Gardier despite the fact that he wore one of their uniforms. He had skin like a drowned corpse and his face was far too smooth, his features subtly malformed, as if he had been badly burned and no amount of sorcerous healing had been adequate to make the damaged flesh grow again.

The man moved forward with a slight limp, speaking rapidly in the Gardier language. The guards hesitated, looking to an officer. The officer reluctantly nodded, as if confirming the strange man's order.

The guards stepped back, motioning for them to continue.

Everyone looked uncertainly at Halian, who swallowed hard and looked at Giliead. Moving like a sleepwalker, Giliead straightened slowly and followed the guards.

The Gardier prodded them down a series of low tunnels starkly lit by bare electric bulbs, then into a long room where corrugated metal walls covered the stone. They passed heavy doors with narrow barred grilles in the center and Gerard could hear the soft movements and voices of the prisoners within. He caught a few disjointed words in Bisran, Aderassi, Rienish, Parscian.

They were prodded through a door at the far end into a long room with a barred cell along one side. Giliead hesitated, threw a glance back at the guns that were pointed at them, then entered the cell. Gerard followed with the others and the door slammed behind them with a note of finality.

The guards departed and everyone breathed a little more freely, shifting to try to find comfortable positions. It was narrow and there was barely enough room for all of them to crouch on the floor. Gerard rolled his shoulder tentatively, wincing. Everyone seemed to be nursing injuries. Gyan moved around so he could sit next to Dyani. Watching Gerard gravely, he leaned past her to say, "Thank you."

"No trouble at all," Gerard replied automatically. He wasn't sure what the Gardier had wanted with her, but from Intelligence sources in Adera it was rumored that when the Gardier took prisoners they simply murdered anyone too young or too old or too sick to work. The girl was short and very young; they might have thought her a child.

He heard someone whisper, "Who did we lose?"

"Barias, Kevlead," someone else reported softly.

"Jian and Nias, too," another voice added.

The tally continued with other names Gerard didn't recognize; they had lost nine men altogether. Halian swore softly, looking away.

Giliead hadn't moved, though Gerard saw a muscle jump in his cheek as the names of the dead men were spoken. He was staring at the door into the cell area. Waiting. There was a little space around him as if the others had unconsciously drawn back, even Halian.

From what he had observed, Gerard could think of only one man who could make Giliead react that way. He shifted toward him to ask, "That was Ixion?"

Giliead glanced at him, so tense that the movement was stiff. "Yes."

"Ah." Gerard hesitated. To say he was on sensitive ground was a vast understatement. "I understood he was decapitated."

"So did we," Gyan muttered.

"He was," Halian put in grimly. "I saw the severed head."

Giliead's head jerked up. "Quiet."

A moment later Gerard heard the footfalls outside in the tunnel. An uneasy rustle swept over the group and Dyani burrowed further back between Gyan and Gerard. Then the door rattled and swung open.

An armed Gardier entered first, followed by Ixion.

Gerard's eyes narrowed as he studied the Syprian wizard. A sorcerer capable of the transformations Giliead and Ilias had described would be capable of advanced healing spells but . . . *How do you cast without a head?* The man must have prepared it all ahead of time, creating something like the architecture of a Great Spell: a magical construct so powerful, so carefully crafted that it would stand alone without a sorcerer to manipulate it. *Something that would activate just at his death.* . . . Gerard lifted his brows. *Chancy, but apparently it worked.*

Ixion stepped close to the bars near Giliead, saying, "It's all right, they can't speak Syrnaic." He eased down into a sitting position with a grimace of pain. "The amulets they use to speak to their enemies don't work with our language, either." He glanced up at the other two Gardier who had followed him in. One was a guard, but the other was an officer, wearing one of the translator disks. His eyes met Ixion's with barely concealed contempt and disgust.

Ixion shook his head, smiling as he turned back to Giliead. "They're very odd. If you were invading a foreign land, wouldn't you learn the language first?" His voice was cultured and mild, somehow not what Gerard would have expected. "They don't even seem to understand the concept of learning a different tongue, even their scholars. The ones who learn even a few words are looked down on. Ridiculous, isn't it?"

Gerard filed that information away for hopefully future use. Giliead's stony expression didn't alter. He said, "You looked better dead."

"Oh, yes." Ixion sighed, but his eyes were like chips of agate. "I had to re-create myself. Thanks to you and Ilias." He looked around at the others. His eyes lingered for a moment on Gerard. "I see he isn't here."

"No." Giliead smiled, his mouth a thin cold line. "You missed him."

Ixion turned back toward him, something deliberate and snakelike in the motion. He watched Giliead thoughtfully. "We both know he'll come after you."

Giliead looked away, but his expression didn't change. *He doesn't believe they can come back,* Gerard realized. He wondered what Ixion had done that made Giliead feel Ilias was better off now. That being trapped in a strange world was a preferable fate for his friend.

Ixion shifted forward. "And when he comes, I want you to take me with you."

Giliead's eyes flicked up but he studied Ixion without surprise. "Which part of you would you like me to take this time?"

Ixion laughed. "I was lucky I had already started growing this body. When you severed my head I had only a few instants to transfer my consciousness." He let out a sad sigh. "I was alone for a very long time, in the dark. I missed you both."

Giliead jerked his chin at the Gardier. "You made new friends."

"I only helped them because I had to." Ixion widened his eyes. "They're holding me prisoner."

"Were they holding your leviathan prisoner too?"

"Now, if I didn't help them capture you, I wouldn't have a way off the island. I had actually made the creature before you killed me; it was sleeping in the bottom of one of the sea caves, and I woke it to help them search for you." He considered Giliead again. "They want to know where the wizard is, the one who killed my poor leviathan."

Giliead's gaze didn't waver. "He went back to his own land when the ship went down."

"Ah." Ixion spoke to the Gardier officer, who received this information with a grunt.

They saw the portal open and close, Gerard thought. Perhaps their sorcerers could sense it, somehow, at least when it was within eyeshot.

The Gardier stared at them narrowly, then replied to Ixion. Ixion sighed, and told Giliead, "He says you're lying. They think everybody is lying." He frowned. "Why were you helping a foreign wizard?"

"He found your curse." Giliead looked at him thoughtfully. "Right under the hearthstone where you left it. I destroyed it myself, stabbed it right through the heart. It screamed like a stuck pig."

"Did he?" Ixion blinked. His half-formed features were hard to read. He seemed able to express exaggerated emotions, but Gerard suspected the real, spontaneous ones were too subtle to convey. His gaze returned to Gerard. "I don't recognize your new friend."

Gerard went still. Giliead didn't react, but beside him Gerard felt Halian tense.

Gerard knew his mistake almost immediately. Halian was the only one of the others looking at Ixion. The other men were looking at the walls, the ceiling, at Halian or Giliead. Dyani had her head buried against Gyan's arm. Gerard had been scrutinizing the sorcerer with thoughtful interest and that had set him apart, at least for Ixion. He smiled grimly, thinking, *Well, I might not be able to do anything to the Gardier but I'll be happy to have a go at you.*

His white face expressionless, Ixion said, "I can smell my own kind, you know. There were two foreign wizards on the *Swift*. The second is no longer here. But perhaps he's left something behind and will soon be back for it, like Ilias." He stood slowly, and his gaze flicked from Giliead to Gerard. He said, "I could tell them, but they wouldn't like me the better for it."

Ixion walked out of the cell, the Gardier officer following him, barking questions, the other guards behind him. As the outer door clanged shut, the men made muttered exclamations of relief. Gerard leaned back against the stone wall, feeling his tension drain away and the pain of various bruises return.

"We're well and truly in it," Gyan said softly.

"You said it," Arites agreed, sounding glum.

Halian was watching Giliead, who glared contemplatively at the cell door. Then Giliead turned his head slightly, saying, "Two wizards."

"What?" Halian asked sharply.

Giliead stirred, turning toward them. "He said there were two wizards on the *Swift*."

Gerard nodded, considering the man's words thoughtfully. "He did."

Halian glanced at Gerard, frowning. "Florian is part wizard, isn't she? That must be what set him off."

"Yes, I suppose it could be," Gerard agreed reluctantly. He could think of one other prospect, but it seemed unlikely. At least he hoped it was unlikely.

Chapter 18

Tremaine asked Niles's secretary Giaren to find some warm clothes for Ilias to supplement his own, which were inadequate for the weather. Then she found a room for him down the hall from hers and gave a brief lesson in how to work the bathroom taps. While he was changing, she went downstairs; there were a couple of things she had to do before they could go to town.

One of those things should have been a nap but the strong coffee she had been drinking for the past hour had made sleep impossible. She went back to the temporary infirmary but the nurse wouldn't let her see Florian and Ander, claiming that while Ander seemed improved, he was still in serious condition and that Florian needed to rest. Muttering to herself, Tremaine went through a green baize doorway at the bottom of the stairs and found her way through the cramped hall beyond it. The muted buzz of the wireless led her to the room where the hotel's switchboards were located. She knocked on the partly open door and peered around it to see a crowded little room packed with telephone equipment. A young man was seated in the old operator's chair going through a pile of logbooks. He looked up with a frown. "Yes? Can I help you?"

Tremaine pasted an affable smile on her face. "I need to make a trunk call."

"Oh?" The operator looked doubtful. Personal calls were supposed to be kept to a minimum at all times.

"I'm Tremaine Valiarde. I need to call my uncle Galiard

and let him know I'm all right before he leaves town."
Tremaine widened her eyes and concentrated on looking
earnest. "He gets so worried."

Even though the Institute was under government control
now, the Valiarde name still worked. "Well, all right, of
course you'll have to keep it short. . . ." He pushed the set
toward her.

"Oh, of course." Tremaine picked up the receiver, feeling that rush of excitement that was becoming almost familiar. Familiarity hadn't diminished its appeal. Now she
understood a little better how her father, Uncle Arisilde, all
the others she had met over the years, could become ad-
dicted to this. When the switchboard operator answered,
she said, "Garbardin 34222."

She saw the wireless man glance up briefly. It wasn't a
particularly good neighborhood but it was a very old one
and it would make sense that the Valiardes might have
connections there. The man would probably be very surprised, possibly fatally so, to find out what kind of connections they were. While she was waiting for the operator
to respond, the wireless man said, "I'm from Garbardin
and I don't recognize that exchange."

Damn. Her heart pounding, Tremaine covered the receiver. "It's a private one." She rolled her eyes and smiled.
"You know how these old families are." *He's going to think
I'm a fatuous moron but that's fine as long as I get the
damn call through.*

The wireless man gave her a polite smile back and nodded, returning to his logs. In her ear the tinny voice of the
switchboard operator said, "One hour delay."

Goddammit. But it was only to be expected; the wires
were probably swamped with calls. The army might even
have started cutting them, to keep the Gardier from making use of the system. Tremaine hesitated. She could ask
for the Institute priority code that would get the call put
through immediately, but that would just draw attention to
it. "Right." She hung up, smiled at the wireless man again,
and strolled out into the hall.

Tremaine tapped her teeth thoughtfully, her eyes on

the door to Colonel Averi's office. *Now the hard part.*
The staff would be destroying the official military documents by now. The Institute people who hadn't already
left were getting rid of theirs down in the ballroom.
Here goes nothing.

She walked in briskly. This had probably been the office
of one of the hotel's lesser managers: It had the same fine
wood wainscoting and lily-shaped light fixtures of the
more public rooms, but it was small and low-ceilinged.
The original furniture had been removed and replaced with
a makeshift desk fashioned out of a console table and
paper file boxes were stacked on the floor. She smiled at
the secretary, an older woman in an army auxiliary uniform, and said, "I'd like to see Colonel Averi, please."
Tremaine had watched Averi leave the hotel while she was
looking for Niles's assistant.

The woman glanced up at her uncertainly. She was sorting documents out of a file box, setting a stack aside on
the desk. The discards, the ones that would be burned so
they didn't fall into Gardier hands, were on the floor in a
wooden packing crate. "He isn't here, miss. He's gone
down to the docks."

Tremaine looked a little flustered. "Oh. He was supposed to leave a letter for me. Can you see if it's in his
desk?"

The woman obligingly got up and stepped into the inner
office. Tremaine had a few quick seconds to burrow
through the discard box. These weren't secret documents—the secretary wouldn't have been allowed to handle those. But Tremaine didn't need secrets, she just
needed the standard form that the Vienne War Office used
to send Averi his orders. She found an old one almost immediately, giving Averi authorization to bring Captain
Feraim in on the Institute's project. *Perfect.*

She had the paper folded and shoved into a pocket and
was waiting demurely when the secretary came back in to
say, "I'm sorry, miss, but I can't find it."

"Well, maybe I misunderstood him. You know, I'll go
down to the dock and ask him."

As she turned to go the door to the hall swung open and a tall dark-haired man in army uniform stepped in. Captain Dommen, Averi's second-in-command. He eyed Tremaine thoughtfully. "Can I help you, Miss Valiarde?"

"She stopped by to see Colonel Averi," the secretary said helpfully.

He stepped forward, extending his hand. "I was so glad to hear you and the others had survived the mission after all."

Tremaine shook hands, her face starting to hurt a little from all the unaccustomed smiling. She noted he hadn't mentioned Gerard. Deciding the fatuous moron persona would work with Dommen also, she said, "Colonel Averi is such a nice man, isn't he?"

Dommen nodded. "He's said a number of good things about you."

Really? Because he's given me the impression he thinks I'm a huge liability to the Institute and possibly the entire war effort. Dommen was making an effort to be unctuous but she could tell it wasn't easy for him. She suspected his normal attitude was a good deal more direct.

"What did you want to see Averi about?" Dommen asked, watching her with a smile that didn't reach his eyes.

"Oh, it was nothing. I'm just going to run down to the dock—"

The telephone on the desk rang and the secretary answered it. Tremaine had a moment of foreboding. Her luck with the document had been too good. The woman listened, then said, "Oh, miss, your call to Vienne was put through."

Dommen's brows lifted and he looked at her inquiringly.

Tremaine's normal temperament would have required her to stare back at him blankly until he asked her outright what the call was about, but she thought helpful dumbness was more productive right now. "That's my uncle. I wanted to talk to him before he left the city."

"Ah, I see. Go ahead and take it here then." Dommen gestured politely for the secretary to hand her the receiver.

"Thank you." Tremaine showed her teeth back at him,

thinking, *That was one damn short hour.* She took the receiver, heard the line click thoughtfully a couple of times as the call was put through, then it was picked up on the second ring. "Hullo?" a low voice queried cautiously.

"This is Tremaine Valiarde." There was a faint gasp at the other end. "I can't speak long"—family code for *someone is listening*—"but I needed to let Uncle Galiard know that I'm all right." *I need help and I need it now.*

"You got a way out of the country? Himself asks me ten times a day. He's worried about you." The rough voice was reproachful.

Tremaine managed not to roll her eyes. *Yes, I need parental guilt from men who look after me because they're afraid my father will come back from the dead and gut them.* "I've taken care of that."

"All right. What do you need?"

"I need a reference," Tremaine told him, hoping she had the code right. Damn Dommen anyway, standing there listening and pretending not to. At least the secretary had gone back to sorting documents.

"For what? Oh, oh, I get you. You want a forger?"

"Yes."

"What you want that for at a time like this? Get yourself to Parscia like everybody else with any sense."

Tremaine half covered the receiver, saying airily, "It'll be just a moment, Captain Dommen. I don't mean to tie up a military wire."

Dommen nodded fake-pleasantly and there was a long-suffering sigh from the other end of the line. He gave her the address and said, "Be careful with this sort. And get out of there, wherever you are!"

"I'm doing my best," she said, and rang off. "Well, I'd better be going." She spoke over Dommen's attempt to interrupt, backing toward the door. "So many things to take care of, you know." She made it out the door and beat a hasty retreat down the corridor, her heart pounding.

She found Ilias exploring the lobby, somewhat to the consternation of a couple of the Institute researchers, who were watching him with wary curiosity. He was wearing his own pants and boots with a heavy knitted sweater and a dark fatigue coat that hung past his knees. He looked almost like he belonged here, except for the earrings, the silver mark on his cheek and the mane of fluffy blond hair.

She said, "Ilias, let's go see the *Ravenna*."

Outside, Ilias followed Tremaine down the rickety wooden stairs to one of the piers stretching out to the dark waters of the bay. The sky was just lightening from black to purple-gray and heavy mist was drifting in from the sea. The extra clothes made a big difference in holding off the damp cold and he was grateful for the loan. Tremaine had made it clear this ship, the *Ravenna*, was essential in her plan to convince her people they could still destroy the Gardier outpost and he was anxious to see it himself.

At first all he could see at the end of the dock were three gray towers, the whole floating high above a gray metal wall. He was impressed by the size of the giant metal building, but wondered where the ship she was pointing at was. When he finally understood that was it, he almost fell down from shock.

"That can't possibly float," Ilias said, pressed against the wall of a wooden shed as far from the immense gray metal mountain as he could get.

A building that size was one thing; the Chaeans and the Argoti had fortresses and palaces even larger, but a ship that huge must have a soul big enough to eat people. And he couldn't get over the feeling that it was about to topple over on him.

"It's floating now," she said, obviously enjoying his shock and horror. "And it's fast. It can make the run to Capidara in three days."

Unable to stop himself from rising to the bait, Ilias said, "So?"

"That would take a ship the size of the *Swift* ninety days."

He glanced at her skeptically. There were small yellow

wizard lights on the pier, just enough to keep you from falling off in the dark, and he could see her expression. She had that look he was beginning to recognize. He said, "You're making that up."

"All right, I am," she admitted readily enough. "But it would be a really long time."

He was willing to believe the ship was fast. It was so big the crew should find a god, elect a lawgiver and call it a peninsula. It could tow the big iron boats of the Gardier behind it like helpless dinghies. That image was appealing, but still . . . He couldn't tell whether it was scaring him or giving him a hard-on. "Why don't they use her to attack the wizards—the Gardier?"

"The Gardier can destroy its engines with their spells." She studied the big ship regretfully. "It wasn't really made for attacking things. It's mainly good for transporting a lot of people someplace very quickly, or being a mobile fort. The original plan was to use it as a troop transport, once the Gardier base had been taken."

"Don't call her 'it,' " Ilias told her, eyeing the ship warily. "At least not where she can hear you."

Tremaine looked like she was going to argue, but stared up at the ship, frowning thoughtfully, and instead said only, "All right."

Tremaine turned to go and Ilias pushed cautiously away from the dockhouse and backed away from the enormous ship, not liking to turn his back on it. "She needs eyes," he told Tremaine. The empty, faceless bow just made her look all the more monstrous.

After that, the car was less of a shock.

There was no traffic on the road as few people would be fleeing toward the dangerous coast, and absolutely no one was going toward Vienne.

On impulse Tremaine decided to use the extra time to make a brief stop at Coldcourt. She hadn't squarely faced this fact before, but with the Gardier invasion imminent she wouldn't be going back there again. She wasn't sure what she was going to do, but it seemed necessary.

The sky was just beginning to gray with dawn when they reached Coldcourt. Visible over the tops of garden walls or past winter-bare trees Tremaine could see the neighboring houses were all still dark; she knew most of them had been closed for some months as the inhabitants had left the city for safer areas. The ironwork gates stood open at the top of Coldcourt's drive and she turned the car in, slowing to creep down the gravel road.

The sprawling gray stone house lay at the end of a wide sweep of overgrown lawn, broken only by the one large ancient oak. There had never been any garden around the house; open ground provided no cover for intruders to approach and allowed a clear field of fire for defense. The three towers hung over the house, just big shadowy shapes in the dimness. She pulled up in the circular drive and Ilias bailed out before she cut the engine, staggering away from the car and leaning on the stone balustrade that lined the steps up to the door.

Tremaine killed the engine and climbed out, eyeing him sympathetically. Even in the bad light she could tell he was going pale under his tan. "Is it that bad?"

"No." He took one more deep breath and straightened up, wiping his mouth on his sleeve. His gaze moved up the front of the house, where the gray light had just started to reveal the cutout shapes of the ornamental crenellations and the chunky lines of carving below them. "You live here?" He sounded not so much doubtful as resigned, as if after the *Ravenna* and automobiles, this unpleasant fact was nothing.

Walking around the car, Tremaine had to admit Coldcourt had always looked like the villain's secret hideout in a melodrama. No wonder Nicholas had liked it. It had actually belonged to his foster father, Edouard Viller, long before Nicholas had owned it, but then Edouard must have had strange taste or he wouldn't have chosen Nicholas for a son.

She started up the few steps to the lead-plated front

doors, absently patting her pockets. "Until it's overrun by the Gardier." *Keep saying it, maybe you'll get used to the idea. Gardier.* She stopped suddenly and smacked herself in the forehead with the heel of her hand. "Of course they won't have to break in, because Gervas has the goddamn key." In the scramble to pick up the scattered supplies, she had left her latchkey on the table in the Gardier interrogation room.

"Key?" Ilias had recovered enough to follow her up to the entrance. "You put locks in your house doors?"

"Yes, so we can lose our keys and look like idiots—" She tried the knob out of desperation and halted abruptly as it turned. The heavy door started to swing open and she stepped back hurriedly, bumping into Ilias. "Someone's been here."

"The Gardier?" he asked sharply, pulling her back away from the door.

Tremaine turned to examine the drive; now that she looked she could see the prints in the wet gravel where one car, a large sedan, had rested near the house. *That's funny.* It was a nearly deserted neighborhood, but would a Gardier spy be incautious enough to park in front of the house? And if he was, why not just break down the door? *And Gervas had the key, not the address,* she reminded herself. Though it wouldn't be that hard for a local spy to find out where the infamous Valiardes lived. No, that didn't feel right. This was something else. She turned thoughtfully back to the door, stepping up to it again. "Let's see."

Ander would have argued; Ilias just came with her, trusting her judgment on her own ground, a tense and hyperalert reassurance at her side. Tremaine pulled the heavy door open to see the dim tiled hall. Ilias shifted in front of her, padding silently down the hall. Tremaine followed, but the fine hair at the back of her neck didn't itch. The cold house sounded, and felt, empty. She was a little shocked at the deserted musty smell of it. She hadn't been gone that long. *It must have smelled like this while you were living here. God, I could be one of those old people who has fifty years' worth of newspapers and gas company pamphlets stuffed in all the drawers.* It wasn't a pretty picture.

The library door stood open but the interior was pitch-dark. She reached in and pressed the button for the lights. The electric bulb leapt to life in the overhead fixture, making Ilias flinch.

"Sorry," Tremaine muttered, stepping inside. On the surface nothing seemed disturbed. But the cabinet where the sphere had been kept looked less crammed with paper, as if some of the folios and documents were missing from the shelves. She crossed the room to the big carved desk and squatted, reaching underneath the dusty wood to feel for a hidden catch. She popped it, then scrambled around to open the secret panel in the leather-embossed side. The drawers there were empty. She sat back, tapping her chin thoughtfully. There had been nothing in here except family items, papers, photos, old letters.

"So, was it Gardier?" Ilias asked. He was standing beside the empty hearth, looking around the room warily.

Tremaine glanced up, distracted for a moment by the incongruity of seeing him in this familiar setting. Even with the borrowed coat and sweater over his own clothes and his wild hair tied back, he still didn't look as if he belonged. She shook her head slightly, getting to her feet. "No, these were my father's people. They left the door unlocked so I'd know they'd been here. Me, and anyone else who came to the house." It was an old custom of theirs, when they had to abandon any hideaway. Leave the doors open and the traps sprung, let any pursuers know that they were too late, anticipated, and outmaneuvered. It could also, in its way, be a declaration of war.

Next she went upstairs to find the wardstones missing, taken so the Gardier wouldn't know there had ever been any sorcery associated with the house, and checked that all the rest of Edouard Villers's old gadgets had been cleared out of the attics. Her own room seemed untouched. Standing there, trying to think what to take, she shrugged finally and scooped the tangled contents of her jewelry box into an empty pillowcase. She added her lock picks and an old stage makeup set from a drawer and that was that.

Coming back down into the hall, she stood there a moment, staring at nothing, then shook her head. "They were better at it than I would have been." She pushed a hand through her hair. *This house isn't you.* Maybe it wasn't even Nicholas. Maybe he had just needed to pretend it was in order to be who he had decided to be. "I don't even know why I wanted to stop here in the first place."

"To say good-bye?" Ilias followed her to the door, casting a dubious look back at the cold dusty place.

"I'm not a very sentimental person," Tremaine told him.

He pretended to be startled. "No, really?"

Tremaine pulled the door shut, her mouth twisted wryly. She didn't know how she felt. Except that she was glad she hadn't come here alone.

Ilias had figured out almost immediately that Tremaine didn't want to tell him about the paper she was going to the city to get. She was almost as bad a liar as Giliead when her heart wasn't in the deception, so it was fairly easy to get the truth out of her. Braced uncomfortably in the front bench of the car, he told her, "It's stealing."

"It's not stealing," Tremaine assured him earnestly. "That's when you take something that doesn't belong to you. The *Ravenna* is supposed to belong to me. Us. The Viller Institute."

As the morning light grew less dim and gray, he could see the trees and fields whizzing rapidly by and it did even more unpleasant things to his stomach. And the car smelled horrible, like the flying whale; he would rather ride in a barrel strapped under an oxcart. Other cars, some of them very large with wizard lights blazing in the dimness, passed them going the other way and most seemed to stray unnecessarily close to their vehicle. He shielded his eyes, concentrating on Tremaine. "You take a paper that says one thing, and you have someone change the paper to say it gives you the *Ravenna*." She had explained the ship was called after a great queen; as far as he was concerned, naming the ship after a person just made her already too-large soul even bigger. "That's stealing."

"It's not stealing." Leaning over the wheel that controlled the car, she grinned suddenly, a manic expression that was not reassuring. "It's forgery. At least that's what the magistrate's charge will say."

Those words *forgery* and *magistrate* hadn't meant anything but the import was clear anyway. "The stealing part will be in there somewhere, trust me." If it would help them get back to free Giliead and the others, he was all for it, but he wasn't sure it would work. His nerves jumped with the thought that they were wasting time with this when a better plan might be formed, but since he didn't have a clue what that better plan could be, they were stuck with this one.

Reaching the city was a relief. Not only did Tremaine have to slow the car down, but it was light enough by now to really see the structures they had been passing for some time. Ilias found the variety fascinating. There were little cottages and farmhouses with trees and gardens not much different than those he had been familiar with all his life, but there were also buildings of strange-colored stone with carvings and towers and pillars and shapes that were surely impossible.

He hadn't expected it to be this big, though after seeing the *Ravenna*, maybe that was naive. He realized it must also be very old when the car approached a high city wall constructed of huge stones and surmounted with guard towers. The houses had grown right up to it on both sides and for that to happen it must have been many years since there had been any need to keep it unencumbered for defense. There was some difficulty getting in, because a large crowd of people and cars seemed to be trying to get out.

After that everything just got bigger and even more impressive. He sank down in the seat, craning his neck to look up at big graceful stone buildings decorated with statues and columns. Some had strange deformed monsters like Ixion's creatures carved along the pediments and windows filled with glass of rich, jewel-like colors. Tremaine took the car down a street so large there was a row of trees down the middle, bare and leafless from the winter. More cars moved down it, all of different sizes and shapes, and a few small wagons drawn by one or two horses. People made their way along on foot too, most bundled up against the cold and dressed in drab colors that contrasted oddly with the richness of the background.

Then further down the street he saw a looming structure with a green-tinged dome. Except the dome was damaged, chunks knocked out as if a giant had taken a hammer to it. He remembered abruptly that these people were at war, and it was a war they were on the verge of losing. He looked more closely at the passersby in the street, seeing how they moved hurriedly, shoulders hunched, their faces preoccupied or drawn or just plain frightened. *This could be Cineth,* he thought, the idea making him sicker than the miasma issuing from the car. It wouldn't take many of the bomb-things the Gardier had burned the village with to turn Cineth into a hole in the ground.

"I'm going to leave the car here," Tremaine said, guiding it into an open space on the edge of the street near a row of other such craft. "I don't want to take it into the part of town where we have to go."

Ilias just nodded, relieved that they would be getting out of the damn thing.

As soon as the car came to a halt, Ilias fumbled with the catch on the door and leapt out, happy to stand on solid ground again. Broad as the street was, the stone buildings loomed over it, though not high enough to blot out the expanse of cloudy gray sky. The air wasn't much better out here, stinking of the cars and tainted with too many strange odors, bitter and acrid like the stench that hung over the Gardier tunnels. Underneath it were more familiar scents of wet earth and human waste and cooking.

As people hurried by Ilias noticed they cast him curious glances but everyone seemed too wrapped up in their own concerns to take real notice. Tremaine had said this city was more used to strangers than Cineth and that with all the refugees pouring in and everyone told to evacuate, he wouldn't cause that much comment. She had convinced him to tie all his hair back and it made his neck feel naked and exposed. He scratched self-consciously at the curse mark on his cheek but reminded himself these people wouldn't know what it meant. And even if they did, it probably still wouldn't make much difference, as accustomed to wizards as they were.

Tremaine led the way past a stone building with beautiful colored glass in its small windows to another with some kind of horrible creatures carved on it. Some had wings and all had hunched bodies and leering faces. As she started up a flight of stone steps toward double wooden doors bound with copper-colored metal, he hesitated. "Uh . . ." Uncertain this was a good idea, he caught her sleeve to stop her. "What's in there?" In the Syrnai the skulls of large predators were sometimes posted to warn travelers what was in the area and these carvings looked like a similar system.

"It's a bank. We keep money and . . ." She gestured vaguely. "Valuable things in it."

"Oh." He nodded, understanding now that the stone monsters were meant to scare off thieves, not warn you of what lurked inside.

"There's a ward here," she explained, stopping under the doorway. "It keeps people from bringing in enspelled objects that might be used to steal something. It's not going to stop us since you know we don't have anything like that."

Ilias was barely listening. Inside was a big high-ceilinged room, the dim wizard lights housed in elaborate confections of bright bronzed metal and white glass. It was floored with black-veined marble, with rich dark wood everywhere. On one wall there was a painting, a giant one, a bird's-eye view of an incredible city with domes and towers and ships on the river winding through it. He had to tear his gaze away to look around at the rest of the place. There were a few people here, sitting at tables writing or speaking in hushed tones.

Across the back were wooden stalls, with odd little grilles in the front and people inside. His first impulse was to think they were cells or cages, except the back seemed to be completely open for the inhabitants to come and go at will.

Tremaine looked around, smiling faintly. "Yes, it's a little much, isn't it. Sort of like a temple to money. This is the main branch of the Bank of Ile-Rien. I've got to get something to pay the man who's going to help . . . change the document. It's lucky we got here this early; it looks like they're getting ready to shut the place down. Wait here. I'll be back in a moment." She started across toward the row of stalls.

He watched while she talked to someone through the grille in the front. Then the person emerged from around the back to lead her across to a door in the far wall. Ilias waited, studying the paintings. He would have felt conspicuous standing around with nothing to do, except that several others who looked far more out of place than he did came in to hold brief conferences with the people in the stalls. It wasn't long before Tremaine came out with a leather case tucked under her arm.

As they went back down the steps to the street, she said, "It's kind of ironic that we keep some of our accounts there, because my father actually robbed the place once."

"He was a thief?" Ilias asked, startled. Gerard had explained that Tremaine's father and a wizard companion had been the ones to track the Gardier from this land to the vicinity of the Isle of Storms. He and Giliead had both assumed that meant he was a warleader or explorer.

She opened the case to poke through it, saying with a shrug, "He didn't steal money. Well, depending on whose money it was, sometimes he did. He took some documents from the bank that he wanted to use to prove that this March Baron was stealing royal land grants that were supposed to go to pensioners and . . . it was complicated."

Concentrating on the papers in the case, she was absently heading toward the edge of the walk and the muddy water pooled at the side of the street. Ilias took her elbow, steering her back. "So he was kind of like a lawgiver?"

"Sort of. I mean, he did illegal things, but it was all in the cause of . . ." They reached an intersection with another more narrow street and she turned down it. ". . . getting back at people he didn't like. But they were bad people. Usually."

All right, Ilias thought, deciding to drop the issue there. They walked down the street for some distance, until the elaborate carving and columns and colored glass gave way to dingy stained stone and boarded-up windows. Here they saw people loading bundles of belongings into cars and wagons, and other heavily laden vehicles moving slowly up the street. Then they stopped at a cross street where Ilias could see an entire section of houses had been reduced to rubble. There had been a fire too; the air still smelled of smoke and charred wood. Soot had been swept back out of the street to pile up on the remnants of the walk. "Damn," Tremaine muttered. "I hope he's still there. I hadn't thought about that."

"You think he left the city?" Ilias asked, looking away from the evidence of destruction. He was still thinking of Cineth. So much smaller, so much easier to destroy.

"No. People in his profession are like very persistent rats. They won't leave even when the ship sinks." Tremaine gazed at a trail sign carved into a remaining wall, then led the way down another cross street. "He probably thinks he can do good business during the occupation."

Ilias snorted at the stupidity of it. "With the Gardier?"

"He's in for a surprise," Tremaine agreed, sounding as if she was looking forward to it.

Ilias was hoping to see inside another one of the bigger doorways, but she chose one of the smaller ones, with no glass windows and stone with flaking red paint. Tremaine tried the door handle and when it didn't turn, applied her shoulder to it and popped it open.

Inside was a dark room, dirty and smelling of cooked cabbage, poorly lit by a couple of bare wizard lights hanging from the ceiling. A wooden counter blocked off the back part of the room, which was filled with shelves stuffed with moldering paper.

Behind the counter there was a boy, not much older than Dyani, lounging in a chair beside a little round iron stove, and an older woman, with ragged hair and a white puffy face.

Tremaine leaned on the counter and spoke to the woman, who answered, coming forward and shaking her head in agitation.

Then the boy got up and came around the counter, showing his teeth in a nasty grin, moving with slow threat. Ilias waited until he got just close enough, then shoved him back a few steps. Snarling angrily, the boy surged forward, throwing a punch that caught Ilias in the jaw. Not much inconvenienced by the punch—Giliead had hit him harder than that by accident—Ilias just looked at him, one brow lifted ironically. Still determined, the boy drew a knife, so Ilias slapped it out of his hand and slammed the boy's head into the wall.

"Is he all right?" Tremaine asked, more curious than concerned as Ilias hauled him up by the collar and draped him over the counter.

"Sure," he told her with a shrug. "I'm not going to kill him, he's a kid."

"Good. I'll be right back."

The back room was cleaner, better lit, though also crammed with paper and musty books. The faded old man who hunched over the old-fashioned writing desk looked like a large gnome. He turned slightly as she shut the door behind her, the light catching his thick spectacles. "Miss Valiarde." He eyed her a trifle nervously. "Are you here representing your father?"

She should have expected that question. Nicholas Valiarde had disappeared before, faking his death or the death of one of his personas, though he had never stayed out of sight for quite this long. The criminal element in Ile-Rien would never be quite sure he was really gone. *If he is.* She hesitated, trying to decide on an answer, then realized her inadvertently enigmatic stare was intimidating him more than any lie. She said, "I'm here representing myself."

He blinked owlishly. She could tell he didn't believe her. Nicholas had never involved his daughter in his business activities; he had never trusted her to get things right. But this man wouldn't realize that. He said, "I see. You have . . . something you would like me to take a look at?"

She stepped forward, taking the papers out of the dispatch case. This man wasn't the best forger in Ile-Rien, but then this document only had to survive a cursory inspection. "I need you to make another copy of this document with Minister Servaine's signature, but with today's date, and change the wording to read that Colonel Averi has permission to use the HRM *Ravenna* at his discretion. The exact wording is . . ." She fumbled with the papers for a moment, then dumped the whole case on the desk. "It's all here."

He took the documents, his brows quirking. He said with a trace of amusement, "One is usually more circumspect. You imply the document is a folio of historical interest which you want me to value for you, for example."

"I don't have time for that. Oh." She dug in her other pocket and pulled out two of the gold coins she had removed from the deposit box. She knew that after the next few days paper royals would only be good for starting fires but gold ones should still be worth something. "This enough?"

He sighed, apparently at the impatience of youth. "We can discuss the fee when I produce the finished result, in . . . ?"

"An hour."

He lifted his brows. Tremaine met his eyes. "An hour," she repeated.

He sighed again, nodding. "Very well."

She went back to the outer room where the female clerk had retreated into a corner and the bullyboy was on the floor, nursing a bloody nose and what were going to be two wonderful black eyes. Ilias was studying the bookcases. He glanced at her inquiringly and she nodded. He was relying on her, she realized suddenly. To get them through this, to get him back home. At the moment she didn't feel very reliable.

As Tremaine made her way through the piles of books, the bullyboy said thickly, "Has he got brass knuckles?"

"No, that was all him," she replied, patting her pockets to make sure she had everything, trying to gather her thoughts. She was tempted to tell the bullyboy that if he tried rowing a galley on the open ocean, he might develop hands that hard too, but there didn't seem to be much point in it. She asked Ilias, "You want to get something to eat?"

Ilias followed Tremaine back up toward the huge street with the trees, where they stopped at a place with little tables and chairs under a dark green awning. There were a few other people already seated there, some with bags of belongings piled around their chairs, looking at papers or maps and talking in urgent voices. As they sat down a man in a white shirt brought them two more cups of the horrible stuff everyone drank here. Tremaine held a brief conversation with him, then as he left reported, "He says they've still got food. They don't want to leave any for the Gardier, so they're trying to use it all up before they go." She propped her chin on her hand. "I haven't had mutton stew with truffles in forever."

Ilias had time to notice how drawn her face was before she dropped her eyes and said suddenly, "I have to tell you something. I'm not—" Her fingers tapped at the table, impatient with herself. "I'm not as reliable as you think I am. If, that is, you think I am—"

Knowing the tangent might go on for a while, Ilias interrupted quietly, "You're fey."

She frowned slowly, not meeting his eyes. She had a shadow over her right enough. He could understand it, at least partly; her home was about to be destroyed. Ilias had seen cities lost in war, villages falling prey to outlaws or

wizards, and this place had that same air of dying desperation. It stank of fear worse than it stank of smoke. But it
was the same for all the others, Florian and Gerard and
Ander, and they hadn't had that fey light in their eyes.
Tremaine's shadow was more complicated than that. "I
saw it in the caves," he told her. He tasted the drink absently. It was still awful, but not as awful as the last one.
"Gil was too, for a long time."

Tremaine looked at him narrowly, as if trying to gauge
his sincerity. "Gil was? Because of his sister and the others
Ixion killed?"

Ilias nodded. "Gil blamed himself for that, though it was
just as much my fault. Gil thought he should have recognized what Ixion was. But when we met him, and he was
pretending to be normal, he didn't use any curses. We
didn't know Gil couldn't tell a wizard was a wizard unless
he was doing a curse." He hesitated, absently turning the
cup around. "And he blamed himself for me ending up
with this." He touched the symbol burned into his cheek.

"Dyani told us it was a curse mark." Tremaine paused,
obviously weighing how far to pry. "How was it Gil's
fault?"

Ilias had promised himself if any of the Rienish ever
asked, he would tell them, even though it couldn't mean
to her people what it did to his. "When we followed
Ixion to the island, he caught me." He glanced up warily, then reminded himself that none of the people at the
other tables could understand their conversation. "He
cursed me, a transformation curse. Gil thought he'd
have to kill me. But when Gil killed—cut Ixion's head
off—it went away."

He knew it wouldn't mean the same thing to Tremaine,
raised not to see wizards as a corrupting evil, but she still
managed to surprise him. Instead of revealing even mild
shock, she looked at him, her eyes assessing. "The scars on
your back. That's where they came from. They didn't look
like normal scars."

He nodded, distracted by the realization that it was easier to tell her than he thought it would be. "Years ago in

most of the cities of the Syrnai, if you survived any kind of a curse, the lawgivers would kill you. They were afraid the evil was still inside you, even if it wasn't on the outside anymore. Now they don't, but you still have to wear this mark. And any obligations toward you, family or marriage, don't count anymore."

Tremaine's brows drew together. "But Halian and Karima and the others didn't . . ."

"No, they didn't. But they're different."

She studied the tabletop a moment, then asked carefully, "Why did you have to get the mark? It seems like Giliead could have prevented it."

That one he had no moral obligation to answer, but he had the feeling that she was seeing past his words a little deeper than he intended. In which case there was no point in not answering. He looked down, rubbing idly at one of the stains on the much-abused wood, hunting for the right words. "I didn't have to get it." No, it was all his own choice. *Be very clear about that.* That mix of willful pride and self-hate and self-pity was something you could manage only all on your own. "I thought it would make me feel better. I hated the way I felt, I couldn't stand it anymore. I could have left Andrien, gone somewhere inland where nobody had ever heard of us all, but I didn't want that, either. So I went to Cineth and got the curse mark. Gil caught me halfway there and practically went crazy trying to stop me. I didn't think he was going to feel the way he did over it." He hadn't thought about anything except himself. But he still didn't exactly regret it, maybe because it was a lesson he had had to learn and it was just as well he had finally learned it and got it over with.

She lifted her cup and put it down again, apparently just to examine the brown ring it made on the table. Her gaze had turned abstracted, as if what he had said had sparked some new thought and she was turning it over carefully, examining it from all angles. "You wanted to change everything."

Ilias hesitated. "What do you mean?"

"When everything hurts too much, you want to get away

from it but you can't, because it's inside you. So you do something drastic because you know it will change everything." She shrugged slightly, her eyes on the street. "Doing something drastic like that usually does."

"Maybe you're right," he said slowly. He waited until she shook herself slightly and her eyes were seeing him again. He asked, "So why are you fey?"

Tremaine gave him that unexpected, faintly self-mocking smile. "I don't know." She looked out at the rainy street, her expression turning sober again. "I lost a lot of people in this war, but so has everyone else. I lost my father. Not that I was that close to him. He's not somebody anyone gets close to. Because of him, of what he did, I was accused of being crazy once, and locked up. Though not for very long." She let out a frustrated breath. "Maybe that's not it. A lot of people found out about it and it was humiliating, but it doesn't sound like much compared to . . ." She shook her head wearily. "If I knew, maybe I wouldn't be fey."

"You had plenty of opportunity to die," Ilias pointed out. "Maybe you're not as fey as you think you are."

"Maybe." But her eyes were opaque again and he couldn't tell if she believed it or not.

The rain was still falling as they returned to the book-binder's. The bullyboy was there but instead of starting trouble he seemed more inclined to slump against the wall and study Ilias with hostility and poorly concealed admiration. Tremaine went to the back room again, leaving Ilias in the foyer.

Tremaine's thoughts were still mostly on their conversation. The reflective pain etched in his face, and all the torment that lay under the simple honesty of the way he had spoken about it, told her it was all so much worse than he was making it sound. It made her own problems seem more like a failure of resolve than anything the world had done to her. Maybe she just needed some perspective. She needed something, she was pretty sure of that. But talking to Ilias had given her a wariness about reaching for that something without being absolutely sure it would do the trick. If it looked easy, then it probably wasn't an answer at all.

Preoccupied with that as she stepped into the inner room, she wasn't aware of anything out of the ordinary. Then a man stepped out from behind the door, shoving it closed behind her and turning the lock. She stopped, eyeing him thoughtfully. He was another version of the bully-boy in the outer room, though a little older and bigger. He sneered nastily at her, an expression that began to turn a bit disconcerted under Tremaine's steady regard.

She looked at the old man, still seated at his desk. He smiled thinly, saying, "I think perhaps I would like a little more for my work. You understand."

This close to her goal, Tremaine was tempted to just grab the marble paperweight on the worktable and beat him to death. But she supposed that since Ilias had objected to the entire scheme on principle, he would also balk at allowing her to kill a sexagenarian. She raised her voice slightly and said, "Ilias."

The door slammed open, the broken lock hanging by one screw, and Ilias strolled in. The older bullyboy looked him over, then backed away slowly, absently studying the ceiling as if he was standing on a corner waiting for an omnibus. "What's wrong?" Ilias asked. The light rain had flattened his hair down and he didn't look nearly as fluffy. With the dark clothes, his scar and the strange silver mark on his cheek, he did look exotic and dangerous.

The old man wet his lips. "I didn't realize you had company. My mistake."

Since it had worked the first time, Tremaine just stared at him. The Valiarde name combined with the appearance of actual muscle had convinced him he had made an error in judgment, but she wasn't in that good a mood. She took the document off the desk and read it over in silence broken only by the old man's nervous wheezing. Satisfied, she tucked it into the dispatch case, tossed one of the gold coins onto the desk, then told Ilias, "Let's go."

She didn't realize the younger bullyboy from the front

office had followed them out into the street until Ilias suddenly whipped around and grabbed him by the collar.

The bullyboy winced, holding up his hands in surrender. "You a Valiarde? You hiring?" he asked Tremaine hurriedly.

"He wants a job," she explained to Ilias in Syrnaic.

He lifted a brow and released the boy, who stepped back, self-consciously tugging his jacket back into place. It was nice to know somebody considered them the winning team, but Tremaine wasn't so sure. She told the boy, "You don't want this job. Do what the government says and leave town."

He watched them walk away, scuffing his boots in the dirty puddles on the sidewalk.

Someone was waiting for them when they got back to the car. Leaning casually against the passenger side was an older man with long graying hair. He was dressed in an expensive greatcoat over a dark suit that made Niles's careful style of dress look cheap. His arms were folded and he was holding an ebony walking stick topped with a silver lion's head. As they drew near, Tremaine frowned, trying to remember if she had seen him before. Despite his age he was a very handsome man and she was sure she would have remembered him.

He watched her approach with a thoughtful expression. "Tremaine? I've been waiting for you."

She glanced uncertainly at Ilias, who said pointedly, "I'm not going to beat up an old man either."

"I didn't bring you along to— Never mind." She addressed the stranger, switching back to Rienish. "I don't believe I know you?"

He smiled. "I'm your uncle Galiard."

"Oh." Tremaine stared at him, nonplussed. She had long wondered who her other guardian was, but she had never expected him to simply wander up one day and introduce himself. Particularly this day. "Is that your real name?"

"Of course not. I'm actually your uncle Reynard." He

pushed away from the car, leaning on the cane, and eyed Ilias with a hint of challenge. "And this is . . . ?"

"This is my friend Ilias. He's . . . not from around here. He doesn't speak Rienish." She turned to Ilias to explain in Syrnaic, "It's all right; he's an old friend of my father's."

This caused Ilias to eye Reynard warily. He jerked his chin toward the other side of the street. "There's two men watching us from over there"—his eyes moved over the passersby, settling on a man standing near the lamppost on the corner—"and one more up there."

Tremaine turned back to Reynard, who was waiting with polite curiosity. She said, "He's spotted three of your bodyguards. Any others?"

Reynard's blue eyes were amused. He stroked his neat mustache. "No, he got them all. Very good. He's much better than that playboy you used to go around with." He lifted his brows inquiringly. "Whatever happened to him?"

"He's a captain in the Army Intelligence corps, and I wasn't 'going around' with him." Tremaine cocked her head, finally remembering where she had seen him before. The newspapers. He was Reynard Morane. "You should know; you're Captain of the Queen's Guard." She hoped she was keeping her face expressionless but she wanted to reel. It was hard to believe that this man had ever known Nicholas, except in a superficial social way. She could see them as opponents, but not as allies, friends even, with Morane privy to all of Nicholas's secrets. And to be her other guardian, Morane must have known everything there was to know.

"Retired." Reynard looked away across the street, his eyes narrowing. His expression turning serious, he said, "We've never met before because it was important for a number of reasons, past and present, that no one suspect I was ever associated with your father. That's not going to matter now."

Tremaine nodded slowly. After what Averi had told her, and what she had seen today in the city, it didn't come as a shock. "You're evacuating the royal family?"

"They went early this morning. The city will be under siege by tomorrow, maybe the next day if we're lucky. In the Philosopher's Cross the street barricades are going up." His gaze came back to her and turned kind again. "I wanted to make sure you had a way out of Ile-Rien."

"That's what this was about." She hugged the leather case to her chest. The man on the other end of the Garbardin exchange would have told him about her wanting the bookbinder's address, but she didn't want to go into details. Reynard would know all about the Institute's project anyway. "We're leaving, but we have some people we have to pick up first."

Reynard nodded but asked sharply, "Where's Gerard?"

"Ah . . . he's one of the people we're picking up."

"Well, that's all right then." He stepped away from the car, tucking the cane under his arm and adjusting the fit of his gloves. "I've got to go."

She had to ask. "To Parscia?" He didn't look like someone who was about to run away. He didn't look like someone who had ever run away from anything.

"No, I'm staying here. Your father's organization is going to work for the government-in-exile, whether most of the members know it or not. Fortunately, going underground won't be anything new for them." He met her eyes. "I've never taken advantage of my contact with them except to fulfill my obligations to you. Using them as a resource for the Crown would have been a betrayal I was not prepared to make, even after Nicholas's death. But I know in this situation that he would want me to use them against the Gardier in any way I could." He hesitated a moment, then added, "I was a friend of your mother's, too."

Tremaine didn't want to go down that road. "Don't tell me I look like her."

He smiled a trifle ruefully. "No, I'm afraid there's more resemblance to a portrait of Denzil Alsene in the palace."

Tremaine frowned. "Who?"

He snorted, looking amused. "He's a less than illustrious ancestor of yours. We all have them, but your father was very sensitive on the subject." He watched her gravely for a moment, then nodded to her and to Ilias. He propped the cane on his shoulder and walked away.

Chapter 19

The routes out of the city were crowded but the Chaire road to the coast was still relatively clear. Most of the civilian populace would be going the other way, trying to seek refuge in the Low Countries or Parscia. *For now,* Tremaine thought as she drove past a line of cars waiting to turn onto the Street of Flowers. The Gardier would surely take those lands next.

Tremaine had much to occupy her thoughts but the trip back to Port Rel was fairly serene, except the one time she had to pull over to the side of the road so Ilias could be sick. It was dusk by the time they reached the town and she found a place for Gerard's car under the trees on the street behind the hotel.

As Tremaine climbed out, she saw three men in military uniform walking briskly toward them down the cobbled path through the overgrown lawn. Her first thought was that Averi had been more optimistic than he had appeared and had sent them to wait for her arrival, so when she brought back the document they could get things under way immediately. She had discarded this theory by the time they reached the car and decided instead that they hadn't recognized her and were coming to warn her off the hotel property. "Miss Valiarde," the first one said, and that theory went down in flames too. "I'm afraid I have to take your friend into custody."

She stared at him. *I will not be stopped now.* She took a step forward. "What? Are you out of your mind? Under whose orders?"

The man looked more than a little taken aback, possibly not expecting Tremaine to respond quite so forcefully. "I was told he was a security risk."

Made uneasy by Tremaine's anger and an agitated conversation he couldn't understand, Ilias eyed the corporal aggressively. Tremaine put a hand on his shoulder to keep him from doing anything rash. She said, "He and his friend blew up a Gardier airship. Two, actually. That was before the Gardier burned the village near where he lives, sank the ship he was on and killed or captured most of his friends and family. That's a little much for a secret agent, isn't it? And he doesn't speak Rienish, so it isn't as if he could overhear our plans, now could he?"

One of the other men gave the corporal a rather accusing glare. Tremaine suspected that despite Averi's caution the story of the destroyed airships had already filtered through to what was left of the military detachment. She had just confirmed it for the enlisted men and surely most of them would see Ilias as a hero.

The corporal mulishly persisted, "It's not my decision, ma'am. I'm sorry, but—"

"Who ordered this? It wasn't Colonel Averi." It had better not be. He hadn't given any indication of it earlier.

The corporal fumbled in a pocket, pulling out a folded paper. "It was his signature—"

Tremaine snatched it out of his hand. "So you didn't talk to him?" She looked it over as best she could in the gathering dusk. It looked as real as the orders she had in the leather document case tucked under her arm. But she didn't know Averi's signature to judge if it was genuine or not. She swallowed a snarl and made herself say reasonably, "Look, there has to be some mistake. I spoke to Averi and Niles just before we left for town to see Minister Servaine. Why were you told to take Ilias?"

"All I know is what is on that order, ma'am—"

"Let me speak to Averi first."

"You can do that, ma'am, but I have to take him into custody."

Tremaine fumed, *I need to talk to Averi. This is . . . very wrong.* What if it wasn't wrong? What could she do, kill Averi? Tempting thought, but it would be a needless complication. "Why don't you just wait? Until I can talk to Averi."

The corporal sighed. "Ma'am, it's only house arrest. We're holding him at the hotel, in the room he's been assigned. Nothing is going to happen to him."

Dammit. Tremaine looked away. Considering Ilias might have ended up locked in a guardroom somewhere, this was lenient. But why lock him up at all? *Averi knows I went to the city with him this morning.* She had conscientiously signed them both out with the frantically busy duty officer and no one had said a word about it. Something was going on here and she had to find out what it was.

She let out her breath and pushed her hair back, trying to look distracted and upset rather than homicidal. With the air of giving in reluctantly under great duress, she said, "All right, but just let me explain it to him. He doesn't understand two words of Rienish, he doesn't have any idea what's happening."

The corporal looked relieved. "Very good, ma'am."

Tremaine turned to an increasingly worried Ilias. She took a breath, gathering her thoughts, and said in Syrnaic, "Something's wrong. They're going to take you to the room in the . . ." No word for hotel. "In the big house, the one you changed clothes in. They're going to lock you in, but wait until it's dark and you can climb out the window and reach my room, which should be three windows to the left. Go there and wait for me. I need to check on some things and try to find out what's going on, then I'll meet you there." She had seen Ilias climb through the caves like a mountain goat, she didn't think he would have any trouble with the ornamental ledges and scrollwork on the outside of the hotel.

He eyed the two guards resentfully and nodded. "All right."

"Good . . . ah, look resigned or something."

Ilias rolled his eyes and folded his arms.

"That'll have to do." She turned to the corporal, switching back to Rienish. "He'll go with you now."

The men took Ilias up the steps of the hotel's back entrance, past the moldering wicker furniture in the boarded-over conservatory. Following, Tremaine veered off as they reached the main foyer and headed toward the ballroom.

The high figured ceiling and lily chandeliers made a strange contrast with the packing crates of books and astronomical equipment stacked on the parquet floor. Only a few of the Institute's personnel were still there, engaged in sorting documents in wooden file boxes and feeding most of them into the fire in one of the large marble hearths. "I'm not sure," a young man she vaguely recognized as one of the astronomers who had worked with Tiamarc told her when she asked about Niles. "He's supposed to be here." He adjusted his spectacles with a frown. "I haven't seen him since late this afternoon."

Feeling uneasy, she went to the infirmary next. The screens were stacked against the wall and all the beds were empty.

A clatter led her to the serving hatches. She looked inside to see the nurse in the pantry area packing up medical supplies. "Where's Florian and Ander?" she demanded.

The woman jumped, startled. "Why, they were taken to the hospital."

"By who?"

"I'm not sure. I wasn't here. Captain Dommen told me they were sent away by ambulance this afternoon." She looked puzzled. "I don't know why. Florian was fine. I thought the doctor would discharge her after lunch and Captain Destan had woken several times and seemed much better."

"Thank you." Tremaine went back out into the corridor. She stood and stared at the faded floral wallpaper for a long moment, tapping her chin. *Oh yes, something's wrong.*

An hour later, feeling as if she had a target painted on her back, Tremaine went back upstairs to her room.

The lock stuck as usual, forcing her to wrestle with it. She had thought she was fairly calm, but had to restrain herself from screaming, kicking the door and going for the fire ax. *Note to self: I am not calm.* Finally she managed to turn the key and slip inside.

Shutting the door behind her, she put her hand on the wall switch in the foyer, whispering, "Ilias, it's me."

As the overhead light flickered to life, he stepped out from around the corner. Tremaine, though she was expecting him, almost jumped out of her skin.

"What did you find out?" he demanded as she stepped past him. He had closed the window again but a few dead leaves had blown in, caught in the cushions of the window seat amid the shattered glass from the pane he had broken to open it.

"I can't find Florian, Ander or Niles." She plopped down on the little settee and he sat on his heels in front of her. "I haven't seen Averi, either. Everyone seems to think Captain Dommen is in charge. I've been watching Averi's office, and I just saw Captain Dommen come out and go into this little pavilion in the hotel's garden. I don't have anything to go on, but he shouldn't be there, he should be down at the docks supervising the evacuation preparations." She scratched her head absently, still trying to put all the pieces together.

Ilias shook his head, not understanding. "So why would he go there?"

"To meet with Averi and the other spies. The Gardier agent that killed Tiamarc can't have been the only one here." Tremaine was convinced now that Averi was involved in the plot. The colonel hadn't objected to her trip to Vienne because he wanted them out of the way. *Bastard.*

Ilias watched her, troubled. "If the Gardier are there and they have Florian and Ander, they could kill them," he said urgently.

"I know." Tremaine nodded, distractedly chewing on a fingernail. "I think we're just going to have to get in there and get them out." She dug in a pocket, pulling out the bundle of keys. "This locking people in rooms thing worried me, so I took these out of Niles's desk in his room. If the one to the pavilion isn't here, I can probably pick it. They put warded doors with secure locks on the boathouse and the main part of the hotel, but they didn't bother with any of the outbuildings." She flipped through the keys, frowning thoughtfully. "So what do you think—" She glanced up to see Ilias sitting back on his heels, smiling faintly. "What?"

"Nothing."

"Did I have you worried? I worry myself a lot," Tremaine admitted.

"No, you didn't have me worried." He got to his feet. "Let's go."

The night air was dank and cold, a good complement to the garden's overgrown shrubbery and weedy flower beds. Over the hedges Tremaine could see the pavilion's conical red-shingled roof, black against the charcoal color of the evening sky. It was a little round building, two stories, probably used for the elaborate garden parties that had been held here before the war. The path turned and Tremaine could see there were slivers of light leaking past the shades in the pavilion's windows, reflecting off the ornamental pond that curved around the right side. Ilias stopped her, saying softly, "Someone's there."

She peered hard at the shadows near the doorway and saw one particularly lumpy blotch of darkness move. There was a guard at the door now. There hadn't been one when she had watched Dommen enter earlier. But it had still been light then and someone might have seen and wondered why the disused pavilion merited guarding. She touched Ilias's arm. "We need to get rid of him."

"Distract him," he whispered back, stepping into the bushes with barely a rustle.

Right, Tremaine thought. She dropped the coil of rope and the torch she had stolen from the hotel's garage into a weedy flower bed. Sauntering forward, hands in her pockets, she tried to look as if she was just out for a walk on the grounds of the moldering old hotel.

She turned up the path toward the pavilion, her shoes scraping on the wood planks that bridged the little stream. She could make out the man's shape against the white wall now. He hadn't moved and probably didn't realize she could see him. "Nice night for it," she remarked.

Obviously expecting to startle her and finding himself startled instead, the man twitched uncertainly. "Ma'am?"

"Nice night for it," Tremaine repeated briskly. She saw Ilias, or at least a dark Ilias-shaped shadow, creeping along the portico. He must have gotten behind the building by going through the hedges and was now edging along the curve of the wall, easing up behind the guard. He still had ten or so feet to go.

The guard tried to recapture the initiative, saying, "I'm afraid you're not permitted here, ma'am," as he stepped forward. His tone was polite but she could see he had one hand on his holstered pistol. "Are you alone?"

"Now that's a very personal question." Tremaine cocked her head to one side. It was also the question someone who was planning to knock her out and dump her in the pond would ask.

He moved toward her and in another instant Ilias had him, a forearm across his throat choking off any outcry. Dodging a frantic kick, Tremaine grabbed up a rock and smashed it on the man's gun hand. He let go of the pistol and she snatched it from the holster.

The guard's struggles slowed and Tremaine watched in consternation; she had forgotten to tell Ilias not to kill anyone, just in case she was wrong, but she didn't want to distract him right now. Finally Ilias lowered a limp body to the ground. She leaned over the man and poked him in the ribs. He wheezed in response and she straightened up, relieved.

As Ilias dragged him back up the gravel path into the brush, Tremaine hastily retrieved the rope and the torch. She checked the pistol to make sure it was loaded and shoved it into her pocket.

They got the man gagged with a couple of handkerchiefs and bound, then approached the pavilion again.
Ilias tugged on her sleeve, gesturing for her to follow him
through the overgrown garden around the pond, back up
onto the little building's porch. "There are windows on the
bottom floor," she told him softly. "Shouldn't we go in
that way?"

He shook his head, replying in a bare whisper, "I heard
voices in the front part of the house."

She noticed again he didn't object to the "we" part.
Maybe because Ander had first met her as Tremaine
Valiarde, playwright and nutty girl about town, and Ilias
had encountered her as Tremaine, intrepid cave explorer.
First impressions were important. "Were they speaking
Gardier?"

"No, your language."

"That's funny," Tremaine murmured thoughtfully. She
had had her heart set on a nest of Gardier spies. But Rienish spies in the pay of the Gardier would do just as well.

There was no portico along the back of the pavilion, but
there were trellises hung with winter-dry vines that
climbed the plank-paneled wall to the second floor. There
were three windows up there, one dimly lit. "That's the
best way in," he told her in a whisper. "But they're going
to hear it if I break the glass."

"Don't break it, just open it," she told him with some
asperity.

"Those are the same as in the hotel?"

Tremaine gazed up at the window. "Probably, why?"

"I could barely figure out how to open one from the
inside."

"Oh, that's right." She realized she hadn't seen a Syprian
house with glass or sash windows. "Here, use this." She
pulled out the metal file she had in her pocket and briefly
explained how to jimmy a window latch from the outside.

Ilias shed his coat and swarmed up the trellis. She saw
him hang outside the lit window for a moment, then work
his way along the ledge to a dark one that must open in the
next room. After some slight fumbling, he got the latch

jimmied and she saw the sash lift. He slipped inside, sliding it carefully shut behind him.

Tremaine waited, arms folded tightly, feeling the cold damp creep into her bones. It was quiet except for the occasional sound of a car from the road past the garden and the distant roar of the ocean. In the distance the army defense battery's searchlights played over the clouds. Then she heard a quiet hiss above her.

Squinting, she saw Ilias leaning out the lit window and motioning for her to come up. *Up there?* Tremaine thought, brows lifted. *Well, he's an optimist.* The problem with people who had confidence in you was that they also expected you to perform. She kicked off her shoes, grabbed the trellis and started up. It wasn't fair; he had to weigh more than she did but the thing creaked loudly as she climbed. Trembling with the fear of falling, she reached the window and he grasped her arm to haul her in.

Tremaine scrambled over the sill, whispering, "I will never wear a tweed skirt again." She stumbled on a rough wooden floor. It was a dimly lit room piled with boxes and furniture draped with white dustcovers. Straightening up again, she winced. After the long car ride, her sore muscles from horseback riding had become petrified and weren't taking well to the exercise.

"Should I untie him?" Ilias asked, patiently watching her.

"What?" Tremaine looked up, for the first time realizing they weren't alone. There was a figure in naval uniform sprawled unconscious on the floor just past a stack of old packing crates. She moved around the crates to see a man seated on a wooden bench, bound and gagged and glaring at her. "That's Colonel Averi," she whispered. "Dammit." She had been sure he was a traitor.

Ilias moved to untie him and Tremaine followed, seeing the chair the guard must have occupied, the battery lamp on the little table next to it and the folded newspaper that had kept him company. As Ilias cut Averi's hands free the colonel yanked the gag out of his mouth, spit, and said quietly, "Who else is with you?"

"It's just us. Where's Florian and Ander?" Tremaine demanded, picking up the newspaper. It was a Chaire edition, dated yesterday, carrying evacuation news and not much else. "Downstairs?"

Averi, tearing the ropes off his ankles, looked up, a flash of astonishment crossing his sallow face. "There's no one else?"

Tremaine looked at Ilias, who was standing with his hands planted on his hips, waiting for a translation. "He was hoping for better rescuers," she interpreted. Ilias rolled his eyes.

"You'll just have to make do with us," she told Averi. "Where are the others?"

"Downstairs, in the front room. They have Ander, Niles, and Florian. There's a man on the front door—"

"Not anymore."

"—and four with the others."

"It's Dommen who did this, isn't it?" Tremaine said. "He's the ringleader of a band of Gardier spies." *If they have Niles they have the sphere. Dammit.*

"No. His corporal, Mirsone, is the ringleader. Dommen seems to be subordinate to him from what I could see. There are also two civilians I didn't recognize." Averi leaned over the unconscious guard, taking his gun from the holster, then stood. "You go for help."

"I brought help already. The only people here I trust are down there." In case there was any doubt, Tremaine amended, "I'm talking about Niles and Florian and Ander."

"Tremaine, dammit, you can't—" Averi began.

"This is just like home," Ilias interrupted in exasperation. "Everybody argues. Did he say how many were down there?"

"Four," Tremaine supplied.

Averi demanded, "What did he say—" Wood creaked in the hall on the other side of the closed door.

Ilias moved instantly, silently springing over the prone guard and flattening himself against the wall by the door. Averi stepped sideways behind a set of shelves, the gun at ready. Caught flat-footed, Tremaine swore under her breath and just managed to crouch awkwardly behind a crate before the door opened.

Tremaine's view was bad but she saw a man in civilian dress start to step into the room. But before he moved into Ilias's reach, his eyes found the man sprawled on the floor. He backpedaled rapidly, pulling a pistol out of his coat and shouting, "Someone's here!"

Running footsteps answered the shout and Ilias slammed the door shut, bracing his shoulder against it. As the men on the other side pounded and shoved at it, Averi moved swiftly to help.

Realizing belatedly that Averi was right about calling for help, Tremaine pushed to her feet and ran back to the open window. Pulling out the pistol she had taken from the door guard, she leaned out and fired into the air.

Three shots blasting out into the night temporarily halted everybody and the pounding on the door ceased. Then she heard running feet hurrying away as the men bolted.

Ilias yanked the door open and he and Averi ran after them. Tremaine shoved the pistol in her pocket and followed.

Outside the room there was a dusty, badly lit hall, ending in a narrow staircase. She hurried down after Ilias and Averi.

The stairs ended in an open foyer and just as Tremaine reached it, the outer door slammed open and half a dozen uniformed soldiers burst in. The two fleeing civilians stopped in shock and Ilias skidded to a halt, not knowing if these were allies or enemies. Not sure of that herself, Tremaine ducked reflexively behind the banister. If the sentries who guarded the hotel grounds were traitors too, they were all dead.

But the man in front spotted Averi and halted in confusion, saying, "Colonel, what—"

"Arrest those men, they're traitors!" Averi said, shoving the nearest civilian toward the sentries.

Only a few feet from Tremaine, the door at the bottom of the stairs swung open. Captain Dommen stood there, his face white and his eyes desperate. She managed to yelp and point.

Dommen stepped back and moved to slam the door but Ilias flung himself against it, wedging himself in to keep it open. Averi shouted an order and the soldiers surged forward to help.

Tremaine clung to the banister, trying to stay out of the way. Ilias had managed to keep the door open and as the first two soldiers joined their weight and strength to his it flew back.

More people ran in from the front entrance and Tremaine recognized Giaren and some other members of Niles's staff who had been working in the ballroom earlier. Tremaine shoved herself to her feet, making it to the door ahead of them.

She pushed through in time to see a big room with large conservatory windows all covered by heavy blackout cloth. A couple of army cots stood near the far wall with two motionless figures stretched out on them—Ander and Niles. Florian was seated in a straight chair near them, her hands bound in front of her. She was still wearing a drab hospital gown and robe. Dommen backed away from the door and another man in a corporal's uniform raised a pistol.

Averi fired first and the man staggered back, falling to the floor. Then Dommen dragged Florian out of the chair, holding the gun to her head. Tremaine heard her say wearily, "Not again."

Everyone halted, the sentries pointing their rifles and the Institute personnel frozen in shock behind them. "Let her go," Averi snapped. "Or do you want me to call a sorcerer?"

Wild-eyed with desperation, Dommen shouted, "Get back!"

Tremaine looked around, just as desperate. She saw the sphere on a nearby table next to a small wireless set and some notepads. *Maybe we don't need to call a sorcerer,* she thought, eyeing the sphere. It was trembling on the table, spinning itself into a frenzy. Her palms were sweating as she weighed her options, but there was no way she could reach the sphere. Out of his head with panic, Dommen might kill Florian if any of them so much as twitched.

Ilias looked from Averi to Dommen, frustrated, but he knew better than to move. The colonel stared at Dommen, his jaw working as he brought himself under control. He put the pistol aside on a chair and lifted empty hands, saying cautiously, "You have to realize it's over. Let the girl go."

Dommen said thickly, "Tell them to back away from the door."

Tremaine stared at the sphere, willing it to hear her. *Why do I have to touch you,* she thought, *you helped Gerard kill the leviathan from a distance. I know you can hear me. Make the pistol hot, make him drop it—*

"Tell them—" The words dissolved into an agonized yell as Dommen flung the pistol down. Florian yanked away from him, falling back into the chair. Dommen stumbled away, clutching a badly burned hand.

There was a surge forward but Ilias reached him first. He grabbed Dommen by the jacket and threw him down on the floor. The sentries surrounded him.

Tremaine shoved through the confusion to Florian, kneeling to untie her hands. "What kept you?" the girl said blearily.

"It was the traffic in Vienne," Tremaine told her, working the knots free. "It was terrible."

Averi looked around, frowning. "Who did that?" His eyes fell on Niles's secretary. "Giaren, I didn't realize you were a sorcerer."

Across the room Giaren, bending anxiously over Niles, glanced up to say, "I'm not. That wasn't me."

"It was the sphere," Tremaine said, more occupied with Florian. The girl's face was stark white and she had dark circles under her eyes. "Are you all right?" Tremaine asked her, worried. "You don't look too good."

"They're Gardier?" someone asked.

"He's not a Gardier." Averi looked down at Dommen coldly. "I know his family."

"I'm fine," Florian told Tremaine with vague assurance.

She dropped her head into her hands. "They gave us some kind of drug. And I think I'm going to be sick."

Tremaine helped her up and one of the Institute workers hurriedly led them to a bare little washroom off the foyer. Florian leaned over the sink, splashing water on her face, and Tremaine left her to the other woman's care.

She returned to the other room where someone had draped a coat over the sprawled form of Corporal Mirsone. More military personnel had arrived and the two civilian members of the conspiracy were handcuffed and standing back against the wall. Averi and a few others surrounded Dommen, who sat on the floor staring at his hand. It was uninjured, all evidence of what had been a terrible burn vanished.

Reminded, Tremaine went to the table and picked up the sphere. It clicked happily at her. It hadn't used the spell she had read about to turn metal objects red-hot; it had done something else, making Dommen see and feel that his hand had been burned without actually injuring him. If only Niles had been conscious to witness it. *Speaking of*... She looked around, found Ilias nearby and dumped the sphere into his hands before he could back away. "Here, take care of this."

He would have been less appalled if she had handed him a live snake. He swallowed and gave her a desperate look. "Uh—"

"Just stand there with it." She patted his shoulder reassuringly. "Don't worry, it likes you."

She went to the cots where Niles and Ander lay. Giaren was sitting on Niles's cot, trying to revive the deeply unconscious sorcerer with smelling salts. It was the first time she had seen Niles looked disheveled; with his sleek blond hair mussed and without his suit coat, he seemed much younger. Ander just looked like Ander, wearing a robe and green hospital-issue pajamas. He twitched and stirred, so she sat on the edge of his cot.

She heard Averi ask Dommen, "Why?"

The man looked up. His uniform was disarrayed, his expression bleak. "Last year on the Aderassi front, I was captured. I knew it was hopeless. They convinced me—"

"You told them about the project," Averi interrupted. He must have realized that he didn't want to hear Dommen's reasons. "You gave them the target point for the Pilot Boat. You arranged for the Gardier assassin who killed Tiamarc."

"Yes."

"Do they know that Captain Destan and the others returned?"

"We couldn't report." He looked toward the little wireless. "Our communication device had Gardier crystals in it so we could use it without being detected. That . . . thing destroyed them as soon as we brought it in here."

Good sphere, Tremaine thought. Another Institute worker hurried over with wet towels and more smelling salts. Tremaine selected one of the towels and slapped Ander with it. He snorted, batting at her, but managed to get his eyes open.

"You all right?" she asked, peering at him.

He tried to nod, then grabbed his head with a moan.

"How did you know Dommen was a traitor?"

It was Averi, standing at her side. The soldiers were taking Dommen and the others away. "He looked suspicious." She shrugged. "I thought you were one too."

As Averi stared at her, Ander lifted his head wearily and said, "That's funny, I thought you were a traitor."

She stared at him. It was almost flattering. Actually, it was flattering. "I offered, but they wouldn't take me."

Not in the mood for humor, Ander grunted, "Great. Now help me up."

"Tremaine, are you in there?" she heard Florian call.

She leaned toward the door to shout, "I'm in Gerard's room." She had come to get Gerard's things and she was in the middle of packing his shaving kit, trying to find room for it among the books already stuffed into the bag. It might seem overly optimistic to pack at all but there seemed even less point in not packing. His room was just like hers, faded patterns on the once-fine bedclothes and carpet, blackout curtains instead of filmy silk, dingy wallpaper. At least he had managed to bag a bedside lamp that worked, though in keeping with the hotel's decor the shades were glass tulips.

Tremaine and everyone else had been wrapped up in last-minute preparations before breaking up to gather what they needed and head for the ship. Ander, though still a little shaky on his feet, was leading a small group of volunteers back through the portal with Tremaine, Florian and Ilias. Ilias was still with him now, explaining the layout of the caves. Their goal was much the same as it had been before: to destroy the base or at least incapacitate it long enough for the *Ravenna* to pass through the portal herself. Though now she would be doing it without the troops originally promised and her purpose would be to carry refugees past the Gardier blockade. Tremaine's goal, and Ilias's too, was to rescue Gerard and the others, though she hadn't mentioned that to Averi.

The colonel had had legitimate concerns, mainly that Dommen and Mirsone must have told the Gardier about the *Ravenna;* she would have undoubtedly been a prime target already if Ilias and Giliead hadn't destroyed one of the airships and partially crippled the base. As it was, the spies might have tried sabotage and a team of Institute and navy volunteers had been sent to search the ship for damage.

Tremaine just wanted Averi to hurry before somebody from Vienne Command contacted them and Averi discovered that the *Ravenna's* side trip to send them back through the portal was unauthorized. During the meeting, Averi had been called to the communications room and she had held her breath; when he had come back to tell them that Vienne Command had shut down all transmissions for final evacuation, she had almost said, "Thank God!" aloud.

Tremaine glanced up from rifling Gerard's bedside table for his spare spectacles as Florian entered the room. The other girl paused at the end of the little hallway, her face drawn and still pale from her near drowning and her encounter with Dommen and Mirsone. "You all right?" Tremaine asked, a little worried. "Where did you go?"

"I was just in the wireless room, sending a telegram to my family." Florian pushed her hair back. She had changed into a pair of khaki knickers and a pullover sweater. "Niles told me he offered to send us back with Ilias," she said flatly.

Tremaine nodded, distracted by finally locating the spectacles. "Yes, he did."

"Going back there to fight the Gardier, that's one thing, going back there to hide—" Florian hesitated, her face taut with tension. "You were willing to do that? Abandon Ile-Rien?"

Tremaine turned to regard her, feeling a little blank. "It didn't come to that."

"If it had, would you?" she demanded.

Tremaine went back to Gerard's battered leather bag, jamming in the few items of spare clothing he had brought. She didn't want to talk about this, not now. "I have a hard time caring about things."

"No you don't." Florian shook her head, frustrated. "You cared enough to get us out of that room at the Gardier base, to find Ilias, to get through those caves, to rescue us from Dommen—"

"That was different," Tremaine cut the litany off abruptly. Most of that had been luck, or Ilias.

"How?" Florian gestured in exasperation. "It's like you're two people. One of them is a flighty artist, and I like her. The other one is bloody-minded and ruthless and finds scary things funny, and I'm not sure I like her very much; but whenever we're about to die, she's the one who gets all three of us through it alive." She pressed her lips together, then asked seriously, "Which one are you? I'd really like to know."

Tremaine abandoned the bag's stubborn clasp, letting out a frustrated breath and rubbing her eyes. She wasn't happy to hear something said aloud that she herself had been mentally dancing around for far too long. She couldn't tell Florian which one she really was when she didn't know herself.

She had chosen the flighty artist, she could see that now in a way she hadn't before. It had enabled her to forget her past, make a new person of herself. But it was the other her she needed now, the one her father had raised and trained, and Tremaine wasn't sure she liked that other self either. "You want me to defend the palace gates with a bloody flag wrapped around me, that's not going to happen. You want me to fight Gardier, that I can do." *That Gardier Gervas thought I was pathetic. Never mind that's what I wanted him to think, never mind this was personal long before that. I'm going to take the Gardier's world away.* That was all the reason she could articulate to herself at the moment and it wasn't what Florian wanted. Lying forgotten on the bed, the sphere clicked slowly, its inner gears spinning into motion, stirred by Tremaine's agitation. *Dammit.* "The sphere's getting upset. Can you take it to Niles?"

"I'm sorry." Her cheeks flushed, Florian stepped to the bed to collect it.

Tremaine watched her go, then went back to fiddling with the clasp on Gerard's bag. *You were raised by an emotionally frozen master criminal and an opium addict sorcerer,* she told herself. *It's a wonder you're only two people.* Maybe she shouldn't have shared any confidences with Florian. *I don't belong here with these people.* She didn't think like them, and if she managed to behave like them, it was only because she was a better actress than Niles thought. She rubbed her forehead wearily. She felt she was back in the caves walking on that narrow bridge over the chasm and had deliberately looked down.

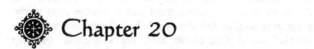

Chapter 20

T he night was well advanced when Tremaine and Ilias headed for the *Ravenna*. Preparations on the dock were quiet but frantic as the skeleton crew readied the ship to sail. Trucks and cars lined the road above the dock, empty now that their passengers had boarded. Only a few stragglers seemed to be left on the dock itself.

Tremaine had changed back into her Syprian clothes, adding her own stout walking boots and a sweater to hold off the cold on the way over to the dock. Her rationale for this was that they were better for swimming, though mostly she had done it because she wanted to wear them. Her small bag of belongings was even lighter since she was leaving behind both her tweed skirts. She had left them draped over the glass tulip lampshades, for the Gardier to puzzle over when they overran the place.

She glanced back at Ilias. Trailing behind her with Gerard's bag slung over his shoulder, he was eyeing the ship with a combination of dread and resignation. "Why don't you like it?" she asked him, frustrated. The *Ravenna* was the first thing she had ever stolen and she was pretty damn proud of it.

"She needs eyes," he said, not looking up at the bow high above their heads. "Without them she's like a . . . giant with no face."

"Oh." Heading on down the dock, Tremaine thought that over. It was hard to argue with.

A scaffold with metal stairs had been erected to allow access to the ship; Rel had never been a port for vessels of this size and didn't have the gangway structure that would normally be used to board. A group of Institute workers were carefully scaling the steps as the structure shook with the wind; it looked like a toothpick sculpture next to the giant gray wall of the *Ravenna*'s hull. Tremaine was more worried about that climb than she was about the trip through the spell portal. She hadn't thought to bring a torch and was relieved someone had strung a few work lights along the handrail.

Florian was waiting at the bottom of the steps, jittering impatiently as the guards checked them off on the list. She was carrying a battered travel case. Not wanting a return to their last topic of conversation, Tremaine asked quickly, "Did your telegram get an answer?"

She shook her head, looking away. "There was a message waiting for me in my room. My family started for Parscia yesterday." She shrugged regretfully as she shouldered her case. "I didn't have a chance to tell my mother where I am. Though considering what we're about to do, that might be a good thing."

"Oh. Sorry," Tremaine said, feeling inadequate.

"I'm sure they're all right," Florian said, but it was automatic. Her face was still shadowed. "Before the wireless room shut down I sent a telegram to my aunt's house in Belaise, just to tell them I'm all right and I have a way out of the country. I'm sure they'll stop there on the way."

"It'll be all right," Tremaine told her, patting the girl's shoulder awkwardly. She wasn't good at reassurance. *Probably,* she reflected, *because the flighty artist half is too flighty, and the bloody-minded one knows just how badly things might turn out.*

Ilias, who was good at reassurance, just stepped up and pulled Florian into a hug. It was the first time he had touched Florian since finding out she could use magic. *He's getting over it, or past it,* Tremaine thought, *whether he realizes it or not. Next maybe he'll even be able to look at Niles without baring his teeth.*

"I'm a little nervous about using the sphere again," Florian admitted as they climbed the wooden stairs up toward the shipside door. The cold breeze picked at their clothes and tossed their hair and made Tremaine cling nervously to the handrail. Florian added reluctantly, "I'm afraid of what happened before. I know the spells, but I'm just not sure I know what I'm doing with the sphere. It's so powerful."

"You got us here," Tremaine pointed out, trying to be supportive. "And you brought us in right to the boathouse, so you must be better at it than you think."

"I brought us into the boathouse?" Florian threw a puzzled glance back down at her, the stark electric light throwing her sharp features into high relief.

"Yes. You don't remember it because you were drowning."

"But we were on the very edge of the target point," Florian protested. "The boathouse is in the center. To change the spot where we came through, I would have had to change the connecting points in the reverse adjuration."

They reached the top of the scaffold where a wooden gangway extended to vanish into the large black hole of the door. It was dark inside except for a few emergency lights illuminating the shadowy passage into the boarding hall. "So, you must have done that," Tremaine said, distractedly twitching hair out of her eyes. Supposedly the ship had been pronounced clear of bombs or spells planted by Gardier spies; since there was an awful lot of ship to search, she thought that was probably optimism rather than certainty.

She glanced back at Ilias as he reached the top of the stairs behind her. He still looked like someone who was being dragged to his execution, but while she groped for a reassuring comment, Florian said seriously, "Tremaine, I can't do that kind of etheric math in my head. Maybe on paper, but not off the cuff when I'm panicking because we're about to be attacked by a . . . whatever that was. I'd need references and charts and . . . more confidence."

"Well . . ." Tremaine began, then couldn't think of a way to finish that sentence. She shrugged and pointed for Florian to go on inside. "We'll figure it out later."

Florian pulled an electric torch out of the sphere's leather carrying case and switched it on, lighting their way down the short black corridor through the ship's hull. Tremaine followed hurriedly; it was a relief to get out of the wind and off the rickety stairs.

The passage opened into a big room, silent and lit sporadically by little round emergency battery lights set high in the walls. The group of people just ahead of them were across the room, their torches flashing around as they tried to decide which corridor to take. Tremaine knew this was the Cabin Class Entrance Hall, but it was hard to make out any detail as they crossed the tile floor. The place had the slightly dusty, temporarily deserted air of a large hotel late at night. Florian flicked the torch over the signs next to the corridor entrances, finding the right one.

As they went down the wood-paneled hallway Tremaine could feel the ship coming to life around them, though the rooms they passed were still dark. The crew members who weren't helping out on the dock would all be belowdecks, spread out among the boilers, the engine rooms and the generating stations. Somewhere in the bowels of the ship a head of steam was being raised and extra turbines run up, ready to take the additional electrical load once they got under way.

She realized Ilias hadn't said anything for a while and looked back. He was following them, head down, hands jammed into the pockets of his coat, the set of his shoulders conveying tension. She remembered what he had said about the bareness of the Gardier quarters, how sterile and alien it had felt, and wondered if the ship struck him the same way.

"Hey, look at this." Tremaine stopped in a doorway and felt for the light switch. Ilias stepped up beside her, curious and wary. The overheads buzzed, flickered and came to life, revealing what the discreet panel on the door claimed was the Cabin Class reading lounge. Most of the furniture was missing, but the walls were covered with wood burnished until its grain was like watered silk. The crystalline fixtures softened the electric light and it played over a patterned carpet in soft reds and golds and a marble mantel with a carved mural of leaping deer above it.

Ilias leaned on the doorframe and whistled softly in wonder. He glanced at her. "Is it all like this?"

She explained, "They were supposed to take out all the fancy bits when they made it into a troop ship, but there was never time. And most of the navy was destroyed, and there was nowhere to send troops."

He nodded, stepping back from the door. "I can see why you wanted to steal her."

"I didn't steal her." She flipped the lights off, not sure if they needed to conserve electricity or not.

"What?" Florian had come back to look for them, her torch playing along the carpet. "Who did Tremaine steal?" she demanded.

"Nothing," Tremaine told her hurriedly in Rienish. "He's overreacting."

"That paper she brought back from the city that said we could use the ship didn't come from a lawgiver; she got some old man to write it for her," Ilias explained matter-of-factly to Florian.

"Oh my God." Wide-eyed, Florian stepped forward and shined the light in Tremaine's face. "Is that true? What were you thinking?"

"Hey!" Wincing, Tremaine pushed the torch away. She turned to Ilias, saying in exasperation, "Didn't I ask you not to tell anyone?"

"No," he said, and added with devastating candor, "you were counting on me not being able to speak your language."

Florian gestured helplessly. "Tremaine!"

"What, so I'll get in trouble?" Annoyed, she shrugged and moved on up the corridor. "Maybe they'll force me to go to another world and fight heavily armed sorcerers who— Oh, wait, we're doing that already."

"Tremaine . . ." Shaking her head in consternation but obviously at a loss for what to say, Florian followed.

Making their way further into the ship, they found more of the corridor lights lit and started to hear voices and see civilian sailors, military personnel and Institute members hurrying by. They found the steward's office open and empty and dropped the bags there, then located Niles, deep in conversation with Averi near the head of a stairwell. Averi had his usual thunderous expression and Niles looked harassed and desperate. "Good, you're here," he said hurriedly. "We're almost ready to cast off."

"Are we?" Florian asked, startled. "I thought there'd be more people coming with us."

Averi shook his head. "Most of the military and Viller Institute personnel agreed to come, especially those who still have families here and had no other way to evacuate them. We sent out a quick general call, but very few of the people still left in Rel wanted to risk it."

"Can we watch the ship cast off? You don't need us yet, do you?" Tremaine interjected, wanting to offer Florian a distraction so the alleged theft of the *Ravenna* wouldn't suddenly come up in conversation. Ilias, worried about his friends and impatient to get on with this, looked like he was badly in need of a distraction too.

It became rapidly clear that Niles and Averi didn't care what anyone did as long as it didn't bother them now. Tremaine found the way up the metal stairwells to the deck and as soon as Ilias pushed open the hatch, it became obvious that the *Ravenna*'s bulk had been shielding them from the worst of the weather. The cold damp wind tore at them and pushed them toward the bulkhead. They were up near the bow, on the main deck, and there was a fine view of the bay, the waves rolling in up the white beach, the darkened port and the hotel above it. The air flickered, seeming alternately thick with a misty distortion, then clear. "That's the wards." Florian raised her voice to be heard over the wind. "The ones that keep the ship from being visible from above are tied to the hull so they'll follow us out."

Ilias squinted up into the dark air somewhat warily. Tremaine impatiently led the way toward the front of the ship, where they could look down on the decks extending out from the bow and the ocean dock far below. She could hear a few shouts and bangs that must be accompanying the closing of the shipside door. They would be casting off the moorings now. Her stomach tightened and she sympathized with Florian's nerves; only a little while now.

The wind made it more comfortable for both women to huddle next to Ilias, for the warmth and the security against being swept off the deck by a gust. Below in the dark choppy water, they could see a tug edging itself into position and a gentle thrumming was beginning to issue from somewhere deep within the bowels of the ship.

Tremaine looked up to see a cloud of released steam puff up from the giant stack looming above them. Her chest felt tight for some reason, and it wasn't nerves from thinking about returning to the island or her anxiety for Gerard and Giliead and the others. The *Ravenna*, languishing in dock for so long, a virtual prisoner of the Gardier, was stretching her legs. Tremaine was anything but an optimist, but this just had to be good. "We're nearly ready . . ." She trailed off, staring down at the dock that seemed to be rapidly rolling away below. Then she realized the ship was already moving. She saw the tug cross the bow again, its running lights revealing frantic activity aboard.

"We're going to hit that building," Florian pointed out, sounding a little alarmed.

The bow seemed to be angling toward a three-story warehouse on the end of the pier. Tremaine nodded, fascinated. "Looks like it."

Ilias craned his neck, trying unsuccessfully to see over the bulk of the bow deck below this level. "And she's going to shear off the end of the dock." He sounded impressed.

"I don't think it'll hurt the hull." Tremaine's brows lifted as the warehouse's rounded metal roof suddenly crumpled and slid out of sight. If a tremor had passed through the great ship, she hadn't felt it. It had crushed the building with as little effort as a truck rolling over a tin cup. The shriek of tearing wood and metal followed them as the *Ravenna* steamed out into the bay toward the dark horizon of the open ocean, gathering speed. They were high above the water but she could still feel the deck sway under her feet; it was a strange sensation, different from any smaller ship she had ever been on. It was as if the great vessel's weight was making the whole earth move. *We're making our secret escape in the biggest boat in this hemisphere,* she thought, admiring the irony.

"We'd better go back in. They'll be starting soon." Florian rubbed her arms briskly, looking back at the port. There was already little to see; few lights were lit and the wards along the dock caused a thickening in the air, as if the buildings were draped in mist. Rel seemed deserted already, a ghost town above an ancient ruined port. "I hope nobody was in that warehouse. Of course, you'd have to be crazy to be on the dock while this was going on," Florian added matter-of-factly, spoiling the poetic image Tremaine had been constructing.

Turning her head away from the battering wind and feeling her way along the rail, Tremaine felt oddly obligated to defend the *Ravenna*. "I heard they brought her into dock at Chaire once without using tugs."

"I wish we had that captain on the tiller," Ilias commented dryly, taking one last look back.

They met Niles again at the entrance to the Cabin Class ballroom. "Hurry," he said, waving at them to come in. "They sent word from the bridge that we're almost in position."

It hadn't taken very long, but the *Ravenna*'s engines were so powerful she moved at more than thirty knots under full steam. They would still be far from the Gardier blockade, but it was dangerous for the ship to remain in these waters too long, even with her camouflage paint and concealing wards.

The spell circle was in the main ballroom, one of the largest rooms in the ship. The circle was a much-expanded version of the one at the boathouse and had been permanently painted onto the marble tile. It enclosed most of the long rectangular room, leaving only a few feet of space along the walls. Little ward signs circled the enameled red support pillars to exclude them from transport when the spell was initiated.

From what Niles had said, taking the *Ravenna* through herself would be easier than sending a few people through at a time. Like the way they had used the boathouse circle to send the Pilot Boat through, it would only be a matter of adjusting the spell's parameters outward slightly. *If we don't fail,* Tremaine reminded herself, feeling her stomach twist with nerves. *If we don't fail, the rest will be easy.*

Most of the big room was unlit and the glimpses of dark wood paneling and red velvet drapes increased the atmosphere of a rich but shadowy vastness. There was a stage at the far end for use when the room doubled as a theater, and the remaining tables and chairs had been dragged out into the foyer. A few crystal sconces on the pillars were lit, providing enough light to move around in.

Ander and the other men who had volunteered for the mission were in the foyer, sealing up the last of the waterproofed wooden cases they were using to carry supplies and weapons. Among other things, they were taking a small portable wireless and a buoy that they could send back through the portal to let the *Ravenna* know if their mission was successful. The cases would also double as flotation devices, since they were going to land in the water again.

Dommen had admitted that their Gardier contact had seemed roughly able to detect when the Pilot Boat had passed through the portal. Niles was betting this was because of the disturbance in etheric vibrations caused by so large an object's sudden appearance. His guess was that smaller disturbances, such as a few people passing through, wouldn't cause detectable vibrations.

One of the men hurried up to Tremaine and Florian, carrying navy-issue life jackets. "Miss, what's it like over there?" the man asked, handing one to Tremaine.

"Uh . . ." Tremaine remembered that his name was Rulan; she had noticed him because he was Parscian and had helped Stanis work on the Pilot Boat's engine once. She groped for a way to describe it. "It's nice, except for the Gardier."

"It's summer there," Florian elaborated, distracted as she buckled herself into the jacket.

He didn't look much enlightened by this description, but Tremaine was too busy to think of a better one. She pulled off her sweater and tossed it onto a chair as Rulan moved on.

Ilias was looking around at the preparations, practically twitching with impatience. He watched Tremaine and Florian struggle into the life jackets as if he thought it was a strange and unlikely thing to do under the circumstances. "What are those?"

"They float, they're to help you swim," Florian explained, buckling her last strap. "You want one?"

He shook his head. "I don't need help swimming." He pulled off his coat and the sweater under it, revealing his Syprian clothes.

For a moment it was quiet as the other men moved around the shadowy room making last-minute checks of equipment, getting into life jackets.

"All right, everyone." Ander stepped forward, his gaze serious. "We're going to go in stages. Ilias, Florian and I will go first, then the rest of you in groups of three, then Tremaine last."

Tremaine didn't care if she was last or not. She was ready to go.

This time they underestimated the distance.

Tremaine had an instant's view of a wall of blue-gray water and a heartbeat to realize it was all around her. Then the displaced sea rushed in with torrential force.

She surfaced, coughing, eyes and nose streaming. Florian bobbed next to her, clutching the sphere's bag. "Little more altitude next time," Tremaine told her, wiping salt water out of her eyes and taking a quick look around. Mist hung heavily overhead, blotting out the sun, and the sea moved in lazy swells. The water was cool but not bone-freezingly cold like the sea at Port Rel.

"There's Ander," Florian said, paddling with one arm. The others were treading water nearby, using the cases as floats. Ander twisted around with a frown, obviously doing a quick head count of the other men. They looked variously startled, shocked and amazed to be alive.

Tremaine paddled toward him, asking, "Where's Ilias?"

"Scouting to make sure we're in the right place," he told her, turning his head away from the splash of her arrival. He gave Florian a hand as she drew closer, helping her grab hold of a floating case. "I don't want to waste our strength swimming in the wrong direction."

"Good, because—" Tremaine said just in time to catch a swell in the face. She coughed up water, gasping. "Never mind, it wasn't important."

Floating nearby, one of the men said tensely, "He's coming back, Captain." He was a hard-faced, wiry man whose name Tremaine thought was Basimi.

She looked and saw Ilias swimming toward them through the mist. He moved quickly, with a minimum of splashing. Still about ten yards away, he paused, treading water, and waved to Ander.

"Right." Ander nodded, turning to tell the others, "Let's go."

The men swam awkwardly as they towed the cases, making Tremaine feel vulnerable and glad for the concealing mist. Giant black rocks loomed suddenly ahead of them, the water lapping at their rough surfaces. They made it past without the waves slamming anyone into the stone and Ilias swam back to report, "The cave mouth ahead leads to the inlet where the entrance is."

As Ander translated for the others, Ilias turned to Tremaine. "Are you all right?"

"Why, do I look like I'm drowning?" she asked, right before another swell swamped her.

Ilias hauled her up by the collar and she shook the water out of her ears in time to hear Ander say, "Tremaine, will you hold on to one of the goddamn cases?"

"We're nearly there." She kept swimming. She was going to do this on her own if she had to dog-paddle the whole way.

Dark cliffs draped with the sour-colored greenery materialized out of the drifting fog. They followed Ilias toward an opening tucked into a fold of the rock. Gray light inside showed the cave was open to the sky somewhere not far ahead. The waves grew rougher, buffeting them against the steep sides as they worked their way along. After much cursing, gasping and bruises the passage spilled abruptly into an open well with a little gravelly beach along the rough rock wall.

The men reached it first, hastily hauling the supply cases up onto the gritty sand. Tremaine felt for the bottom and found it, her feet slipping on the gravel. Florian, some paces ahead of her, stood up with an exclamation of relief. Rulan waded out to her to drag her case ashore.

Tremaine staggered up after them. Under the bulging folds of the cliff were the dark pockets of several cave mouths. One was larger than the others, leading back deep into the rock. The familiar smell of dank decay hung over the little inlet and the purplish plants clung to every crack.

"Here we go again," Florian said under her breath, plopping down on the sand and pulling off her boots to dump out the water. Under Ander's direction, the men pried open the waterproofed cases.

"I think we're a little better prepared this time," Ander commented, lifting one of the crossbows out and checking the stock and string for dampness. They had also brought brown coveralls, confiscated from an abandoned textile mill in Rel. Ander had pronounced them close enough in color and style to the Gardier uniforms and worker outfits to fool an observer at a distance or in bad light.

Sitting on his heels, Ilias leaned over to inspect the crossbow. He didn't look impressed. "They're small. They have good pull?"

"Good enough." Ander handed one to him and knelt beside the case with the torches and other equipment. "It's what we used on the Aderassi front. The Gardier's spells for disrupting machinery and electrical equipment won't work on them." He shook his head suddenly, wincing at some memory, and looked around to make sure the other men weren't having trouble arming themselves. "Didn't help much against firearms, but it was something."

Basimi came over, wearing one of the coveralls over his wet clothes and checking the set of his equipment. His eyes moved over their little group and Tremaine wondered what he saw: one Intelligence captain recently wounded and still laboring under a burden of exhaustion, one wild native guide, plus one half-trained underage witch and one dilettante flake. Then Basimi said, "Are we sure we can trust him, the native?"

Rulan, sitting nearby checking the batteries of the torches, glanced up, frowning a little.

Ander flicked a grim glance at Basimi. "The native's killed more Gardier than all of us put together," he said. Startled, Basimi gave Ilias another searching look.

Tremaine was a little surprised at how correctly she had guessed Basimi's estimation of them. Surprised, but not particularly gratified. She shifted over to Ilias, trying to look as if she was asking about the crossbow, and said in Syrnaic, "Are we sure we can trust them?"

"That's what I was wondering," Florian said in the same language. "If Colonel Averi thinks he didn't find all the spies—"

Loading bolts into a quiver, Ander said flatly, "No, we aren't sure we can trust them."

Ilias lifted a brow at this information, then rolled the shoulder he had injured and glanced uneasily back at the cave entrance. "I wish I had my sword."

Tremaine looked at the other men, most of whom were busy arming themselves. "I wish you had your sword too," she said under her breath.

W hat about the disappearing curse?" one of the men demanded.

"The what?" Gerard asked, baffled.

"The one you did to the *Swift*, that didn't work," Dyani interpreted, shifting around to find a more comfortable spot in their crowded cell.

It had been a long timeless interval and they had no idea if it was day or night. The Gardier hadn't provided any food and their source of water was a trickle of foul-tasting liquid leaking down the rock walls. That may have been just as well; the sanitary facilities consisted of the back corner of the cell. The chains, not comfortable to begin with, had painfully abraded everyone's wrists. The crowded conditions would have been intolerable, except that most Syprians were apparently sociably inclined individuals with the body modesty of cats. And this group had obviously already been through trying circumstances together in the past. Giliead was really the only withdrawn one, set apart more by his reticence than his status as the god's Chosen Vessel.

"The disappearing curse did work," Arites protested. "There's no leviathans here, so maybe—"

Gerard shook his head. "No, I don't have the materials to create that ward again." The Syprians were taking their enforced proximity to a sorcerer fairly well, though Gerard was still glad Giliead and Halian were his allies.

There had been one awkward incident not long after Ixion left. At some muttered commentary near the back of the group, Halian had lifted his head, singled out the ringleader by eye, and demanded, "What did you say, Darien?"

Darien had shrugged uneasily. "He's a wizard too."

"He's killed wizards." Giliead hadn't bothered to turn his head, but his voice was as hard as steel. "Haven't you?"

"I have." Gerard eyed his audience thoughtfully. "I can describe the occasion if it would help."

To his surprise nearly everyone had nodded. After relating the time he had fought a rogue Bisran sorcerer-priest, he followed it up with a couple of Nicholas and Arisilde's more violent adventures. He had noticed that some of the men still avoided his eyes and had shifted to the back of the cell to avoid any accidental contact, but others were obviously hoping he could help.

Gerard had been racking his brain for something that might get them out of here, but the Gardier were proof against any direct attempts at offensive spells. He added, "The cell door and the corridor are too small; if one of you tried to slip out, even warded, the Gardier would be aware of it. They can detect wards at close quarters."

Halian grunted thoughtfully. He hadn't asked the frantic questions that the others had, but Gerard sensed he was just as eager to take any weapon that lay to hand.

"There's got to be something." The quiet voice was Giliead's. He leaned against the bars, staring toward the cell door.

The others went silent. *Respect or fear?* Gerard wondered. Looking at the other men's faces, he thought it was mostly respect, but the fear was there too. He said slowly, "This may be a ridiculous question, but there's no possibility that Ixion might be trusted, in this one instance?" He shifted uncomfortably, leaning back against the damp wall. "He knows what I am. Even if he's holding that fact back as insurance, a way to bribe the Gardier for his safety . . ."

Giliead shook his head, brows drawn together almost in pain. For a moment he looked young and uncertain. "I can't . . . he's done this before. When he tricked his way into our house, he didn't just pretend to be someone else. He made himself our friend, he kept it up for months when he could have killed us at any time." He turned urgently toward Gerard, as if willing him to understand. "Just telling them who you are is too easy for him."

"He's right," Halian put in with grim resignation. "This could just be a game to him."

"And he's drawing it out for his own amusement," Gerard finished thoughtfully, rubbing his aching shoulder again. He found himself wishing Ixion could encounter Nicholas Valiarde. Tremaine's father had disliked men who used other people as playthings, whether they were sorcerers or not, and his response to them had tended to be fatally efficient. *They always have a weakness . . . Now there's a thought.* He wondered if perhaps he was looking at Ixion's weakness, or at least one of them. "He didn't kill you because he didn't want to," Gerard told Giliead.

Giliead looked at him, not understanding. "The game is more important to him than winning," Gerard clarified. "It makes him vulnerable. We, on the other hand, are only interested in winning."

He watched Giliead turn that thought over. Halian said doubtfully, "You think we should make a deal with him."

"Then kill him?" Gyan put in, hopeful.

"Exactly. If we can." Gerard saw they all seemed a little startled, and he added honestly, "As I said, we have mad sorcerers in Ile-Rien also, and they have to be dealt with without mercy; they're too dangerous for honorable means."

Giliead actually cracked a smile. "I know."

Thinking about Nicholas Valiarde had led Gerard's mind back to the old days before the Viller Institute. He wasn't sure he had ever been in this tight a situation before, though there had been some interesting times. "That's it." Gerard sat up suddenly. He had been trying to think of a complicated spell, but perhaps the answer lay in something simple. If Ixion could be persuaded to get them, or at least Giliead, out of this cell even as a cruel trick, they might just be able to play a cruel trick on him. "I haven't used this in years—it wouldn't work against the Gardier. It's a charm that can disarm a sorcerer, or a Rienish sorcerer at any rate, temporarily. It may work on Ixion as well. It's certainly worth a try."

"How temporarily?" Halian demanded.

"Very temporarily, only a few moments, but if you're quick—"

"—That's all I'll need," Giliead finished, watching him intently.

Distracted, Gerard looked around, absently patting his non-existent pockets. "The spell requires a few simple ingredients." Spittle, a bit of thread, those were accessible enough. "I need some strands of hair from a virgin."

He hadn't realized the implications of that until he had said it aloud. Before the sudden silence could become embarrassing, someone in the back said, "Well, Arites?"

"Very funny." Arites twisted around to glare at the offender.

"Hah." Dyani gave them a determined smile, sitting up

in the circle of Gyan's arm and picking at one of her braids. "Now you lot can't say I wasn't useful for something."

With the battery torches and the carbide lantern, the cavern passages weren't as dark—at least Tremaine kept telling herself that. These tunnels were definitely more cramped and narrow than those nearer to the underground city.

Ilias led the way with Ander, Tremaine stumbled along not far behind, and Florian followed with the sphere, the other men behind her. They had all put on the coveralls and Tremaine was sweating under hers. She had had to roll up the arms and legs to keep from tripping and the extra rolls of bulky fabric didn't help.

A hiss from Ilias abruptly silenced them and they waited, tense and expectant. Then he poked his head around the turn and whispered, "Douse the lights!"

Ander hurriedly translated for the others and the lights winked out along the line. Still keeping his voice low, Ilias explained, "There's a new break in the wall ahead, leading into a room or a passage I didn't know about, and there's wizard light."

As he spoke Tremaine's eyes adjusted and she could see the dim white glow ahead.

"Let's take a look." Ander eased forward after Ilias.

Tremaine started to follow when a hand on her arm stopped her, and Ander said, "No, you and Florian stay back here."

"Why?" Tremaine demanded. If he said "because it's dangerous" she was going to laugh hysterically.

"Because I don't want the sphere deciding it doesn't like what we see," Ander told her in a tense whisper. "I don't want to announce us to the whole island just yet."

"Oh." *Well, that makes sense.* Tremaine settled back against the rock.

She waited impatiently, listening to the tense breathing of the men and her own pounding heartbeat. The faint white radiance grew a little brighter, but it wasn't enough to make out anyone's face. Muffled clicking from the sphere was accompanied by the sound of Florian shaking the bag and murmuring, "Stop that, right now."

"Is it moving?" Tremaine asked quietly.

"A little," Florian admitted, shifting around for a more comfortable position. "It's not whirring, you know, like it does right before it"—Tremaine could almost hear her veer off the words "blows things up"—"does something."

"Does it do that a lot?" one of the men asked softly, sounding both amused and worried.

Tremaine recognized Rulan's deep voice. Florian explained, "It reacts to the Gardier and to anything it considers hostile."

We won't raise the point that it's making those decisions on its own, Tremaine thought, *and has decided it can practice sorcery without benefit of human intervention.* The sphere was their best weapon; they couldn't stop using it just because it had developed a mind of its own.

Then Ander's voice, rough with suppressed excitement, sounded from just ahead. "You've got to see this."

Tremaine got hastily to her feet and threaded her way through a narrow stretch of jagged rock, the others behind her. "What is it?" she demanded, remembering to keep her voice low.

Ducking under a low knob of rock, Ander said, "You remember—Florian, you worked on this at the Institute, didn't you?—in the airship that went down in Adera, there was no sign of any magical objects except those crystals in the control area. No hint of how they managed the trip between this world and ours?"

"Yes, but—" Florian began.

Following them around a boulder, Tremaine saw a large crack in the rock with a white light shining up through it. In its radiance she could see Ilias crouching near it, looking just as puzzled as she was.

"Look in there." Ander motioned for them to move ahead.

Florian knelt beside Ilias and looked. "Hot damn," she breathed.

Frustrated, Tremaine nudged her aside to see a large cave, strung with bare bulbs like the other sections of the cavern the Gardier had turned into their base. But etched into the smooth stone of the floor was a rough circle of symbols. Many of them were incomprehensible but she recognized a few—they were the same symbols as in Arisilde's spell circle.

Tremaine opened her mouth but couldn't say anything. Too many pieces were falling into place. In the center of the circle was a metal tripod that was obviously meant to hold something about half the size of the sphere.

Florian gripped her elbow. "This is what they found, Tremaine. Your father and Arisilde Damal. Not this room, not here in this world, but somewhere. This is how Arisilde got the underlying symbols for the spell circle."

"They must have found one in Adera." Ander was nodding, the light casting half his face into shadow. "And Damal used the sphere in place of whatever goes there, in that stand."

Florian sat back, looking urgently up at Ander. "We have to destroy it. Somehow this is letting their airships go through portals to the coast of Ile-Rien."

Tremaine stared at her. They could still complete their interrupted mission. She knew it was important, but she didn't want it to derail the rescue.

Basimi and the other men had been listening, fascinated. One of the navy men Deric, put in, "That crack is wide enough to drop a stick of explosive through."

Ander tapped his chin thoughtfully. "If that's our only option. . . . But if it didn't break the circle, it might just bring all the Gardier down on us without disrupting their spell."

"Even if it brought the cave roof down on it, it might not disrupt the circle," Florian pointed out. "I did some reading up on it when I started learning the reverse adjuration. Spell circles, like fayre rings, can still work even if they're buried underground." She shook her head. "Burying it under rock might just make it impossible for us to get to. We can't be sure it's destroyed unless we actually break the circle itself."

Tremaine realized she was hogging the best view and moved back so the others could take a look. Basimi immediately stepped forward to take her place. Ilias shifted over next to her, asking in frustration, "Is it good or bad?"

She realized they had been speaking in Rienish and explained, "Once we found that the Gardier were coming from here, we still didn't know how they were doing it. I mean, we knew how we were doing it, but there didn't seem to be anything comparable on the airships. No symbols like the ones we used, no spheres, just a few crystals mounted above the place they steer." She took a deep breath. "Now it looks like they do use a spell circle, but those crystals must somehow connect their ships to it, so they can use the circle from a distance." There was still so much they didn't know.

"So their crystals work like he does." Ilias pointed to the sphere's bag, which gave a muffled cluck.

"Yes." Tremaine eyed it thoughtfully. The bag had come open a little, revealing metal that gleamed faintly in the radiance of the reflected electric light. She reached to tug the bag closed. *Yes, it's definitely reacting to everybody. It knew Ilias pointed at it, for God's sake.* She looked at Ilias, frowning. "Why do you call it 'he'?"

"That's what you call gods. That's like a god, isn't it?"

"I don't really know what it is. I thought I did, but . . ."

"Come on," Ander said, shouldering his pack again and grabbing the torch. "We've got to find a way down there to wreck that thing."

G iliead watched Gerard braid the broken strands of Dyani's hair, moving deftly despite his chains. Gerard had used threads plucked from his own shirt, moistening each with spittle before plaiting it. Giliead had never seen Ixion or any other wizards do this, using a few simple things to make a curse come to life. He wondered if they knew how.

"But wizards' curses don't work on the god's Chosen

Vessel," Maceum said, craning his neck to look past Arites. "How is this different from what Gil normally does?"

"Curses don't work on him," Gyan replied shortly. "But that doesn't do him any good when the wizard curses a ship to fall on him."

Giliead lifted a brow at Halian, who smiled ruefully. They had lost the *Seeker* that way while she was in dry-dock in Calaide and Giliead had spent three days unconscious.

"This is a very old charm," Gerard said, in the tone of someone giving a lesson, an attitude he seemed to fall into unconsciously, "though it's not generally known. It was developed by a court sorcerer called Morthekai Deroi for use by— But I suppose that's not relevant now." He tied the thread, bit off the end, and continued, "Now, what you must do is place this in Ixion's hand so it's in contact with his skin, and say the words *Berea-deist-dei.* It will immobilize him and prevent him from using his powers for a few moments." Gerard glanced up as he held out the braided skein, noticing the other men were uneasy. He smiled. "Don't worry, it only works on sorcerers."

Giliead took it, turning it over curiously. *In Ixion's hand. I can't believe he's not dead.* He should have known, but he hadn't wanted Ilias to be right. He hadn't wanted to go through all this again. Seeing Ixion felt as if it had drained the life right out of him. *Don't think about it; at least Ilias isn't here.* Giliead repeated the phrase slowly, trying to get the odd accent right. He couldn't feel any curses in it at all. *Like their sphere.* "What do the words mean?"

Gerard met his eyes. "Blood stand still."

Giliead nodded slowly. He believed the man, and not just because the god had said he could, or because Gerard had kept faith with them so far. Gerard had looked at Ixion the way Ixion looked at rival wizards; as if something in Ixion woke the same killer instinct in Gerard. Giliead believed Gerard had fought wizards in his own land before. Fought them and won.

Giliead heard footsteps on stone outside the door and

stiffened. "They're coming back." He tucked the skein inside his shirt and everybody shifted around, chains clanking, trying to look like they hadn't been watching a foreign wizard do a curse.

The door creaked open and three Gardier entered, all carrying the wizard weapons. They lined up in the space opposite the bars of the cell, pointing their weapons into it. *That does not look good,* Giliead thought, a sick sensation settling in his gut. The others stirred uneasily and Halian threw him a tense look. Gerard said softly, "Oh, no."

Giliead heard Ixion's voice out in the corridor, speaking the harsh Gardier language and sounding querulous. Then the leader Gardier came in, the one with the amulet that let him speak Rienish but not Syrnaic. He carried a crystalline rock in one hand. *A rock?* Giliead thought, baffled. It looked like an ordinary gray rock, half-covered with white fragments of crystal.

Halian whispered to Gerard, "What's that?"

"I . . . don't know." Gerard shook his head, eyeing it worriedly.

Ixion trailed in last, still making his complaint, but his eyes were alight with interest.

"Ixion, what are they doing?" Giliead asked sharply.

Ixion threw a glance at him but didn't answer.

The leader lifted the rock and spoke to it. *He's as mad as Ixion,* Giliead had time to think before the crystal started to glow and light fountained gently up from it like beads of water.

Giliead looked at Gerard, who was staring, blank with shock. "Oh God, it's like the sphere," he breathed. "That explains so much."

"Not to me," Halian muttered.

The gentle radiance bathed the Gardier's sharp features and his face was rapt with concentration. Then the light abruptly died. He looked up in grim triumph and pointed at Gerard.

Giliead swore, surging to his feet with the others. The Gardier shouted and the deafening blast of a wizard weapon rang out. Giliead ducked instinctively, dazed by the loud noise. Someone cried out and Giliead looked up to see it was Arites. He was on the ground, gripping his shoulder, blood streaming from between his fingers. The others were crouched on the floor or had fallen back against the wall, temporarily frozen in shock. Gerard was the only one still on his feet.

The Gardier pointed the weapons at them, the meaning obvious. The leader shouted orders and one of the others started to unlock the cell door. Halian leaned over Arites, helping him sit up, and Gerard knelt next to the wounded man. He looked at the wound, then pressed his hand over it.

Gyan, Kias, and several others tensed, ready to charge the door. Halian told them roughly, "It's no good, stay where you are."

"Yes," Gerard seconded hastily, looking around at them all. "Don't risk yourselves; they'd kill all of you."

They'll kill all of us anyway, Giliead thought, but Gerard and Halian were right. Even if several of them rushed the door, it was too small and the Gardier weapons were too fast and too deadly.

Gerard stood as the guard jerked the cell door open. The Gardier eased closer, pointing their weapons, and the one with the crystal touched his amulet and spoke to Gerard. It was the Rienish language, Giliead could tell that much. Gerard answered with a dark expression and stepped out of the cell. Three of the guards seized him and hauled him through the outer door.

Giliead swore and exchanged a bleak look with Halian. He hoped that wasn't the last they saw of Gerard.

"Are you all right?" Dyani asked Arites urgently. She looked at Giliead. "If it doesn't kill you right away, does that mean it's all right?"

"It doesn't . . . it doesn't hurt as much." White and trembling, Arites lifted his hand carefully and Giliead leaned over to look. "Gerard did a curse to stop the bleeding."

Arites was right. Giliead could see the lacerated flesh where the curse from the weapon had torn into his shoulder, but it wasn't bleeding. Giliead met Arites' eyes. *I thought he was trying to staunch the blood with his hand,* he thought. No curse to heal a wound like that could be evil. "Gerard did a *spell* to stop the bleeding," Giliead corrected, using the Rienish word.

He looked up as Halian said softly, "I don't like this."

Ixion was arguing with the Gardier leader in their language. One guard remained, still pointing his weapon at the cell, but his eyes were on his leader; he was obviously waiting for an order. *They don't need us anymore,* Giliead thought grimly.

The leader spoke sharply to Ixion, made a "go ahead" gesture at the last guard, and followed the men who had taken Gerard. *Dammit.* Giliead shoved to his feet, pressing against the bars. "Ixion, I'll help you get off the island, whatever you want."

Ixion flicked a glance at him. He turned to the remaining guard, stepping in front of him and gesturing back at the cell, as if offering another alternative. The guard shook his head angrily, lifting his weapon and motioning for the wizard to get out of his way.

Ixion moved like a striking snake, slapping the weapon away and catching the Gardier by the throat, squeezing off his outcry. He shoved him back against the wall, forcing him down despite the man's frantic struggles. Giliead caught his breath, knowing what was coming. Behind him someone murmured in horror.

Ixion breathed into the Gardier's face and the breath became a gray mist. It clung to the skin, the mist turning into a solid mass that filled the nose and the gaping mouth.

The guard clawed at Ixion's hands but his eyes went still and his struggles ceased. Ixion stepped back, his expression oddly blank, and wiped his hands on the coarse brown garment.

"Let us out," Giliead said softly.

Ixion turned to him and for a heartbeat it was as if Giliead was looking at someone else, another man in the wizard's makeshift body. Someone who wasn't mad. Ixion reached for the lock, then his face changed. "Just you," he said, and smiled.

Half expecting it, Giliead glared. "All of us."

"Of course not. I don't need all of you." The wizard glanced toward the outer door. "Hurry. If they don't hear the weapon fire and screaming soon, they'll surely come back to see what the delay is."

Giliead turned to face the others. *Gerard was right.* It gave him renewed confidence as he slipped the cursed skein out of his shirt. His friends were all carefully not looking at each other or him, tense with anticipation and fear of giving the game away. Arites was the only one staring wide-eyed at Ixion. Halian, standing behind him, was regarding Giliead gravely. He said, "Go ahead, Gil." There was almost a crack in his voice. "Don't worry about us."

Giliead gripped Halian's shoulder, silently mouthed "Don't overdo it," and nodded sharply. He turned back to Ixion, trying to let all his hate and none of his anticipation show in his eyes.

"Very sensible." Ixion put the key in the lock. His eyes hardening, he said, "The rest of you, don't try anything unwise. I may be trapped by these Gardier fools, but I can still strike you blind, boil your blood, turn your innards to burning coals."

The others stirred fearfully and Halian folded his arms, watching the wizard grimly.

Ixion turned the key and jerked the heavy door open. Giliead stepped out and Ixion shoved the door shut again, locking it. He turned toward Giliead with a cold patronizing smile, reaching for the chains at his wrists.

"Ixion." Giliead slapped the charm into the wizard's open palm. *"Blood stand still."*

Ixion froze, mouth open, shock growing in his eyes. It was only an instant before Giliead's joined fists, gripping the heavy metal chain, struck him in the chin. He dropped like a dead man.

Giliead found the key on the floor and unlocked the cell, wrenching open the door.

"Is he dead?" Halian demanded as he stepped out.

"He's not breathing," Giliead reported, leaning over Ixion as the others hurriedly stepped past the wizard's inert body. He couldn't find a heartbeat either. Not that that meant anything where Ixion was concerned. He grimaced. "For what that's worth."

"Cut his head off again," Gyan suggested, helping Arites out of the cell. "That'll slow him down, at least."

"With what?" Giliead interrupted the general chorus of approval. He wasn't going to use the Gardier weapon that still lay where it had fallen; for one thing, he hadn't a clue how it worked. He managed to pry Ixion's eyes open to see the pupils were still and dead. He sat back, thinking it over. It was damn problematic trying to kill someone who seemed to be stone dead already.

"We've got to do something with him," Halian pointed out.

"Right." Giliead hauled Ixion up and deposited him in the empty cell, shutting the door again and tugging on it to make sure it had locked.

Jivan had the key to their cell and was trying it in everyone's manacles without success. "This isn't going to work," he said, frustrated.

Kias, cautiously surveying the outer room, ducked back in, saying, "Hey, there's all these others here locked up. Maybe that key works on these doors too. Should we try?"

"Yes, let them all out," Halian told him with a firm nod. "We're not leaving anybody behind."

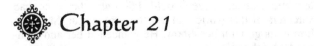

Chapter 21

Light came through chinks in the rock, telling Tremaine
that they were traveling parallel to a passage within
the Gardier base. Everyone was tense, moving in strained
silence.

Ilias stopped at a wider crack in the rock. Through it
Tremaine could glimpse a rough corridor strung with electric bulbs. They crouched on the floor of the narrow cavity to wait as he and Ander held a consultation in such low
tones Tremaine couldn't hear them no matter how close
she edged. Finally Ander turned back, elbowing Tremaine
to move her out of the way, leaning toward Basimi to
whisper, "We're going to try to get to the chamber where
the portal is by cutting through here. Florian, do the illusion now."

Florian nodded hastily, slipping the sphere's bag off her
shoulder and passing it to Tremaine. "Wouldn't want to accidentally put an illusion on the whole island," she said
under her breath.

"Ha ha, right." Tremaine put the sphere on the ground,
anxiously edging it away with her foot and hoping it didn't
decide to help anyway. The men eyed it doubtfully.

Florian closed her eyes in concentration, murmuring a
few ritual words. Back in Rel, Florian and Niles had discussed illusions and wards that were most likely to remain
undetected by the Gardier. They had settled on the simplest
of illusions, just a faint clouding of sight that would blend
shadow and the expectation of the viewer to obscure their
passage. In the knife-edged light from the corridor,

Tremaine saw Ilias watching Florian. His shoulders were a little hunched and his body tight with tension. She was beginning to realize he still didn't like magic at close quarters and probably never would; Ixion and the other mad sorcerers of this world had left too deep a scar. She gave him a nudge with her elbow. He glanced at her and managed a brief smile.

Looking back at the others, she caught Basimi and Deric exchanging a dubious expression; they were used to sorcerers providing support in combat, but Florian was very young.

Florian opened her eyes and nodded firmly. "That's it." She stretched to pick up the sphere's bag again.

Ander glanced at the others, possibly seeing the same doubt Tremaine had noted. He leaned forward, listening, then slipped out of the gap down into the corridor. Ilias followed immediately. Tremaine clambered after them, relieved that the other men followed despite their doubts.

They made their way step by step down the Gardier corridor. After six paces Tremaine would rather have been at home removing her own teeth with a pair of pliers; anything was preferable to this tension that made her stomach churn and her heart beat somewhere in the region of her throat.

Just as they reached the mouth of a short cross passage, Ilias stopped, his head cocked alertly. An instant later Tremaine heard the sound of footfalls and Gardier voices. The men tensed, lifted their crossbows, but Ander motioned sharply to hold back. Florian took Tremaine's hand, either for reassurance or a possible boost from the sphere, Tremaine couldn't tell. The girl's palm was cold and damp with sweat but her expression was calm and intent. Tremaine just hoped the sphere didn't decide to help by doing something drastic.

Three Gardier passed the mouth of the connecting corridor, not twenty paces away. One glanced casually at them, his expression obscured by shadow, but he must have seen nothing but the illusion. Then the Gardier were gone and it had lasted only a heartbeat. *Close enough to spit at*, Tremaine thought, exchanging a relieved look with Ilias.

They moved on, but the next connecting tunnel led the other way. Tremaine could just see that it opened into a jagged hole that looked down on some large shadowy space. Intriguing sounds echoed from it, voices and machinery clanking and the buzzing of the big arc lights. It had to be the large cavern the Gardier used as a work area.

Obviously coming to the same conclusion, Ander hesitated, but couldn't resist the chance to reconnoiter. He turned into the short tunnel.

There were only a couple of bulbs lit here and the shadow gave the illusion of security. Some tumbled rocks near the open edge also afforded some cover. Two of the men stayed up near the mouth to watch the corridor as the others edged into position around the opening. Tremaine managed to shoulder her way forward, crouching next to Ilias.

The opening gave a view of the main cavern from a different angle than Tremaine had seen before. They were about twenty feet above the floor and almost directly opposite the tunnel entrances, the wooden stairs and platforms and the mesh cage that marked the slave pens. The giant ring frames of the half-completed dirigible still lay atop the construction scaffolds, glittering in the glare from the buzzing arc lights. From this angle she could see several generators, about fifty yards along the cavern wall, at the center of a cluster of power lines that ran snakelike across the stone floor.

"Taking those generators out would help," Basimi said softly. From the murmurs of agreement he was voicing everyone's thought.

None of the slaves were out and most of the Gardier who were visible weren't working on the airship. *They're getting ready for something,* Tremaine thought. She was relieved to see only a few howlers, squatting sullenly in a makeshift pen near the other tunnel entrances.

Ilias sat up suddenly with a muttered exclamation. He nudged her arm and pointed. At first she couldn't see anything, but then a flash of green and white amid the brown and gray caught her eye.

A group of Gardier were emerging from one of the tunnels near the stairs. They were hustling along a figure in Syprian clothing. Even at this distance through the cavern's shadowy spaces and too-bright pools of electric light, she recognized his walk.

Tremaine's eyes widened. It was Gerard and he was alive. "It's Gerard! Come on, let's go get him!" She started to stand.

Ander grabbed her arm, yanking her back down. He whispered furiously, "Tremaine, we can't take that chance. We have to destroy their portal."

"We have to do both," she told him firmly, jerking her arm free.

They were speaking in Rienish. Unable to follow their conversation, Ilias looked frustrated. He twisted around suddenly, staring back up the tunnel, then hissed a warning. Tremaine turned to look just as two Gardier appeared, framed in the opening into the corridor.

Discipline held and everyone went still. The first Gardier just glanced down the shadowy cavity and kept moving. The second hesitated. *Just keep moving, you bastard,* Tremaine thought in annoyance. She couldn't make out his expression but suspicion was eloquent in the very way the man stood. Then he reached for one of the devices on his belt.

Grimacing, Ander signaled for the men to be ready. The second Gardier returned impatiently but the first ignored him, studying the device in his hand. It was the one that looked like a cigar lighter with crystals attached. *The same kind that patrol leader used when Florian tried to do an illusion,* Tremaine thought helplessly. *Oh, damn.* At least it hadn't been her idea to come down this tunnel. Beside her Florian shifted nervously.

Then the Gardier made a shocked exclamation and his head jerked up. He stared directly at them.

Ander made a sharp motion. Both Gardier barely had time to reach for their sidearms before crossbow bolts struck them. One staggered back, clawing at the bolt, crying out. Shouts and running bootsteps echoed down the tunnel. "That's it, we're done," someone said. Ander swore, snapping out orders.

Basimi shoved Tremaine down behind the rocks and she pushed back against the wall. Florian landed beside her as the men surged forward.

Tremaine sat up on her knees, risking a peek. Ander, Ilias and the others were holding the end of the tunnel. She heard two gunshots, loud as explosions in the close space. She saw Basimi and Rulan duck back against the wall. Then Ilias took his crossbow by the stock and swung it up, smashing the lightbulb overhead and the passage was cloaked in darkness.

Tremaine sank back down, trying to think. In the dim light, she saw Florian wince and the other girl didn't bother to ask how bad it was. Out in the cavern the Gardier were looking up, running toward the tunnel entrances.

There's an idea. . . . Tremaine sat up, leaning forward to see. There was no one near the generators and this part of the cavern was nearly dark. She caught Florian's eye and jerked her head toward the opening. "Give it a try?"

Florian studied the situation, brows drawn together. "Why the hell not."

Tremaine nodded, grimacing. Maybe she wished Florian had refused, but it wasn't as if they had a lot of options. Tremaine edged forward, finding the lip of the crevice in the dark, carefully feeling for footholds. Florian followed her, the sphere making annoyed clucking noises as its bag thumped against the rock.

It was only about twenty feet but Tremaine's hands were sweaty and shaking, reflecting the state of her insides, and it made the climb difficult. A buzzing alarm started to sound somewhere in the Gardier tunnels, echoing off the walls. Across the cavern, agitated guards and workers ran in and out of the entrances, shouting instructions and questions. The howlers near the chain mesh fence hissed uneasily.

Tremaine reached the ground and sank down next to the wall, grateful for the shadow. She couldn't see where the

Gardier had taken Gerard. Florian crouched beside her, wondering, "Why are they running that way? I'm glad they're doing it, but it doesn't make sense." Most of the Gardier seemed to be heading toward the tunnel entrances on the opposite side of the cavern.

Tremaine nodded. "There's something else going on." She couldn't worry about that right now. She squinted, assessing their chances of reaching the generators. It looked like they could make their way along the cavern wall. They would have to pass two tunnel entrances strung with electric bulbs, but heading directly across the open floor was impossible. "Still got the illusion?" she asked Florian.

She nodded glumly. "For what it's worth."

Tremaine took a deep breath. "Let's go."

They hurried along the wall, dodging around tumbled rocks and the bundles of electrical cables that led toward the humming generators. Tremaine heard voices up the second tunnel entrance, but no one came running out to shoot at them.

They reached the first of the generators, the vibration of it making Tremaine's teeth ache. In the dim light it was just a tall collection of odd metal shapes, stinking of smoke and oil. The shadows helped their illusory shield, but it was hard for her to see what they should do. She realized she had stupidly been expecting a big lever they could pull or something similar. "Any ideas?" she asked Florian helplessly.

Florian studied the machine grimly. "Yes." She pulled the sphere's bag around, undoing the buckle. "If it knows the Gardier translation spell, it knows their mechanical disruption spell."

"Oh." *Good point*, Tremaine thought. She hesitated as Florian held the sphere out to her. "How do I . . . ?"

"Just ask it, like before." Florian flinched as a Gardier stepped out of the nearest tunnel entrance, fumbling for one of his belt devices. "Hurry!"

"Dammit!" Tremaine grabbed the sphere. It was hot to the touch and trembling as the wheels inside spun frantically. Her eyes on the Gardier, she didn't have time to think about the spell. Behind her the generators suddenly gave a metallic shriek, ending in a horrible grinding noise that made her teeth ache.

Florian's head jerked up, her eyes wide with fear. "Too soon— Run—!"

Shit. Tremaine shoved the sphere under her arm as they bolted away across the cavern floor.

Gardier shouted, a shot fired, then the grinding rose to a grating crash and the lights went out.

W hy are you with the natives?" Gervas said, eyeing Gerard with poorly disguised curiosity. He held the translator disk in one hand and the sorcerous crystal in the other. Beads of sweat formed on the Gardier's forehead and he didn't look like a man with much time to waste in questions.

Gerard would have given a great deal to know what exactly that crystal was. It was obviously kin to the ones recovered from the crashed Gardier airship and seeing Gervas use it, he thought it must function along the same lines as the Viller spheres. "It's a long story, you wouldn't be interested," he replied.

They had taken him from the prison area through a giant cavern converted to a staging ground for the airships. Gerard would have been fascinated had he not had other things to worry about at the moment. They had passed out of the cavern and down another tunnel to a sort of administrative area with smaller rooms sectioned off from the rock by the corrugated metal walls. This one was small and bare, with a wooden table and only one door. Gervas had two armed guards with him and his hands were still chained. The stone floor was cold against his bare feet and he found himself wishing he hadn't abandoned his boots.

"Perhaps not so long," Gervas said, eyes narrow. "We have many informers in your world. They told us that a Rienish sorcerer was left behind here. There is no point in not answering my questions."

Gerard made his expression stay noncommittal. "If you have so many well-informed spies, then there's no point in asking your questions."

Lips twitching, Gervas glanced down at the crystal he held. It sparked briefly and a sudden sharp pain in the gut doubled Gerard over. He gasped as it faded and stumbled back against the wall, leaning on the rough metal for support. *This can't end well*, he told himself grimly. He just hoped the Gardier intended to keep the Syprians alive for their worker pool. When the guards had entered the cell and lined up as if for a firing squad, he had feared the worst.

"I will ask you only once more." Gervas's face said that wasn't an idle threat.

Gerard straightened with difficulty, his chest aching from the phantom pain, and faced Gervas. "You won't get an answer then, either."

Gervas shook his head, more annoyed than angry. "You are foolish. There is nothing you can do to escape us. If you tell me what I want to know, it will save you discomfort before you are sent to our Central Command, to be converted."

"Converted?" Gerard repeated, trying to keep the man talking.

Gervas lifted the crystal and said significantly, "For useful employment."

Gerard was baffled. "What?" Did they use sorcerers as slaves too? It seemed unlikely at best. He supposed there could be some sort of brainwashing or mind control but—

A muted crash echoed through the rock and the overhead light sparked and went out. Seizing his chance, Gerard shoved away from the wall, charging Gervas. He came up against a solid body and swung his bound hands up toward where he hoped the man's jaw was, using his chains as a club. The man fell away and Gerard ran.

He found the opposite wall by slamming full tilt into it. The fabricated panel shook but didn't give way and he groped along it for the exit. The other men shouted and a battery lamp flared just as Gerard found the door.

He crashed through and stumbled out into the dark corridor. The wildly waving light from the room behind him was the only illumination. Gerard ran back the way he had come. *I can lose the guards, release the other prisoners—* A shot rang out behind him, striking the wall near his head and showering him with rock chips, emphasizing the difficulties of that ambitious plan. He ducked, running faster. *If I can just stay alive.*

He whispered a quick illusion charm, clumsily managing to make the gesture to initiate it with his chained hands. It filled the corridor behind him with a brief blaze of blue light and fog and the next shot went wild.

Gerard reached the cross corridor, whipping around a corner into sudden firelight. He skidded to a halt, finding himself staring at Giliead and Halian. Behind them was Gyan, holding a makeshift torch.

Gerard gasped, "Thank God—"

Giliead reached out a long arm, grabbed Gerard's shirt and yanked him forward. Gerard fell back against the wall and Giliead stepped to the edge of the corridor, Halian ducking across to take the other side.

A heartbeat later the two Gardier pelted around the corner. Giliead swung a heavy spanner, striking the first in the head, and Halian got the second one with a metal bar.

Breathing hard, Gerard looked back down the corridor. In the flare of torchlight he saw other familiar Syprian faces and several men and women wearing Gardier slave uniforms. Everyone looked wild-eyed with excitement and fear and clutched assorted tools as makeshift weapons.

"Here, let him get your chains off," Gyan said, taking Gerard's arm and motioning toward the other prisoners. A young Parscian man carrying a large metal cutting tool pushed forward. With relief Gerard stretched his manacle chain out. "He's good at it," Gyan added, smiling at the young man.

"You speak Rienish?" Gerard asked the Parscian as he cut the chain.

"Yes!" He looked up, startled and relieved. He spoke the language with an educated accent. "These men released us from the cells. Is the base under attack?"

"I hope so," Gerard replied honestly. He turned back to Giliead and the others and asked in Syrnaic, "Did you destroy the generators?"

Keeping watch at the corner, Giliead glanced back, frowning. "The what?"

"The—things that make the wizard light," Gerard clarified hurriedly, wondering if they could have done it by accident.

"No." Halian turned to him with a puzzled expression. "We thought you must have done that."

"It certainly wasn't me." Brows lifted, Gerard said, "I think we're all being rescued."

Tremaine lifted her head, dazed, her ears ringing from the explosion. She lay sprawled on the stone floor, her hands stinging from sliding in the gravel. Smaller lights had sprung up all over the pitch darkness of the cavern, handlamps held by the Gardier. They illuminated brief flashes of frightened faces, running figures, fragments of the airship's skeleton. Huge shadows leapt on the rock walls. Shouting voices and the enraged cries of the howlers echoed off the stone, confusing her. Behind her what was left of the generators still popped and crackled.

"Ow," Florian said quietly beside her.

"You all right?" Tremaine asked hurriedly, pushing herself up. Her knees were scraped, even through the tough material of her pants.

Florian gasped and sat up. "Yes, just hurt my elbow when we fell." They had run into the center of the cavern and flung themselves down as the generators exploded. As the lights crackled and failed, metal debris had rained down all around them. Nothing had struck them and Tremaine wasn't sure whether they had luck or the sphere to thank for that.

As if stirred by that thought, the sphere started to emit a blue glow. Tremaine grabbed it and shook it vigorously. "No! No glowing! Stop that!" She looked around wildly.

There were Gardier everywhere and their guns still worked; she didn't want to present a perfect target.

The glow obediently died and Florian said in amazement, "That thing is getting so . . . so . . . alive."

"You said it." Clutching the sphere, Tremaine climbed awkwardly to her feet, Florian struggling up after her. They both froze as a figure ran toward them.

In the dark the man pounded past without stopping. Florian let out a relieved breath, whispering, "Let's get back to the others."

Tremaine wasn't good on direction at the best of times, but Florian got them pointed back the right way. They blundered in the dark, holding on to each other, until they drew near the wall and heard soft voices arguing in Rienish. Not wanting to get shot by accident, Tremaine whispered, "Hey, it's us!"

A figure appeared out of the dark. The sphere clicked happily at it and Ilias's voice demanded, "Where did you go? Did you do this?"

"The sphere did it," Florian answered. "It—"

Before she could explain, another figure loomed out of the dimness. "Tremaine!" The furious voice belonged to Ander.

Ilias turned to block Ander's path and Tremaine grabbed the back of his coverall to stay behind him. "There wasn't time to discuss it!" she said defensively.

Ander swore. "We don't have time for this."

"Well, what do we have time for?" Tremaine wanted to know.

Ilias said over his shoulder, "The slaves are loose, but the wizards are turning the howlers on them."

"We can stop them!" Determined, Florian pushed forward. "I can do another illusion and we can get over there—"

"We need you to get us to the portal so we can destroy it," Ander objected. "That has to come first—"

"We could split up," Florian interrupted. "The sphere worked just for Tremaine. She could use it to wreck the portal—it would be better than trying to use explosives—and I could help with the howlers."

"No, dammit." Ander turned to her impatiently. "Tremaine couldn't possibly—"

"Ander, you can't send everybody down there, the Gardier will realize what we're trying to do. Keep them busy elsewhere and just a few of us could do it." Tremaine took a sharp breath. The wave of anxiety and doubt was probably understandable under the circumstances, but she didn't have time for it. "Ilias can find it. Send a couple of your men with us—" Basimi didn't trust Ilias, she didn't want him. "Deric or somebody who can use the dynamite in case the sphere doesn't work."

"I'll go, Captain," Rulan's voice said out of the dark. "She's right, just the three of us could get down there without being noticed, especially if they think there's a full-scale attack up here."

Ander said nothing. In the dark Tremaine couldn't see his face, but he was breathing hard, struggling with the decision. With his doubt and mistrust of her.

Next to her Ilias nudged her impatiently, demanding, "What are we doing?"

They had been speaking in Rienish, leaving him out of the conversation again. Tremaine answered in Syrnaic, "I'm asking him if you and I can take the sphere and destroy the portal while they're helping the others."

He didn't hesitate. "Good."

"So, Ander? We don't have a lot of time," Tremaine prompted. The sphere clanked loudly in her arms and everyone flinched back. Its gears spun up, hissing, and blue lights sparked deep inside. "Somebody agrees with me," she added under her breath, shifting her grip on the hot metal.

Ander said quietly, "Can you do that, Tremaine? Destroy the portal yourself?"

I won't be by myself. She put all the confidence she didn't have into one word. "Yes."

"All right," Ander said sharply, already turning away. "Go."

G erard awkwardly braced his feet on the table and shoved at the light wooden ceiling panel, barely able to see what he was doing in the firelit darkness. The panel gave only a few inches before jamming up against the rock just above. He swore and reached for the next panel.

His voice desperate, Gyan called, "Any luck?" He was steadying the table and Gerard could hardly hear him over the shouting and milling confusion of the freed prisoners.

They had become trapped in this suite of rooms by howlers driven by the Gardier. Giliead's idea was to go up through the ceiling into the cave passages and down into an open corridor, but so far they hadn't been able to find a space large enough for anyone to squeeze through. "No good." Gerard jumped down from the table and he and Gyan shoved it over another few feet to try again.

Across the room, in the light of a captured battery lamp, Giliead and a few others had their shoulders braced against the makeshift barricade of chain-link mesh they had propped across the doors. The chain link had come from the slave pen and Gerard again blessed the forethought of the young man who had found the metal cutters during the escape. The howlers tore at the other side of the doors, shrieking in rage and hunger and fear of their masters, pounding their bodies against the barrier.

Gerard tried the other side of the room and couldn't even get the ceiling panels to move. From the shouts and calls in the other rooms, no one else was having any luck either. Swearing, he jumped down again to shove the table over.

The door thumped open a few inches and howler claws wedged through the gap, scrabbling frantically. The men threw their weight against the barricade, but the creature pushed most of its upper torso through, wedging the door partly open. Giliead grabbed its head, shoving it back, grimly turning his face away as it clawed for him. Gerard started forward, but Gyan leapt past him, grabbing a stick of wood from a shattered chair and beating at the thing's flailing arms.

A young woman in a prisoner's coverall stumbled back into him and Gerard caught her shoulders to steady her. "Who are these people?" she gasped in Bisran.

"Syprians, from the mainland," Gerard explained, gently moving her aside. "Our allies."

Forcing the creature back through the gap, the men managed to shove the door shut, slumping against it and breathing hard. Giliead's arms were streaked with bloody scratches. Then the shrieking on the other side of the barricade abruptly ceased.

"Quiet," Giliead yelled, and Gerard repeated the command in Bisran and Rienish. As the confused babble died away they could hear nothing outside, no renewed burst of effort from the howlers, no shouts in Gardier.

"It's a trick," Gyan whispered harshly.

Then, made distant by the thickness of the doors, a voice called in Rienish, "Hello, is anyone in there?"

"God, that sounded like—" Incredulous, Gerard moved toward the barricaded door. "Ander, is that you?"

"Gerard? Yes, it's us!"

In the dark behind him people moved uncertainly, frightened voices whispered. Gerard thought of three different charms of revealing he could do to make sure it was really Ander out there, but he didn't have the right preparations for any of them. He looked at Giliead, who was still braced against the door. "It sounds like him, but if it's a ruse—"

Giliead shook his head, his expression going distant. "It's not a curse."

Gerard nodded slowly. He had forgotten about Giliead's abilities. "That's good enough for me."

Giliead motioned sharply to the others and they pulled at the mesh.

The door opened slowly, the men still braced to slam it shut. Gerard saw howler bodies sprawled in the corridor, bristling with crossbow bolts. Someone called a warning as figures moved past the dead creatures. Then Florian's red-brown hair caught the torchlight and she pushed forward. "Gerard!" She waved excitedly at him. "You're all right!"

Giliead hauled on the barricade and the others moved hastily to help.

"I'm very glad to see you," Gerard said in relief as

Ander, Florian and a number of armed men crowded through the door, stepping over the dead howlers. He looked past them, frowning, as another familiar face failed to appear. "Where's Tremaine?"

Ander caught his arm to draw him aside. "We think we located the Gardier's spell circle for their portal. Tremaine and Ilias are using the sphere to destroy it," he explained in Rienish.

"What did he say?" Giliead demanded, suddenly standing at Gerard's shoulder.

The man was nearly rigid with tension. "Ilias is with Tremaine," Gerard translated quickly, knowing how concerned Giliead must be for his friend. "They're trying to destroy the Gardier's—" He turned to Ander, suddenly realizing what the young man had just said. "You found the Gardier's portal?"

"Yes, we found a circle—"

"It's a long story." Florian urgently shouldered in between the men. "Gerard, Niles gave me some different herbs and a bunch of premixed powders and effusions. Can we do something about the howlers?"

"Yes, if he sent the right things." Gerard shook his head, trying to get his mind back on the essentials. First they had to do something about the howlers or the Gardier could use them to retake the base. "If the Gardier are using Ixion's spells to control these creatures—"

"What are you going to do?" Florian asked, pulling the various bags and packets out of her pockets.

Gerard nodded to himself. "Counter his spell."

Following Ilias down the dark tunnel, Tremaine realized she was clutching the sphere in a death grip. Rulan was keeping his electric torch shielded with his hand so there was just barely enough light to make their way along without tripping. The dark was a little easier on her nerves; she felt far less exposed with the overhead lights out.

Ahead, Ilias paused. Tremaine could barely see an opening in the rock wall. He turned back to say, "This is it."

Tremaine stepped up to look inside, pulling her torch out of the coverall's pocket and switching it on. She flashed it over the circle of symbols etched into the stone floor and the metal tripod in the center. The tripod was still empty. It made her wonder what was supposed to be there and where it was now, and what the Gardier were doing with it. The rest of the chamber seemed just bare rock, the walls shining with moisture and a purplish moss.

On impulse, Tremaine turned to Rulan. "Can you stay out here and keep an eye out for . . . you know."

He looked past her into the room, then nodded. "Yes, ma'am. I'll go back a little way to that last branch corridor."

Tremaine watched him go, then took a deep breath and moved further into the chamber, approaching the edge of the circle. Ilias followed her, walking as if there was slime on the floor. He had shed his coverall at the earliest opportunity and looked far more comfortable without it. She had rolled up the sleeves and opened the front of hers, but hadn't taken the time to get rid of the bulky garment.

"Let's get this over with." Tremaine tucked the torch under her arm and pulled the sphere out, tossing the bag down. She hesitated, frowning. It was still spinning and the metal was hot. Not quite hot enough to burn, but warm enough that it wasn't easy to handle. "It's been like this all along."

"What?" Ilias stepped closer, peering at it warily.

"Stirred up. Like there's something it didn't like. Now that we're in here, it must be this circle, but . . ." She shook her head, not quite happy. "I guess it must have been reacting to this thing the whole time we've been here."

Ilias squeezed her shoulder. "Better hurry."

"Right." *He thinks I'm nervous; well, he's right.* Tremaine just hoped the sphere didn't get moody and decide not to listen to her. This would be a fine time for a disaster, just when she had been stupid enough to ask for an important job. She stared down at the metal ball, trying to concentrate on what she wanted it to do. Before she could arrange her thoughts she heard a faint sound. Ilias twitched, looking toward the door. She asked in a whisper, "What was that?"

He shook his head, starting toward the opening. "Some-one called out."

Rulan appeared in the door, caught in the light of the electric torch Tremaine still had tucked under her arm. He had something in his hands. She frowned, her first thought that he had found something and had brought it to show them. "What—" It was a rifle.

A familiar figure in Gardier uniform stepped up beside him. Tremaine said sharply, "Ilias, stop." Her stomach clenched. She had been caught flat-footed and it was not a pleasant sensation.

Ilias halted in place, head cocked, watching Rulan and the Gardier warily.

Gervas stepped forward, clutching his translator disk. His narrow face was pale and gray in the unflattering glare of the light. He said, "Very good. Tell him to turn around."

Instead Tremaine dropped her torch. It hit the floor and winked out but several balls of sorcerous light sprang to life overhead, illuminating the chamber with a faint white glow. Ilias, braced to jump Rulan, fell back a step, startled. *Did we decide Gervas was a sorcerer?* Tremaine wondered, backing away, her heart pounding.

"Do as I say and you will be unharmed," Gervas said. He spoke by rote, as if he didn't believe it and didn't care if she did either. "Tell the native to turn around."

Tremaine translated for Ilias, who gave both Rulan and the Gardier an impartial glare and turned his back, saying, "Try to stall him—"

"Stop!" Gervas shouted suddenly. He lowered his voice with an effort, grating out, "Tell him not to speak or I'll kill him."

"He doesn't want us to talk—" Tremaine began in Syrnaic.

"That's enough!" Gervas moved further into the room, eyeing her suspiciously. "So it is the little woman from Maiuta."

"That's me." From here Tremaine could see the crystalline rock he held. It looked about the right size to fit into the tripod behind her. *That's not good.* "You've met Rulan, I see."

Gervas flicked a glance toward the young man at his side. "He recognizes his place is to help us."

"Really?" Tremaine lifted her brows. "You recognize that, Rulan?"

Rulan's face was expressionless. "I had relatives on the Southern Islands; they have them hostage." He stepped closer to Ilias, covering him with the rifle.

It was pointless to argue with someone who would turn traitor for such an irrational reason, but Tremaine tried anyway. "And you think they'll let them go if you do this?" she asked skeptically.

"I know what they'll do if I don't." Rulan poked Ilias in the back for emphasis. *Mistake,* Tremaine thought as Ilias spun and grabbed for the rifle barrel. That poke had told him exactly where the other man was standing. Rulan stumbled back as Ilias wrenched at the gun. Tremaine surged forward to help. But Ilias suddenly lost his hold on the gun and collapsed.

Tremaine stumbled to a halt, horrified, but she hadn't heard a shot. Then she saw the crystal in Gervas's hands spark. "You leave him alone," she said, not realizing she had spoken until the words were out of her mouth. The sphere was ticking in her hands like a time bomb. *Blow Gervas up,* she told it, *go on, you can do it. What are you waiting for?*

Ilias pushed himself up off the floor to his knees, breathing hard. *He can't get up,* Tremaine realized. *Some kind of disabling spell.* He tossed his hair out of his eyes, glaring up at Gervas, but she could tell he had been badly shocked. Rulan straightened from a fighting crouch, leveling the rifle at Ilias again, glancing at the Gardier.

"I will if you do as I say. You will answer my one question—" Gervas began.

"Then you're a fortunate man if you have only one question—" Tremaine started with no idea of where she was going.

"Shut up or I'll kill the native now," Gervas grated.

Tremaine shut up. Fear again. Gervas was desperate and afraid. Maybe it was so easy for her to tell that because she shared both emotions. She tightened her hold on the sphere; her hands were sweating and this would be a bad time to drop it. Ilias looked from her to Gervas, frustrated with his helplessness.

Gervas took a breath and fixed his gaze on Tremaine. "Our avatar detected two sorcerers on the native craft we destroyed. How did you conceal your power from me when you were captured before?"

My power? "I'm not a sorcerer. Your thing must have detected someone else." Had Gervas forgotten about Florian? He knew she was a witch. He had been rather snide about it at the time, Tremaine remembered that distinctly.

Gervas looked down at the crystalline rock and an eddy of light crossed its rough surface. With a loud pop the electric torch she had dropped exploded into fragments. Ilias recoiled and Tremaine flinched away from the fragments that struck her boots. The sphere just whirled a little faster, the metal growing warmer. It must have deflected the spell to destroy mechanical objects again.

Gervas's brows lifted suddenly in startled realization. In a thoughtful tone, he said, "I see. It was not you I detected."

Ilias said suddenly, "Tremaine—" He was staring at her feet. Tremaine looked down and realized she had stepped back over the edge of the Gardier spell circle etched into the rock. Little points of light sparkled above the incised symbols. "Uh oh," Tremaine breathed. The sphere had done something to the portal, made it react in some way. *I'd like to get out of here but I'm not sure I want to do it with their portal.* And Ilias wasn't inside the circle.

"So you of Rien have the avatars also," Gervas sounded almost relieved. "You will tell me how you came by the knowledge to create that one."

"I don't know what an avatar is. I know what the word means but I don't . . ." *Except that's not the word you're using.* The translation spell would choose the closest equivalent for an unfamiliar term, the way the sphere did with Rienish and Syrnaic. An avatar was an incarnated god.

Tremaine stared at the crystal the man was holding, thinking of how Ilias had compared the sphere to Cineth's god. "You mean a . . . receptacle."

"Call it what you will." Gervas was impatient. "You will tell me what method you used to transfer the sorcerer's consciousness into that device."

"You put a living person in that crystal? He— It does your spells for you?" Things started to fall into place and she said in a rush, "That's why you can't heal yourselves and your magic is so limited. You aren't sorcerers. You've got that one there, and the other smaller crystals are smaller sorcerers— No, no, Florian and Ander were right, the little crystals just connect to the big one. They're like the early spheres the Institute made, they're like the cylinders in a music box, they only have certain spells recorded in them." The implications all fell into place and she couldn't believe it. She wasn't usually a sympathetic person but this turned her stomach. "My God, who did you put in that thing? Was he alive when you did it?"

"You may pretend you don't understand, but it does you no good," Gervas thundered. "Now give me the avatar or I'll kill the native!"

"This is not an avatar, this is—" *This is a sphere that Arisilde built to do tricks for a twelve-year-old girl.* It was like Edouard Viller's original spheres: It boosted the sorcerous abilities of a person with a limited magical talent, letting them perform simple spells. *Which is all it did, until Arisilde vanished. Then it not only let Gerard correctly operate the architecture of Arisilde's Great Spell, but sucked the spells out of a Gardier translator and used that information to decipher the wards on the Gardier airship and destroy them. Since then it made friends with a Syprian god, woke you because Gerard was hunting Ixion's curse, boosted Gerard's death spell from a distance, recognized people who have no magical talent like Ilias and Ander. . . . That's after it established enough of a connection to this world to influence your writing . . .* It acted like a living sorcerer. *Niles was right, a sphere couldn't do those things. It would have to be a human mind.*

"Now!" Gervas snapped impatiently.

"All right, all right. Just . . ." *Give me a moment to have a brilliant idea.* And maybe now she knew what the sphere was waiting for. It must be evenly matched against the disembodied consciousness in the crystal Gervas held. It had to take Gervas quickly, before he had a chance to harm her or Ilias. There was one way to do that and it was right under her feet. Tremaine swallowed in a dry throat. "Arisilde," she said under her breath, "if you're in there, see what I'm thinking, see what you need to do. I don't know the spells, but you do." The sphere clicked at her and the inner motion of its wheels slowed, but the outer surface grew painfully hot. She started toward Gervas, holding it out.

Ilias, who had been unable to understand the Rienish conversation, struggled helplessly to stand. "No, don't!"

In Syrnaic, she said, "It's all right. I'm about to try something—get ready."

Ilias subsided, watching her worriedly, and Gervas nodded, relieved at her surrender. "Very good. Now give me—"

Tremaine lurched forward and grabbed Gervas's arm, yanking him off-balance and across the lip of the portal.

The Gardier wizard staggered forward and Tremaine fell back. As they hit the ground both vanished, as if the stone under them had gone liquid, then hardened again in a heartbeat. Though Ilias had experienced it before himself, watching it was a stomach-churning shock; he pushed at the ground to surge to his feet and realized abruptly that he could move his legs; the curse had disappeared with Gervas. And Rulan didn't know it.

Rulan took a step toward the edge of the circle, uneasily shifting his hold on his weapon, the sweat gleaming on his forehead in the light from the remaining torch. Ilias eased back into a half-sitting position, wiped his mouth on his arm and wriggled his toes to make sure he could move. He just hoped Tremaine wasn't dead.

Rulan threw a wary glance at him, and Ilias bared his teeth, trying to look thwarted and defenseless. The other man snapped some words in Rienish that Ilias didn't understand, then looked at the circle again. He paced closer to the edge, studying the empty space in frustration. Ilias waited, silently urging him closer; he was fairly sure the only part of the weapon that was dangerous was the open end of the long tube. It was still pointed toward him, but Rulan's attention was more and more focused on the circle.

Rulan took that last step and Ilias surged to his feet, throwing himself forward and grabbing the weapon, wrenching it upward.

Tremaine fell backward and kept falling. She struck hard-packed sand, the breath knocked out of her, Gervas landing heavily nearby. Wheezing, she twisted, kicking out at him. Caught by surprise and badly shocked, he lost his grip on the avatar crystal and it rolled free. Clutching the sphere tightly, Tremaine grabbed the crystal with her free hand. She rolled away from Gervas, pushing herself awkwardly to her knees.

They were above the scrub desert, atop one of the hills, further away from the wall she had mistaken for a cliff. From this angle it was obvious it was a structure, crudely made with enormous slabs of rock propped up against each other. It was at least the size of the *Ravenna*.

Gervas twisted around, his face working. Tremaine read horror, shock, rage. *Oh yes.* This was a good feeling. She said through gritted teeth, "Have a go at these natives, why don't you?"

Gervas shoved to his feet, reaching for her.

The stone floor smacked into her and Tremaine found herself sprawled on it, groaning. She felt like she had been run over by a milk truck.

The cool dampness of the rock revived her a little. She heard scuffling nearby and shook her head dazedly, pushing herself up on her hands and knees. Rulan would still have the gun and she needed to help Ilias. The sphere lay near her right hand, spinning itself like a top. The crystal with its imprisoned Gardier sorcerer lay near her left. "Hold on, I'll be there—" She looked up to see Ilias had Rulan on the ground, one knee planted between his shoulder blades, determinedly strangling him with the Gardier rifle. "Never mind, I see you're dealing with that."

Tremaine made a few awkward grabs at the sphere before it slowed its spinning motion enough for her to catch it. She stumbled to her feet, bending down again to pick up the crystal. Staggering, she made it to the edge of the portal and sat down on the floor. The symbols of the spell circle were melted and blurred now, as if the stone had turned liquid with heat.

Rulan went limp. Ilias dropped him and shoved him away. He stood to smash the rifle against the stone floor until the stock fell off and metal bits went flying. "Hey," Tremaine objected belatedly, "don't do that unless it's unloaded."

He whipped around, dropping the remnants of the rifle, staring at her. "You're back! I thought you were . . . gone."

"No, that was the plan," she explained as he knelt beside her. She leaned against him, needing the support. "Gervas is gone."

"Where did you take him?" Ilias put an arm around her, holding her up.

"That place we went by accident, the desert with the giant."

"Good," Ilias commented. He looked grimly at the circle, taking a deep breath. "I hope he enjoys it."

Tremaine sat the sphere in her lap and picked up the crystal, looking into it. White light played in its depths, very like the distant blue sparks in the inner layers of the sphere. Very like. "Gervas said there's a wizard imprisoned in this. That's how the Gardier get their magic."

"Imprisoned?" Ilias leaned over the crystal doubtfully. "You mean, somebody's soul is in there? But that's . . ." She could almost hear him sorting through words. ". . . perverted. Even if it's a wizard. Are you sure he wasn't lying?"

Tremaine looked at the sphere. *Oh, Arisilde, how did this happen?* "Pretty sure." She lifted the crystal, testing its weight. "You don't think he went in there voluntarily, do you?"

Ilias was still skeptical. "If he's in there, he didn't ask for it. I'd bet the harvest on that."

Me too. Tremaine hefted the crystal and smashed it down onto the floor.

It broke like glass. Milky white light fountained up out of the shattered mass. Tremaine yelped, grabbing the sphere, and Ilias grabbed her, scrambling to his feet. It rushed for them like water, but parted a few inches before Ilias's boots, streaming away on either side of them. The light faded, dissipating in trickles, dying away. Ilias set Tremaine on her feet again. He looked aghast. "There was something in there all right. It really was a person?"

Tremaine nodded grimly. "It really was."

Ilias led the way back through a different passage in case Gervas had brought friends. It narrowed to nearly a crack before opening into the main cavern. At least Tremaine thought it was the main cavern; it was a great dark empty space where lights flashed at random, illuminating running figures. Noise made it more confusing as people shouted in a variety of languages and rifle fire echoed from down the rocky passages. "Oh, great," she said sourly, propping her weary body against the cool stone. "How are we going to find the others?" She didn't hear anyone yelling in Gardier; that was promising.

Ilias paused, another shadow-shape in the dark, one hand on her arm to keep track of her. The sphere had tried to make light for them back in the passage, but Tremaine had desperately convinced it/him not to so they could move around with a little more circumspection. Ilias tugged her back into the passage impatiently. "Most of the fighting is back this way."

"Oh, good," Tremaine muttered, taking his word for it.

After a long scramble through the dark, Tremaine dimly

heard gunfire and Ander's voice yelling, "Cease fire, cease fire! Shooting at it doesn't help!" The passage abruptly opened into a ledge looking down on a view of a huge dark cavern, or a different branch of the one they had just come from. In the erratic light of a few battery lamps, torches and several balls of sorcerous light, Tremaine could see a large wooden platform not far below them with moving figures, stacked crates and big metal tanks. Then in midair a huge patch of the darkness seemed to shift. The light caught it and she realized it was the black skin of a Gardier airship, turning away from the platform and moving slowly down the cavern. The hollow rushing sound of its engine reverberated through the enormous space, rising to a roar as it glided further away.

Ilias stepped to the lip of the rocky ledge, swearing under his breath. "They're running. There's nothing we can do."

"Running," Tremaine repeated almost absently, watching the jagged tail fins as they vanished into the shadows. "I don't think they can use the portal anymore. They can't get to Ile-Rien. But they can fly to another base. If they've already sent a message— But only if they're using magic to communicate. They can't get a conventional radio signal out of these caves."

Ilias stared at her, then eyed the sphere suspiciously. "Who are you arguing with?"

"Myself." But the ruthless bitch and the twitchy poet were in agreement on this one. Tremaine addressed the ball of metal and wheels and sorcerous power softly. "We can't let them go, Arisilde. Stop the airship."

A sort of rushing thump, like a giant gas stove being lit, echoed off the cavern walls. The airship had moved perhaps three hundred yards away down the huge passage, out of reach of any of the lights. But spots of red blossomed in the dark, apparently in midair, throwing orange reflections on the rock; fire growing inside the dirigible's membrane, traveling from cell to cell through the hull. Tremaine nodded to herself, satisfied with her deductions and the result. "The wards were already gone. All the spells on this base, all the other crystals in their gadgets, must have been tied into that big one."

The orange glow grew and uneasily, Ilias pulled her back from the opening. Tremaine hesitated, wanting to watch, but let him draw her away.

Back down the passage they found a dark corridor now chaotically lit by firelight and battery lamps and crowded with freed slaves in Gardier worker coveralls. Tremaine was relieved to recognize some of the Syprians and a couple of Ander's men among the unfamiliar faces. Everyone was filthy and flushed from the heat.

"Gil!" Ilias shouted suddenly and bolted past, shouldering a path through the press and sending people staggering out of his way.

One of the bigger figures turned. Tremaine had a glimpse of Giliead's face—startled, relieved—before Ilias flung himself into his arms.

"Tremaine!" Florian called from behind her. Tremaine turned and saw Gerard striding toward her. As he reached her, she automatically tried to hand him the sphere. He took it, passed it off to Florian behind him and pulled Tremaine into a tight hug. He released her and she couldn't think of anything to say. "You smell funny," she blurted.

He smiled, raising his voice to be heard over the babble. "It's one of Niles's old college charms. I used it to confuse the howlers. Hopefully it will wear off eventually."

"Did you get the portal?" Ander demanded, appearing next to them.

Tremaine nodded, not really sure where to start. "We destroyed their sorcerer and Arisilde got the airship—"

Florian was pounding her on the back. "I knew you could do it."

"Wait, what?" Ander stepped closer, frowning. "Their what?"

A deep-throated roar rolled down the tunnel, bringing an acrid cloud of smoke. There was a general instinctive surge back toward the main cavern, away from the wash of reflected light and heat.

An arm still around her shoulders, Gerard urged her after the others. Sounding puzzled, he asked, "Who did you say got the airship?"

Tremaine took a sharp breath. This wasn't going to be easy to explain. "I found Arisilde."

Chapter 22

With the Gardier gone, the caves were silent again. The light from his torch throwing twitching shadows over the rock, Ilias picked his way through the big cavern to where Giliead stood by the skeleton of the half-completed flying whale. No thumping, no buzzing lights; it was obvious all the Gardier's magic had fled. It was a relief to hear nothing but the whisper of wind through the air shafts far above, the soft voices of the Rienish and an occasional clank as someone tripped over debris in the dark. The lines that connected the wizard lights, the artificial walls, were just lifeless trappings, so much litter cluttering the ancient stone.

Giliead held his torch high, the warm light striking coppery sparks off the metal ribs arching up into darkness. "How many more of those do you think they have?" Ilias asked him softly.

Giliead shook his head, his gaze still caught by the metal beast. "If Ander is right about those markings on the maps, that they represent more Gardier strongholds—"

"Too many." Ilias answered his own question, wishing he hadn't asked it. He was just trying to avoid what they had to do next anyway. "Come on, we're putting it off." He turned away brusquely, but Giliead caught up with him in a few steps, dropping an arm around his shoulders.

They went down the narrow tunnel that led through the Gardier's quarters, threading their way through the slap-dash barricades already pulled down by the Rienish. The howlers had hauled off most of the bodies as they escaped into the tunnels, Gardier and freed slave. A door in one of the fake walls stood open and Ilias saw Ander and his men inside, tearing open cabinets and drawers in their haste to search. Ilias noted with approval that they were destroying some of the strange Gardier devices too; Gerard had said the crystal boxes didn't all hold captured wizards, that some of them must only be useful for specific curses and that they might not work now that the main crystal was destroyed. But he was glad to see them in shattered pieces.

Ander, studying a sheaf of paper he had just pulled out of a drawer, looked up and spotted them in the doorway. "Don't stay down here too long. We're almost done here and we need to evacuate the area soon."

Ilias cocked a brow and glanced up at Giliead. *Like we need him to tell us that.* Giliead just said imperturbably, "We'll be right behind you."

They moved on, making their way back through to the dark warren of the prison area. When they were out of earshot, Giliead said, "I wish I was that young again."

Ilias snorted. "No, you don't."

They found a few more Gardier dead, the bodies torn apart by howlers. There were also a few dead slaves in similar condition, huddled in the back corners of open cells or sprawled across the doorways; stragglers who had been reluctant to trust their Syprian rescuers or just too afraid of the Gardier to attempt escape.

Still they made sure all the cells in the prison area were empty. Halian was leading the *Swift*'s crew on a similar search in the other parts of the wizards' caves. Once they left for the surface, anyone who remained behind would end up howler food.

Finally there was only one more place to look. Giliead pushed open the heavy metal door to the chamber where he and the others had been held. The torchlight flickered and for an instant Ilias couldn't see anything on the other side of the wall of bars. Then he made out the sprawled form and took a deep breath to slow his pounding heart. Ilias held the torches as Giliead knelt and cautiously reached through to touch the wizard's body.

"He still feels dead." Frowning, Giliead stood, brushing his hands off on his pants. "He's cold, but not as cold as he should be."

"He doesn't look as dead as he did last time," Ilias pointed out, watching Ixion's unmoving form uneasily.

Giliead lifted his brows. "Good point."

They stood in silence for a moment.

Giliead grimaced, planting his hands on his hips and looking away. "I think he moved."

Ilias fell back a step in pure reflex, then glared at his friend. "That's not funny."

Giliead shook his head, frustrated. "No, no, from when we first put him in there. I think he's moved."

"Oh." Ilias eyed the inert form again warily. It might be Giliead's imagination, but he wasn't willing to count on that.

"He could do it again." Giliead wearily rubbed his forehead as if his head hurt. "He could have bodies growing all over this place we'd never find, not before the Gardier come back."

They regarded each other with glum resignation. Ilias took a deep breath. "We'll have to take him with us."

Are you sure?" Gerard asked again.

He and Tremaine were seated on a dark stone block on a bluff overlooking the sea. This had been a plaza or meeting area about the time the underwater city had been built. Dark flat-roofed stone buildings formed two sides of it, one concealing a shaft leading to the caves and the other a rough set of stairs down the rocky overgrown hill to one of the canals. The twisted trees and thick vegetation had eaten away much of the stone paving but the outline of the plaza was still visible. The misty sky was a heavy gray and waves washed against the rocks below, twisted into fantastic shapes by wind and water. Tremaine sighed. "No. For the last time, no. If you want to be sure, ask it. 'Are you Arisilde? One click for yes, two clicks for no.' " She knew she was hovering on the edge of exhausted collapse, but she couldn't seem to manage it. All she could do was sit here being dimly surprised her aching body was still upright and argue with Gerard.

Nearby some of Ander's men had set up the small portable wireless brought with the other supplies from Ile-Rien. Earlier, Deric had climbed on top of the taller stone building to string up the wire that worked as an antenna. If the *Ravenna* managed to successfully cross through the portal, she would signal them, but so far they had heard nothing but dead air. The wounded Arites, his arm in a sling to keep him from moving his injured shoulder, had been pressed into service as a radio operator. He sat cross-legged in front of the little device, studying it with wary curiosity.

The freed prisoners roamed over the plaza, some gathered in groups talking excitedly, others sitting alone or staring dully into the distance. They came mainly from the Southern Seas, from Maiuta, Khiuai, the other islands, though there were people of all nationalities mixed in. There were a number of Parscians and citizens of the Low Countries who could speak Rienish well and translate for the others. They hadn't seen the sun since they had been brought to the Gardier base and even the misty glow through the island's fog must have been a relief. Florian and Dyani were moving among them, calming them, looking for wounded, offering water.

There were also eleven Gardier prisoners, captured by a force led by Halian and Ander. Their hands bound with their own chains, they sat in a little group, guarded by Basimi and a group of freed slaves. Their faces were closed and still; it was hard to tell how they were taking their captivity. Only one seemed to be an officer.

Tremaine wasn't keen on having them here. After discovering Arisilde's fate, she would have rather left them underground for the howlers and grend to find. Or just shot them.

Before she and Gerard had left the caves, Ilias and a few others had gone back to look for Rulan, but he hadn't been in the portal chamber. They had found howlers feeding on a body that might have been his in one of the other tunnels, but they couldn't be sure.

"I don't want to ask it if it's Arisilde," Gerard said, eyeing the sphere almost warily. "This explains so much. Its ability to construct new spells of incredible complexity, to initiate attacks." He shook his head slowly. "It must be a living hell. The Gardier have certainly proved themselves to be callous in the extreme of human life, but to use this as the entire basis for their magical craft . . ."

Tremaine didn't want to talk about it, though she could see why Gerard was unwillingly fascinated by the subject. It was undoubtedly what the Gardier would have done to him eventually. There was no telling how many captured sorcerers from Ile-Rien, Adera, Parscia and everywhere else had already shared that fate. "I don't know. I mean, yes, I'm sure it's horrible for the Gardier sorcerers, especially, you know, right when they put them in the crystal. But I don't think Arisilde remembers being a person." At least she hoped he didn't. She didn't want to think about the gentle, kind man she had known trapped in a metal prison. "If he did, wouldn't he have tried to communicate with us, warn us about what he found here?" She ran a hand through her hair, grimacing at the gritty feel of the sand and dirt in it. "I think he's been asleep and using the sphere just started to gradually wake him up."

"Almost asleep." Gerard glanced at her. "It was undoubtedly his influence that allowed events from this world to appear in your writing."

Tremaine shook her head. There were still so many things she didn't understand. "But how did he know things about Ilias and Giliead? They never met him."

"Arisilde was—is?—an extraordinarily powerful sorcerer," Gerard said slowly. "He obviously maintained some sort of connection with this world, even from a sphere locked in a dusty cabinet at Coldcourt. The Syprian god did greet him rather readily, if you remember. And the god, whether it's an elemental or a spirit that was at one time human, would know about the events you described, from communicating with Giliead." Gerard winced, rubbing the bridge of his nose. "I can't think what it must be like. Trapped inside a metal prison, drifting in and out of awareness, trying, perhaps unconsciously, to reach your mind. It's a wonder you didn't receive any more impressions from him. Anything worse, I mean."

It hit Tremaine like a punch in the stomach. "He was giving up." She stared at nothing. The images that had come to her, working their way into her play and the smattering of magazine stories, that had been the attempts to communicate. But she hadn't responded and the sphere had been left in the cabinet, untouched. Arisilde, left without hope in whatever part of his consciousness that was still functioning, had started to die.

And you wanted to die. Her feelings of overwhelming resignation, of being trapped, useless, hopeless. It wasn't all him. She had been despondent enough on her own, probably with a borderline case of shell shock. That probably hadn't helped either, when the only connection Arisilde had had was with someone who just fed his own despair.

"This is all speculation," Gerard was saying, "and it doesn't tell us what happened to your father." He looked at her gravely. "Nicholas could still be alive. He may have sent Arisilde back for help and to warn us about the Gardier. But something happened during the spell and Arisilde ended up in the sphere at Coldcourt."

Tremaine swallowed in a dry throat. She didn't want to talk about this to Gerard yet. Maybe later, when she was sure. She looked out at the mist hanging above the sea, trying to focus on the here and now. Across the plaza, Florian and Dyani were trying to convince a woman with a stunned expression to drink some water. "Or the Gardier captured them, killed Nicholas and tried to make Arisilde . . . Tried to put him into one of their crystals. And Arisilde escaped. The hard way."

Gerard pressed his lips together and shook his head. "Why didn't he warn you about Rulan?"

"Maybe he didn't know how." Tremaine lifted her brows as another thought occurred. "Or maybe Arisilde wanted to see Gervas. One last time." *I know I would've done that, but would Arisilde?*

As Gerard mulled that over, Ander, Halian and Gyan, with the other Syprians and Rienish, emerged from the stone building that concealed the surface shaft. The Syprians stopped to douse their torches and Ander came wearily toward Tremaine and Gerard. He rested one foot on the block, leaning on his knee. "Anything on the wireless?"

Gerard shook his head. "Nothing yet."

"Why don't you sit down before you fall down?" Tremaine told Ander. Before they had evacuated the caves, she and Ander had taken the buoy back out through the passage to the little cove they had landed in. The sphere had been able to send the buoy back through the portal from there, so at least the *Ravenna* had still been intact and roughly where she was supposed to be at that point. They had all expected the ship to come through immediately, but that had been hours ago.

He smiled, lifting his brows. "Why, Tremaine, it's as if you care."

"Put the accent on the 'as if.' " She saw Gerard staring at her and explained, "Ander and I are developing a new relationship where we're completely honest with each other."

"I see." Gerard's glance at her was dry. "That should make the time just speed by."

Ilias and Giliead came out of the stone building, both dragging along something wrapped up in a tarp. Knowing Syprian reluctance to touch anything that had belonged to the Gardier, Tremaine stared in surprise. She couldn't think what they had found down there that they actually wanted to keep.

They dumped it on the pavement and stepped back, staring down at it bleakly. *Not that they look like it's something they want to keep,* she thought.

Ander frowned down at it and Tremaine asked, "What's that?"

Ilias rubbed his eyes. "You don't want to know."

Giliead, more literal-minded, said, "It's Ixion."

Now everyone stared at the bundle. Tremaine stood up and approached it carefully. She had never laid eyes on Ixion and was tempted to ask them to open it so she could take a look. Deciding reluctantly that that might be seen as inappropriate under the circumstances, she looked up at Giliead, asking, "You think he might be growing another body somewhere?"

Giliead nodded, pressing his lips together.

Halian let out a breath. "I know your reasons, but what are we going to do with it?"

Gerard stepped up beside Tremaine, eyeing the bundle grimly. "I can cast a ward around it, that's a start." He glanced back at the sphere and shook his head slightly. "I should say, we can cast a ward around it."

A crackle from the radio interrupted. "It sings!" Arites yelped.

The singing Arites had heard was the rapid beeps and clicks of a Rienish code signal. The transmission was garbled, perhaps from the weather, perhaps from the lingering remnants of the etheric disturbances around the island, but it was in the newest military code. After their experience with Dommen, Tremaine didn't find that terribly reassuring.

Once it was translated into words, the message on the radio had briefly explained the delay, saying that a call for evacuation assistance had been received from Chaire and the *Ravenna* had paused to pick up more passengers. In response Ander had tapped out a series of instructions over the wireless to meet them at the cove the Syprians called Dead Tree Point. They couldn't reach the harbor the Gardier had used without going back through the caves, and Halian had said that was the best alternate spot for a boat to come in.

With Ander in charge at the plaza and as strong a ward as Gerard and the sphere could cast around Ixion's body, Tremaine, Gerard, Ilias and Giliead made their way down the canal to Dead Tree Point. Florian had followed them to the edge of the canal, watching them anxiously. They had left the sphere with her, just in case.

Though no one was willing to say out loud that this might be a trap, they had discussed alternate plans; if this wasn't the *Ravenna,* they still needed a way off the island or a way to summon help from Cineth. Ander and some of the others had raided the Gardier stores for rations, but food and clean water were going to be an issue soon. The best alternate solution was to risk the caves again and make for the Gardier harbor and the transport ship docked there. If the few surviving Gardier hadn't already taken it for their escape.

If this wasn't the *Ravenna,* Tremaine thought they were probably all dead.

They reached the cove late in the afternoon and the gray clouds overhead were beginning to darken with the threat of rain. Walking out onto the bluff where there was a good view of the cove below and the gray-green sea past the sheltering rocks, Tremaine found herself missing the *Swift.* She wondered if Ilias and Giliead felt the same. She shielded her eyes from the watery glare, staring into the mist that lay across the waves like a cotton wool blanket. "I don't see anything."

Gerard lowered the field glasses, his brow furrowed with anxiety. "But the mist is very thick out there and with the *Ravenna*'s camouflage, she might fade into it."

Giliead frowned in concentration. "I hear something."

After a moment Tremaine heard it too. Her stomach jittered and she found herself wanting to bounce nervously on her heels. "That's an engine."

Squinting, Ilias pointed. "There, it's a boat."

Gerard lifted the glasses again, then lowered them with a relieved smile. "It's one of the *Ravenna*'s launches. I can see Niles in the prow."

In another few moments they could all see the small boat chugging toward them, slowing as it drew near the cove. Tremaine couldn't see Niles without the field glasses, but she could see that the man at the wheel, and the others behind him, wore dark blue Rienish navy uniforms. Then the clouds parted, sunlight temporarily thinning the mist just long enough for them to glimpse in the distance the distinctive silhouette of the enormous hull and the three stacks. The *Ravenna* was hanging back offshore at the edge of the deep water.

Giliead stepped back with a startled curse. He turned a shocked expression to Ilias, who said pointedly, "I told you. She's as big as a mountain."

"Now we can get off this damn island," Gerard breathed fervently, turning for the trail that led down to the little beach.

Tremaine folded her arms, smiling. "That's right." *Now we can go after the Gardier.*

If you enjoyed reading

The Wizard Hunters,

then read the following selection from

The Ships of Air,

available in hardcover from Eos in July 2004.

The wall rose out of the sea and the fog, up and up, bigger than a mountain, taking up all the horizon like another sky....

"*Ravenna*'s Voyage to the Unknown Eastlands,"
Abignon Translation

Tremaine thought the water in the cove was rough but as the launch left the shelter of the rocks, the high waves flung it into a violent roll. She slid from her seat to the deck, clutching the bench and trying valiantly to keep her stomach down where it was supposed to be. She hadn't ever been seasick before but the waves tossed the boat like a tin cup.

Gerard pushed his way up to the bow and held on to the rail next to the sailor wrestling with the wheel. Everyone else was clinging to the seats, trying to brace themselves. Ilias was beside Tremaine, gripping a stanchion, and Giliead was braced next to him. Even with the wind and the spray in their faces they were watching something with awed expressions. Whatever it was Tremaine didn't think she wanted to see it. The sudden onset of nausea had sucked any interest in staying alive right out of her; it was almost like being back home again. Then the wind died suddenly and she realized the sea was less violent, the boat's wild dips and sways less agonizing. She grabbed the rail and dragged herself up a little to look.

At first all she saw was a giant gray wall. She thought it

was mist or a low cloud formation, then she realized it was
the *Ravenna*, looming over the little boat like an avalanche.
Ilias and Giliead must have been watching her advance and
turn.

The pilot turned from the wheel to shout, "We're all
right now! She's come to our windward side so we're in
her lee."

Oh good, an optimist, Tremaine thought. "She's shielding us from the wind," she translated it into Syrnaic for the
Syprians, though being sailors they probably didn't need
her to tell them what had happened.

The boat chugged rapidly toward the *Ravenna* now,
making good progress over the still rough sea. Peering up
at the ship, Tremaine could see a few lights glowing along
the upper decks and a searchlight sweeping the water, fix-
ing on the launch to guide it in. The gray paint made the
ship fade into the heavy overcast sky and her upper decks
were draped in mist. It fell over the ship like a giant's
shroud, catching in diaphanous streamers on the three
enormous smokestacks. She didn't dwarf the island behind
them in actual physical size, but she gave the impression
she wanted to try. The *Ravenna* had been built to be a passenger liner, the largest in the Lenaire Solar line, and she
was far from home, just like everyone else from Ile-Rien.

Somehow approaching the liner by sea was more daunting than just walking up to her on the dock; the *Ravenna*
was free now and all powerful in her element. As they drew
steadily closer to that great gray wall, Tremaine suddenly
remembered the smashed warehouse and the sheared-off
pier, victims of a miscalculation during the ship's leave-
taking from Port Rel. It had seemed funny at the time; it
didn't now.

The pilot brought the little boat alongside the wall between dangling cables, then worked frantically with the
other crewman to get them locked in place at either end of
the boat. With the others, Tremaine stared nervously at the
huge hull so dangerously close that she could count rivets.
Gerard stood at the wheel, holding it steady as the two seamen worked. She saw Gyan on the other side, up toward

the bow with Arites and Dyani; he looked a little better though his face was gray in the dim light. He was staring at the *Ravenna* with nervous astonishment. Halian shouldered his way back through the others, his face intent, leaning over to ask Tremaine, "What are they doing?"

Giliead and Ilias both leaned in to hear her answer. She swallowed to clear her throat and said, "They hook those cables to the front and the back and then there's an electric winch to haul the boat up to the deck where they uh . . . keep boats." She knew about the procedure in principle but had never gone through it herself.

Giliead and Halian exchanged a dubious look and Ilias leaned back on the rail, craning his neck to look up at the height above them.

Halian nodded in resignation, squeezed her arm and said, "Don't tell anyone else."

Finally one of the seamen signaled to those waiting above and the lifeboat started to lift, moving a little in the wind. Some men shifted and called out in alarm but Halian snapped at them to be quiet. It seemed to take forever and Tremaine tightened her grip on the bench, reminding herself that if the Rienish woman who was supposed to be blasé about all this got hysterical everybody else was bound to do it too. She saw portholes in the *Ravenna*'s side, then larger windows streaked with water from the spray, then suddenly the boat swayed in toward an open deck, bumping against the ship's railing.

Tremaine stumbled as she stood and Giliead caught her arm to help her. A seaman held a gate in the ship's railing open and she stepped up on a bench and climbed through it, finding herself on the *Ravenna*'s polished wooden deck in a milling confusion of sailors, freed prisoners and people she vaguely recognized from the Viller Institute. The deck was rolling but it was nothing after being thrown around in the little launch. The wind was still harsh but the other stowed lifeboats, their canopies flattened down, hung overhead in their curved davits, forming a sheltering partial roof for the deck.

A little dazed, Tremaine noticed some of the sailors

were women, their hair cropped short or tightly bound back under their caps. Early losses at the beginning of the war meant there were now more women serving in the army and fragments left of the navy than ever before in Rienish history. It didn't surprise Tremaine that the *Ravenna,* designated as a last-ditch evacuation transport when the pilot boat had failed to return with the sphere, had ended with a lot of female crew. It also meant they would all have only a few years' experience at most and that none had ever worked on a ship like this before.

Tremaine watched the others clamber off the boat and then Gerard appeared at her side, guiding her to an open hatch. A seaman stood beside it, motioning for them to hurry. Tremaine dragged her feet, looking back to make sure the Syprians were following, then ducked inside.

Getting out of the wind was an immediate relief; with everyone else Tremaine jostled down a narrow wood-paneled stairwell that opened abruptly into a large area, brightly lit and teeming with refugees from the Gardier base, more Viller Institute staff and crew members trying to get them all to go somewhere. Voices spoke urgently in Rienish, Maiutan, Parscian; freed slaves who had held together throughout the battle and the trek across the island were falling down on the tiled floor and weeping with relief. Tremaine stumbled and leaned on a wall of finely polished cherrywood. Over the heads of the crowd, she spotted green marble pillars and the top of a glassed-in kiosk. "Promenade deck," she said to herself, relieved. Now she had her bearings; they had come down a full level from the boat deck above and were in the ship's main hall and shopping arcade. Past the people clustering around she could see that the glass cabinets for the shops along the walls were dark and empty.

"Gerard!" Someone forced his way through the crowd. "There you are," he said, as if Gerard had been deliberately concealing himself. It was Breidan Niles, the sorcerer who had brought the *Queen Ravenna* through the etheric world gate to this temporary safety. He had narrow features, fair hair slicked back and wore an exquisitely tailored country walking suit. Despite the appearance of a man who should be lounging decoratively at one of the expensive and fashionable cafés along the Boulevard of Flowers, Niles had been working on the Viller Institute's defense project as long as Gerard. As the other primary sorcerer on the project, his role had been to stay in Ile-Rien to watch over things there; this evacuation had been his first chance to travel through the gate.

Before Niles could continue, Gerard interrupted. "There's a problem. We're holding an enemy sorcerer called Ixion." Gerard gestured toward the damp canvas-wrapped bundle Giliead was just depositing on the floor. "He isn't a Gardier; he's a native collaborator. He's apparently perfected a consciousness-transference spell that can take effect at the moment of his death. Now he seems to be in some sort of comatose state. Giliead here is something of an expert on this subject and he believes it's very possible that Ixion has another body waiting somewhere that he can transfer into if we attempt to harm this one."

"I see." The crowd noise rose and fell around them but Niles stroked his chin thoughtfully, eyeing the quiescent bundle as if they were standing in a quiet library. "No chance we could tempt him over to our side?"

Gerard's mouth twisted in distaste. "I rather doubt it. From what our allies tell us the Syprian sorcerers are all quite mad. My experience with Ixion certainly bears that out."

Niles' frown deepened. He pulled a booklet with a printed cover out of his coat pocket and began to flip hurriedly through it. Tremaine stared. It looked like a tourist brochure. "What is that?" she demanded.

"A map of the ship for passengers," Niles explained. "There were bundles of them in the Purser's office. They come in handy since so many of the crew were assigned here just yesterday." He glanced at Gerard. "Thorny problem. But this Ixion isn't resistant to our spells like the Gardier?"

"No, not resistant at all, fortunately." Gerard pushed damp hair out of his face. "Does the ship have a brig?"

"No, but there's a secure area meant for stowaways. That's where your Gardier prisoners have been packed off to." Niles' brows lifted as he studied the map. "The ship does have an extensive cold storage capability."

Gerard smiled thinly. "That's a thought."

Giliead touched Tremaine's arm, asking uneasily, "What are they saying about Ixion?"

Tremaine started. Standing here listening to Gerard and Niles talk, she had almost drifted off. "They've thought of a place to keep him," she explained, switching back to Syrnaic with an effort and trying to look alert. "A locked cold room somewhere."

He nodded, pressing his lips together. "I'll take him there."

"No!" One of the Syprians protested. Tremaine craned her neck and saw it was Dannor. *Of course.* "You brought us here, you stay with us."

Tremaine saw Halian's face suffuse with red. Ilias muttered something under his breath that hadn't been included in the sphere's translation spell. But it was obvious the others agreed, except maybe Arites who was staring around in anxious curiosity. *It's a good thing they don't know Niles is a sorcerer,* Tremaine realized. Ilias knew from his brief visit to Ile-Rien, but he didn't look inclined to mention it. The Syprians had gotten used to Gerard but there was no telling how they would react to another Rienish sorcerer, especially as unsettled as they were now.

Watching with concern, Gerard told Giliead, "It's all right, we can take care of it ourselves. I still have a ward of impermeability on Ixion."

Giliead hesitated, threw a dark look at Dannor, then said reluctantly, "All right."

"Very well." Gerard turned to Tremaine as Niles called over a couple of men to take Ixion. "Will you let me have the sphere?"

She nodded, handing him the bag wordlessly. The lights were too bright and everything was taking on a surreal tint, probably a product of her exhaustion. As he pushed off after Niles, Florian appeared, saying, "Were you the last, did everyone make it?"

Tremaine stared at her blankly. Florian, with her red hair tied tightly back and her face pale, seemed oddly normal against the chaotic background. Tremaine shook herself and nodded a shade too rapidly. "Yes, we were the last. Everyone made it."

"Good." Florian relaxed in relief. "I've got to go, I need to help them get some people down to the hospital."

"Good luck," Tremaine managed as the other girl slipped away through the crowd. She looked at the Syprians gathered around her. Dyani had fetched up next to Tremaine and she anxiously eyed the light in the wall above their heads. It was encased in a smooth crystal sheath mounted in a brass base. It took Tremaine a moment to realize what was wrong, then she said hurriedly, "The lights aren't magic, they just look that way." *We need to get out of here,* she thought wearily. She stood on tiptoes to see over the heads of the crowd; her legs felt like rubber.

"This way," she said in Syrnaic and turned to follow the wall around. By this method she found the grand stairway at the back of the large chamber. She led the way down the carpeted steps, feeling the tension in her nerves ease as they left the noisy crowd behind. She glanced back to make sure the Syprians were following and saw Giliead and Halian both looking around, probably doing head-counts. Gyan was walking by himself but holding on to the wooden bannister with another man at his elbow watching him worriedly. Dannor, who had started the mutiny, looked wary and she was glad to see Ilias was right behind him.

The next deck was the First Class entrance hall she, Florian and Ilias had passed through when they had boarded the *Ravenna* in Port Rel. It was brightly lit now, the fine wood walls and the marble-tiled floor gleaming, and nearly as crowded as the main hall. Tremaine continued down to the next deck, finding a smaller carpeted lounge, mercifully unoccupied, with one wall taken up by the Steward's office. It was covered in sleek wood and had etched glass windows; there was a light on inside and the door was standing open. Tremaine hesitated and decided not to bother them. If she did, it would just give someone the opportunity to give her a lot of unnecessary instructions and orders.

Four large corridors led off from here, two toward the bow and two toward the stern. She picked the nearest and led the way down toward what should be the First Class staterooms. The corridor seemed to run most of the length of the ship, the patterned carpet making her a little dizzy as her eye followed it. The doors were in little vestibules opening off the corridor and she picked one at random. There was only one doorway in this vestibule so she hoped that meant it was a big room. "This is the place," she said over her shoulder, trying the handle. It was locked.